I0789015

The Life of Marek Zaczek

Volume 2: Embers of Love and War

David Trawinski

The Life of Marek Zaczek Volume 2:

Embers of Love and War

By David Trawinski

Thanks to Sophie Hodorowicz Knab for her assistance..

I have used an extensive number of quotes within this volume from published sources taken from several of the works listed in Appendix A: Sources Materials and Historical Readings. In order to differentiate these quotes from any given character's fictionalized dialogue, I have presented them in center-justified blue bold, italicized font. Even in black and white editions, these quotes should readily stand out. I have also foot-noted them to the volumes listed in the appendix, and annotated them to the specific page numbers within those references. Where possible, I have listed the original sources attributed within those volumes.

Note that in a select few cases I have intentionally used a character's quote out of context or before the occurrence of when it may have actually been said or written. General Kościuszko's referencing Napoleon's comments about religion in 1804 (that were not actually made until 1806) is an example, but I decided to use the quote to show the Emperor's long held state of thought. My apologies to anyone offended by this atypical usage.

I have a habit of italicizing foreign terms as well as the names of ships of war, but these are not in bold. I suspect there will be no confusion to the reader. Note that the term Ships-of-the-Line used throughout this volume refers to the most powerful warships of the day, most carrying from 60 to over 120 guns, or naval cannons.

If you wish to follow the array of countries that made up the various coalitions that Napoleon faced off against during his many wars, I've included a guide in Appendix C (Coalitions relative to this volume) & Appendix D (those that will play a role in future volumes).

Finally, if you are looking for a Polish pronunciation reference, please consult Appendices E (terms) & F (characters) at the end of this volume.

This novel is dedicated to

the people of Ukraine,

who in their suffering

under assault by a more powerful

and greedy neighbor state,

remind the world of the need for a vigilant

Coalition of the Just.

Map of Europe and Napoleon's Movements 1804-1806

(Holy Roman Empire Shaded)

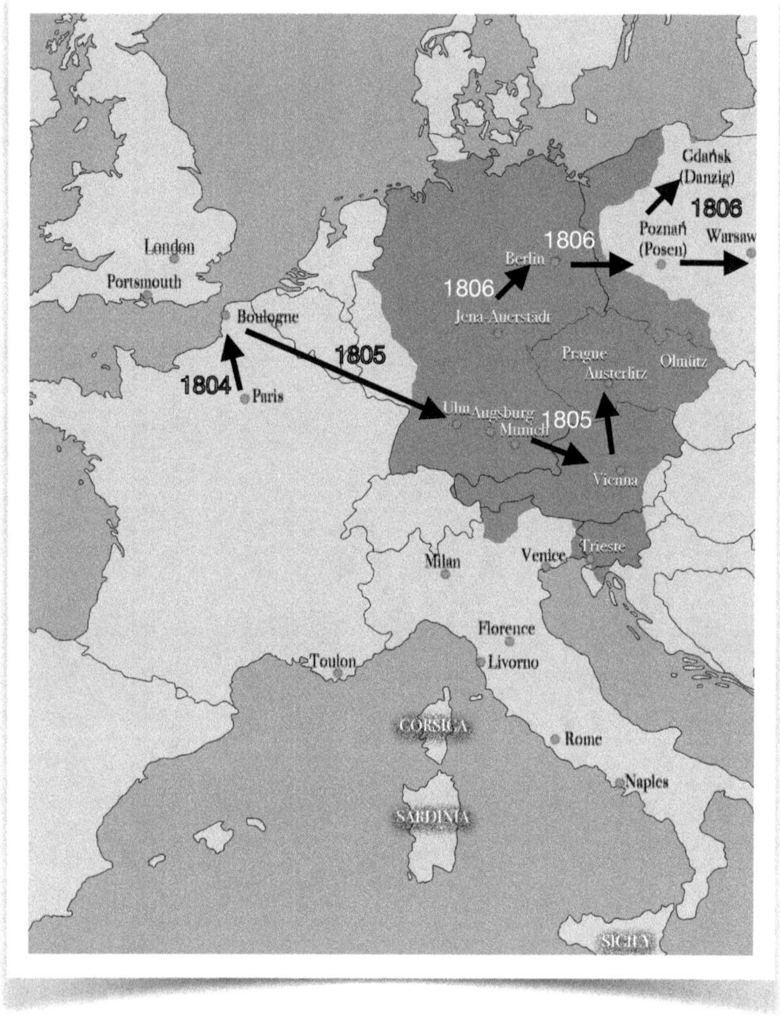

Figure 1: Europe of 1806

(Current Borders Shown for Reference)

Figure 2: Napoleon's Prussian Campaign of
October 1806 through January 1807

Part One:

Admirals and Generals

"Revolutions have never lightened the
burden of tyranny; they have only
shifted it to another shoulder."

George Bernard Shaw

Figure 3: Napoleon Bonaparte Crossing the Alps at the Saint Bernard Pass, by Jacques-Louis David

Chapter 1: Paris

October 9th, 1804

Confidence is the armor of youth. Forged on a false anvil of immortality, quenched in the waters of self-deception, its highly polished, sculpted skin is thought to protect the wearer from the brutal onslaught of a belligerent reality. With each blow of the enemy's assault deflected, the wearer senses his armor begins to glisten, then ever so subtly to shine, as honest and pure as the most tender tear ever wept from the eye of a child. Yet in the end, the armor will falter, and the wearer will come to understand both the folly of his myth, and the infallibility of his foe - time.

Marek Zaczek lay on his back, exhausted and slack. His every muscle enfeebled and loose. His conquest was over, his objective had been subdued. Every quantum of his energy had been exerted in achieving absolute dominion over his prey. Marek left not the least reserve with which to defend himself.

Marek, at the age of thirty-two, a man by all standards, lay naked in the sleigh bed. He was unclothed except for his unseen armor, a carryover from his misspent youth, which he never shed. Through the attic apartment's elegant dormer windows, flung open inwardly, like himself gasping for air, he could hear the melodious call of the Latin Quarter street vendors clamoring from their wagons below. The sweat of his body dampened the sheets, the finest made in all of France. The autumn Parisian air was heavy; it lingered with the mixed fragrances of perfume and performance.

A slight breeze crested and then dropped from the left bank rooftops. It fell steeply, as if to scoop up the cacophony rising from the cobblestones below, only to offer the slurry of sound up through the open dormer and roll it as a balm upon his sweaty skin.

A short time later Marek's partner recovered herself, and rolled up on to her side. Her desire to look once more upon his chiseled naked form taxed a great effort from her, one paid without any semblance of grace. She struggled to right herself like a listing ship whose sails billowed wildly in the first winds of a returning gale. She steadied herself upon an elbow propped at an indecent angle. The storm that had raged between the two of them had passed, but they both knew from those scant first winds that it threatened to return.

"That was amazing," she gasped as she attempted to calm the still raging beating of her heart. "You are such a savage lover."

Marek looked upon her naked skin, glistening with beaded sweat. "*Oui, ma petite puce,* it is you who brings out the most primal instincts of my desire."

"It does not take much, after all. Tell me again, *cheri*," she whispered as she reached with her free hand to trace the outline of the muscles that even in their spent state ripped across his chest.

"You know it all," he said in a bored voice, "you've heard that story many times. So many that I should have you tell it to me."

"A good story lives forever in its retelling," she whispered.

"And a true soldier's heart," Marek responded, "dies a little each time he repeats tales of his own conquests."

"Tell me, my sweet Marek" she insisted more forcibly. She knew he preferred her voice firm when making demands of him, rather than to softly plead or beg.

"Tell me about the attack of the Cossacks and what you feared they would do to your lovely Maya," she demanded.

Her fingers traced the edges of the plateau of his chest, and followed the contour until it melded into the damp softness of his armpit. She then rode it along the ridge line of his powerful bicep.

"She was heavy with child," he said, giving in once more to her command. "I saw the two Cossacks approaching the barn on horseback, so I had Maya and her mother hide in the carriage after I closed its doors. The two horsemen then rushed me on either side, as Cossacks will do. They did not realize I was an Austrian Uhlan, for I was clothed as a peasant, and they did not expect me to be carrying a pair of pistols. They charged me. I shot the one on my right in his chest, and he was driven by the ball from his saddle. But with the gun in my left hand I fired and missed the other as he drove past me."

Her fingers had found the scarred wedge on his left forearm. Its texture was radically different from the rest of his supple skin. The flayed area was smooth, almost like glass. Her fingers seemed to skate atop its icy surface.

"That second Cossack sliced you here with his sabre as he passed," she said in a husky and strangely animated voice. "You knew he would wheel his horse around and return to kill you. You knew he would afterwards defile your woman, even with her being so far along in carrying that child."

Marek felt his jaw tightening. He hated retelling this story, but knew it always aroused her in some very strange and primitive way. So, he decided to go on, to flush the wild beast from the bush.

"No one ever truly knows what a Cossack will do," he said as if he had just stated the obvious, "but one never wishes to find out just how heinous and debased are the limits of the acts in which their wild souls are willing to engage."

"His horse charged you," she breathed excitedly as she leaned over him, drew her arm high, "and he raised his sabre high to strike you dead."

"I did not have time enough to unsheath my own sabre, so I raised it up within its metal scabbard to blunt the blow."

"And the Cossack's blade struck it and broke in two," she said, her voice hungry with expectation.

"Yes," Marek said, "and had it not, I would likely not be here listening to you retell my story."

She ignored his quip. "The broken end of the blade snapped free and cut you deep across here," she said, as the fingers of her left hand found the long scar of his chest. Her eyes had taken on a menaced look of fear mixed with lust, as if she herself was at risk of being ravaged next by the attacking Cossack.

"Indeed it did," Marek said, "and it sliced open the back of my right hand as well, but the jolt of the breaking sabre's blade during the Cossack's wild thrust caused him to lose his balance and fall from his saddle. I was quickly over him, pinned his weapon hand under my boot, although it held by then but half a sword and…"

"You killed him," she said, her tongue dancing wildly on the beat of the words, "by sinking the tip of your own sabre deep into his Russian heart."

The lusty fire in her eyes distilled into a pure, even more intoxicating sensuality, primal and unrestrained. It re-ignited in Marek a raging desire of his own.

"Truly, I did so, but Cossacks do not like to be thought of simply as Russians," Marek corrected her, "as they are an independent people. They come from the wild lands that lie between Poland and Russia, mostly from the Steppes in the South, along the rivers of the Ukraine."

"You killed him," she seethed, ignoring his rebuttal, "and watched as the last sparks of life drained slowly from his eyes."

Her right hand wandered south from his triangular scar to explore another feature of his still recovering body.

"I was forced to," Marek confessed, "for he was still a threat to kill me, and then do whatever to Maya and her mother…"

For the first time his voice struggled slightly as her right hand explored his condition. Then she pressed down hard with her left hand upon his scarred chest to raise herself over him.

"But not the second Cossack, the one you had first shot who had fallen from his saddle…"

"He was badly wounded," Marek admitted, "and dying a slow, painful death."

He felt her weight then shift fully onto the arm driving into his chest as she threw her bare leg over and straddled him.

"They both cursed you with their last breaths," she said, as she leaned forward and crawled atop him. Her body was hungry again, the beast driven out from its hiding. Marek wondered why each time this story's telling produced the same response in her. Did she imagine herself being defenseless at the hands of these two brutal warriors? Why did it excite her in such a dramatic fashion? "Tell me how you put the second Cossack out of his misery. Tell me, tell me now!"

She eased herself down upon him. He reached up and placed his hands over her ribs, not so much to steady her, but to guide her such that it pleasured him most. When their union was complete, she bent forward over him. He raised his head to nibble on her ear as she slowly increased the pace of her writhing.

"Tell me," she gasped, "leave nothing out. Not a single detail."

"There is not much to say," Marek demurred, "I merely placed the tip of my sabre over his throat…"

She released the wounded sigh of a beast as he spoke…

"… and with the flick of my wrist, I sliced open the vein in his neck to free his blood, and release him from his painful fate."

Her moan continued throughout his saying this, but became so guttural that Marek could feel its pulse upon their joined bodies.

With this Marek rolled her over, flipped her body wildly beneath him as it bashed hard against his own.

"This excites you?" Marek teased. "Why does hearing how another man dies excite you so?"

She grunted as she ground herself harder against him. He found her rhythm, and the two were as one again synched in the joint motion of pleasure.

"Your husband cannot release this demon in you with such stories of war, can he?" Marek taunted her between his thrusts.

"No." she gasped between heaving breaths. "He is such a weak man, do not speak of him…"

"But, he is in the business of war…" Marek teased further, not easing his motions in any way. He timed his breaths to his words: "His weapons buy you this life… your lovely clothes… your mansion home… this exquisite apartment set aside just for us." He stabbed the last phrase hard.

She was breathing in ragged, sharply edged breaths.

"He loves war …" she gasped, pausing to wince from the deep pleasure within her, "only to make money…" she winced again. She released another moan atop a ragged breath. "Stop talking, damn you, Marek, and take me, take me hard…"

Her body clung tightly to his, as if it demanded he apply even more force to break it free.

"So, it is the danger and the threat of harm that your mind craves…" Marek was nearly yelling at her now, "… while forcing your hungry body to crave something altogether different."

"Yes," she panted. Her eyes stared at him like hot irons just drawn from a bed of red embers in a fireplace.

"The threat of being taken by a man," Marek caught his breath, "against your own will excites you."

"Yes," she gasped. She was at the pinnacle.

Marek knew exactly what to say to release her. He held the words on the tip of his tongue, waiting for the exact moment to release them. Finally, he unsheathed them like a fatal weapon, "You thought that just perhaps," he paused to suck for air, "as he ravaged you, a man like myself would come forth to your rescue."

"Yes!" she moaned, but now in a slow, release of ecstasy.

"And that after saving you, I would merely take you again, this time for my own wanton needs."

She said nothing more. He felt her body clutch his own, twitch and slowly release him. She was gone, to wherever it is that women go in this, their most delicate and delicious moment.

As the afternoon slipped into night, Marek and his woman would engage in this dance of sinful pleasure again and again. It was not until the physical fatigue of them both yielded in the vast darkness of the night, when sleep overcame them both. First it claimed her, and soon she lay placidly with her head upon his strongly sculpted chest. The soothing repetition of her deep breaths ebbed him into a restive cove of solitude. Once there, Marek began to take measure of his life.

That introspection always lead him to reflect upon his life's greatest regret, having allowed his love, Maya, to slip out away from his reach.

Marek thought upon the contours of that most beautiful face he had not seen for a decade. Yet, still he recalled its features so strongly in his memory that as he slipped across to the other realm, from his state of restless fatigue into the restive escape of slumber, its image stood out in the emptiness of his being.

As the dream state came upon him, he remembered Maya in her vibrant youth, long before she was stained by the unwanted burden of childbearing so viciously thrust upon her. She had been his companion since his earliest remembrances. He saw her face smooth, unworried, and beaming with great pride. The daughter of a Duke, she was his unexpected partner, for Marek was merely a peasant boy. But to his great joy, fate had paired him with her throughout childhood. She became the pleasure he knew he would never be allowed to enjoy. She blossomed into the passion he knew he would never quench. He chased the memory of her pure face as it faded into his mind's dimmer recesses.

Suddenly, that twilight was swept away by the vibrant, brilliant azure skies of his youth. Marek swept like a breeze over golden fields atop the *folwark's* fastest Arabian. The tips of the harvest stalks polished against his roughshod peasant boots as the regal equine beneath him galloped furiously. Marek could see his Uncle Jacek, who had just saddled the steed, watching along the field's edge standing next to Marek's father, Bronisław, the salt miner, and his mother, Magda, the peasant housekeeper of the Duke's mansion. All their eyes were upon him as the frenzy of the beast beneath him unfurled into a furious rage, astonished that Marek remained atop the steed, its master, in full control. Slowly his parents and his uncle faded in his peripheral vision, leaving him only with the pure joy of commanding the Arabian.

Marek could feel the winds of the heavens as they filtered first through the beast's onyx black mane, then rushed through the long locks of his own youthful blonde hair. Everything was perfect. Everything was pure.

Marek then felt his mount abruptly come to sliding halt. It resisted his commands to continue on. Instead it finally, hesitatingly moved forward at merely a cautious trot. Only then could he make out two shadowy figures lurking within the stalky grasses ahead. Marek rose in his stirrups to recognize the taller menacing form of the Duke Sdanowicz, master of the *folwark,* and under his left arm was his daughter, Maya. Upon her face was an impish, inviting grin. The Duke beckoned for Marek to come join himself and Maya by taking the place alongside his right side.

Sensing the ominous portends of the vision, Marek refused. With an angry flip of the Duke's wrist, Marek's father and uncle were vanquished as if their figures were made only of a fine powder, stripped away, layer by layer, by a rush of commanded winds. His sobbing *matka* was then left all alone.

Marek felt a dread overcome him. He commanded the Arabian to turn and gallop in the opposite direction, but it seemed constrained to obey. He was overtaken by several of the Duke's horsemen. They led him away to a spit of rock surrounded on three sides by the Vistula River. His only option was to surrender himself or cast his body into the *Wisła's* swift flowing waters.

The aqueous fabric of the dream rippled and Marek soon found himself suspended, immersed fully in the river's waters, as he thrashed wildly and struggled for his life. Something pulled him down like a weight deeper into the *Wisła's* murky depths. He could not breath, his desperate grasps clutched only at river water that squeezed helplessly between his fingers. He felt himself sinking in the *Wisła's* currents as they became colder, cloudier and hid the threat his senses could not measure, but his heart feared in terror.

Marek awoke covered in a cold sweat. He had always loved the simplicity of his peasant childhood and every year he came to cherish it more. So why the recurrence of this nightmare of dread and panic supplanting the peace and placid years of his youth?

Awakened now, Marek consciously assessed his earliest memories, when even as a child he demonstrated a mastery for riding for which there was no equal in all of Europe (as he himself was even now quick to openly profess). Even in his youth, he had come to love and respect the noble creature that was the horse. The animals had already been his life's passion even before Duke Sdanowicz had taken a favored interest in him. The Duke soon found he could enhance young Marek's natural riding talents best not through the force of training, but more so by the sheer joy of repetition. The child's skills were shaped and sharpened by the hours he spent atop the Duke's most vigorous mounts. In this way, Marek had come to love the animal, not any singular horse, *per se*, but the beauty of all things equine.

Marek's natural equestrian abilities soon led to his achieving his childhood ambition of becoming an Austrian Uhlan cavalry rider. He impressed his superiors with his prowess in the saddle, but it was in weapons training that his warrior instincts were discovered. These innate capabilities were quickly honed to a deadly edge by the Austrians. It was that very training which allowed him to prevail against the two Cossacks on that day of the Battle of Maciejowice. This was the assault that always so deftly enflamed the lust of his lover.

During that fight, occurring nearly a decade ago to the day, Marek prevailed over the two Cossacks, saving the life of his love, Maya. Unfortunately, he failed at completing his primary order - the abduction of the Polish General Tadeusz Kościuszko. Marek was stripped from his stirrups, demoted by the Austrians from being a prestigious Uhlan cavalier to the punitive role of a mere, dispensable infantryman.

Marek knew he had not only been denied his place of esteem on horseback, but, far worse, he had become nothing more than raw fodder for the Austrians to sacrifice to the cannons of their most feared enemy - the atheistic armies of the French Revolution.

Marek knew as a Polish soldier he would be sacrificed on the front lines first, in order to preserve the lives of soldiers of true Austrian descent. So it was, the aged Habsburg generals cobbled together boys from the furthest corners of the empire's conquered lands to form the forward most lines against the French cannons in the northern Italian provinces of Piedmont and Lombardy.

The French Revolution had no love for royalty in any form. In their eyes, the Austrian, Prussian and Russian peoples were ripe for revolution of their own, ready to rise up against their emperors, kings and tsars. It was exactly these thoughts and words of the French revolutionaries, who had already murdered their own king, that terrified the other monarchs of Europe.

It was one thing for the mayhem of the revolution to be cordoned off within the borders of France, but this regicidal fervor had since 1792 threatened to be spread across all of Continental Europe by the French Revolutionary Army.

The remaining monarchs, be they king, tsar or emperor, knew the French must be stopped before conquering the lands to France's east and snuffing out their own royal bloodlines: the Habsburgs of Austria and the Holy Roman Empire; the Hohenzollerns of Prussia; and the Romanovs of Russia.

Over this same period, these monarchs watched as the French increasingly yielded control to the maneuvering of a single man: a young Corsican named Napoleon Bonaparte. By 1804, that man had risen to the greatest position in France. In May of that year, he had himself declared Emperor. Napoleon's coronation, set for the second of December, was now but weeks away.

The British, safely removed from the Continent by both geography and mindset, watched cautiously from across the Channel. They had no love for the French in general, but Britons perhaps best understood the mayhem of the French Revolution. Over a century and a half earlier in 1649, they had, in a fervor of haste they would later regret, beheaded their own King Charles I.

What really concerned the Brits was this sole leader who had emerged so unexpectedly from the revolution's chaos and disorder. Young General Bonaparte arose from the mayhem to first grasp notoriety, then seized control and finally consolidated power in a very effective manner. His organizational skills, in both military strategy and civilian governance, were far too formidable not to be recognized. If there was one dynamic leader that the British could envision unifying the long warring cultures of the Continent, it was this Corsican. Napoleon only grew stronger on the Continent as they watched. The British knew they had but a singular advantage on which to rely over Napoleon's feared army: their Royal Navy that controlled the seas that all but encircled Europe, that is, all but the extensive land border with Russia.

Napoleon Bonaparte had been spotted early as he rose from obscurity under the very eyes of the English. The ships of the British Navy had participated in the siege of the French port of Toulon in August 1793, which began only seven months after the execution of King Louis XVI. British ships were still present in that port when Marie Antoinette was executed that October. It was almost as if the last throes of leadership had been cleared away in order for Napoleon to emerge. In Toulon, Napoleon took command of the French artillery, ordered it elevated high on a hillside overlooking the harbor, and rained his cannon fire down upon the blockading ships. By the end of December, the siege was lifted, and Napoleon emerged as a national hero. At the age of only twenty-four, he was promoted to brigadier general.

Three years later, he was given command of the entire French *Armée d'Italie*. Napoleon faced off against and defeated the vaunted Austrian forces. He prevailed in battle after battle using tactics of speed and troop positioning. He would later state that it was after the May 1796 Battle of Lodi, for control of that town's critical bridge crossing over the fast moving River Adda, that he first recognized his own true greatness:

"It was only on the evening of Lodi that I believed myself a superior man, and that the ambition came to me of executing the great things which so far had been occupying my thoughts only as a fantastic dream." [1]

This was the very battle that earned Napoleon the affectionate nickname *"le petit caporal" or "the Little Corporal"* [2] from his troops for positioning artillery with his own two hands. It was also here where the twenty-four year old Marek Zaczek was forced to fight as infantry for the Austrians. At Lodi, he would make the most fortunate decision of his life. Marek was at that point still discovering his true self that lay hidden deep beneath his youthful exterior.

Marek had already learned in battle that he possessed the ability to remain calm even under the most frightening of conditions, such as the assault of enemy cannon fire. It was not that Marek did know fear; he felt it in his very bones like any other man. But he could function under its grip, whereas as others found the fear disabling. He could still weigh which actions he might take to improve his chances of survival. Logical reasoning under fire is rare, but Marek found he could suppress the panic known to scatter battlefield minds into disarray.

---

[1] *"The Campaigns of Napoleon"*, David Chandler, Folio Society Edition, Vol. I, p. 84
Sourced to "Napoleon" by Felix Markham, 1963, p.28

[2] *"The Life of Napoleon Buonaparte"*, J.G. Lockhart, Bickers and Son, Leicester Square, London 1889

One such incident occurred when he, as an Austrian infantryman, dug into his position nearest the bridge. There, as the shelling commenced, he spotted the most beautiful horse he had ever seen - a pure white charger - bolt frantically and riderless across that besieged bridge from the enemy side. Marek overcame his fear and moved under heavy fire onto the structure to rescue the glorious but horror-struck animal.

After abandoning his assigned position at the base of the bridge, Marek ran forth onto the wooden span under intense shelling and gunfire. He knew he must rescue the magnificent horse, since the Austrians would surely butcher the splendid animal if only out of sheer retaliation. He raised his arms as high as he could near the center of the bridge, and was able to arrest the animal's flight. He then scrambled up into its saddle, and led it back over to the French side of the river. The mount turned out to be that of none other than *the Little Corporal,* the young French General Napoleon Bonaparte. Napoleon was quick to associate Marek's daring rescue with his own good fortune at Lodi.

Marek recalled this event as if it had happened yesterday, although it had occurred eight years in the past. Soon the same man then known to his troops as the *"le petit caporal"* would be crowned Emperor of the French. Ever since his defection at Lodi, Marek had fought valiantly for the French *Armée d'Italie* as a member of the Polish Legions assembled under General Jan Henryk Dąbrowski. The General was a hero who had emigrated from Poland after having served with distinction in the Kościuszko Uprising of 1794, where his cavalry had defeated the highly regarded Prussian cavaliers in battle.

Napoleon had been quick to recognize the mastery of the Poles as light cavalry, and valued the bravery of these most able horsemen. He ordered Marek remanded over to General Dąbrowski's legions. Dąbrowski would tell Marek that Bonaparte had many times over the next eight years asked as to Zaczek's abilities, and followed his career with great personal interest.

Marek took naturally to the mortal skills of warfare he was forced to hone. He soon needed a release for his enraged emotions. He learned to temper these through the conquest of the fairer sex, a world Marek had been initiated into, ever so coarsely, by the alluring Hungarian prostitute, Reka, in Kraków years before.

Admittedly, it had been a rough and awkward introduction. Yet, despite this, Marek soon came to master the art of seduction. He found that the secret to lovemaking was to allow himself to let go of all restraint. Since joining the ranks of the Polish Legionnaires of the French army, he had much practice, first with the voluptuous women of the Italian provinces.

In Piedmont, Lombardy, Milan, Venice and even Rome, he sharpened his skills of pursuit, capture and conquest. Those years in Italy had passed with many successes in both battle and *boudoir.* By 1804, Dąbrowski's Legions had been pulled back to the French capital. In Paris, Marek's lovemaking skills would flourish further.

Marek had become something of an instant darling of the salon *fêtes*. He soon exchanged his rakish delights of the peasant girls of Italy for the more nuanced seduction of the refined French women of Paris. Before the Revolution, these women were socialites and aristocrats. In 1804, the country was still stabilizing. Wealth was slowly beginning to reappear in Paris, but not openly, not flagrantly. Paris under Bonaparte was rebuilding its civil structure from the chaotic wreckage of the Revolution. This meant the re-establishment of the classes, which was done through the industries supporting Napoleonic France's greatest export - War.

Those engaged with the state in providing war materials to the French army had become very prosperous. Prosperity breeds adventure, and none were more adventurous than the wives of this suddenly thriving merchant class.

These elegant women were drawn like moths to the flame of Marek's persona by his stories of danger, intrigue, and physical daring. Their gazes feasted upon his impressive uniformed presence, adorned over a strong, delicious physique. To them, Marek might simply be viewed as another amorous foreigner. Yet, it was far more than the Pole's charming etiquette and chivalrous displays that beguiled these baronesses and salon patronesses. He radiated a certain allure simply from basking in Napoleon's favor.

Of course, Marek could be quite charming even without the shadow of Napoleon enshrouding him. For instance, there was the romantic way in which Marek spoke, not only in his choice of words, but more so within the timbre of his voice. In it there existed a deep yearning for the country of his birth that existed no longer. There was the melancholy of nostalgia laced in his words, along with a haunted gaze in his piercing blue eyes that so irresistibly complemented his mystique as a man of action and conquest. Marek was idolized by these women as one who seemingly always got what, and *who,* he wanted, until he no longer desired neither it nor *them* and moved on to his next tryst.

These socialites desired nothing other than to be the subject of his seduction, and ultimately the dominion of his conquest. It was not enough for these *nouveau riche* to merely attract Marek's attention to themselves, or to ever so deftly *"allow"* him to possess them in the throes of passion. It was necessary that they should not only hold but dominate his romantic intentions. They must remain the ambition of his desires, even against ever-emerging fresh and more youthful threats also vying for this gallant Pole's attentions.

These women were nothing more than seducers themselves. After all, they had lived through the extreme, radical era of the Revolution. In it, each year seemed like a decade, where events could turn rapidly, often to viciously consume those who had only weeks or days before been held in the highest of favor. These women would live not only for the day, but for every minute of their unpredictable lives. Especially those fleeting moments in which they could imagine themselves becoming this young officer's lover, his concubine, and if lucky, his romantic consort.

Marek had taken to the game quickly, and had changed partners several times since arriving in Paris. Each lover was followed by one more prosperous, and of a higher social standing. His sequence of "affections" had elevated him amongst the ranks of the socialites until he had settled on a very prominent patroness.

The Baroness Charlotte Larouche was Marek's current conquest, or perhaps he was hers. Madame Larouche's husband was profiting indecently from the sale of cannon shot to the army. He knew of and actually encouraged his wife's amorous liaisons, so long as they were with highly placed military officers. His rationale was that she surely would take a lover of her own in any case, so best be it that his business should profit from that man being a favored military officer of Napoleon Bonaparte. To this end, he paid dearly to keep that finely appointed apartment just for his wife's *"clandestine"* encounters. It was here that Marek, long since awake, found himself under the rays of the *soleil du matin.*

Marek lazed in that morning sun which sluiced through the shutters of the Baroness' elegant apartment and across her bed. He was covered by nothing more that a strategically placed coiling of sheet that draped across his muscular flank. She was perhaps five years his senior, but it still pleased him to watch her at the vanity of her *boudoir,* her *toilette*, as the Parisian women are prone to say. To Marek, her shape was still beguiling, her gentle movements still endearing, and her sexual appetites still voracious. Of the latter, Marek knew how to ignite them, but was just as quick to recognize her icy demeanor return once her needs were fully satisfied.

Marek was always amazed at how significantly her personality could morph during the course of their overnight *rendezvous*. The wild lust-seized animal of the night transformed into the socialite madame by morning. She spoke of their raptures from the evening before, but in a much more civilized and refined voice. He preferred the raw passion of her cries in the darkness.

"Did I please you last night, my warrior?" she called out, not breaking her gaze upon her own image in the mirror.

"Like no one else has ever done, *mon petite chou*," he replied with an impish smile.

"Yet it was far from our first time together! Am I still competing with myself in your eyes?" she queried.

"It is a competition you shall never lose," Marek said, proud of his repartee, "for each encounter with you grows sweeter than the last, if by nothing other than sheer anticipation."

"Then, I can *'anticipate'* you will be at my *soirée* this evening?" Madame Charlotte asked in a demanding tone. "You must, for I am *fêting* one of your countrymen visiting Paris."

"I see," Marek said. "I have given you a taste for the men of Poland, only for you to desire more of the same?"

"Don't be ridiculous, *mon ami,*" she answered. "No other man from Poland or all of Europe can satisfy me in so many ways as you do. You enjoy it, *no? Oui,* you enjoy your lovely distractions, and for that I am most grateful. I want you to attend this evening so all my friends will be made green with envy. They all want you, you know. But I want to remind them that you are mine alone. It will not be said outright, but they will know after the *soirée* that I alone am yours, my love. Besides, this countryman of yours is actually a woman, a princess in her own right. Perhaps you know her, Princess Izabela Czartoryska?"

Hearing her name spoken aloud froze Marek in thought. *Can it be? The same woman who had attended to what otherwise would have been my mortal wounds at the Czartoryski Palace in the town of Puławy? Whose tender touch and adept hands healed me after my fight to the death with those two Cossacks? She who provided the carriage which saved the lives of Maya, her mother and myself just hours before the Russians plundered the palace?*

When the fog of his thoughts had lifted, Marek moved to pull up the sheets, covering more of his immodest pose. It was as if merely mention of the name of the Polish princess had somehow brought her physically into the room.

"What is the matter, my lovely legionnaire?" Madame Charlotte said, turning from her mirror to take in his reaction. "You appear to have seen King Louis' ghost!"

"I know this Princess Czartoryska," he admitted. "Let us just say I visited her at her family's estate once, long ago."

"She must have been rather pleasing to your touch for you to become so white like talc recalling it," Madame Larouche teased. "Do you know that she asked about you? She wished to be assured that you would be present at her reception. Perhaps tonight I will not only be competing with myself after all?"

The Baroness cast an accusatory glance at the Polish cavalryman that she so loved to tease.

"I have never touched the woman," Marek said, "although I cannot say that she has not touched me. You see these scars, the very ones that excited you so wildly last night, it was the Princess who cared for these wounds. It was she who attended me when I thought I might die. It was she who delivered me to the safety of the Austrian controlled lands of Poland. I owe her my life."

Marek thought briefly of the pregnant Maya in the carriage that he led, bleeding profusely on horseback to the gates of the Princess' palace. He remembered, the relief he had felt in making it to its magnificent grounds, which were openly known to be a refuge for all who fought with General Kościuszko against the Russians. Marek knew the women would be safe there, and only then gave into the pain he had so arduously resisted to that point, and collapsed. He truly expected to die there, having delivered the two women from the advancing Russians. Yet, this woman, the Princess Czartoryska, had brought him back from the brink of expiring. He remembered her caring, healing touch vividly.

"You are so amusing, my warrior," Madame Charlotte teased. "Even in recalling your nearly having died, you still have to differentiate the lands of your youth as the *'lands of Poland controlled by Austria.'* It has been too long, my sweet, nearly a decade now, I am afraid the Poland that still lives in your heart is forever dead, never to return. Your country is but a thing of the past, my love."

Marek sprung forth excitedly from the bed, his nakedness no longer a concern. He reacted to her words as if they were flaming spears. For she had struck the one nerve that was most sensitive in all patriotic Poles - that which denied or even questioned the true sovereignty of their homeland, or dared to justify in the least the criminality of the Partitions of Poland.

"That is where you are so wrong, my Baroness. It is exactly why General Dąbrowski and all we Poles fight for Napoleon so fanatically. The Emperor has said many times that the Partitions of Poland by the Austrians, Prussians and Russians was a crime for which all of Europe shall pay. He will restore our country's sovereignty! *Vive l'Emperor!*"

The baroness looked upon his naked form, muscular and lean, and thought herself a fortunate woman. She was sure she had captured this most desired Polish cavalryman's heart, but feared her comments may have bruised the romance of its idealism.

"Well, I see my words can still arouse you, my love," she replied calmly to his outburst, "even if it is not always in the way I desire most. You and your countrymen fight for France, not Napoleon. But beware, my Marek, for Napoleon, despite declaring himself so, is not yet Emperor until the upcoming coronation. In Revolutionary France, many surprises have awaited its leaders. King Louis, Queen Marie Antoinette, Danton, Robespierre - all lost their heads to the guillotine in the *Place de la Revolution*. Napoleon has already dodged a few attempts on his own life, no?"

"Alas, my sweet," Marek replied, "the Revolution is now behind us, ever since Napoleon declared himself Emperor this past May, we have entered the Imperial Napoleonic reign. Indeed, he will be crowned Emperor of the French soon enough, in fact, in only a matter of weeks. Then his troops, myself proudly included, will defeat the Austrians, the Prussians and most deservedly the Russians in battle. Those who so callously sliced apart my country, partition by partition, will feel his wrath. From those spoils, the Emperor will carve out a renewed and loyal Poland. The sovereignty of the land of the White Eagle will be restored, and for that reason alone, the allegiance of all Poles is not to France, but to the very man, Napoleon, who will be our nation's liberator!"

A wry smile crept over her face hearing him profess this so.

"Ah, my sweet Marek, it is your fiery emotion that stirs the very mortar that binds our love."

Marek looked cautiously at her, as if weighing his next reply. Then, having thought through the situation, he released the words from his lips:

"My darling Baroness Charlotte, let us not delude ourselves. There is no depth of love channeling between us, only the shallowest fords of lust and lasciviousness do we enjoy."

Her wry smile broadened in a wretched delight.

"Ah, but at least for now, my Marek," she answered after hesitating, "these are enjoyments we both still crave, no?"

Chapter 2: Britain
Ruler of the High Seas

Duty, above all else, lures the seaman to his life's call upon the waves. It trumps valor and victory alike, for few if any warships, armadas, or navies will forever avoid the bitter taste of defeat. Yet, no country had more often demonstrated its mastery of the seas than had Britain over the centuries. Her sailors were well trained, and her officers were of the soundest tactical judgement. But perhaps what differentiated her navy from all others was its generational regard of her every sailor to do their duty for their island nation. Britons had long realized that their future was tied to their navy's dominance. Duty of her seamen was more than merely expected, it was demanded, even in the face of disastrous peril.

> *"If I had been censured every time I have run my ship, or fleets under my command, into great danger, I should long ago been out of service, and never in the House of Peers."* [3]

was once said by Britain's greatest Lord of the Seas. He was born on the East Coast of England, in the countryside known as Norfolk, where the nation's green lands absorb the stormy wrath of the North Sea. Thereupon lies a small town named Burnham Thorpe, where in 1758 a son was born to the family of Reverend Edmund Nelson.

---

[3] *"The Life of Nelson"*, Captain A.T. Mahan, Easton Press Edition of 1897 text, Vol. I, p.19.

Horatio was the sixth of eleven children, of which three would not survive infancy, and only two would grow to an old age. He was named after his godfather, Horatio Walpole, the Earl of Orford and nephew of the highly respected former Prime Minister Robert Walpole. These great men were distant relatives of his mother's lineage. She died when Horatio was only nine, so little could Catherine (*nee* Suckling) Nelson ever imagine that one day her son's name would become more highly esteemed by all classes of her nation than that of either of her prestigious ancestors.

At the age of twelve, the widowed Reverend Nelson committed young Horatio's life to the sea, not by any assessment of skill or temperament, but by mere chance of familial opportunity. Under the tutelage of his maternal uncle, Captain Maurice Suckling of the Royal Navy, Horatio was made a coxswain, as was the custom afforded to ship's captains of the day.

Horatio Nelson's very personality was forged upon the waves. His first transit was upon the *HMS Raisonnable,* aptly still bearing the French name of this earlier captured warship. Captain Suckling set sail for the far off Falkland Islands in the first dispute over those isles, then being contested with Spain. While the *HMS Raisonnable* never saw battle in that affair before it was settled in England's favor, the voyage took young Horatio across the expansive Atlantic Ocean.

After that journey, he was separated from his uncle. Horatio would undertake expeditions to Jamaica and Tobago. Seaman Nelson next joined an Arctic exploration, coming as close as ten degrees from reaching the North Pole before the icecap became frozen solid and thus impassible. The tale is told of Horatio deserting his watch duty to pursue a polar bear he had spotted atop the ice floes before being recalled by his ship's captain. When reprimanded and asked as to his lack of judgement, Nelson merely said he wished to bring the animal's skin home to his father as a souvenir. No fear dwelled within this able seaman.

So in only his first two and a half years on the seas, Nelson had crossed oceans and neared the Polar icecap. The young sailor would next transit to the far off lands of the East.

Nelson sailed for India aboard the *HMS Seahorse* in late 1773 at the age of fifteen. There in mid-February 1775, he had his first taste of battle. Unfortunately, early in the following year, he contracted malaria and was sent back to England to recuperate. After recovering, the eighteen year old Horatio passed his lieutenant's boards and was made an officer in 1776.

Nelson spent much time in the Caribbean thereafter and was in those seas while the American War of Independence was being fought. He again contracted illness in 1780, at age twenty-two, this time thought to be either dysentery or yellow fever. He recovered, but would for the rest of his life be plagued by a sickly constitution. Nonetheless, up until this time, he had demonstrated expertise in navigation, temperament in judgement, and most of all, the ability to inspire and lead men.

By 1781, at the ripened age of twenty-three, Nelson was elevated to the rank of captain, and given his first command of the 28 gun frigate *HMS Albemarle*. When the American Revolutionary War ended in 1783, Captain Nelson returned to Britain.

The victory of the Americans that year owed much to the interdiction of the French Navy, whose blockade of the Chesapeake Bay two years earlier prevented the British Navy from evacuating General Cornwallis' troops, who had found themselves surrounded on the Yorktown Peninsula by the Continental Army. While no one can pinpoint the exact origin of Nelson's intense hatred for the French, the British held a generational enmity dating back to the Hundred Years' War and beyond. Nelson's limited recollections of his own mother included her loathing the French. Certainly, the French Navy's belittling of the Royal Navy and having forced the surrender of the British army, contributed to Nelson's deep distain.

The next year, Nelson took command of another ship, the *HMS Boreas,* and again was chartered to sail throughout the British West Indies. It was in the British Leeward Islands where Nelson faced his first major crisis of command.

After the American War of Independence, the governors of those British islands were actively trading with American merchant ships, despite the British Navigation Act being still on the books. That act forbade British possessions from trading with foreign-flagged vessels. Nelson determined that it was his duty to enforce the laws of the Crown, not to give in to the demands of the local British Governors and merchants. He soon began seizing any American ships that entered British harbors. Complaints were leveled against him. Eventually, Nelson was exonerated by the King's Home Government, but his vigilant enforcement of trade law left a bad taste in the mouths of influential merchants. Many of these men had longstanding relationships with Nelson's superiors.

On the island of Nevis during this time, Nelson met and courted the recently widowed Frances "Fanny" Nisbet in 1785. Nisbet was only a few months older than the twenty-seven year old captain. Fanny was the niece of the island's premiere plantation owner, John Richardson Herbert, who was also President of the Council of Nevis. By other than mere coincidence, he had been one of the few merchants who had supported Nelson's actions during the trade dispute. Perhaps Herbert's objective was to have his freshly widowed niece re-married so that neither she nor her young son, Josiah, would any longer be his financial responsibility.

After marrying Fanny in March of 1787, Captain Nelson brought his new wife and step-son back to Burnham Thorpe in England. Meanwhile in London, the overseas merchants' accusations of Nelson's far too vigorous enforcement of post-war trade restrictions caught up to the young captain. He soon found himself in a period devoid of war and without a command. He was placed on reserve and thus half-pay for the next five years.

It was a dark time for the young captain, who only wished for a ship to command and the respect of his peers. Over these five years, Nelson often requested from the Admiralty any craft, regardless of size or function. Each request was denied. Few warships sailed on the tides of peace. This half-decade of being run aground became a trying time for the new husband and provider.

Yet, fate has a way of affording opportunity to those of its choosing when it is least expected. The French Revolution had begun in 1789, and its Reign of Terror evolved beginning in 1792. Ironically, Nelson would come to owe the restoration of his professional career to the French that he abhorred so.

England's King George III watched in horror, along with the other monarchs of Europe as the French beheaded King Louis XVI in January of 1793. France then declared war against all the monarchies of Europe, including Britain, which brought Horatio Nelson back into the full service of the Admiralty. It was the French themselves who had saved Nelson's career.

Captain Nelson was soon dispatched to the Mediterranean Sea aboard the *HMS Agamemnon*. France still suffered internally from the Revolution's raging civil war, with the revolutionary Republican forces pitched against the Royalists, those still loyal to the Bourbon Monarchy. The French Royalist troops had forcibly taken control of the Mediterranean port of Toulon. The town was quickly under counter-attack by the French Republican Army and the British Royal Navy was dispatched to aid the Royalists by blockading Toulon's harbor.

Nelson was ordered to Naples to raise local reinforcements and transport them to fight the French. There he called on the longstanding British Ambassador, Sir William Hamilton, for assistance in raising these troops. It was then that Nelson was introduced to Lady Emma Hamilton, the Ambassadors's energetic and vivacious wife, thirty-five years younger than her esteemed husband.

This chance meeting would eventually spark a relationship that would dominate the rest of Nelson's controversial personal life. He would not meet Emma again for another five years.

As fate would have it, Toulon was the very same French port where a young Republican artillery officer named Napoleon Bonaparte would begin his meteoric rise to fame. As the French port fell to Napoleon and the French Revolutionary forces, the British fleet was driven off into the open Mediterranean Sea. Being denied the harbor at Toulon, the British then needed a strategically located seaport from which to resupply their ships.

The Royal Navy looked to overtake control of the ports of Napoleon's home island of Corsica from the French. Nelson's ship became involved in the blockade of the island's seaports. He then led an assault on the coastal town of Calvi. During that landing, Nelson was fired upon with grapeshot. The cannon's load missed him directly but kicked up a terrible spray of sand and debris that wounded his right eye. Nelson would surrender his sight in that eye just as the seaports of Corsica were surrendered to the British.

Figure 5: Captain Nelson, 1781, age 22

Figure 6: Napoleon Bonaparte (unfinished)

Chapter 3: Paris
Baroness Larouche's Soirée

The evening's gathering was cloaked in mystique, and anticipation edged the air that filled the salon under the high Rococo-style ceiling. The crystalline notes of a piano sparkled softly, as if not to compete with the delicate fragrances of rose and lily flowered vases that lined every wall. The massive chandelier above the guests' heads held no fewer than two hundred tapered candles. The salon was abuzz with the trilling of tongues. The hostess, Baroness Charlotte Larouche, was draped in an elegantly brocaded violet gown, outshining the impressive evening wear of the her many resplendent guests. Her husband, Baron Larouche, was not present, as he was away in Flanders on business, which, quite frankly, the hostess preferred.

It was by then in 1804 only becoming permissive to show wealth once again in the capital as the sharpest pangs of the Revolution had receded. Riches and even subdued extravagance, were once more enjoyed, mostly in private. Yet, the one remaining sin that would not be forgiven was that of being named a Royalist. Any mention of restoring the throne to any descendent of the Bourbon kings was still treason and enough for one to be executed.

But to host a *soirée*, which only a few years past could cost one their head, was once more allowed, so long as it was done discreetly and not flaunted in the face of the still excitable poor.

Marek, fitted out in his finest parade dress uniform, milled about the salon, not openly as Madame Charlotte's beau, although most all there plainly knew that to be the case. Instead, he was supposedly there to receive Princess Czartoryska as her countryman in exile. The Princess had not yet arrived, and all were anxious for her entrance, none more so than Marek Zaczek himself. As he smiled politely at the others present, his mind was engaged on the exact words in Polish with which he would greet the beautiful Princess Izabela.

The Princess' carriage arrived, and Marek's throat seemed to tighten along with his anxiety. A few minutes later, the guest of honor was announced to the *soirée* as Princess Izabela Czartoryska of Poland. This introduction was a consolation Madame Larouche had afforded Marek, introducing her as royalty from a country which had not existed for nearly a full decade.

Princess Izabela entered the room looking just as Marek remembered her from the Czartoryski Palace at Puławy. She was as beautiful as that fateful evening ten years ago. Her face was long and thin, but not unattractively so. Her cheeks and lips were of the softest complementary hues of rose petals dusted atop her pale skin not unlike the milkiness of lilies. Marek wondered if the flowers along the walls were selected to mimic this most personal feature of the Princess' appearance, rose upon lily, deciding that it was the sort of touch to which his lover would have paid great attention. The contrast enhanced the tenderness of the Princess' eyes as they took in the French socialites awaiting to receive her.

Princess Izabela wore her hair up like an exotic crown. Her burnt umber locks were streaked with cocoa brown highlights. Her dress was of a most subtle shade of green, reminding Marek of asparagus or artichoke, although he would later learn it was the color Celadon, named after the hues of rare Chinese ceramics. She was, after all, a collector of many works of fine art, and it reflected in her carefully cultivated style of dress.

Her beauty was not so much breathtaking, as it was elegant, subdued and natural, all in one stroke. It was not affected; it was hewn from the elements of her own innate persona. Few could so readily replicate it, he thought, although many had tried only to come off as pretentious.

Marek knew few women who could meld these qualities and do so effortlessly. Yet, even in his nearly unbearable suffering that night a decade earlier, he recalled her in exactly these ways. It had been on this very evening, on 10 October 1794, after Poland's military leader, General Tadeusz Kościuszko had been defeated and captured by the Russians at the Battle of Maciejowice that the Princess herself had attended to Marek's wounds.

Marek was then an Uhlan cavalier and had been sent by the Austrians to capture the General and bring him back to their territory of Galicia. They desired his leadership in controlling the Southern Poles in their annexed lands. Having been beaten to capturing Kościuszko by the Russians, Marek then decided that as his primary mission had been denied him, he would go on to rescue his childhood love, Maya, hiding nearby on a farm where which she had been living.

Marek came upon his love there, but shortly thereafter so did two pillaging Cossacks. He disposed of each of the horsemen, but not before taking on significant wounds of his own. That night, after delivering the pregnant Maya and her accompanying mother safely to the Czartoryski Palace in the nearby town of Puławy, Marek collapsed at the palace gates. He recalled his wounds were treated by Princess Izabela herself later that evening.

Madame Charlotte Larouche welcomed her prestigious visitor, and as she did so, beckoned gracefully for Marek to join her. She began with the single Polish word, *"Witamy,"* meaning welcome, that Marek had taught her. After which Marek gently took the Princess' hand, and in a graceful succession, lowered himself to one knee. The warrior kissed her hand with the greatest respect, and raising his head slowly, said in their native Polish tongue, "I am honored to welcome you this evening, Princess Czartoryska. It is the greatest pleasure for my eyes to rest upon your beauty once again. I am *Pan* Marek Zaczek of Wieliczka, your servant, forever indebted to your family's support of our country and to your personal grace."

His words, understandable to no one else other than he and the Princess, drew from her an unusual response. Despite not speaking the language, the guests must have noticed her reserved reaction.

"Have I had the pleasure of meeting *Pan* Zaczek in the past?" she asked. "I am sorry, but if so, it escapes me now."

Then it was Marek's turn to display a quizzical countenance of his own. His eyes accused her, as the words stabbed at him, as if intended to bring back the pain of that night a decade past. She had re-opened those wounds with her denial of their very existence.

After she reflected on her words, and his reaction to them, she felt them to be perhaps too harsh. The Princess softened them, saying, "It is my pleasure to *meet* you, *Pan* Zaczek."

"But we have met before," the young warrior insisted. "You saved my very life by attending to my wounds the night of the Battle of Maciejowice, when I arrived terribly gored at the gates of your palace in Puławy. By God's intent, it seems, it was ten years ago on this very night."

The Princess had noticed that the French hostess and her guests were waiting patiently while she and Marek conversed in Polish. It was quite stylish for the well-bred of Poland to speak fluent French in those days, but none of even the most celebrated of Frenchmen had taken the time to master the very difficult Polish language.

"Yes, I recall now that your *matka* said that you were there that terrible night. However, I was not. It was most unfortunate that I wasn't, but it appears my servants took exceedingly good care of you and your wounds, or perhaps you would not be here today. I must also tell you before I move on to the French guests collected here that I carry a letter for you at your mother's request."

"I am surprised that you would even know my mother…"

"War has an awkward way of forging friendships," the Princess interrupted him. "I met *Pani* Magdalena in Warsaw, and when I told her I was coming to see First Consul Napoleon, she asked if I would be kind enough to carry a letter for you with me."

"My *matka* was in Warsaw? Prussian Warsaw? I thought she was in Austrian Kraków?"

"Well, *Pan* Zaczek, I look forward to continuing this discussion after I am properly received by our hostess and her other guests," she said to him, all in Polish, before turning to her hostess. The Princess then said in near perfect French, "Forgive my delay in thanking you, Madame Larouche, for going to the trouble of having me greeted in my own native tongue. It was such an unexpected but welcome consideration that I fear I have dwelled a bit too long in its familiarity. What a wonderful reception you have troubled yourself to provide me."

"I had hoped to have General Jan Henryk Dąbrowski here to welcome you as well, but I am afraid he had a pressing military engagement from which he could not free himself. However, he promised to stop by later in the evening. Come, Princess, I have so many dear friends and associates to introduce to you. They are all waiting eagerly to meet you, for they know you to be such a fine collector of and patron to the arts."

"Yes, of course, *avec plaisir*," Princess Izabela said as Madame Larouche took her by the arm. "It will be splendid to see the General later in the evening, as I have some business to discuss with him. May I request of you a room to that end, where General Dąbrowski and *Pan* Zaczek and I can speak in private? I do not wish to affront your guests by the three of us having a prolonged conversation in a foreign tongue in front of them. That would be terribly rude, I'm afraid."

"Of course, my Princess, I will arrange it. You can have the privacy of my husband's study for that purpose." And so Madame Larouche took the Polish Princess Czartoryska by the arm and began the personal introductions to the awaiting crowd of guests assembled.

Marek, having risen to his feet, felt as though there was a vast misunderstanding between himself and the Princess. Their brief encounter left him with a series of unsettling questions, which ate away with self-doubt at the surety of his recollections.

Why would my mother who lives in Austrian Kraków be in Prussian Warsaw to see the Princess? Why would the Princess refer to her as Pani Magdalena and not Duchess Magdalena? Why would his mother not merely dispatch a messenger of her own with a letter for me? She is certainly wealthy enough to do so. What could be so terribly important that she would impose the burden upon Princess Izabela to carry the note?

The evening droned on for Marek, until after the entertainment of the pianist's performance, when the hostess, Baroness Larouche, returned with the Princess to Marek's side.

"Marek tells me your Puławy Palace in Poland is quite exquisite," the Baroness Larouche said as she rejoined the two.

"Our family was fortunate to have many beautiful properties before the Partitions," Princess Izabela replied, "but the palace at Puławy was always my favorite. I am afraid it is only now returning to the full beauty it possessed before it was desecrated by the Russians a decade ago. But just as forest fires make way for new growth, so too the palace has been renewed somewhat. A few years ago, in 1801, I was able to open portions of it as a museum for the people. We have lovely Greek classical structures, including the Temple of the Sybil, which now houses many of the most important artifacts of Polish history and culture."

"How wonderful," Madame Larouche said with a slightly dismissive smile. "Marek tells me that he escaped only the night before the Russians attacked your palace. He says that you were kind enough to attend to his wounds and offer your personal carriage to carry him, his Maya and her mother away to safety."

"It is just as I have said," Marek added. "How many times have I told that very story to you, Baroness?"

"Perhaps just as you remembered, *Pan* Zaczek," the Princess countered, "but you see, Baroness, I was not there. I was in England with my two sons at the time."

"But I remember you so clearly," Marek protested, "your beautiful face peered down at me as you cleansed my wounds with the most tender touch. I recall your gentle humming as you did, and it relaxed me so, as even then I feared death awaited me. I cannot possibly be mistaken."

"It is quite possible there is another explanation. Can you remember what I was wearing that night?" Izabela asked.

"Yes, of course," Marek replied. "That night you also wore a beautiful green gown. Not as beautiful as this one, of course, but in a similar shade."

"As I might have thought," the Princess said. "Certainly, you were in great pain, my brave hero. Your mind was dealing with the stress of your injuries. Under those conditions, suffering plays such tricks on even the strongest of us. You surely were looking up at my portrait in our receiving hall as my staff attended to you."

"No, no, I felt the touch of your hands," Marek said, "the scent of your perfume, and the gentle soothing of your voice."

"The portrait is just as you describe," the Princess continued. "The Russians swarmed over the palace only hours after the coach carrying you left. You are lucky to be alive, *Pan* Zaczek. As it is, our chambermaids were all ravaged and carried away by the Russians, those not killed outright. I am sure one of them attended to you. I am sorry it was not me, for anyone maimed doing battle with the Russians that day deserved my personal attention. But alas, I was in England, and in the days that followed my sons and I tried to make our way back to Puławy, but the Austrians took us as prisoners upon our return to the Continent."

"How dreadful for you, my Princess!" Madame Larouche decried. "By what means did you make your escape?"

"I was ransomed and set free in due course," Izabela answered, "but my sons were not so fortunate. They were turned over to the Russians, and at the command of Tsarina Catherine were kept as political prisoners in Saint Petersburg. She came to take an interest in both Adam Jerzy and Konstanty Adam, and they won her favor shortly before the Tsarina died. Then, they were shown compassion by her son, Tsar Paul, and after he was murdered a few years later, by the friendship of his son and heir, Tsar Alexander."

The Baroness displayed great outrage upon her face over the plight of her guest's children. Her jaw dropped in disgust.

"So where are your sons now?" Madame Larouche asked.

Marek answered for her. "My Baroness, Princess Czartoryska's older son, Adam Jerzy, serves as the Minister of Foreign Affairs to Tsar Alexander. Of this I am aware. I am sorry, Princess, but I am unaware of your younger son's whereabouts."

"Konstanty Adam has since returned to Warsaw, thank you," the Princess added. "You seem to know much about my family, *Pan* Zaczek, even if your recollections are somewhat tainted, but most understandably so."

Marek appeared to be flustered by her last remark. He had been sure over the past ten years that she herself had administered to him that night. He still did not fully accept her explanation of his suffering and the portrait being the source of his memory.

"Forgive me, your Highness," Marek said in a highly conciliatory voice. "I am ashamed that I did not know about your being detained and ransomed by the Austrians, for whom I have no respect. I had assumed your two sons were captured at your Palace at Puławy. I am embarrassed to have been so confused. Please accept my apologies."

Marek then lowered his head before her in disgrace.

Princess Czartoryska reached out and taking his chin in her fingertips, raised his head until his eyes met hers, then she responded, "I have just thought of a wonderful way for you to make amends, my countryman."

As they had been speaking in French, the baroness became visibly perturbed at the Princess' suggestion. Princess Izabela was known to have had many dalliances, and her two sons were rumored to have been fathered by two different men, neither of which were reported to be her husband. Her elder son was said to be from an affair with a Russian diplomat in Warsaw; the younger son from a liaison with a French nobleman here in Paris. They were both raised by her husband as his own. But before the baroness could even think of a manner in which to protest the Princess' solicitation of Marek, the discussion was interrupted by the announcement of the arrival of General Jan Henryk Dąbrowski.

The Baroness reluctantly left Marek and Princess Izabela to make her way to the entrance in order to greet the General. As she slowly accompanied him back through the onslaught of guests, they delayed him to give thanks for his service to France. This gave Marek and the Princess a few moments alone together.

"I did not wish to put you in an awkward position in front of our hostess," Marek said to Princess Czartoryska in Polish, "but it is well known that your son has advised the young Tsar to declare war against the French, and that he has no regard personally for our Emperor Bonaparte. It is also understood that your Highness was invited to come to Paris by the Emperor himself. I can only assume that he wishes to discuss this with you to understand the nature of your son's reservations."

Marek knew he was being forward with her, but inwardly still stoked a feeling of resentment at her not remembering him. *She was there, he was sure it was her. Why would she lie?*

The Princess sipped from her flute of champagne, as if she wished to find a way to sweeten the words she was about to speak.

"You are quite perceptive, *Pan* Zaczek. For this very reason, I have asked General Dąbrowski to attend this evening so that I might share my thoughts with someone of *his importance.* Let us await his joining us before we discuss this any further."

Her words stung Marek, implying that the young legionnaire's lack of both rank and status should have precluded him from confronting her, even if done so only in private.

"Please forgive my being so forthright, my Princess, but I only fear what is most important," Marek continued, sidestepping her. "If *Pan* Adam Jerzy Czartoryski continues to advise the Tsar not only to stay aligned with the Austrians, but also to solicit the aid of the Prussians, he will find himself as much an enemy of our Emperor as any man in Europe. That can be a very poor position for a man as ambitious as your son."

"*Pan* Zaczek," the Princess replied, "you continue to refer to First Consul Bonaparte as Emperor, a title not yet fully bestowed upon him. I understand the Holy Father will be here at the Cathedral of Notre Dame in December to do so…"

"A mere technicality," interrupted Marek. "The Senate proclaimed him Emperor this past May…"

Marek found himself cut off in return by the Princess, who eyed their hostess approaching with General Dąbrowski in tow, and wished him not to hear the words she spoke next.

"… but it is a technicality that Bonaparte desperately needs to satisfy, no? He may be all powerful within France, but it is still ill advised to have his armies being viewed as fighting against Christianity itself. Yet, they appear to do so as they face off against the combined Austrians and Prussian forces of the Holy Roman Empire, or even the Orthodox Russians. Bonaparte needs to be viewed as having the Pope's blessing for legitimacy, does he not?"

"Austria, Prussia and Russia! The same three so-called Christian Kingdoms who collaborated to so devilishly devour our pious Catholic land of Poland lying so peacefully between them?" Marek baited her with his own questions. "And yet, your son would have them unite once more to fight against any hope of our every recovering the sovereignty of our homeland?"

"My son works from inside the Tsar's court to restore our country to freedom," she said with an abruptness that stung him.

"Forgive me, my Princess," he said, "but that is like asking the devil himself to give up sinning. It will never come to pass."

Madame Larouche then returned with her newly arrived guest. She led Princess Czartoryska, Marek Zaczek and General Dąbrowski to her husband's study. Its walls were paneled floor to ceiling with flawless mahogany overlaid with fine millwork of a most intricate design. Near the window was a precious *Louis Quatorze* style writing desk and chair. Baroness Larouche waited for the servant lighting the oil lamps to finish and leave the room, after which she herself departed their company.

As she did, she said, "Please take all the time you need. I will be with my guests just outside these doors should you need anything at all." She pulled the doors closed behind her.

Marek, who had fought for the French *Armée d'Italie* under Dąbrowski against the Austrians for the last eight years, was excited to introduce him to the Princess.

"General Dąbrowski, please allow me to intro…," Marek began in the trio's native tongue, before being interrupted again.

"No introduction is necessary, Zaczek," General Dąbrowski said, offering to take the hand of the Princess in his own. "The Czartoryskis are well known to me. They have hosted me at their estates in Warsaw, at Puławy, and even at their Sieniawa home in Austrian Galicia many times. My dearest Princess Izabela, it is so wonderful to have you honor us here in Paris with your presence."

The Princess gently laid her hand in the General's own, upon which he dropped to one knee and kissed the back of it out of sheer respect, just as Marek had done before him.

"It is delightful to see you again, General Jan Henryk," the Princess replied using the familiar form of his name. "Adam Kazimierz sends his regards."

"Ah, yes," General Dąbrowski said, "how is my most celebrated countryman, your husband?"

"Slightly ill, I am afraid," she responded, "not seriously so, but certainly too sick at this time to make the long journey. But I was happy to do so, always wishing to find an excuse to come and see the art collections of Paris."

"Well, you must visit the *Musée Napoléon* in the old Louvre Palace," General Dąbrowski replied. " I am sure you will find time for that, but it is hardly the reason for my invitation."

The Princess took her gaze off her family's old friend and turned to Marek. "I am afraid your officer, Lieutenant Zaczek, does not realize I am here at your bidding."

"Ah, but only on Emperor Bonaparte's behalf," General Dąbrowski clarified. "His Imperial Majesty Napoleon is eager to your meeting in two days hence."

"Yes, of course," Princess Czartoryska continued. "Your officer Zaczek is however very astute as to why Bonaparte might wish to have a private audience with someone who commands no political power herself."

"Your Highness has all the power of the world at her fingertips," Marek interjected, "as mother to the Foreign Minister to Tsar Alexander of Russia. Surely the Emperor views your presence as an opportunity to influence your son, so he in turn can advise the Tsar in matters on France's behalf."

Marek's outburst caught the Polish general off guard.

"And so now I see the meaning of your comment regarding Lieutenant Zaczek," Dąbrowski said to Princess Izabela, if only to save her the embarrassment of having to respond to Marek's brash, but accurate, observation. "Zaczek can often be a little too eager to show off his skills, and it is apparent that extends to his deductive reasoning, as well as his battlefield disciplines. He is old enough to have learned that it is not always to a good soldier's advantage to reveal all the weapons arrayed in his arsenal."

Marek was embarrassed, as if he were merely a child being scolded in the company of adults. Despite this, he refused to hang his head. He held it high, taking the brunt of the General's insult.

"Technically, Russia is already at war with the French, alongside the Austrians," Princess Izabela stated. "My son thinks that the young Tsar is perhaps overly eager to engage in battle."

"The Emperor is said to have received word," General Dąbrowski replied, "that your son is advocating for Tsar Alexander to persuade Prussia to join the Coalition with Russia and Austria. The Tsar so far has resisted this advice. Russia has only recently begun to prepare to move its troops eastward against France. The Emperor has much regard for the young Tsar, and believes there is time to alter his foolish ambitions."

"Well," the Princess replied, "allow me too say that my son, Adam Jerzy, has no trust to place in the hearts of the Prussians, for theirs are hearts full of treachery. And as I have said, war with France has already been declared. Yet while the Tsar's troops prepare for war, the Prussians continue to remain neutral."

"Emperor Bonaparte knows there is still plenty of time to soften the young Tsar's alliance with Austria. Your son could be influential in making this occur, instead of advocating against us. The Emperor would be willing to bestow great riches and titles to your family. After all, it would be best if all this is done before Napoleon is coronated at the second of December ceremony."

"In that way," Dąbrowski continued, "there can be no accusation by the enemies of Tsar Alexander of his acting out of fear to Bonaparte's increased power. Emperor Bonaparte is no threat to Mother Russia. He only desires for the Tsar and the Russian people to be France's easternmost allies."

"But before his coronation?" chided the Princess. "Why does he even await the Pope? Why not coronate himself now? And why stop at calling himself Emperor? Why not simply declare himself king of France?"

"France has no use for kings, Madame," replied Dąbrowski. "The people will never again allow a throne to reign over them."

"Ah, but has not Napoleon already taken a throne as Emperor?" the Princess asked boldly. "Perhaps it will be the sheer audacity of this man Bonaparte that will eventually convince the citizens of France to return the Bourbons to reign over them."

Marek listened intently to the discussion as it passed like a shuttlecock between the General and the Princess. He had decided to hold his tongue, and was surprised to hear Princess Izabela say that her son had no trust of the Prussians. Yet, this same man aligned himself so prominently to the equally treacherous Tsar and his Russian army that had already taken so much of Poland.

"General Dąbrowski," the Princess asked after a few moments, "were you able to arrange the meeting I had requested for tomorrow? I am quite adamant that it must occur before I meet with Bonaparte."

"On that account, I have both good news and bad for you, my Princess," Dąbrowski responded. "I have made the meeting appointment for tomorrow that you have requested. However, Emperor Bonaparte demands my presence at Fontainebleau, so I will be unable to escort you to Berville."

"I see," Princess Izabela said. "I thought your time might prove too valuable a commodity to squander on a visiting dignitary as inconsequential as myself, so perhaps *Pan* Zaczek could escort me in your stead?"

"Of course, your request is granted," the General answered without hesitation. "Lieutenant Zaczek will be the perfect companion for your journey."

"But, General Dąbrowski," Zaczek protested, "I am scheduled to lead the drills of the lancers among your Polish Legions tomorrow at the *Champs de Mars*."

"Yes, my Princess," Dąbrowski said, ignoring Marek's embarrassing outburst. "I agree Zaczek would be a most appropriate escort. I only ask that you assure he does not attempt to kidnap the man with whom you intend to meet. But then again, he was not very successful in doing so a decade ago."

"You mean we are to meet with General Kościuszko?" Marek blurted, drawing laughter from the Princess and Dąbrowski.

"Yes, Marek," Princess Izabela replied after her giggling subdued, "tomorrow, we will meet with the great patriot, General Tadeusz Kościuszko. He met several years ago with Napoleon, and although his recollections will be somewhat aged, I would like his insights into the man you are so eager to call Emperor."

"It will be my honor," Marek said, straightening his already rigid stance. "I have never had the honor to meet him. I knew he had come back to Paris from America."

"Nearly six years ago, now," General Dąbrowski said. "Kościuszko is treated as a hero on both continents. When he left Philadelphia with the assistance of Thomas Jefferson, he left behind a Last Will and Testament to use all the back pay owed him by the Continental Army to free slaves in that country. It was an honor to fight under him in Poland for freedom, even if it ended ultimately in defeat."

"Then it is settled," Princess Czartoryska said. "Marek will escort me. He will ride with me in my coach, and as an accommodation to yourself, General, I will ask him to sit in with General Kościuszko and myself. In that way, he can report back to you all that is discussed."

"Then it is agreed," Dąbrowski said.

"And Lieutenant Zaczek," the Princess called to Marek.

"Yes, Princess Czartoryska?"

"I will be sure to bring along the letter your mother asked me to carry. I am quite certain it must be of great importance for her to have made such a request of me directly."

Chapter 4: Nelson and The Birth of a Hero

The tortured soul rips and tears at itself, but when the pain of its self-inflicted wounds drive it to incoherence, that confused creature soon redirects its anger and lashes outward at those around it.

Nations, like individuals, have personalities. For France, since 1789, her personality was highly schizophrenic. She condemned herself for having allowed the prosperous elites, in their palaces of grandeur, to take advantage of her starving masses of peasants. She tore at her own limbs - the monarchy, the church, the aristocracy, nearly all conventions of society - to rid the guilt from her long history of misdeeds. Then in 1793, shortly after the crucible of her anger bubbled over with the beheading of King Louis XVI, she was surprised to discover the nation's wrath still remained unresolved. Civil war between the Revolutionaries and the Royalists intensified, and the Reign of Terror soon reached its full demonic bloom. Sensing her own internal lesions not pacified, surely not conquered, she lashed out at those devils surrounding her and feeding that insurrection. France struck out at her neighbor states and declared war on all the monarchies of Europe!

That declaration of war by France restored Horatio Nelson to command; his spirits billowed like his ship's sails on the winds of the open seas. That new ship that he would captain was the sixty-four gun *HMS Agamemnon*, his first command of a Ship-of-the-Line, named after the Greek king who had led his massive army outside the gates of Troy. Indeed, if Helen was the woman who had launched a thousand ships, then the *HMS Agamemnon* was the ship that launched a thousand glories for Horatio Nelson. It would not be his last command, and certainly not the greatest, for both those fates were reserved for his flagship when he would later become Rear Admiral Nelson. That last flagship would be aptly named the *HMS Victory.*

Over the five years he had been grounded in England, Nelson's affections for his wife "Fanny" had not yet cooled. He could have fallen prey to the human frailty of associating his loss of command with having brought Fanny and Josiah back to England. Instead, Nelson professed nothing but love for Fanny, despite her never having told him that she could not bear his children. Yet, even with this becoming evident over the years of their marriage, he took a keen interest in her son, Josiah, to the point that when Nelson captained the *Agamemnon*, he convinced Fanny to allow him to take young Josiah into service with him. At twelve years old, Josiah began a seaman's life under Nelson, just as the young captain once had under his own uncle. Fanny was left behind at the Norfolk parsonage to care for Nelson's aging father.

But thanks to the war with France in 1793, everything had indeed changed for Nelson. In May, he had set sail commanding the *HMS Agamemnon* as a Ship-of-the-Line in Admiral Hotham's fleet supporting the Siege of Toulon. It was the first of Nelson's war engagements with Napoleon, although the pair would never be pitted directly against each other in the same specific battle. Napoleon was by then merely an unknown colonel of the artillery, while Nelson was already established as an accomplished, if not infamous, naval captain.

Nelson, as has been earlier noted, was ordered to Naples to conscript reinforcements from that kingdom. He engaged Sir William Hamilton, and in doing so met the British Ambassador's young, vivacious wife, Emma. But there is nothing to indicate the meeting distracted him away from his mission. It would be another five years until they were to meet again, and a very consequential five years for Nelson's career those would be.

In fact, the incredible remainder of Nelson's life's journey would last but another twelve years. Over those same dozen years, Napoleon's star would rise from his daring exploits as leader of the Revolutionary Republican Army in northern Italy, to his first great victory as Emperor.

Captain Nelson spent the majority of his and the *HMS Agamemnon's* time in the Mediterranean Sea. After losing the sight of his right eye in the taking of the Corsican port of Calvi, Nelson would go on to engage the enemy in a series of confrontations.

In 1795, Nelson and the *HMS Agamemnon* became part of the British fleet tasked with orders to prevent the French from retaking Corsica. In March, the two fleets met, and Nelson's sixty-four gun *HMS Agamemnon* engaged a much larger French vessel, the eighty-four gun *Ça Ira.*

That French ship had collided into another vessel of its own fleet on the open sea. The collision's impact snapped her upper masts, which then hung uselessly over her port side, blocking her cannons on that side from defending her. As the de-masted *Ça Ira* fell behind the rest of the French fleet, Nelson rapidly approached from her blinded port side, settled in on her stern and blasted her with cannon fire, disabling the *Ça Ira.* Nelson had done extensive damage to the French vessel before *HMS Agamemnon* was driven off by other returning French warships. One was the massive one-hundred-and-twenty gun French Ship-of-the-Line *Sans Cullottes,* which would later face Nelson in battle once again after having been renamed as *L'Orient.*

Figure 8: Nelson's HMS Agamemnon Engages the French Warships Ça Ira and Censeur

The *HMS Agamemnon* and other British ships shadowed the French fleet into the next morning. The heavily damaged *Ça Ira* was, by then, being towed by the seventy-four gun French Ship-of-the-Line *Censeur*. Being near Genoa, the British and French fleets re-engaged as Nelson attacked the severely damaged French warship and the companion vessel that towed it.

Nelson's *Agamemnon* would boldly end up taking both ships as the rest of the British fleet engaged to hold off the remaining French Ships-of-the-Line. When the French fleet eventually sailed off, effectively surrendering both the *Censeur* and the *Ça Ira* to the British, Captain Nelson urged Admiral Hotham to pursue and re-engage the escaping enemy ships. Hotham thought the day won. Nelson considered the incident only a partial victory, and viewed his Admiral as having allowed the bulk of the French fleet to escape. This limited British victory kept Corsica under British control for a few years longer, but as a result of Hotham's cautious leadership, France was allowed to retain the bulk of its considerable naval presence in the Mediterranean.

Captain Nelson was recognized as a naval hero for his decisive actions during the battle. He wrote affectionately to his wife Fanny after the initial *Ça Ira* engagement, expressing,

"It is with an inexpressible pleasure I have received your letters, with our father's. I rejoice that my conduct gives you pleasure, and I trust I shall never do anything which will bring a blush on your face. Rest assured you are never
absent from my thoughts." [4]

The *Ça Ira* incident brought Nelson notoriety within the Admiralty. He returned to England and was soon promoted to commodore in 1796, the last rank below Admiral. By the following year Commodore Nelson was in command of another Ship-of-the-Line, the *HMS Captain.*

By January of 1797, much had changed in the war. The Spanish had aligned their navy with the French. The combined Franco-Spanish fleet rivaled that of the British, at least on paper. The French fleet was of its own doing a formidable foe, but as for the Spanish Navy, while it possessed some of the finest and largest warships built at that time, it lacked the discipline and ability of both its commanders and crew to effectively wield them in battle.

The tides of war forced Britain to eventually withdraw from both the islands of Corsica and Elba. As they were doing so, their fifteen ship fleet now came under the command of Admiral Sir John Jervis, a more aggressive leader who had replaced the tentative Admiral Hotham. Admiral Jervis soon tracked down and engaged a much larger thirty-eight ship Spanish fleet. Nelson would lead his *HMS Captain* crew into that conflict which would become known as the Battle of Cape Saint Vincent, named after the site along the Spanish coast. The British ships attacked in a single column, and bisected the line of the enemy fleet.

---

[4] *"The Life of Nelson"*, Captain A.T. Mahan, Easton Press Edition of 1897 text, Vol. I, p.173."

The British column separated the Spanish line of ships into two parts. Nelson's command, the *HMS Captain,* was near the rear of the British column, which had passed through the Spanish line and was turning in a broad circle to re-engage the enemy's formations. However, Nelson saw that the forward segment of the British line would not re-engage fast enough, and that the two parts of the Spanish fleet would rejoin into one, creating a much more formidable opponent.

Of his own initiative, Nelson boldly broke his ship away from its assigned position near the end of the British column after it had just passed through the Spanish line. The *HMS Captain* turned back, and Nelson engaged the much larger ships of the Spanish. His ship was soon under tremendous enemy fire, but Nelson's unordered initiative proved successful in keeping the two enemy groupings from joining together again. Soon the *HMS Captain* was assisted by other British warships and together they engaged three massive Spanish Ships-of-the-Line.

In the end, Nelson personally led a boarding party onto two of the Spanish ships' decks and demanded their surrender. When the British fleet prevailed, news soon reached England of another great victory at sea. Once again, as was the case with the *Ça Ira* incident, Nelson was in the center of the action.

Admiral Jervis was named Earl Saint Vincent for his leadership of this great conquest. He was quick to acknowledge Commodore Nelson's valor and bravery in combat. Nelson would be honored by King George III as a Knight of the Bath. Lord Nelson's name became widely known across the land. He was well on his way to being hailed as a hero of renown in all of England.

Despite this, in the heat of the Battle of Cape Saint Vincent, Nelson had ignored direct commands from Admiral Jervis by breaking formation and attacking the Spanish vessels. Jervis, who otherwise thought highly of his Commodore, deferred on officially reprimanding the officer, given the tremendous outcome and overall success of the attack. Yet, despite what very well could have been pressed as insubordination, Nelson came out of the battle as a tremendously respected naval leader, and was soon after promoted to the Rank of Rear Admiral of the Blue.

It would not be the last time Nelson would defy a superior's direct orders, including those ushered forth from his wife. Fanny pleaded for her husband to be more cautious at sea. She asked him, now as a Rear Admiral, to allow the captains of his fleet to take on the most hazardous duties, such as boarding enemy vessels in battle. As an admiral, she surely would have argued, Nelson owed it to the country to stay safely out of harm's way to assure a continuity of leadership.

Nelson, of course, would not hear of such a thing, as he would have responded that it was his duty to be in the very thick of things. Having tasted the benefits of hero recognition by the public and the increase in status by the Admiralty, there was no possibility of containing or throttling back his courageous naval exploits.

Nelson had prophetically written to his wife, Fanny, regarding a failed attack on Cádiz after the Battle of Saint Vincent:

"My late affair here will not, I believe, lower me in the opinion of the world. I have had flattery enough to make me vain, and success enough to make me confident." [5]

His knighthood by King George III surely stroked his vanity, while his hero's welcome had made him overly confident.

Later in that same year of 1797, Rear Admiral Nelson took to the sea aboard his first flagship as Admiral, the *HMS Theseus*. He was still subordinated to Admiral Jervis, the recently made Earl Saint Vincent, but the two men respected each other nearly as equals. While Jervis was awaiting a joint Franco-Spanish fleet to leave the port of Cádiz, Nelson laid out a daring plan to capture the treasures of Spanish gold ships returning from the New World.

The treasure ships were known to regularly stop at the Spanish Canary Islands. Nelson took a portion of Jervis' fleet to the islands' capital, Santa Cruz de Tenerife to assault the enemy's fortification, the *Castillo de San Cristóbal*, by amphibious landing. After the initial wave of landings had failed at the hands of his captains, Admiral Nelson himself led the next wave of the assault, in direct defiance of his wife's earlier pleadings. He even took along her son, Lieutenant Josiah Nisbet, and to good purpose, for young Josiah would end up saving the life of his stepfather.

In what came to be known as the Battle of Tenerife, a hastily planned and ill advised affair, the enemy swept the British landing parties with grapeshot and musket fire. Nelson's right arm was hit by a musket ball, crushing his humerus bone. His main artery was severed, and he surely would have died if not for the quick thinking Lieutenant Josiah Nisbet who used his handkerchief to tie off the wound and stopped the extensive bleeding.

---

[5] *"The Life of Nelson"*, Captain A.T. Mahan, Easton Press Edition of 1897 text,
   Vol. I, p.295"

This was critical as Admiral Nelson then refused to be taken to the nearby *HMS Seahorse*, insisting to be taken further out to his own flagship. He also would accept no assistance to board the *Theseus*, telling the others,"

"Let me alone! I have yet legs left and one arm. Tell the surgeon to make haste and get his instruments. I know I must lose my right arm and the sooner it is off, the better."

Nelson was then to have said directly to the surgeon,

"Doctor, I want to get rid of this useless piece of flesh here." [6]

Thanks to his stepson Josiah's quick thinking and rapid actions, Nelson lived not only long enough to lose his right arm to amputation, but more importantly to continue to fight on behalf of England on for another eight years. The culmination of that added span being the salvation of England from Napoleon's clutches.

The assault at Tenerife was a horrendous failure of an overconfident leader, but despite this, Nelson's injuries garnered sympathy for the national hero. He returned to England to convalesce at the town of Bath. The public, who refused to criticize his leadership for the debacle, laid that blame elsewhere within the Admiralty. Instead, Nelson was exalted for risking his own safety in an attempt to secure a national victory. His countrymen must have wondered, *What more could be asked of Nelson?*

So, after the Battle of Tenerife, the famous sea admiral had use of neither his right eye nor his right arm. During his recovery at Bath, initially after the amputation of his arm, he had become quite maudlin. Nelson had to learn to write using his left hand, among so many other things. He wrote to his friend, telling Admiral Jervis,

---

[6] Quotes commonly attributed to Nelson, contextually supported by the text of *"The Life of Nelson"*, Captain A.T. Mahan, Easton Press Edition of 1897 text, Vol. I, p. 304

Figure 10: Nelson Loses His Arm at Tenerife

"I am become a burthen to my friends and useless to my Country. When I leave your command I become dead to the world; I go hence and am no more seen." [7]

Nelson's slow recovery at Bath lasted months. It was a terribly painful healing process, until the ligament irritating him was finally sloughed free. All the while he felt that the Tenerife debacle could have been successful.

---

[7] *"The Life of Nelson"*, Captain A.T. Mahan, Easton Press Edition of 1897 text, Vol. I, p.306.

Nelson would later write,

*"Had I been with the first party, I have reason to believe
complete success would have crowned our efforts.
My pride suffered."* [8]

He eventually came to accept the reality that he could still effectively lead a fleet into battle. He would wear his wounds like badges of honor, especially the loss of his arm. He refused to hide his empty sleeve, instead he pinned it boldly across his chest as if it were a commemorative sash or a ribbon of merit.

Nelson recovered from his amputation wounds over the remainder of the year and into 1798. He returned to service in the spring aboard a new flagship *HMS Vanguard*, and rejoined Admiral Jervis, still off shore at Cádiz. Under Jervis' orders, Nelson would separate from the overall command at Cádiz to lead a fleet into the Mediterranean Sea in search of Napoleon Bonaparte and a French expeditionary fleet of 40,000 soldiers.

---

[8] *"The Life of Nelson"*, Captain A.T. Mahan, Easton Press Edition of 1897 text, Vol. I, p.307.

Chapter 5: Paris
The Road to Kościuszko

Rare is the personality who truly learns from the past, and rarer still is one afforded the opportunity to consult with those who already bear the scars of history. Marek was blessed in this regard when he was selected to escort Princess Izabela Czartoryska to her visit with the Polish General Tadeusz Kościuszko as preparation for her meeting with Napoleon. Kościuszko was the man who Marek, in his days as an Austrian Uhlan, had been assigned to kidnap and return to Galicia - the lands of Poland so covetously stolen by the Habsburgs.

Of course, Marek failed to capture the General that day, as the Russians had already beaten him to this objective during the Battle of Maciejowice. General Kościuszko, badly wounded from the fighting on the battlefield, was transported back to Russia, accompanied by a guard detail of no less than two thousand Russian soldiers, lest he escape and return to lead the Polish Uprising. In Saint Petersburg, he was kept in the Peter-Paul Prison as a political captive until the death of Tsarina Catherine the Great. Kościuszko was released, along with many other foreign prisoners by her son, Tsar Paul I, when he ascended to the throne.

The General, despite being very sickly along with the festered wounds from his forced imprisonment, made his way back to the United States and resided for a short period of time in a Philadelphia boarding house during his recovery.

Kościuszko was visited there often by his good friend, then Vice-President Thomas Jefferson. When Kościuszko received a letter in early 1798 from the French Minister Charles Maurice de Talleyrand, he immediately made plans to return to Paris. After arriving there, Kościuszko met on two separate occasions with First Consul Bonaparte and Talleyrand, but refused Napoleon's offer of commanding the Polish Forces within the French army. Although those meetings had been six years in the past by the time of the Princess' visit, she nonetheless wanted to hear Kościuszko's opinions of Napoleon. The Princess would meet the very next day with the man who in only weeks was to be crowned Emperor.

Marek and the Princess Czartoryska rode in an ornate carriage that Madame Larouche had made available for their use while in Paris. They travelled to Kościuszko's home in Berville, on the outskirts of Paris, not far from Fontainebleau, the palatial hunting lodge of the kings of France. Marek sat opposite the Princess and her lovely young blonde-haired lady in waiting, an attendant who she introduced only as Kobieta.

After initial pleasantries were exchanged, the carriage ride became tense with a heavy silence accompanied by awkward glances and brittle smiles. Marek knew he must break through the icy chasm that had opened itself between he and the Princess, but his inner voice instantly weighed and rejected every line with which he sought to initiate a conversation.

"*Pan* Zaczek," Princess Czartoryska finally said, relieving him of this problem by asking, "do you know why I asked General Dąbrowski to allow you to escort me this day?"

"No, your Highness," he confessed, "I honestly haven't the slightest inkling of your motive in that regard."

She smiled knowingly at him. "Is it true what is rumored?"

"And to which particular rumor do you refer?"

"The rumor that you were assigned by the Austrians to kidnap General Kościuszko at Maciejowice…" she replied.

"Yes, that is true," he answered casually.

"…and that you abandoned this task to rescue your childhood love from the threat of advancing Cossacks used by the Russians as forward scouts?"

"That," Marek declared, "is a misconception. The General had already been captured by the Russian soldiers, thus ending my assignment."

"But you did thereafter seek out your childhood love, the pregnant daughter of the Duke named Maya?" asked the Princess.

"She was at a farm nearby," Marek explained. "She was a friend in distress. Of course I went there to offer my assistance."

The Princess traded glances with the beautiful Kobieta, who looked down and blushed, as if by Marek's downplaying his relationship to Maya he had been caught in a lie of the heart.

"I was told by my servants who survived the Russian onslaught of our palace that she carried *your* child?" asked, more than stated, Princess Izabela.

"She carried *a* child," Marek corrected her, "but it was not my own."

Again the Princess looked to Kobieta, as if the two of them shared a great secret. Marek noted the glance between them both.

"So I see," the Princess said. "That is so unfortunate. I had for so very long wished it to be true. I thought it to be romantic. A young man, fighting two Cossacks to the death to protect his wife and unborn child. Then delivering them, against all adversities, mind you, to the gates of our palace despite being so terribly injured himself that my servants would find him collapsed on the grounds outside our gates. I was told that your wounds included a large swath of flesh flayed from your forearm."

"Yes, it is so, your Highness," he said, adding, "but it is all healed now, only the scar remains."

With this, the Princess appeared to become very nervous. She again looked at Kobieta, who smirked as if she knew the request that came next.

"Would you think it terrible of me if I asked to see it?"

"My scar?" Marek repeated, caught off guard by the unusual request.

"I know that it is a very intrusive petition," the Princess apologized, "but it all seems so chivalrous for a young man to risk his own life to kill two Cossacks in order to save a woman and the child in her womb. My feminine heart finds it so gallant."

"A woman, her child *and* her mother," added Marek, as he crouched over his seat to strip off his greatcoat and uniform jacket. After sitting again, he began rolling up his sleeve, finishing his joke, "Although I admit I had long thought Maya's mother more fierce than both of the two slain Cossacks together."

Princess Czartoryska smirked at his comment. "Tell me, Marek, how are the young mother and child today? Did they all survive the ordeal of the coach ride to Galicia, as you did? Where are they today? In Poland? At least those lands that once were our country."

"Your Highness," Marek began, "you will be happy to know that both the mother, Maya, and her young child, Władek, are in splendid health. I do not hear from them much, as they are in Kraków, which as you know is in Austrian Galicia. With France being in a state of war with Austria, there is no means of our easily communicating with each other. I have been away from home for nearly a decade myself, but every now and then my mother, the Duchess Magdalena, finds a way to sneak a letter through. She can be quite resourceful when she needs to be."

Marek smiled at the Princess, having delivered a stealthy reminder to her for his mother's letter that she carried.

"My apologies, *Pan* Zaczek," Princess Izabela said, "I have nearly forgotten your mother's letter. Allow me to present it to you." She retrieved it from Kobieta, who had it at the ready within her purse, and handed it to the Princess, who in turn presented it to the young soldier. Marek reached for it with his right arm. He had by then had exposed the glazed-over skin of scar on his left forearm where a large wedge of flesh had been flayed clean away.

The Princess inspected the scarred-over wound quite closely, as if to assure it identified that the young cavalryman was indeed who he claimed to be. Only then did she give him the letter.

"Quite remarkable," the Princess said. "Do you desire to look upon it, Kobieta? You do not mind, *Pan* Zaczek?"

"Not at all," Marek replied, "let the young maiden's eyes remark upon the hazards of war. I hope they should never come to be inflicted upon anyone that you may love."

His words seemed to draw a slight wince from the Princess, as if on behalf of Kobieta. The maiden herself ignored the comment as she leaned forward in an awkward position to closely inspect the wound. She studied its scarred-over flesh with intrigue, as if it had great meaning to her. Kobieta then said with sympathy, "At least it is in such a place that it does not show, *Pan* Zaczek."

"But how I wish it was out in the open," Marek boasted, "so that all could see it as my badge of honor. Lesser men would see it and shy away. But perhaps other Cossacks would see it and be motivated to exact their revenge. In attempting to do so, they would only bring me further honor when I disposed of them also."

"Despite your wishes, *Pan* Zaczek," the Princess said, "I am very happy that it did no harm to your manly face. Every Polish girl would be honored to have as handsome a soldier as you to fight for her virtue. Don't you think so, Kobieta?"

"Of course, My Lady," Kobieta answered, and again her face blushed. Marek pulled back his arm from her and slowly rolled down his sleeve. As he did this, he questioned the Princess.

"So, Princess Czartoryska, you requested my presence as an escort only so that you and the beautiful *Pani* Kobieta might inspect my scars?" He smiled as he said this, by then feeling closer to them both. His recollections returned of the Princess at Puławy when she attended to his wounds. Yet, just the night before she had denied she was even there at all. It was suggested to him that this had all been the work of his feverish imagination. It was suggested that he merely had a lengthy discourse with a painting that hung on the wall overhead.

"No," Princess Czartoryska said, laughing gently, "I wished only for you to finally get close to General Kościuszko. He is one of the greatest defenders of Poland's freedom throughout all our country's history. I hold him in the same level of esteem as King Jan III Sobieski and Queen Jadwiga herself. It was a disgrace, an injustice, what the Russians did to the man, but at least they did not kill him. You deserve to hear the wisdom of this warrior, when he reveals his thoughts on your Emperor-to-be Bonaparte with myself. You need to hear his perspective on *First Consul* Napoleon's proclaimed intentions to restore our country to its rightful sovereignty."

The streets of Paris swept by them outside the coach. As they did, they became less prosperous and more rife with squalor. Marek knew the city well, but was conscious only of what the Princess would think of its poorer areas. She looked with pity on the destitute, surely thinking of all the suffering they had to endure before and during the Revolution merely to survive.

"One can almost feel the hatred for the monarchy by the populace here that caused these peasants to rebel so violently," said Princess Izabela as she looked out of the coach.

"Poland, like France," she continued, "no longer has a king, but unlike France is no longer a country. At least the revolution of these peasants has placed their country into their own hands. I fear *First Consul* Bonaparte only wishes to pry it forever from their grasp."

"You must not speak of the Emperor so, your Highness," Marek protested mildly, "for it is Napoleon who will fight to restore our homeland to once more be among the sovereign nations of Europe. He has said often what a horrible crime against all humanity the Partitions of Poland were."

"My son, Adam Jerzy," she said, returning her gaze to him, "advises the young Tsar that Bonaparte only uses this rhetoric to touch the hearts of Poles such as yourself and inspire you to fight for France. Bonaparte will never honor his words with action."

"I fear your son leads the Tsar directly into a path that will bear the full brunt of the Emperor's action," replied Marek.

Tsar Alexander I, who had taken over the Russian throne upon the assassination of his father, Tsar Paul, three years earlier in 1801, was reported to have been keen to engage his troops in battle. Entirely too keen, for because of his youth, Alexander had never observed the true butchery of war. His heart ached only for its glory.

"Tell me, *Pan* Zaczek, why do the French people love this man Bonaparte so? What has he actually done for them?"

Marek was amazed that she could ask such a question.

"He has stabilized France, My Lady," the cavalryman answered. "After the mayhem of the Revolution over the past decade and a half, Emperor Napoleon has restored order, and he has brought back a long forgotten hope."

"And exactly how has he done so?" the Princess probed.

"Well, first there are the military victories," Marek answered, "in Toulon, and then throughout the northern Italian lands. He defeated the Austrians, and took the prize of Milan. He ended the eleven hundred year reign of the Doges of Venice. I was among the four thousand troops that entered that city and its surrounding islands as their empire crumbled."

"Yes, I am well aware of Napoleon's successes in Italy," she said. "Was it not in Lodi where you rescued his steed and gained his confidence?"

"Yes, that was the year earlier," Marek confessed. "Lodi was in 1796, Lido and Venice in 1797. Battle after battle became only a succession of victories against the Austrians and their allies. My head became dizzied by all our successes."

"Apparently, so did Napoleon's," Princess Izabela demurred. "But despite the peace accords reached then, he still today is at war with the Austrians. The peace did not last for long."

"But that is the will of the Austrians," Marek responded, "and now they align themselves with the British and the Russians. Certainly, the Emperor wishes you to influence your son to advise the Tsar to return Russia to neutrality, to back away from its declaration of war with France."

"I must remind you, *Pan* Marek," she smiled sweetly on calling him by his given name for the first time, "despite Napoleon declaring himself so in May of this year, he has not yet been coronated Emperor as such. The man who had the vanity to name himself *First Consul for Life*, is still not satisfied. Now he demands to be called Emperor?"

Her use of his given name suggested that despite their banter, she had warmed to the young officer. It was appropriate for her to initiate its use, with her being his respected elder. Of course, he would never dare to address her openly as *"Princess Izabela."*

"But your Highness," Marek responded, perhaps a little too energetically as his words tread upon the very fall of her last utterance, "the people have already overwhelmingly accepted him as Emperor. Not so much only for him to bear the fruits of that title, but for France to be adorned with the honor of the title *Empire*. Besides, what is different for him to be *First Consul for Life*, or even *Emperor*, when the Russian Tsars and Holy Roman Emperors take their own titles until their deaths."

"*Pan* Marek, that is my point exactly," the Princess attested. "Like them, this man becomes a dictator, nothing more. France may as well have a king once more."

"No, My Lady," he rejected her reasoning, "Napoleon fights the royalists at every turn. It was General Bonaparte himself who led the defense against an uprising of Royalists in October of 1795, when throngs of the Bourbon supporters amassed in the streets of Paris. These mobs threatened the safety of the National Convention itself, those who were the very heart of the Revolution. It was Napoleon who saved that Convention. He told his troops, to give the amassed Royalists *'a whiff of grapeshot.'*[9] You know this term, your Highness?"

"I know very well that grapeshot is a cluster of miniature lead balls sprayed from the barrels of cannons, used to kill as many soldiers as possible. And yet Napoleon turns it on his fellow Frenchmen, killing some fourteen hundred that single day. He massacres his own people and yet they still love him so! *Pan* Marek, can you explain to me how this can be?"

"Ah, yes, exactly because the Emperor is so committed to the Revolution. Those he killed were traitors to it, wanting only to return the corrupt Bourbon kings to power. Napoleon vowed to not only defend the Revolution, but to export it to all of Europe."

---

[9] *"The French Revolution: A History,"* by Thomas Carlyle, 1837, Easton Press 2008 Edition, Volume 3, Page 297.

"And Europe trembles at the thought," Princess Izabela replied. "But even in his failures, most embarrassingly demonstrated in his Egyptian campaign, Napoleon returns home to Frenchmen who not only still hold him dearly in their hearts, but actually revere him!"

"With the greatest respect," Marek responded, "I would argue, your Highness, that you cannot call the conquest of Egypt anything but a grand success. Consider the Emperor's tremendous victory over the fierce Mamelukes at the Battle of the Pyramids."

"While the whole of his fleet was destroyed by the British Navy along the banks of the Nile," she contested. Despite her addressing him more casually, Marek was becoming exasperated at the Princess' deriding his Emperor's triumphs at every turn.

"A failure of the French Navy, this is true," Marek admitted, "but at that point they were not under his command, were they? It was not his doing that they lined up like sitting ducks for the guns of British Admiral Nelson's ships, was it? But instead consider how Emperor Bonaparte had the foresight to take a legion of scientists from the French Academy with him. They returned with many Egyptian artifacts that enflamed the imagination of all Paris. And after conquering Egypt itself, Emperor Bonaparte then led his troops across the Sinai into the Holy Lands."

"Where he failed to take the Fortress of Acre," the Princess countered. "He failed at his primary objective of disrupting the British trade routes from India. Still, he spins his failures into gold. Napoleon abandons his troops stranded in Africa and comes back to Paris hailing himself as a conquering hero. The man is a fraud!"

It was clear that the Princess had carefully studied the history of Napoleon's ascent, but her words carried a bitterness that Marek supposed came from the tongue of her son, Adam Jerzy. Her mind had been made up long before she ever left the streets of Warsaw, he recognized.

"I wish not to quarrel with someone as noble as yourself, my Princess," Marek said after taking a few breaths to calm himself, "but neither can I fail to defend the greatness of our Emperor. He is our Polish homeland's greatest hope of recovering its rightful sovereignty."

Princess Czartoryska fought the urge to snap back at Marek, who she new had only the best intentions of their vanquished country at heart. She instead drew a deep breath before speaking as plainly as she could.

"Nor do I wish to argue with you, *Pan* Marek, but from the depths of my heart, I can only hope that when you find out what an ogre your Emperor-to-be truly is, it is not because he has led you to your demise on some bloody foreign battlefield!"

"If it is required of me to lay down my life in protecting Emperor Bonaparte," Marek said, "then I am prepared to do so."

"Of course," she responded, "you are first and foremost a trusted soldier. Your life is the very currency he deals in."

"No!" Marek protested sharply, "If I am required to lay down my life for the Emperor, it is nothing other than to sacrifice my last breaths for Poland itself!"

The tense words of the conversation gave way to the return of a strained reticence of silence. Outside their coach windows the squalor of the poorest sections of Paris had given way to the natural splendor of the open countryside. They progressed along a road with a primeval forest on one side and a grassy meadow on the other.

As the coach rode on, the awkward chasm that again stretched so crisply between them was in many ways welcomed by Marek, the Princess and Kobieta. It was, if nothing else, a muted diversion from the animosity sparked from their opposing positions on the merits of the Bonaparte's leadership.

Soon enough they entered the small country town of Berville. Marek had long since rolled down his sleeve and replaced the jacket and greatcoat of his uniform. He held the letter from his mother, so thoughtfully carried to him by the Princess, high and next to his face. Marek thought he would wait until he returned to the barracks back in Paris that evening to read its contents in private. But at that moment, Marek knew that the three of them must not egress the coach with the harshness of their words remaining between them.

"*Dziękuję bardzo*, my Princess," Marek said removing holding up the unopened letter, "for bringing such a joyous bit of home so far to warm my heart."

Princess Izabela casually tilted her head and with a wave of her hand said, *"Nie ma za co. (It is nothing!)* I only hope your heart has not grown so cold over these past years that you fail to open it fully to consider your mother's requests."

Marek slid the letter inside his jacket as he considered her words. He placed it such that it was secured in his waistband. He then gently ran his thumb over the letter's wax seal which was unbroken. Marek thought the words of the Princess were spoken as if she knew the letter's contents. He raised his view to Kobieta, catching her eye before the young maiden blushed and quickly turned her head away.

Chapter 6: Nelson and The Battle of the Nile

Fate often forges a strange chain of events in order to serve its most wicked desires. This can be no better illustrated then in 1798 when Admiral Horatio Nelson went off in search of Napoleon and his expeditionary forces as they set sail on the waves of the vast Mediterranean.

Admirals Jervis and Nelson had intelligence indicating that the French General Napoleon Bonaparte was preparing a massive movement of an invasion force by sea. They did not have any inkling as to where they might be heading. France had interest in overtaking Sicily, so this was one possibility. But in order for France to invade Sicily, it would need to first take Malta as a territory from which to stage its assault on the larger isle. Therefore, Malta was a second option. Finally, Naples itself might be the target. But in all these cases, the magnitude of the number of troops being prepared to embark, reportedly some 40,000 soldiers, suggested a much more ambitious plan. Nelson assumed that the only logical destination of Napoleon's army was Egypt, with the intention of France using the territory to disrupt British trade routes from their colonial interests in India.

Fate first intervened by conjuring a violent gale which drove Nelson's fleet beyond the French port of Toulon from which the French fleet was expected to depart. Nelson's flagship, the *HMS Vanguard,* rolled so violently in the storm that her topmasts were driven overboard. The ship was forced to enter port for repairs along the Italian coast, during which time the French expeditionary fleet slipped out to sea from Toulon.

Nelson, after repairs to the *HMS Vanguard* were effected, was in a constant search for the French fleet. When he arrived at Sicily, he learned that Malta, under orders of the Grand Master of the Knights Hospitaller *(The Knights of Malta)*, had surrendered to Napoleon. Nelson then was sure the French fleet, just days ahead of them, had passed through those Maltese waters on their way to Egypt, and set a course to intercept the flotilla.

Under the providence of fate, a heavy haze had obscured the surface of the sea. The British and French fleets passed near each other in the night, each unaware of the other's close proximity. Had Nelson's lookouts spotted the French warships, the Admiral surely would have engaged them at sea, attacking the transports bulged full with the thousands of French soldiers aboard. Of course, among these was Napoleon himself. Consider the luck of Bonaparte that Nelson's fleet did not spot them and attack, for Napoleon was sure to have been either killed or captured in their doing so. The entire history of the next seventeen years could have been averted, and millions of men from all across Europe would not have had to perish in the crucibles of the Emperor's wars.

Nelson reached Alexandria but found no sign of the French warships or their troop transport vessels. He did not realize that his fleet had outpaced and arrived ahead of the larger, slower French fleet to the North African harbor. Nelson then moved further east to search the coast of *the Levant* (today's shores of Syria and Lebanon) before returning to Sicily in search of the elusive French. He must have wondered, *How can I not find so massive a flotilla?*

In Sicily, Nelson's fleet confirmed that Egypt was indeed Napoleon's objective. The British fleet then raced back to the shores near Alexandria and found only the unloaded troop transports, which had arrived a few days after the British had left. Nelson searched further down the coast until, on the first of August he came to the mouth of the Nile River at Aboukir Bay, where they found thirteen French Ships-of-the-Line. The French vessels were lined up bow-to-stern along the bay's shallowest waters, presuming that the coastal shoals would protect their port sides.

Nelson quickly saw the folly of this strategy. It rested on the belief that no opposing warship could navigate the shoals between their line of ships and the shoreline. Nelson ordered his fourteen warships to form into two lines at dusk, one attacking from the safe depths of the sea, while the second slipped between the line of French warships and the shore. There, the water was only five fathoms, or thirty feet deep. It was shallow, but was still possible to be navigated with great skill.

One of the first British warships, the *HMS Culloden*, did wander too far to shore and indeed ran aground. Yet, treasure was rendered from tragedy as the *Culloden* made an excellent landmark for the other ships from which to navigate. The result was several British warships slipping between the French line and the shore, opening fire while their companion vessels did the same from sea.

The French fleet had been commanded by Admiral François-Paul Brueys d'Aigalliers. He was as seasoned a naval officer as France possessed, having served with distinction during the American War of Independence. He was aboard his flagship, the one-hundred-and-twenty gun *L'Orient* (the former unimpressively named *Sans Culottes* which had once run off Nelson's *HMS Agamemnon* from the wounded French ship *Ça Ira*). *L'Orient* had taken on extensive damage during the British attack and was ablaze. Admiral Brueys had been wounded in both legs severely.

The other officers aboard *L'Orient* recommended that the French admiral abandon his flagship but Brueys refused, staying bravely upon its burning quarterdeck, surely knowing what was to come.

Ships-of-the-Line of all navies had one fear above all others, that being any fire ignited onboard at sea. In order to charge their massive cannons, with some ships such as *L'Orient* having over one hundred aboard, they carried tremendous amounts of explosive black powder. The powder room where this was stored was the most revered sanctuary aboard the vessel. Its purity could never be defiled by either the presence of metal or an open flame. Metal could produce a spark, and thus have the same effect as a flame. The only light that was allowed to enter into the powder room shone through a window from an adjacent room's lamp. So great was the fear of igniting the massive quantities of powder that access to the "lamp room" was only possible from another deck of the vessel, eliminating any chance of the lamp's flame igniting the stores of powder. These design features were of no use when a ship was already set aflame, as was *L'Orient* by Nelson's attack.

The severely wounded Admiral Brueys awaited his fate patiently, perhaps preferring it to the indignity of being taken prisoner, or having to return to Paris and face the guillotine for his abject failure. The French Admiral, having earlier in the fight lost the use of both his legs to cannon shot, had his sailors strap him into his command chair so as to continue to direct the French defenses. It was useless. Near nine o'clock that evening, the fire gnawed its way through the ship and ignited the powder room. The resulting explosion killed some eight hundred sailors who had remained on board along with their Admiral, all still fighting valiantly. *L'Orient's* fireball could be seen for miles.

Nelson's strategy was pure genius. The destruction of the French fleet was devastating and nearly total. Of the thirteen Ships-of-the-Line, only two escaped.

**Figure 11: Explosion of the French Flagship L'Orient
During the Battle of the Nile, August 1, 1798**

Napoleon had already been ashore with his troops for several weeks. They had landed during the first days of July and captured Alexandria. They then marched to Cairo. But instead of following the Nile, Napoleon, on camelback, led his soldiers across the desert and engaged the Muslim forces made up primarily of Mamelukes, the famed Ottoman warriors, in the Battle of the Pyramids. It was here that Bonaparte famously inspired his troops, saying:

"Think of it, soldiers; from the summit of these pyramids, forty centuries look down upon you." [10]

In that battle, fought within sight of the Pyramids of Giza that followed on July 21, 1798, the French forces routed the Mamelukes with little effort.

---

[10] Oxford Dictionary of Quotes, Sixth Edition, attributed to
Mémoires, Volume 2, Égypte - Bataille des Pyramides, Gaspard Gourgaud (1823)

That great French success came only twelve days before Nelson destroyed the French fleet at the mouth of the Nile. This would foreshadow another time, yet to come, when Napoleon would not fully enjoy his greatest triumph of all, at Austerlitz, because of the exploits of Britain's Horatio Nelson.

As the expedition commander of his *Armée d'Orient*, as it was named, Napoleon realized that without his warships, his soldiers were now stranded in North Africa. He would lead them over the next year across the Nile, through the Sinai desert on camels and mules to the area of Syria and Lebanon then known as the Levant and its medieval fortress of Acre. Napoleon would siege Acre for two months, but fail to overtake the fortress. Bonaparte then attacked and seized some poorly defended coastal towns, but overall would fail in his attempt to establish French dominance over Syria and its ancient capital, Damascus.

Dashed were any desires Bonaparte held to disrupt British influence in the area. So too were all hopes of disrupting Britain's trade routes with India. Napoleon's deep desire to create his own path to Asia, as had Alexander long before him, crumbled with the French naval defeat at the hands of Nelson along the mouth of the Nile.

Napoleon stayed with his *Armée d'Orient* well into 1799, leading them from *the Levant* back into Egypt. Almost exactly a year after Nelson's victory at the Battle of the Nile, Napoleon's troops would fight one last major land battle in Africa. It would be fought on the very same shores off which the British had so thoroughly destroyed his French fleet.

Napoleon's *Armée d'Orient* went up against forces sent aboard ships from the Ottoman Empire under the command of Seid Mustafa Pasha. France still had control of Egypt, and the Ottoman Sultan was intent on taking it back at any cost. It would turn out to be a very tragic and costly assault, indeed.

The battle turned out to be a bloody rout, even with the Ottomans having two and a half times the number of the French forces. Of their 7,700 troops, the French lost only 200 with another 600 wounded. From the Ottoman forces of 20,000 troops, 6,000 were killed in combat while another 11,000 were thought to have drowned as they fled into the sea. Their leader, Seid Mustafa Pasha, was taken prisoner by the French.

Napoleon claimed in his usual overstated manner, that:

"The enemy threw themselves into the water in an attempt to reach the boats which were more than two miles out at sea; they all drowned, the most horrible sight I've seen." [11]

The French army, after its humbling defeat at Acre and after illnesses had rifled through their numbers, had won a massive victory at that battle in the last week of July 1799. Yet, a month to the day later, Napoleon would depart from his *Armée d'Orient*, taking advantage of a break in Britain's blockade of the Egyptian coast. It would take Bonaparte six weeks to return to Paris, cautiously avoiding any and all British ships along the sea route.

Napoleon returned to his country's capital from Egypt to a hero's welcome, much as his idol Julius Caesar had done nearly two millennia earlier at Rome. However, Napoleon's accomplishments were but a mere shadow of what his role model had achieved. The long arc of history would cast dispersions upon the true breadth of the French general's successes in Egypt, regardless of his routing of the Mamelukes at the pyramids and against the Ottomans at Aboukir Bay. His setbacks overshadowed these victories. Still, Napoleon made the most of the situation.

Never being known as one to let facts stand in the way of declaring success, Napoleon had deftly embellished his accomplishments in the reports that he had been sending back to the committee ruling France known as the *Directory*.

---

[11] Napoleon Bonaparte, Correspondence, Volume 5, p. 541.

In fact, Napoleon had cleverly taken along a team of historians, archeologists and botanists which he declared *l'Institut d'Egypte*. Their dispatches of scientific discoveries, including the Rosetta Stone, ignited a wave of Egyptology which soon became the primary obsession of all Paris. Over the coming years, Napoleon's *l'Institut d'Égypte* would produce one of the most beautiful and expansive treatments of Egyptian history and culture in the 20 volume work entitled *Description de l'Égypte*.

While these works further wetted the appetite of France for all things Egyptian, unfortunately, Parisians would never lay eyes upon the most fabled artifact. The Rosetta Stone documented the reign of Egyptian ruler *Ptolemy V Epiphanes* in Ancient Egyptian demotic script and hieroglyphics, as well as in Greek. The Rosetta Stone was ceded to the British in the armistice that followed Nelson's victory at the Battle of the Nile. It remains to this day in the British Museum's collection instead of that of the Louvre.

But Napoleon timed his return to France not just to be received as a returning conqueror, but for far more devious considerations. In only a few weeks after landing on French shores, Napoleon and a handful of others (including his later foreign minister, the *duc de Talleyrand*) plotted to overthrow the ruling *Directory*. That government ruling body of five members was then politically crippled after having lost the support of the French people. Napoleon and his plotters were intent on overthrowing it.

The Coup of 18 Brumaire (the date upon which it started on the Revolutionary Calendar) took place overnight on November 9th into the morning of the 10th, 1799. Napoleon provided the armed power of the miltary to expel the five-member *Directory*, and replaced it with a three-member *Consulate* to lead France. Napoleon and his military stormed the upper legislative body, the Council of Five Hundred. His conspirators had assured Napoleon a seat on the ruling Consulate. But unknown to them, Napoleon was determined to occupy its first, and thus most dominant, chair.

Although his co-conspirators offered a draft constitution giving Bonaparte only limited governing powers, Napoleon recognized the opportunity as he himself, and no one else, held full control of the military. He rapidly rewrote the constitution to proclaim himself as *First Consul.* His re-written constitution effectively made him dictator over the French people. Most historians mark this *Coup d'État* as the end of the French Revolution and the beginning of the Napoleonic Era.

In this *Coup d'État of 1799,* Napoleon had milked as much glory and power as he possibly could from the Egyptian Campaign during the previous two years, which from a sheer military perspective was an utter failure. His critics noted that when the French troops of the *Armée d'Orient* had become infected with, among other illnesses, the bubonic plague, Napoleon, while still with them, had ordered some of his most incurable soldiers to be overdosed with opium. His supporters viewed this action as being humanitarian to the dying soldiers, while his detractors claimed he had simply poisoned his own troops who had become a drag on his army's effectiveness and morale.

Just as controversial was Napoleon's manner of departing from his troops in Egypt. His supporters argued that he had become aware of the weakened state of the *Directory* as a governing body, and was justified to rush to Paris to preclude the government's total collapse. After all, they would argue, Napoleon left his troops under the command of several very capable French generals. His detractors would argue that Bonaparte abandoned his *Armée d'Orient* to fend for itself. In any case, it would not be the last time that Napoleon was accused of abandoning his beleaguered troops after citing an urgent need to travel back to Paris. He would do so again thirteen years later. His last footprints with his troops in 1799 were impressed on the sands of Egypt, but in 1812, they would be sunk even more deeply into the winter snows of Eastern Europe.

Chapter 7: Berville, France

Meeting Kościuszko

Bravery manifests itself in many forms. Upon their arrival in the small country town of Berville, the legendary Polish and American Revolutionary hero presented himself as an old man, riddled with wounds from chasing the sole ambition of his youth: *Freedom*. Despite his life's great ambitions, he wore only the modest clothes of a peasant - a gray smock over short breeches capped off with a modest straw hat.

Tadeusz Kościuszko was only fifty-eight years old on that October day that he received the Princess in 1804, but he had lived through enough revolution for two lifetimes. His wounds inflicted by the Tsarina's troops while he was defending his native Poland a decade earlier had transformed the hero into a man most thought to be two decades older than his true years.

In Marek's eyes, Kościuszko's scars had been taken in vain. In the year following the General's capture the last remnants of the carcass of their country had been stripped away completely by the three jackals: the European powers of Austria, Prussia and Russia. *But now at least,* Marek thought, *we will have the Grande Armée of the Emperor of France with which to correct this injustice.*

"My Princess," Kościuszko said while bowing feebly and taking her hand to kiss, "it is the joy of my heart to lay my eyes upon you once again. Welcome to my modest abode. I regret that its owner, my friend the Swiss gentleman, Monsieur Zetnur, is not here to enjoy your presence. Still, your crossing its threshold will bring this house both greater grace and happiness."

"I am honored to again be in your presence, General," the Princess replied. "Allow me to introduce my young companion, the maiden Kobieta from Puławy, and my military escort supplied by General Dąbrowski, *Pan* Marek Zaczek."

The General then took Kobieta's hand, again bowed slightly and kissed it. "So many lovely flowers grow upon the juncture of where the *Wieprz* flows into the *Wisła*," said Kościuszko, referring to the two rivers merging in the area near the young woman's hometown.

"You are too kind, sir," the sweet Kobieta said. "I am honored to meet today the man who gave so much for our country." She curtsied graciously before him. He then moved his eyes to Marek, who showed his respect by snapping a crisp salute to General Kościuszko.

"This is the greatest moment of my life, my General," Marek said.

"Then you must lead a very boring existence," Kościuszko replied with a gentle laugh as he returned the salute slowly, almost dismissively.

Kościuszko smiled tepidly at the young officer, as if to indicate the words were intended more as an insult to himself than to his warrior guest. However, Marek missed the self-deference of his hero's demeanor.

"I can assure you, sir, that my life has been anything but boring," Marek said, not only to defend himself vigorously, but also to amplify the respect he had intended to Kościuszko.

Kościuszko's grin broadened, until gentle laughter escaped like a poet's verse through his next words.

"You need not assure me, young man," Kościuszko answered, "as General Dąbrowski has already done so. I know all about your exploits, including those at Maciejowice and at Lodi. You are a man of action, there is little doubt as to that."

Marek's face registered both a swell of pride and a scathing shame. "General Dąbrowski has told you about my past?"

"Yes, yes," Kościuszko replied. "The famous Austrian Uhlan broken back to infantry for failing to act out a ridiculous order. This is exactly why the Austrians fail in one war after another. They are too stupid to understand the enemy's strengths and too conceited to see their own weaknesses. I do not blame you for defecting away from their ranks in that Italian river town. I am only concerned that both you and your leader, my good friend General Dąbrowski, have become too impressed with your French overlords. After all, you know the saying from our homeland, *'You become who you befriend.'* Now, please, all of you come inside."

Marek understood the "ridiculous order" of which Kościuszko spoke was his own assignment to kidnap the General at the Battle of Maciejowice. *Dąbrowski shared my secret with his longtime colleague, yet still assigned me to accompany the Princess here,* he thought. *To what end was this done?*

The three figures of Kościuszko, the Princess and Marek made their way into the modest cottage in which General Kościuszko resided. Around it simple fields of crops grew.

Close to the cottage was a great manor, and a paved stone walkway connected the two structures. Kościuszko noticed Marek taking in the grander home adjoining the fields.

"That is the manor house of Monsieur Zetnur," Kościuszko said to Marek. "He has been quite kind to me since my return to France. His generosity has no bounds, it seems."

"But I thought you said you shared his home," replied Zaczek.

"Indeed I do," Kościuszko answered, "but his manor house proved a bit too elegant to my liking, so my friend had his coach house converted to this simple cottage for me. It suits me much better. Also, he allows me to play farmer and tend these small fields. I find that to be quite relaxing."

Kobieta stayed with the coachman to see to the unloading of their bags. Inside, a fire burned brightly in the hearth, and four chairs had been pulled up before it. The small table in front of them was crowded by a single wooden tray, on which four cut crystal glasses rested. Despite their being empty, the crystal's facets glimmered with reflections of the hearth's dancing flames as if sheer valor and truth had cleaved their edges.

The trio took their seats around the fire, saving the outermost chair for Kobieta, who remained with the coachman.

"I do not understand the need for so many bags," Marek said as he watched the coachman hauling in the luggage.

"They are women are they not?" answered Kościuszko. "Did General Dąbrowski not share with you the fact that Princess Izabela will be received by Napoleon tomorrow at the nearby Palace of Fontainebleau? She and *Pani* Kobieta are my overnight guests this evening."

"Then I assume I will return to Paris later with the coach?"

"Marek," Princess Izabela said, "you are to escort me tomorrow to Fontainebleau for my meeting with Napoleon. Was this not made clear to you?"

A contorted look of shock came over Zaczek's face. A thought ran through his head, *Am I being set up, in some way?*

"No, I am not prepared to meet the Emperor," Marek snapped back.

"You are a soldier, Zaczek," Kościuszko replied sharply, "you are always ready, are you not? In the morning you can use my razor and boot black. What more could you possibly need? Besides, the coachman will be residing overnight at the town's *auberge,* he will not return this night to Paris. We will have no more discussion on this matter. The Princess and Kobieta will take my bedroom, and you and I will sleep by the fire tonight. Unless, my Princess, you prefer the manor house accommodations."

"Absolutely not," replied the Princess, "Kobieta and I will be quite comfortable here in your cottage home, General."

The bags then secured, Kobieta rejoined the three of them.

General Kościuszko reached for a hidden object. "I have something a little special for us all to enjoy - a fine bottle of *Żubrówka*. It will warm the parts of you that the fire cannot."

"Bison grass vodka!" Marek exclaimed. "What a wonderful taste of home, but how do you come across it here in France?"

"The Émigrés bring it with them when they visit me here as a gift of courtesy," Kościuszko said. "I am happy to receive them alone, but they somehow feel they must bring me a gift from our Polish homeland. From where they manage to obtain it is a mystery to me, but a happy one, I feel."

Kościuszko held the bottle up proudly for each of them to inspect. He passed it to each of them to hold for a few seconds.

He then poured the clear liquid from the bottle into the cut crystal glasses. As he did, within the bottle swirled a single long blade of grass hand picked from the Białowieża Forest of Poland, a tradition that by then had already existed for three centuries. As the General prepared to pour the spirit into Kobieta's glass, she modestly placed her hand over the rim.

The affronted Kościuszko assured her that she needed to partake in the toast, even if only a to draw a single, slightest sip.

"Kobieta is very modest, my General," Princess Izabela explained. "She refuses all alcohol."

"I am sorry, *Pani* Kobieta," Kościuszko said, "but I must insist you join us. Not only are we partaking of the *Żubrówka,* but doing so in hand-cut crystal from Silesia. This is not merely a toast to you, my guests, but to Poland itself. It would be rude for you not to join us, an insult to our land. I insist and will not accept otherwise. At least allow the spirit to wet your lips, my child."

"Kobieta is as pure as the salt of the earth, my General," the Princess added.

"And in the country that is home to us all, it is said that *without salt the feast is sad.*" General Kościuszko raised his glass, and waited for the three others to join him. Even the scolded Kobieta slowly raised her own. Then Kościuszko bellowed out the customary toast, *"Na zdrowie!",* meaning *"to health!"*

They all said the toast aloud, touched glasses and raised them to their lips. The Princess and Kobieta gently sipped at the clear liquid, while Marek and Kościuszko drained their glasses dry. Slowly, the warmth of companionship between a clutch of countrymen, huddled together far from home, arose in them all.

After much small talk and several more drinks imbibed by the men, Marek felt comfortable enough to profess his inner feelings to General Kościuszko.

"My General," Marek said, "I am so terribly sorry that I failed in my mission at Maciejowice. I wish that I might have saved you from your fate at the hands of the Russians."

Kościuszko then briskly replied with the Polish proverb, *"What has happened can't unhappen,* Marek. If only the mare that I rode had not sunk in to the mud perhaps you would have captured me and not the Russian devils. Well, I jest, my young soldier friend, for we knew what you were up to that day. You would never have gotten close to me, no matter how sly you may have been."

Marek remembered when essentially the same words echoed through his ears about the General's forces knowing too well his mission. They were spoken by his close friend, Tolo, as he delivered him and his mount by raft along the *Wisła* just as the sun had begun to rise the morning of the battle.

"Still, General I am sorry for your suffering at the hands of the Russians, Sir," Marek answered.

"A soldier's life is lived only to endure suffering," Kościuszko said. "Surely you must know that by now. The greedy politicians steal away the glow of valor from the victories, and are quick to assign blame to others for the stench of the defeats, but in the end the soldier is left with nothing more than his suffering, and perhaps, if he is quite fortunate, a few good war stories."

Marek laughed, and thought it amazing that after all this man had endured, he lives out his modest life with such a refined perspective.

"So, as we are talking of greedy politicians," Kościuszko went on, "let us discuss Bonaparte."

"Yes, General Kościuszko," the Princess remarked, "I am eager to hear your impressions of the politics of the man."

"But the Emperor is more of a military man than a politician," decried Marek.

"No, Zaczek," Kościuszko replied, "he showed his true colors when he returned from Egypt in 1799 and soon overthrew the *Directory* by a *Coup d'état*. Yes, he dressed his military takeover in the civilian clothes of a ruling tribunal, but by naming himself as *First Consul,* he declared himself as much a politician as a fighting general. Now, after he has secured his grip on the nation, he dreams only of empire, and with empire comes only war with other empires, as we have seen. Yes, he has defeated the Austrians, only to have them rise again and rejoin the British. They have drawn in the Russians, which greatly concerns Bonaparte."

"That is surely why he has invited you to France, Princess," the aged general continued. "The Czartoryski name is strong with the young Tsar, and your son, the Foreign Minister, has his ear. Napoleon, through Talleyrand, will be so kind as to share with you exactly which words your son must whisper to Tsar Alexander."

"Sir, is it not true that Emperor Bonaparte himself offered for you to lead the legions of Poles who fight for him?" Marek asked in blurted awkwardness.

"Yes, I was excited to receive Talleyrand's letter when it was delivered to me in America. It was full of promise for the revival of our country. But by the time I travelled to Paris, that promise had been laid aside. Talleyrand and Napoleon each feared angering the Russians by doing so, driving them to side with the Austrians. Napoleon offered me only a small role in which to play, commanding troops as does Dąbrowski. I explained to him how much more influence I could have over all the Poles if only our country was to be freed from the Russians, Prussians and Austrians. He called me a fool who overestimated my importance."

"That does not sound like the Emperor I know," Marek stated.

"Perhaps it is because you do not understand the man as General Kościuszko does," Princess Czartoryska replied. "Only this past March, Napoleon kidnapped the Bourbon Duke of Enghien, Louis Antoine, by sending his Dragoons across the Rhine into the lands of Baden, abducted the Duke, and took him back to Paris at the Château de Vincennes where he was executed."

"Yes, but he did so because the Duke had plotted to overthrow the French Government," objected Marek, "and take Emperor Bonaparte's life in doing so."

"The man Bonaparte has no regard for national borders, no respect for life other than his own. Napoleon is nothing more than a ravenous wolf," Princess Izabela exclaimed.

"The wolf carries off its prey a number of times and then eventually is carried off itself," said Kościuszko, quoting another Polish proverb. "Yes, the man is merely a despot out to fill his personal ambitions and nothing more. He will build nothing that lasts beyond his own pre-eminence. Once he falls, and I am quite sure he will, all he has built will tumble inward upon the man and bury him."

Marek felt as though he would be sick as he realized he was huddled amongst nothing more than a group of conspirators.

"I still serve him proudly," Marek boasted, "as Emperor, Napoleon Bonaparte will restore our lost country of Poland."

"Exactly," said Kościuszko, surprising all. "That is exactly the sentiment he will enkindle in you and all our countrymen until the hour when it no longer serves his needs. Beware Zaczek, the man will only ever act to suit his own ends. Empty words are easily uttered along the way, but Napoleon will defer to the Russians and Austrians long before he seriously considers an independent Poland. An empty future is all that awaits both you and our once glorious nation!"

Marek offered no response, but in his heart of hearts, he knew the Emperor would fulfill his promises for the homeland.

"Marek, do not take me wrongly," said General Kościuszko sensing the conflict in the young warrior. "I see the faults of the man, but I equally recognize how great a military mind the man has. You should have no remorse in acceding to his innermost circle and learning all you can from Napoleon. Consider yourself in a most elevated and restricted school. That knowledge one day may be harnessed by yourself in actions to free our homeland. But never fool yourself that Napoleon will free Poland himself, as he will always have personal motives for not fully doing so."

After several minutes more, the subject of religion was raised by General Kościuszko.

"Our Polish culture is based on the existence of and reverence to Our Lord Jesus Christ. The French are not only atheistic, their revolution has destroyed every facet of organized religion. It is against the very fabric of our culture to throw in with this group of anarchists. God's wrath will surely befall them."

Marek could be silent no longer. "But don't you see, the Emperor has already undertaken action to restore the Catholic religion to France by signing the *Concordat* with Rome!"

Marek Zaczek spoke of the agreement that had been signed on Easter Sunday, 1802 that named the Catholic religion as one of the primary religions of France. It also reversed many of the confiscations of Church properties and lifted restrictions enacted by the French Government during the Revolutionary period.

"Don't you see," Zaczek asked, "that the Emperor dutifully respects the need for the church in society? He is committed to re-establishing ties with Rome. He needs the stability of religion."

"What you say is not so far from the truth, Zaczek," replied General Kościuszko, "for Napoleon has been known to say,

'Religion is what keeps the poor from murdering the rich.' [12]

The Corsican has no need for Rome's blessing other than to keep his own social state in order, such that the peasants no longer riot and foment revolutionary ideals. He knows how difficult it is to strike at enemies afield when the very foundation that you stand upon is unstable and prone to crumble under your feet. For this reason alone, he has invited the Pope himself to rest the Crown of Charlemagne upon his head at his coronation. He does not desire this in his heart, but knows he needs the legitimacy of Pius VII."

The discussion went on for many hours more, with General Kościuszko confirming the opinions of Napoleon that Princess Izabela had already held, passed on to her by her son, Adam Jerzy.

---

[12] Napoleon, March 4, 1806, during a meeting of the French National Committee

Marek excused himself before dinner to take fresh air and clear the unpalatable words of the afternoon's discussion from his head. Kobieta asked to join him, and he agreed, leaving the Princess and the General alone together, as Kościuszko's cook prepared a meal of *Haluski*, that being fried cabbage and noodles.

Marek and Kobieta walked alongside each other on the stone walkway that led to the manor house. The cold air bit harshly at them, but compared to the fierce sting of some Polish October winds, it was pleasant enough.

"So, *Pani* Kobieta," Marek said, "this manor house reminds me of a similar home of the Duke on our *folwark* near Wieliczka. I understand you are from the town of Puławy as the princess said?"

"Yes, *Pan* Zaczek," she replied, "my parents worked at the Czartoryski Palace there."

"And they do so today?"

Her eyes lost their sparkle as she averted them to the ground. "I am afraid not, *Pan* Zaczek. They were murdered by the Russians that stormed the palace shortly after you departed."

"Oh, Sorrow of God!" Marek exclaimed.

"My mother herself attended to your wounds," Kobieta said. "I remember watching her do so tenderly. It is among my very last memories of her. It is why I was so interested to see your scar in the carriage."

"You were there?" Marek was amazed at the revelation.

"Yes, but I was then only eight years old," said Kobieta. She had not lifted her gaze from the wind which swept through and gently parted the high stalks of grass nearby. Marek felt the heaviness she bore, and realized under the weight of her memory's crushing pressure she was pierced by the sharpest of pain.

"I cannot imagine how difficult it was to be there as the palace was overrun. Were you forced to watch the deaths of your own parents by those bastards?"

Tears glistened in Kobieta's eyes as she raised them to Marek. He could tell the young woman was on the verge of breaking down completely.

"No, praise be to God, I was not. I was hidden in the woods by a cook. She too was killed after she left me in a place of safety."

"My heart bleeds for you, young Kobieta," Marek said. "To have borne such cruel burdens at so young an age."

"*Dziękuję, Pan* Zaczek," she said, "but there is more. Princess Czartoryska was also there when you arrived with such terrible wounds. She and both her sons were all there. She attended to you alongside my mother…"

Marek was tempted to return to the house on hearing this.

"Then she just made up that fantastic story at Madame Larouche's salon that she was in England for no reason?"

"Even distant tongues can be overheard when the walls have ears. With her son being Foreign Minister to Tsar Alexander, she can take no chances. Most importantly, neither she nor her son Adam Jerzy can admit publicly that they were assisting the armies of Kościuszko that openly fought so earnestly against the Russians. They did escape just before the Russians came, like yourself, but it is true they were later held by the Austrians. The Princess Czartoryska was forced to say they had been in London, and had not directly aided Kościuszko or his forces. The Princess right now is pleading for the General's forgiveness as we speak. She asked me to share all this with you, and in that way she can honestly say that she herself did not divulge this information to you, an enemy of the Russian state, for which her son endeavors."

"I understand. Thank you, Kobieta," Marek said, "but how odd is it that her own son went on to win the favor of Tsar Alexander. It is indeed very sad that he advises those who imprisoned his own family and plundered their lands."

Kobieta's countenance slowly morphed from mournful to apprehensive. Marek spied her hesitation, and cocked his head. "What is it, Kobieta?"

"There is much more terrible news I must share with you, I am afraid," she said as she hung her head again to the ground.

"Do not be afraid, Kobieta, please do not be indirect," Marek said. "Please tell me everything."

She paused for a second, as if to gather her strength.

"The letter the Princess carried for you is indeed from your mother, a woman who has fallen on very hard times. A few years ago, the Austrian Count Von Arndt was successful in having your mother's title rescinded based upon your having defected to the French army. She is no longer the Duchess Magdalena Kowalczyk, and has lost control of the salt mine at Bochnia and the proceeds that came from it. The Count has wickedly stolen all that from her to add to his own fortunes of the Wieliczka *folwark*."

"You mean she now has nothing! But she was so wealthy the last time I was with her. And to think at one point she was actually considering marrying the Count."

Marek felt for how his *matka* had been sunk low once more, but he remembered warning her that the Count's desire was only for her riches. What he could not obtain through marriage, the Count had stolen through whispering into the Austrian Emperor's ear. "God, please give me the opportunity to kill the man who has returned my *matka* to being a peasant."

A gentle smirk raced across Kobieta's face. It embodied mirth, but was tinged with a sullen mournfulness.

"Your mother *Pani* Kowalczyk," Kobieta said, then corrected herself, "excuse me, Marek, *Pani* Zaczek, as she once again calls herself, may no longer be wealthy in her own right, but neither is she quite a peasant either. She had the wherewithal to gather up what funds she had access to before she escaped Austrian Kraków for Prussian Warsaw. Once there, Princess Izabela took sympathy on her plight, and allows her to live near the Royal Castle in a town house owned by the Czartoryski family. Your mother has enough funds stored up to at least give the appearance of wealth, and now lives among the finest people of Warsaw."

"My experience," said Marek, "is that the wealthiest should not be confused with the finest of people. That I learned from Duke Sdanowicz, may the devil's hooves tread and tear eternally upon his greedy soul. But wait, what has become of Maya and her son, *Władek*?"

"They live with your *matka*, as does her sister-in-law, your Aunt Ewelina?"

"And *Ciocia* Ewelina's husband and sons?"

"All still are in the Austrian army," Kobieta explained. "Your uncle still is stationed at the stables of the Imperial Riding School in Vienna. The two boys are infantrymen, stationed only the Lord knows exactly where."

"And *moja Maya Manusca?* Is she married, or does she raise her son Władek alone?"

"Both," Kobieta answered obliquely.

"You mean she married and the bastard ran off from her?"

"Precisely," answered Kobieta.

"Tell me who he is. I will see to it that should I ever cross his path that he shall pay dearly for this travesty."

"I will do better, I will show you him, *Pan* Zaczek."

She led Marek over to a frigid but unfrozen puddle of standing water. Its chilled surface was as tense and still as the emotions that overtook Marek.

"Look down," Kobieta said, "and you will see the bastard." Marek lowered his head to see the reflection of his own face.

"What is the meaning of this joke?" he asked. "I have no time for such games. I had never married Maya. How possibly could I have after her having given birth to that boy?"

Kobieta looked at him with a sweet tenderness.

"That is what I am trying to tell you, Marek. Maya's son, Władek, as he grew, only wished to know who his father was. A natural curiosity for a boy to have. When he was very young, he was told his father died in the war. But when he was six, Count Von Arndt told the child that his father was not brave enough to have died fighting for Austria."

"Instead," she continued, "the Count told him you were his father, and that you had, in great shame, defected to the French army. The child did not care about the supposed shame, but was excited to have found he had a living father. Władek refused to let go of the story, no matter what his mother or *babcia* told him."

"So, when they all reestablished themselves in Warsaw, the child began calling himself by his middle name, Marek. To play along, Maya is now called by all as *Pani* Zaczek."

Marek was stunned. He stood dazed, as he continued to inspect his reflection in the puddle. It was too much information to process in such a brief period. "It all makes no sense. How can the church allow this with no record of our being married? I know my Maya could never live outside the church's blessing."

Kobieta's face sparked anew with an uneasy pride. It was not of her own doing, but of her lady's.

"Princess Izabela took care of that," Kobieta said. "At Puławy, there was a resident priest, Father Stanisław Lee Świętek. Alas, he also was brutally killed by the Russians when they sacked the palace. But Princess Czartoryska attested to the fact that nine months before, Father Świętek had secretly married Maya and yourself in a ceremony on the grounds of the palace. The child, Władek, now calling himself Marek after his soldier father, was said to have been conceived on your honeymoon on the grounds of the palace. That story was accepted by the Polish Church's Primate in Warsaw, along with a rather sizable Czartoryski family donation. The church then fabricated documents to support the story."

"So, while I am away, spiders have woven the thickest and stickiest of webs around my honor," Marek said. "I am trapped."

"It is one of the reasons Princess Izabela needed to see your scar," Kobieta explained, "so there could be no confusion that you were indeed the same young man that had rescued Maya from those barbarian Cossacks. Your healed-over wound proved it without a doubt. So she has told me to explain this all, in order to help you digest the rest of the information in the letter from your *matka*. The Princess thought this would be the only *fair* thing to do, so that when the time comes that you may do the *right* thing."

"Everything is so chaotic," Marek said. "I have been in many skirmishes that were much more orderly than this fiction."

A still moment transpired between them. It was as heavy as the new reality that Marek was being asked to accept. Kobieta sensed Marek's indecision, his hesitancy to accept all this.

"Do you still love your Maya?" Kobieta asked. The question seemed lost on Marek, who searched through a forest full of memories, but in which he failed to find its answer.

"Honestly, I don't know," Marek finally said. "It has been far too long."

"A truthful answer," Kobieta offered."But you will know when you see her,"

"What do you mean, see her?" Marek was most unsettled by her statement.

"Your *Maya Manusca* arrives in Paris in two weeks time. With her will be your son, Władek Marek. Do the right thing for them, *Pan* Zaczek. Do not steal their new truth from them."

"How am I to know what the right thing might be?" asked Marek. "Can a new truth be built over a bed of lies? The child is not my own. Yet you ask me to love him as if he were?"

"The child was sired against Maya's will. God has stricken the offending party by placing his head on a Russian pike. By His Holy Grace, He has allowed the pieces to fall into place for this arrangement. If you decide not to go along with this story, this fiction, as you so callously call it, then your *Maya Manusca* will bear insufferable shame. Her son will go from having a father he has not yet met but idolizes to being returned to the ignominy of being an incestuous bastard. Of course, we all know the real truth of what occurred. God, in His Providence, has given us all we need to resolve what indignities were perpetrated. You and Maya will always know, of course, but your son needs never to learn of this."

"So, *we are to turn the cat around by its tail?*" Marek referenced the Polish proverb that seemed so apt. "I need time to digest all this, to read the letter from my *matka*."

The beautiful Kobieta could see the strain that her words had inflicted on Marek, as if he was pulled at once in different directions. She knew only he could determine his path forward by releasing the past.

"I will walk back to the cottage, *Pan* Zaczek," Kobieta said. "I will be in your view all the way, so I am safe. Do not feel compelled to accompany me. Think over all I have told you. Meld it with what is in your *matka's* letter. What you need to do will come to you. I only pray you will open your heart to its message."

Kobieta turned away and slowly receded along the stone walkway. Marek thought she had done well with a most difficult task. It surely dredged up many painful memories of the death of her own parents at the hands of the Russians. *How clever of the Princess to use her maiden to deliver the news,* he thought For certainly Kobieta could not be thought to be in any way impartial, yet she relayed the points with tremendous respect for the Princess' magnanimous treatment of Marek's mother, aunt and his Maya.

Marek wondered, *Why was the Princess willing to go to such trouble and expense to rescue them all from destitution and perhaps becoming eternal outcasts?*

Marek's thoughts turned to the girl who had once been his life's love, Maya, and of her son that he was being asked to accept as his own. He fished his mother's letter from the waistband of his uniform. So Maya had given up the family name Sdanowicz for his family name of Zaczek. Young Władek was now calling himself Marek, after his warrior father fighting for the French army. How convenient this brave new world was that Maya, his *matka* and the Princess had concocted for themselves in Warsaw. Now, it simply depended on his going along with its fictitious plot.

Marek had last seen his mother years ago in Milan, when it was still under Austrian control. It was before his defection to the French. She was then still considering marrying the Austrian Count Von Arndt. Von Arndt later called off the wedding after Marek defected, not willing to have a stepson who took up arms for the French against Austria. Now, his *matka*, the once Duchess Magdalena, had been robbed of all her holdings by the Count, and was again forced to live upon the generosity of another, albeit still in a high style.

Regarding Maya, his once tender love for her had turned bitter. Marek never recovered since finding her being full with child on the day of her rescue. Even after his mother had explained to him that his love had given herself to no one, the acrimony remained. He was still angry that Maya's innocence had been taken from her so sinisterly by her own uncle. The man had paid his penance to God at the Battle of Maciejowice, with his head at day's end raised high on a Russian pike.

Yet, try as he did, Marek had never fully forgiven Maya. The pure innocent love he once held for her had never returned. It was as if his heart had been blanched of any feeling for her except the clinging remnants of pity. Now, he was being asked to accept her as his wife, and the bastard child, Władek, as his own.

Marek held the hefty, folded letter in his palm. He wondered what its contents could reveal that might be more shocking than what had already been told to him. For a moment he thought of flinging it as far as he could and to go on living his life, ignoring its revelations.

After all, Marek had done well under General Dąbrowski in the Polish Legions of the *Armée d'Italie*. Why should he give any of that up just to answer the request of paving over a lingering past? Beyond that, the Emperor held him, this simple Polish cavalry rider, in high esteem.

That turned out to be the very moment when he knew he must read the letter. He had, after all, spent the entire afternoon arguing that the Emperor was intent on reestablishing the nation state of Poland, independent and sovereign. Had he merely fooled himself all along by stating this as the first objective of his exiled heart? Then, would he not be a hypocrite if he said he never intended to return there after its rebirth?

And any return to Poland first meant a return to his *matka*, Magdalena, to his once loved Maya, and her son. He thought of the Polish proverb that states, *"The greatest love is a mother's, then a dog's, then a sweetheart's."*

Then, almost as a counter argument, he thought of the saying from his land that said, *"The devil can swallow a woman but even he can't digest her."*

Yet, Marek was being asked to digest even more - a dishonored wife, and a child not his own.

Marek slipped his finger under the fold of the heavy letter's paper and broke the seal. The wax was rigid and stiff, he presumed from the length of the long journey. It cracked and separated with the slightest force, not unlike the like dried-out earth after a summer's drought.

He unfolded the fine woven paper, bearing a thick purple ink unlike any he had seen before from his mother. It seemed be a correspondence more befitting a princess than a fallen duchess. Then Marek remembered what Kobieta had said, that his mother was living upon the generosity of the Princess Czartoryska.

The late afternoon sky held just enough light to read the message, but would not for much longer. Marek looked down upon his mother's cursive script, which flowed like the clinging vines of the *folwark* he had been forced to clear throughout his childhood.

Marek strained his eyes to read:

My Dearest Marek,

How terribly I miss you, my son. I hope my letter finds you safe and in good health. How I long for the day to be reunited with you.

By now, you'll have been told of all that has gone on here over the past few years. Due to the cruel greed of Count Von Arndt, I have lost everything - my standing as an Austrian Duchess, my wealth, and even my home. You were right when you said he lusted only after my possessions. I was such a fool.

But do not fear. Your Aunt Ewelina, Maya, Wladek and I live comfortably here in Warsaw thanks to Princess Izabela's generosity in making her townhome available. We want for nothing, and through the Princess I have been introduced to the highest circles of society here.

I understand by the time you read this, all will have been explained to you. I apologize that this "new reality" has been set in motion without your knowledge. Please understand the need for us to uphold Maya's honor, which was stolen from her by force. A young unmarried mother with a fatherless son would otherwise be shunned here. In my heart, I knew I must offer your name as a salve to Maya's wounded past.

I am sending Maya and Władek to Paris so that they may spend a few weeks with you. Please receive them both with a loving heart. The Princess has already arranged this in advance with General Dąbrowski, so that he might release you from some of your duties to spend time with them. Worry not about their accommodations, as the Princess has also generously taken care of this.

Władek is so very excited to meet you. He demands we call him by his middle name, Marek, to honor his soldier father. All the child talks about is becoming a cavalier - an Uhlan, Dragoon or perhaps a Hussar. I have told him many times the story of you and your Uncle Jacek constructing those fanciful Hussars' wings from swan feathers. They now hang so proudly upon his bedroom wall, that is when he has not taken them down to play. The child cherishes them, because they come from your hands.

Finally, I ask of you the most pressing of requests. General Dąbrowski, again through the Princess' intervention, has agreed to release you so you may return to Warsaw with Maya and Władek. My heart hopes most profoundly that you have had enough of war and can join living amongst the peace of our little family here in Warsaw permanently.

I myself have never been happier, except for when Bronisław and I raised you as a peasant child. Those were the best of times for me.

I wish for you to enjoy the pleasure of watching young Władeh grow. Of course, it will be confusing to call out your name and have both you and Władeh respond.

Please come home with Maya and Władeh. I am beginning to grow old, and would love nothing more than for us all to be together here along the banks of the Wisła once more. You have always been the greatest joy of my life.

With all the love of a mother's heart,

Magdalena

Chapter 8: Naples and Nelson's Turn of Heart

The heart demands what the heart demands. So has been the justification since time immemorial of many a man's lustful pursuits in defiance of his vows of marriage. It was so for Admiral Horatio Nelson, who was by necessity very often far away from his wife in England when he attached his heart to the young, vivacious and irrepressible Emma. She was the wife of the British Ambassador to Naples, Sir William Hamilton.

Following the Battle of the Nile, any casual friendship Nelson and Emma had maintained enflamed outright with his return to Naples. She had been known to correspond with him while he was at sea with letters of adulation. Sir Hamilton, it would appear, knew of his wife's hero worship of the increasingly famous Nelson: he who had lost the sight of his right eye at Corsica and the use of his right arm at Tenerife. Emma came to adore Nelson, who commanded those magnificent British Ships-of-the-Line throughout the Mediterranean, keeping the seas, and thus the Kingdom of Naples, safe from the French peril that had already overtaken Piedmont, Lombardy and Venice. These regions were all to the north of Naples, where the Hamiltons lived so opulently. And by then, Emma had come to cherish that opulence, that great affluence.

Lady Hamilton's heart set itself upon Nelson. It would be easy to see how the romantic, beautiful and accomplished young woman (only thirty-three years old in 1798 against her husband's sixty-eight years) could attach herself to this famous naval adventurer. Apparently with her husband's blessing, Emma gave all of herself to Nelson, initiating a fate for each of the three of them that even a dreamer like herself could never have imagined.

Emma Hamilton was indeed a dreamer. Her life was a flurry of all the sowings of her heart's desires being reaped into reality; she envisioned herself an artist, a singer, a model, a patron of the arts and a diplomat's wife, and deservedly or not, became each. When that same heart grew increasingly desirous of the so oft-wounded naval hero, she knew her only recourse was to offer herself as a feminine conquest to this man of action.

Emma was born into poverty in rural England as a blacksmith's daughter named at birth as Amy Lyon. Her father's unexpected death came only months after her arrival. Her family eventually became destitute, and by the time she was twelve, she was forced to work at a nearby manor house to support the family. She was soon released, but even at that youthful age she had caught the eye of the young men from that strata of society. She seemed to enjoy her ability to stoke the desires, and thus the attention of these prosperous men.

As Amy matured, she rebelled by notoriously becoming the mistress of Sir Henry Fetherstonhaugh and in doing so became his hostess for stag parties attended by some of the most debauched young men from families of the aristocracy. She was reported to have danced nude on tabletops at their request, amongst other pleasures. In time, young Amy's beauty had caught the attention of the highly respected Charles Francis Greville, the younger son of the Earl of Warwick. This would be the first of a series of fortuitous relationships that would propel young Amy from the obscurity of poverty to the upper echelons of English social life.

Engaging in her raucous lifestyle, Amy soon found herself pregnant. She was but sixteen years old when she gave birth to a daughter, father uncertain, whom she named Emma Carew. When Sir Fetherstonhaugh rejected Amy after he discovered she was in a family way, it was Charles Francis Greville, who took her on as his own mistress. He did so under the guise of taking on her mother as his housekeeper at his Paddington townhome in London.

Charles Francis Greville refused, however, to take on Amy's illegitimate daughter, Emma Carew, which forced Amy to release her to foster parents. During her stay with him, Greville persuaded Amy to refine her style of dress, as well as to change her name to Emma Hart. Both were in order to retain some semblance of propriety, and perhaps disassociate herself from her earlier frivolous endeavors. He taught her enunciation and schooled her in societal etiquette, as well as the classics and fine arts. Emma Hart proved to be a very quick study.

Greville was a collector of works of fine art and was a close acquaintance of the portrait artist George Romney. Romney became enchanted by young Emma's beauty, and she soon became the artist's muse. His paintings depicted her in classical poses, often in the setting as figures from antiquity, as was the fashion of the time. She became famous throughout London for his many paintings, not only capturing, but sensationalizing upon her raw beauty.

Emma Hart proved to be a sponge for the affections of others, especially young aristocratic men. The attention she received from the Romney paintings stroked the unquenchable vanity that dwelled within her. Perhaps coming from such humble beginnings, she desperately needed the continual reassurances of attention. She loved the life that Greville had brought her into. It is said that during her years with him, she fell madly in love with young aristocrat. It became evident to all other than Emma, that Greville's affections did not match her own.

Greville's lifestyle had soon brought his finances to a precarious state. His only way to increase his wealth and maintain his lifestyle was through marriage. In his late twenties, it was time he began his search for a wife, a wealthy one, in earnest. This would have been hindered by his keeping Emma as a mistress on his grounds. In order to resolve this conflict, Greville persuaded her to take a long Mediterranean vacation at the home of his uncle, the British Ambassador, Sir William Hamilton, in Naples. Greville pledged to join her as soon as he could. What Greville did not share was that he had assured his uncle that Emma would stay on permanently as Sir William's mistress and companion.

Sir William Hamilton had been the Ambassador to Naples since 1765, coincidentally the same year as Emma's birth. He had first come across her while visiting Greville in England in 1784. His wife had died two years earlier, and Sir William became enthralled with the nineteen year old beauty.

Under Greville's deception, Emma would depart to Naples, unsuspecting she was fettered in what could easily be classified today as human trafficking. Greville was even bold enough to send along an invoice to his wealthy uncle for the cost of Emma's refinement and education.

The year was 1786. Emma arrived in April on her twenty-first birthday. She stayed several months with Sir William before the finality of her residence there dawned on her. By then, Emma had not only endeared herself to the Ambassador, thirty-five years her senior, but also to the Neapolitan Queen, Maria Carolina, daughter of Hapsburg Empress Maria Theresa and sister of the then French Queen, Marie Antoinette.

Emma was initially outraged when she learned that Greville had no intention of returning her to England. In fact, she had been anxiously awaiting Greville's arrival. Eventually she came to understand her lover had discarded her by means of deception. By the time this epiphany took place, however, she had grown accustomed to the splendor and elegance of Ambassador Hamilton's *Palazzo Sessa* home. The ambassador was a renown collector of art and classical antiquities, even more so than his nephew, Greville. Perhaps Sir William initially treated Emma in this realm, as merely another beautiful acquisition.

Both Greville and Hamilton would both later remark on Emma's wicked temper. In any case, once her fury abated, she determined it would be to her benefit to fill the role of confidant and companion to Hamilton. She had been respectful of him ever since they she had arrived, and determined life with him suited her. At the time, she had no other real option.

In any case, whether in love, or merely cementing a beneficially mutual relationship, Emma became Lady Hamilton in September of 1791 during a visit back to England. Her mother had also come to live at *Palazzo Sessa* with them, but the ambassador, like Greville before him, refused Emma's request to bring along her daughter, Emma Carew. Nor would Emma and Sir William bear any children of their own together, likely due to his being sterile. Emma would only a few years later prove quite fertile.

By the time of his reappearance in Naples after five years in September 1798, just after his great success at the Battle of the Nile, Horatio Nelson was received as a hero of the British Empire. He was received by none other than King Ferdinand IV, his wife Queen Maria Carolina, and the Hamiltons. Emma was reported as being highly excited to see once more this man she had openly idolized as England's savior upon the seas. The young Captain Nelson she had entertained in 1793 had since been promoted to Admiral, but also had lost an eye and an arm for his country. Upon his arrival, his head was still bandaged from shrapnel wounds he had taken on during the fighting at the Nile.

All of Nelson's infirmities only made Emma desire him all the more. She wanted nothing more than to care for the battle-worn combatant, so much more than she ever had for her own husband. She had already, before Nelson's arrival, written fanatical letters of devotion to him for his feats throughout the Mediterranean. Now, she had the chance to prove just how devoted she was to the man.

After all, Nelson contrasted Sir Hamilton in so many ways that appealed to her. For instance, and most notable, Nelson was a man of action while Sir William was a diplomat, a man of words. But there were other more subtle contrasts, as Nelson was, like herself, from humble beginnings, having worked since he was only twelve years old. Nelson was also, again like herself, not formally educated, but was a committed student of a hard life, having traveled the world.

The thirty-three year old Emma *fêted* Nelson at every chance. Learning that his fortieth birthday was approaching, she organized a massive reception for him, inviting more than eighteen hundred guests. Nelson would remain in Naples over the coming months and years as the palace guest of the Ambassador and his wife.

Nelson's officers, including his own stepson, Josiah, soon noticed the attention Lady Hamilton was lavishing on him. In due course, rumors of their behavior would reach the Admiralty, and eventually the London newspapers. The rumors caught fire upon the inquisitive and sordid imagination of all Britons. What could be more salacious than the hero of the Battle the Nile celebrating abroad in a *ménage à trois* with Her Majesty's Ambassador and his young wife?

The reality was that Emma had given herself fully, heart and soul, not to mention other bodily delights, to Admiral Nelson. Before they left the Kingdom of Naples and Sicily together, she would become impregnated with his daughter. Emma would name her Horatia in his honor. All this was done with the Ambassador's full knowledge, if not blessing. Lady Emma had taken her hero as her lover.

There was but one major concern that had interspersed itself into Emma's dreamy world. She had secured her man of action as her lover, but another man of action had his sights on the lands in which she and her husband not only lived, but made their prosperous living. First Consul Napoleon Bonaparte, after returning from Egypt, had set his sights on all of Italy. While away in Egypt, his old enemy, the Austrians, had retaken much of France's holdings in the north of *"the boot."* Napoleon would retake those holdings by force, but would not be satisfied with only that. He threatened to drive south to the Kingdom of Naples, which until then had eluded his grasp.

When Napoleon returned to France from Egypt to a hero's welcome in October of 1799, Nelson was still reveling in the intoxicating mix of his desirous affections for Emma, as well as the generous hospitality of the Ambassador, and the sheer adulation of the Court of the Kingdom of Naples. By then, Admiral Nelson, had lingered in Naples a full year.

Whenever he was not at sea, Nelson lived with the Hamiltons at their *Palazzo Sessa* home in Naples or at their other palatial property in Palermo. In fact, the Kingdom of Naples included all of the lower portion of *"the boot"* as well as the triangular shaped island of Sicily it appeared to kick. Nelson refused to return to England until he did so along with the Hamiltons when the Ambassador was recalled to London in the summer of 1800.

Over that period of Nelson's time squandered away at Naples, his nemesis, Napoleon was very active. After returning from Egypt in October 1799, within a month Bonaparte had overtaken the governing in a *Coup d'état.* Despite the window dressing of the three-man *Consulate,* France had transitioned from a republic to a dictatorship with Bonaparte as *First Consul.* To assure his ever tightening control over the French people, Napoleon knew he needed military victories to placate them, and launched a procession of new attacks against the Austrians in northern Italy. The *First Consul* famously crossed the Alps, and then again racked up victory after victory over the Austrians. Of these, his most significant would come at Marengo in June 1800.

Napoleon's navy had also successfully retaken both the islands of his homeland Corsica and nearby Elba. He had closed the port of Genoa and other Riviera ports to British ships. He still possessed Malta and Egypt, denying the British their seaports as well. The British had fewer and fewer options for harbors to base their fleet in the Mediterranean. By 1800, Admiral Nelson reported to a new commander in the Mediterranean, Lord Keith.

Lord Keith was adamant that Malta needed to be taken back from the French. He ordered Nelson to join the blockade of the French at Malta and develop a plan for taking the isle's fortified port of Valetta. Nelson deferred, claiming health issues. When Lord Keith insisted, Nelson took along the Hamiltons, making the passage not much more than a pleasure cruise around that island. Upon hearing this, Lord Keith was infuriated.

Nelson set up command in a small fishing village on Malta's east side, where he lived openly ashore with Lady Emma in a small cottage. It is believed this was where their first child, a daughter, was conceived. Emma insisted on naming her Horatia.

Lord Keith was outraged. He ordered Nelson to rejoin his main fleet, but Nelson refused and travelled instead with the Hamiltons as well as the Queen of Naples to the Tuscan port of Livorno. Nelson even wrote to his friend and old superior at the Admiralty, the Earl St. Vincent (Admiral John Jervis) claiming that his health kept him from honoring Lord Keith's order.

Having heard the rumors of Nelson and Emma, St. Vincent's response in his return letter to Nelson was uncharacteristically harsh. Nelson's refusal of any orders from a superior officer could no longer be tolerated. St. Vincent wrote:

> *"I believe I am joined by your many friends here, that you will be more likely to recover your health and strength in England than in an inactive situation at a Foreign Court, however pleasing the respect and gratitude shown to you for your services may be..."* [13]

These could hardly be the words that Nelson had expected in return from the man he considered his good friend and trusted mentor, Lord St. Vincent. He must have sensed the inevitable.

---

[13] *"The Life of Nelson"*, Captain A.T. Mahan, Easton Press Edition of 1897 text, Vol. II p.33.

Of course, Lord Keith was livid. Nelson had disobeyed him directly, and then had written to the Admiralty in London, effectively going over his head. Lord Keith set sail to Livorno to confront Nelson face to face. Once there, he ordered Nelson to put the Hamiltons and the Neapolitan Queen ashore at Livorno and return to Malta. In a most defiant act, Nelson responded by striking his flagship's colors (lowering the ship's flag - the naval sign of surrender).

It appeared that official London had tolerated enough of the "Admiral Nelson and Lady Hamilton" scandal. Nelson was ordered to return to London by the Admiralty, just as the Ambassador, not so coincidentally, was recalled to the capital by the Foreign Office.

Beginning in June 1800, Admiral Nelson would make his way back to London, not by ship, but by an overland carriage shared with the Hamiltons. The three took a circuitous and leisurely paced route through Florence, Trieste, Vienna and several stops in the German provinces before crossing the English Channel in November. They left just in time, for between the Tuscan towns of Liverno and Florence, their carriage came perilously close, perhaps as near as two miles, to Napoleon's advance line of troops.

Nelson was celebrated everywhere they visited. Many who saw the attention so painstakingly paid by Emma to the Admiral throughout their trip could not help but comment. She would sit next to him at dinners and cut his meat for him. The Earl of Malmesbury joined their party in Vienna and commented in a letter to his son:

"Lord Nelson and the Hamiltons dined here the other day;
it is really disgusting to see her with him." [14]

---

[14] *"The Life of Nelson"*, Captain A.T. Mahan, Easton Press Edition of 1897 text, Vol. II p.41.

The Earl went on to say that when the great composer Haydn played for them at a ball on their behalf a few nights later, Lady Hamilton simply sat at a Faro table and played Lord Nelson's cards for him.

"Lady Hamilton is without exception the most coarse, ill-mannered, disagreeable woman I have ever met." [15]

In London, much of the same criticism would await Emma Hamilton. As for Lord Nelson, the Admiralty would walk a fine line in dealing with their insubordinate Admiral who was revered as a national hero. Nelson's wife, Fanny, had long awaited letters from her son, Josiah, to see if the rumors already in print in the London newspapers of her husband and Lady Hamilton held any merit. She would find the truth to be more than she could bear.

---

[15] *"The Life of Nelson"*, Captain A.T. Mahan, Easton Press Edition of 1897 text, Vol. II, p.41.

Chapter 9: Fontainebleau
In The Presence of The Emperor

As the refined elegance of a pearl is enshrouded by the coarse protection of an oyster's shell, the magnificence of the Château de Fontainebleau was shielded by an expanse of dense forest. It was only fitting, for if the pearl is the unexpected product of the oyster's secretions, then Fontainebleau seemed the inevitable product of the forest itself. These dense woods, some fifty miles south-southeast of Paris, attracted the attention of the French kings as early as the twelfth century for its renowned hunting. King Louis VII built the first royal hunting lodge there, and nearly five hundred years later, King Phillip I tore it down to its foundations only to rebuild it on a truly palatial scale.

The carriage transporting Princess Izabela and Lieutenant Marek Zaczek progressed through the shadowed road piercing the secluded forest. All around them were thick growths of primeval woods, interspersed with strangling thickets and clutching brambles. The lane's desired effect was achieved, offsetting the travelers' expectations of Fontainebleau's opulence in the deep isolation of these ancient and thickened woods. Surely, Napoleon had reserved this château for his most private meetings, just because of this very effect, enhancing his personal grandeur without the burdensome history of the Palace at Versailles.

A stillness had crept throughout the interior of the coach as the lurking darkness of the woods enshrouded the carriage. The silence was not of awkwardness as before, but was of a more ominous nature. It seemed to linger like a thief who stole all sound save for the unwanted creaking of the wheels turning beneath them and the clatter of the horses hooves on the rough forest road.

"Marek," the Princess asked in Polish as she broke the silence, "do you know why this place is called *'Fontainebleau'* in French? Is it because the waters of its fountains are especially blue? It seems an unusual name."

Marek looked at her quizzically. He so wanted to address with her all that Kobieta had revealed to him the night before on the stone footpath. Kobieta, whose own parents had been slaughtered by the Russians, had remained behind this morning at Kościuszko's cottage, and would be collected after the two of them met with Emperor Napoleon.

Marek answered the Princess' question. "You speak better French than I do, my Princess. *Fontainebleau* is actually a local contraction for *Fontaine belle eau*, or fountains of beautiful water. Over the centuries, it was shortened to its current form. I myself have never had the honor to be stationed at this residence before, but perhaps soon we will see whether it deserves this name…"

Not long after these words were said, the harsh glare of the morning's sunlight flooded the coach's interior as the forest fell away, after which they rode through an extensively cultivated clearing. Scattered upon it was a massive array of ponds and canals. The grounds were covered with the geometric designs of extravagant gardens unmatched in beauty. Among them sprayed fountains that streamed white arches high into the blue morning sky. Their waters feathered as they fell like the layered wings of angels. Beyond these truly heavenly fountains reclined an earthbound grand structure, poised in the distance, like a hungry lion among the tall grasses of Africa, seemingly ready to pounce.

Figure 14: Château de Fontainebleau

The rough forest road gave way to another road, paved with fine quarried stone. Its surface had become as level as the waters of the calm ponds. The road soon bisected the unmatched, although beautifully balanced, wings of the palace masquerading as a French château. Its facades were set off in decorative earth tones and soaring charcoal-blue rooftops of slate. Fontainebleau's opulence exceeded that of any château or maison known to either of them. The imposing nature of the *"hunting lodge"* was awe-inspiring.

"My God," Princess Izabela gasped, "Puławy would not be fit to be the stable house to this château." She spoke of her own palace in Poland, and dramatic as Marek remembered the Czartoryski estate there being, it could not compare to the elegance through which they rode.

"I wish Kobieta could have seen this," the Princess continued, "for I know that I will never be able to find the words to describe it, in any language."

One of Napoleon's Bonaparte's Imperial Residences in 1804

The carriage continued onward until it was enwrapped by the two wings that towered above them outside either window of the coach. The effect was of having passed the point of no return, with no retreat from the pull of the paved stone central courtyard ahead. It was known as the *la cour du Cheval Blanc, or Courtyard of the White Horse*. To turn and flee now, one would only expect to face a charging line of Napoleon's cavalry closing in from behind to cut off any hope of escape.

The courtyard grew in size as the carriage slowly rolled on. It expanded in volume the closer they drew near, enveloping them like hungry jaws flared wide to swallow whole the coach and them inside it. Soon the carriage could proceed no further, having come fully into the expanse of the château's courtyard enclosure. Two massive, symmetrical curved stone staircases extended out from Fontainebleau as if they formed a pair of muscular arms reaching out to clutch and detain the carriage itself. The coachman had brought the horses to a stop just between the staircases' grasp.

He climbed down from atop the coach to hold open wide its door for them to emerge, but to the surprise of everyone, no elaborate welcoming party awaited. Instead, only two parade-dressed soldiers stood at attention to receive them and lead them to the meeting room.

The guests were escorted up the right staircase and into the grand hall of the château. Their heels clattered noisily on fine marble floors as they were led through a maze of rooms, each more ornately decorated than the one before. Hand painted walls, gilded with long golden fingers reaching ever upwards, were seemingly designed to lead the eyes of visitors to the majesty of the imposing painted ceilings looming overhead. These were decorated with art so breathtaking, that one had no option but to crank their necks as they walked under to absorb every delicate brushstroke of their beauty.

Marek had been to Versailles several times since coming to Paris, albeit his visits had been well after that palace had been plundered by the mobs during the Revolution. Each room he passed through here would have been equally at home there, he thought, even when that royal residence was still in its most grand state.

The footsteps of the Poles and their escorts echoed as they were led from one magnificent chamber into another. Finally, they were shown into a resplendent, although vacuous room. It was too large to be called a study, yet somewhat too small to be described as a ballroom. Nearly empty, save for a few chairs and a single desk, their voices resonated from the Rococo hand-painted wall panels, each gilded in gold trim.

Overhead hung a half dozen spectacular crystal chandeliers. They almost chaotically competed with the artwork floating so lightly overhead. There, a multitude of elegant hand painted panels were interspersed among the beams of the room's massively coffered ceiling.

A fire burned slowly in the hearth. The two guests were offered refreshments, which each graciously refused. Then the attendants left them to begin their wait for Napoleon to arrive.

"Remember that the walls may have ears," the Princess said in Polish to Marek, "and likely an interpreter is at hand to translate whatever we might say in our native tongue while we wait."

"I believe you are being somewhat dramatic, My Lady."

"And I believe you are being somewhat naïve, my legionnaire," she responded.

They settled in on the fine *Louis Quinze* period furnishings, what little there were. Marek recognized this subtle trick of statesmanship, done intentionally to make the visitors feel insignificant in relation to the size and grandeur of the room.

There were only five chairs and a small secretary desk upon which simply sat a vase of fresh cut flowers. The room was quiet, except for their limited chatter and the incessant ticking of a mantle clock centered upon the fireplace. Marek assumed this was the noisiest timepiece that could be found, and that it was selected to be placed there to exaggerate the empty hours they might be forced to wait for the Emperor to appear.

An hour passed with no one entering or leaving the room, followed by another. By then, their throats had become parched, to the point both regretted having refused the initial offering of refreshment. There was no pitcher of water in the room, nor had any servants reappeared for them to request one to be brought in.

Finally, with no introduction, a small door previously unnoticed in the panel of the side wall snapped open and in briskly strode Napoleon, contrasted by the cane-assisted, hobbled limp of his adviser and foreign minister, the *duc de Talleyrand.* Beyond them both trailed none other than General Dąbrowski. After him a half dozen of Napoleon's legendary *Vieille Garde (Old Guard)* followed before protectively fanning out through the room.

"Ah, Princess Czartoryska," Napoleon said as he strode across the room, "for an Emperor, affairs of state can be most demanding of his time." He was careful to assure he did not overtly apologize for her wait, beyond that implied by these carefully selected words.

Napoleon's brisk walk came to a rest and he stood before her, nearly clicking his heels as he took her hand and raised it to his lips. Marek noticed he did so without ever having allowed any appearance of having bowed before her. Every step, every movement seemed to have been carefully choreographed to assure she was shown no outright signs of respect.

"You are as certainly as lovely a woman as I have been told," said Bonaparte. Marek could not help but think that while these words resonated with the warmth of a compliment, their careful selection did not disclose anything in particular. The Emperor could have been told she possessed no beauty at all, and they would still be true. But all knew her beauty was true, so why had the Emperor selected his words so painstakingly?

"Merci Beaucoup," she said, before he rudely cut her off, almost as if she did not deserve to be heard.

"No, Princess Czartoryska, thank you," Napoleon responded, "for traveling so far to meet with me."

He spoke quickly and with authority, intentionally clipping the last syllable uttered of even her simple words of thanks. He seemed to place special emphasis on the phrase *"for traveling so far to meet with me,"* as it was intended to subordinate his guest.

Marek had been in the presence of the Emperor often enough to have an understanding of the man. He hated to waste effort or opportunity. He did everything with great purpose, whether it be the quick pace of his stride, his expeditious but intent manner of inspecting a map, or even the rapid pace with which he consumed his meals.

The Emperor's greatest sin was to waste time. For that reason, in all his residences, be they the Tuileries Palace in Paris, his country home of Malmaison, or here at Fontainebleau, the Emperor always kept his library adjoined to his sleeping quarters. In that way, Napoleon could quickly access his beloved tomes no matter which hour of the night he awoke. Each residence's library was identical, shelf for shelf, book by book, so that no matter where he was, Napoleon wasted no time in searching for a title. Thus, it was no surprise that Bonaparte had little desire to spend any more of the clock's incessant ticking engaged in small talk.

"You are so very welcome, *First Consul* Bonaparte," the Princess said, sweetly enunciating the words of his *passé* title like icing on a cake.

Marek thought he saw Napoleon physically take affront to the title *First Consul,* outdated as it was. It visibly offended him that she refused to refer to his having assumed the title Emperor. The Princess offered no salutation of *Your Excellency*, or *Your Imperial Majesty* or even *Sire,* and most certainly not *Emperor*. She continued, "I am told it is an honor that you see fit to receive me, a mere Polish subject of the Prussian State, here at Fontainebleau, far removed from the Tuileries Palace in Paris."

Napoleon stood before her, his arms joined at the wrist behind his back "Ah, Madame," he interjected, "so skillfully said." With having uttered this, Napoleon remained silent, arched his eyebrows, and gave the slightest nod of his head.

"I do not understand your meaning, sir," the Princess coyly responded, feigning a look of befuddlement. She knew exactly his intention, but wanted him to express his indignation to her.

"*Au contraire,* Madame, you know exactly my meaning! Your words are intended to accuse me of a desire to hide these discussions with yourself from the people of Paris. No? I assure you, Madame, I have nothing to hide from my subjects."

"You are *told* to be in my presence is an honor," he continued, "as if you do not hold that belief yourself! You call yourself a simple Pole from Warsaw, yet that city is controlled by the Prussians who so far have deemed to stay neutral in the looming war. Still, these Prussians are being courted by the Russians to join them and their Austrian allies in the coalition against me. This is the very same Russian Court in which your son advises young Tsar Alexander to encourage the Prussian King Frederick Wilhelm III to take up arms against France."

The Emperor's words were spoken in a parlance that was delivered quickly, and with great intent. There were no pauses, either for effect, or because his intellect needed to search for any specific word. He spoke his mind but once; Napoleon rarely repeated himself.

"All you say is true, *First Consul* Bonaparte, except that my son advises the Tsar to court the Prussians. The love for that country was placed long ago in Tsar Alexander by his father, Tsar Paul, who had great esteem for the Germanic peoples. I assure you, my son does not hold King Frederick Wilhelm in high regard."

Her words were then answered not by Napoleon as she expected, but by a more gentle and conciliatory voice. Whereas Napoleon's words bore the brutality of a frontal assault, Talleyrand's entreaties seemed to waft through the air like a pleasant perfume.

"Is it war that you wish for Warsaw, Madame?" Minister Talleyrand then said, so softly that she leaned forward to hear him. "Is it not best that Prussia, who rules over Warsaw should remain neutral, so that the ravages of conflict do not reach its streets? Your son can assure this, by having the Tsar disengage from courting the Prussians and further to convince him to stand down his own troops that even now plan to move westward from their garrisons in Moscow. France only desires Russia to be our easternmost ally. The reckless wrath of war benefits neither their nor our interests."

"Of course I do not want war, Monsieur Minister Talleyrand," she answered, "but I am merely a patron of the arts. You confuse me with a woman of great political power."

"Ah, Lieutenant Zaczek," Napoleon snapped once again before she had even finished her words, as if the Emperor had just noticed the soldier in full uniform before him. He had intentionally turned his back on the Princess as she spoke, as if having grown tired of her excuses. "I should have known General Dąbrowski would have assigned you the honor to escort Madame here today. I hope at least *you* recognize the honor of being in my presence."

"It is indeed my highest honor, Your Excellency," Marek said, saluting Bonaparte, who returned it somewhat casually. Marek quickly caught on to the subtle derision in Bonaparte's words and actions. After Princess Czartoryska's refusal to address him with proper respect, the Emperor would refer to her only as "Madame." He turned his back on the Princess as Marek spoke, to imply to her how unimportant her presence had become.

As Marek finished speaking, Bonaparte then turned slowly back to the Princess, as if he had given her enough time to fully consider the request made by Talleyrand. He would now entice her further with the full reward of the French Empire offered to those who did his bidding.

"Now, Madame Czartoryska," Napoleon said, "let us dispense with all frivolities and address the matter at hand. I know you are a great patriot of Poland, as are all Czartoryskis. Consider what the *duc de* Talleyrand has expressed. As we meet today, France is now formally at war with Warsaw's neighbors of Russia and Austria. Should your son successfully persuade Tsar Alexander to stand down his troops in the east, negotiate an armistice with France, and restrain from hastening the Prussians to enter the war, your family will be rewarded with great honors in titles and riches after I restore Poland to its rightful place again among the sovereign nations of Europe."

"But, *First Consul* Bonaparte," the Princess replied, using the outdated title once more, this time enunciating it with the sharpness of a dagger pressed against his breast, "my family already has great wealth and titles in Poland."

That last word, "Poland," echoed in the air of the near empty chamber. By intent, no one spoke or moved until its syllables slowly faded into oblivion. It was clear that Napoleon used the suspenseful seconds to accentuate his next point. Marek watched as the Emperor's eyes narrowed and his nostrils flared. It only took a second to recognize the Emperor had reined in his anger, instead of unleashing it in a fury, he channeled its energy into the delivery of his carefully selected words that followed hers.

"*Poland! Ahh, Poland!* May I remind you, Madame, that Poland as such no longer exists!" he snapped. "It only lingers as a memory in her peoples' hearts of what the Prussians, Austrians and Russians have so criminally stolen. Yet, you continue to support your own son who conspires against myself, the only man who has proven himself strong enough to resurrect the country of your birth. Your son is foolish to allow the Tsar to drift toward an alliance with Prussia, just as foolish as he was when he advised Alexander to go to war with me! I am told he also favors the Tsar to strengthen his relations with the British. Soon, that country of war-loving agitators will pay for their offenses against me."

Marek could feel the full weight of the pressure as it descended upon the Princess. He did not believe she could take much more of the Emperor's confrontational style of "discussion."

"Madame," Talleyrand said after a few seconds in a more amicable tone, "we respectfully request for your son to advise Tsar Alexander to declare neutrality and abandon any war claims against France and the French Empire. We wish for this to be accomplished prior to the Emperor's upcoming coronation a few weeks hence. We are quite certain that you are capable of achieving this simple request in that timeframe."

A few seconds of silence followed, before Bonaparte again snapped sharply, "Well, Madame? What is your response?"

His impatience sliced through the air like the freshly honed blade of a warrior's sabre. Princess Czartoryska glanced to General Dąbrowski, who gave her a look as if to say, *Did I not warn you that they would take exactly this approach?*

Princess Czartoryska took another few seconds to compose herself as Napoleon glared impatiently at her from only a few steps away. She felt her throat constrict, followed by a heaviness in her chest. Then she remembered General Kościuszko's description of Bonaparte as a self-serving tyrant and somehow it relaxed her.

"You wish my re…response?" the Princess, still under the great pressure of Napoleon's intense gaze, stammered softly. She breathed in deeply, to compose herself, after which she said in a tense but firm voice, "Here is my response: the two of you would lower yourselves to traffic in a princess' love for her deposed country in hopes of leveraging a mother's love for her son only so that you might achieve your political ends? Shame on you, gentlemen, as you clearly do not understand the workings of a mother's heart. There, *Messieurs,* you have my response."

"And so, you would prefer to have war instead?" posed Napoleon in a brisk reply. "Madame, I cannot protect you should the Prussians elect to join your son's Russian masters and aim their cannons at France's brave soldiers. There will be no mercy given when we furiously respond, as one must, in war. If I were you, Madame, I would fear that the current vast holdings of the Czartoryski family will be impacted adversely."

The Princess did not withdraw her eyes from his gaze. She again collected herself by drawing in a deep breath. "What I fear is that we will have war, *First Consul* Bonaparte," she answered, "so long as the leader of France, regardless of whatever title he chooses to be addressed by, attempts to satisfy his lust for Empire."

Blood flushed to Napoleon's cheeks, unaccustomed to being spoken to in so frank a manner, especially by a woman. He stood completely still before her, his arms clasped behind his back, frozen in place except for the tapping of his boot as it began incessantly slapping the marble floor beneath its sole.

"So, we have your decision, Madame," Napoleon stated before he spun on his heels and moved once more toward Marek Zaczek. Marek could see the contempt in his eyes, and while he knew it was intended for the Princess, it still raised a taste of bile in the cavalier's mouth. Marek Zaczek did not fear the battlefield, but he was very apprehensive of the unknown terrain of diplomacy.

"Lieutenant Zaczek," his Emperor said to him, "you are my witness that all I strive for is the resurrection of your nation of Poland in the East. I know most Poles, those not so maliciously aligned with Russia as are the Czartoryskis, support me in this virtuous labor of justice. You have been with me since Lido. You have been among the troops that have triumphantly entered Milan, Venice and Rome. I know your heart is pure and committed to the Revolution. For this I am rewarding you, Lieutenant Zaczek, by naming you to the command of a company of lancers in my Imperial *Vieille Garde*. You will henceforth be given charge of that cavalry unit as *capitaine* of the *Lanciers Polonais* in the *Chasseurs-à-Cheval de la Garde Impériale!* You will represent your unit next month in that capacity at the coronation. Soldier of France, I bestow this great honor upon you; it is earned through your dedication to our Empire's cause. I recognize all that you sacrifice for freedom, including the preservation of hope for your country's restoration."

At that point General Dąbrowski stepped forward to the Emperor's side.

"Congratulations, *Capitaine* Zaczek, you have been greatly honored by your Emperor," said Dąbrowski. "Your promotion is hard earned and deservedly awarded!"

Bonaparte then spun sharply on his heels, and with merely a tilt of his head said to the Princess, "I give you your leave, Madame. I bid you *adieu*."

Napoleon, hands still clasped behind his back then walked off at the same brisk pace with which he had entered, with Minister Talleyrand and the Imperial Guardsmen following closely behind them. A sole figure remained as an after echo of the Emperor, like the shadowy haze made upon the eyes from a flash of lightning.

General Dąbrowski lingered behind with them in such a way that Marek thought it to have been pre-planned by the two departing leaders in the event that the Princess did not concede to Napoleon's will.

"I would encourage you, Princess, to reconsider the Emperor's request," General Dąbrowski said gently. "It could lead to the recovery of our homeland's sovereignty."

"General Kościuszko does not agree with you, my General," the Princess said. "I shall not meddle in my son's affairs, that is final. What comes next will be of *First Consul* Napoleon's doing, not mine or my son's."

"Then when *Emperor* Napoleon and his armies defeat our country's overlords and he refuses to bestow his graces upon the Czartoryski family in the resurrected Poland, know that I will have no ability to intercede on your behalf. I am sorry, but so it must be, my Princess."

"Yes, of course, General Dąbrowski, I understand," the Princess said with a smile to show she had no hard feelings toward her family's longtime friend. "I understand very clearly that your Emperor will never forgive even the least of perceived slights by those who do not readily align themselves with his wishes."

The General then took her hand into his and raised it to his lips, and bowed slightly as he kissed it. He no longer dared to kneel before her.

"I bid you *adieu*, my Princess," General Dąbrowski said as he rose and turned to depart.

He then turned and walked slowly toward the hidden door, which had been left ajar for him. The echo of the fall of his boots receded with each step, as if they represented the hope of every having Poland reinstated as a sovereign European power. Finally they could only be heard in the distance, as the General had disappeared into the hidden passage. The Princess felt only sadness for the man she now considered a fallen hero.

"I would have preferred to hear him say *do widzenia*," the Princess said softly to Marek after Dąbrowski had left the room.

Marek allowed her words to settle, before adding his own.

"It is most sad that war can have such drastic effects on friendships and families."

They awaited the return of the two soldiers to escort them back to the carriage. The Princess then smiled in an embarrassed manner as she turned her gaze fully to Marek, who she had suddenly realized was due her recognition.

"Oh, forgive me, *Capitaine* Zaczek. Congratulations are due," Princess Izabela said as she recovered from her brief but turbulent encounter with Bonaparte. "Upon you has been bestowed a great honor and with it a tremendous responsibility."

Marek could not help but feel that the Emperor declaring his promotion so boldly in front of her was intentionally done only to emphasize Napoleon's dedication to reconstituting their homeland. At the same time, Marek also felt the Princess had gone too far in so greatly disrespecting the French leader.

"You mean in my being promoted to *capitaine* of the Lancers of the *Vieille Garde?*" Marek replied. "Even though you are aware that the foremost function of the Old Guard is to protect the Emperor in whom you have no faith?"

Marek said the words with only a slightly intended malice, but he could see that they struck the Princess particularly harshly. She initially seemed to curl away as they fell upon her, but recovered gracefully, only to lean in close to him to deliver her response.

"Ah, but my *Capitaine* Zaczek, let me assure you that I have the greatest faith in him, actually," she replied, "all the faith in the world, in fact. I have every expectation that the Emperor you serve will bring the wars he waged in Italy and Egypt to every corner of Europe. All in the vanity of his quest to expand his own personal empire - at any cost. I fear war is what he will deliver to our Polish homeland, not its independence."

Chapter 10: London
Nelson's Return to England

What a dichotomy was Nelson's reception in London in early November of 1800. He returned to thronging crowds that enthusiastically welcomed home the hero of the Battle of the Nile, while in stark contrast, the Admiralty knew not quite what to do with this renegade who repeatedly defied direct orders from his superiors. All the more disturbing to them was the business of his taking up travel and quarters with Ambassador Hamilton and his wife, Emma, before reaching London. This only fueled the incessant rumors about their unconventional relationship.

The Hamilton's had secured a residence at number 23 Piccadilly, while Nelson initially quartered nearby with his wife, Fanny, at Nerot's Hotel on St. James Square. As Nelson was *fêted* at balls and other festivities, it became inevitable that Fanny and Emma Hamilton would continue to come into close contact with one another. Fanny soon after found herself addressed by her husband in a very reserved manner, while she herself had observed him engaging with Lady Emma in a very familiar and far too intimate way. The disparate treatments ground with friction inside her like two tectonic plates stressed under the earth's crust.

Fanny must have been enraged when she learned that Emma Hamilton was pregnant. Although Emma'a large frame and layered clothing hid her condition from most who saw her, clearly Lady Nelson suspected the Ambassador's wife was carrying her own husband's child.

Near Christmas of that year, Lord and Lady Nelson took breakfast with a close friend, when the Admiral spoke glowingly one too many times of Lady Hamilton. Fanny Nelson erupted, and confronted her husband with the following ultimatum:

*"I am sick of hearing of dear Lady Hamilton,
and am resolved that you should give up either her or me."*

Admiral Nelson's response has been preserved for history. He reportedly replied with these famous words:

*"Take care, Fanny, what you say; I love you sincerely but
I cannot forget my obligations to Lady Hamilton
or speak of her otherwise than with
affection and admiration."* [16]

Husband and wife thereafter never lived together again. Instead, Nelson spent as much time as possible with the Hamiltons as the birth of his and Emma's child neared.

As 1800 wound into 1801, the Admiralty named Nelson second-in-command of the Channel fleet under his old friend and superior, Lord Jervis. This was necessary as, even then, the British expected Napoleon to be preparing for a cross-channel invasion of their homeland. The *"Corsican Ogre"* had begun to amass his troops across the Channel at the port of Boulonge-sur-Mer, near Calais. The only barrier to their invading was the Channel, which Napoleon referred to as,

*"a mere ditch, and will be crossed as soon as
someone has the courage to attempt it."* [17]

---

16 *"The Life of Nelson"*, Captain A.T. Mahan, Easton Press Edition of 1897 text, Vol. II, p.53.

17 Oxford Dictionary of Quotes, Sixth Edition, p.556, Letter to Consul Cambacérès, 1803.

In addition to the troops stationed at Boulogne and elsewhere along the Channel coast, the French fleet had been reconstituted after the Battle of the Nile, and was augmented by the ships of their new Spanish allies. Mustering such a large joint fleet could only be viewed as an open challenge to Britain for potential control of the Channel itself. They knew that if Napoleon held any plans for an invasion, he would first have to overtake control of that crucial waterway.

On the first day of 1801, Nelson was promoted from Rear to Vice Admiral. He was assigned to a flagship cruising along with the home fleet protecting the Channel. While Nelson was aboard ship, exactly four weeks later, Emma Hamilton secretly gave birth to his daughter at the 23 Piccadilly residence of Lord Hamilton. Emma had, in fact, hidden her being "in a family way" from friends and acquaintances in London quite successfully. Most assumed her large size related to nothing more than having had enjoyed the extravagant lifestyle in Naples a bit too much.

Emma named the child Horatia. Nelson had wished for his daughter to be named Emma, after her mother, but Lady Hamilton insisted on naming her in honor of her father. With Nelson once more at sea, even if only cruising the waters of the Channel, there was no one to stop her from carrying out this tribute.

A few days later, Lady Hamilton would turn the infant over for another woman to raise away from the probing eyes of the public. Emma took a cab from Mayfair to Little Titchfield Street in London's Marylebone district with Horatia hidden within her winter garb. She left the newborn to the care of a Mrs. Gibson, a widow, who would care for Horatia until such time that Emma requested her child returned. Mrs. Gibson would hire a wet nurse for the infant, a common occurrence at the time. The secretive agreement could have been drawn directly from the pages of a Charles Dickens novel, except for the fact that the author would not even be born himself until the next decade.

Few had known of Emma's pregnancy. But no sooner had she turned over her infant to Mrs. Gibson, Emma brazenly attended a concert at the Duke of Norfolk's home in St. James Square. It was there that she was said to have drawn the attention of the Prince of Wales, the future King George IV. What developed next turned out to be on the level of a royal infatuation.

When word of the Prince of Wales lavishing attention on his Emma reached Nelson at sea, it created a raging jealousy in the Admiral. This was only smoothed over when Ambassador Hamilton wrote Nelson what must have been a truly unusual letter, assuring him that Lady Hamilton had remained faithful to Horatio. One can only imagine the mixture of emotions in a husband writing such a testimony to the lover of his own wife.

In late February, Nelson returned to London and was delighted to finally meet his daughter at Mrs. Gibson's house. He spent every free hour he could doting on Horatia. However, he would not remain in London for very long.

In April 1801, Admiral Nelson sailed under the command of Admiral Sir Hyde Parker to Copenhagen. The Danes, along with the Russians, Swedes and Prussians had tired of the English restricting their ships from conducting commerce with France. These countries formally pushed back against their vessels being boarded by the English in international waters, only to confiscate anything the British viewed declared as contraband. The countries had formed a Baltic resistance known as the Northern Alliance.

Although it was a neutral state, Denmark was considered the key. It controlled the pathway to the Baltic. The Russian and Swedish fleets were still trapped in their winter ports at the other end of the Baltic by a harsh, thick blanket of ice. England wished to bring Copenhagen to its knees and sign an agreement allowing the search and seizure practice to continue before the thaw that would free the other navies to come to the Dane's rescue.

Admiral Sir Hyde Parker was unsuccessful in his diplomatic negotiations with the Danes. Nelson convinced him that the most effective negotiating tactic was to threaten a preemptive strike on the Danish fleet. The entire fleet was squeezed in at Copenhagen harbor. Nelson's real objective was to destroy the Danish fleet before its ships fell into the hands of the French.

In the end, Parker reluctantly agreed with Nelson. When even that threat failed to bring the Danes to the negotiating table, Parker ordered Nelson to press the attack on Copenhagen harbor. Admiral Parker's own ships would remain safely at a distance in the *Kattegat*, the strategic waterway separating the Baltic from the North Sea. Admiral Parker would communicate with Nelson throughout the attack by way of messaging flags, as was the proven method of the day.

Nelson led the attack. Initially, it did not go well, with several British ships running aground. At one point, things became so dire that Parker signaled via flags and gave the order to his subordinate admiral to cut off the attack. Nelson would once more demonstrate his arrogance for his superior's commands, as he knew pulling his ships from an engaged battle would make them vulnerable. In fact, he viewed disengaging his attacking fleet to make it susceptible to being obliterated by the Danish batteries.

When made aware of the raising of Parker's signal by his flagship's Captain, Thomas Foley, Nelson was recorded to have said:

> *"You know, Foley, I have only one eye.*
> *I have a right to be blind sometimes …"*

He then raised the spyglass to his blind eye, and said,

> *"I really do not see the signal."* [18]

---

[18] Oxford Dictionary of Quotes, Sixth Edition, p. 556, attributed to
  "Life of Nelson" by Robert Southey (1822)

Once more refusing a direct order from his superior, Nelson literally turned his blind eye and continued the attack. In the end, the Danish fleet was destroyed and another great naval victory was earned under Nelson's command.

Nelson could not wait to return to London thereafter, to rejoin the Hamiltons at 23 Piccadilly. From there, he would continue to secretly visit his infant daughter at Mrs. Gibson's flat in Marylebone.

Meanwhile, a group of British politicians sought an end to the seemingly perpetual war with Bonaparte. During the autumn of 1801, they brought an end to hostilities between Britain and France. Fighting ceased on 1 October, and by the 25th of March 1802, the Treaty of Amiens was formally signed between the two parties. For the first time in many years, a calm of peace stretched across the turbulent waters of the English Channel.

Nelson was not concerned, however, for he knew in the beating of his embattled heart that this peace could not and would not last for very long.

Chapter 11: Paris

A Visit from the Past

Agony awaits those who tempt to revisit the past; but how much more agonizing it is when the past calls upon those neither willing nor ready to receive it. That was exactly the situation that faced Marek a few weeks after the encounter at Fontainebleau as he awaited the arrival of the coach carrying his childhood love, Maya, and her nine year old son, Władek. Marek waited at the *Place Louis le Grand*, in front of the hotel where the recently departed Princess Izabela had stayed during her visit. In fact, this would be the very same hotel where Maya would reside upon her imminent arrival.

Place Louis le Grand was a stunning square, even though with its corners clipped by the layout of its buildings, it formed more of an octagon than a true square. The Revolution had long ago swept away its impressive centerpiece, a huge bronze casting of the Sun King, Louis XIV, on horseback. Yet even without the monument, the square breathed a sense of space and perspective, so welcome and rare, preserved among Paris' crammed streets. Several years in the future, Napoleon would fill the void at its center with a tribute column cast from the melted metal of the cannons of his many conquered enemies, and would rename it as *Place Vendôme*.

Marek had waited patiently in the square, on the very spot that the messenger sent ahead of the coach had directed. With him was his companion, Rydek, who had befriended him ever since his entry to the Polish Legions of Napoleon's *Armée d'Italie*. They were about the same age, although Rydek came from a different part of the homeland. He hailed from Thorn, as the Prussians then called it, although he knew it better as Toruń, the city most famous for being where the great astronomer Copernicus had studied at its renown university.

The two soldiers sat side by side on their mounts, looking impressive in their full parade dress uniforms. These were romantic reflections of the French Revolution's famous tricolors of *Bleu, Blanc and Rouge:* the *bleu* of the traditional double-breasted plastron-fronted lancer jackets (known as *Kurtas* in Polish) and stovepipe trousers; the proud *rouge* of the jacket's breast-piece and neck collar as well as the trousers' flanking stripes; with all trimmed out by the *blanc* of the broad sashes across their chests, and long gloves covering their forearms, as well as the distinctive feathered plume of their headgear. These *Czapka* headgear were direct throwbacks to their Polish past, squared off just as were the famous *rogatywka* military caps of General Kościuszko's revolt. The *Czapka* though, were inflated versions, rising high over each lancer's head like a mad *rogatywka soufflé*. From their *Épaulettes* dangled loops of brocaded ribbon, while from their hips dangled deadly sabres, their danger sheathed in decorative metal scabbards. Their uniforms were the only decorations on the deserted muted stone square, as if they were the dazzling array of colors on an artist's palette set before a large monotone expanse of canvas.

"So, Marek," Rydek asked, "do you even remember your love Maya's face well enough to recognize her?"

"Somewhat," Marek lied, but then truthfully added, "but my affections for her are such that I should not have the slightest problem in greeting her."

Figure 15: A Polish Lancer at ease

"Ah, but what of her son?" Rydek pressed, "I can tell from your eyes that greeting him will be another matter altogether."

"You know I have never laid eyes on the child," Marek said matter of factly. He had some time ago in those lonely nights that accumulate between battles shared with his friend his own heart's rupture upon when he first saw his pregnant Maya. He had even shared the fact that the child was not his, that his love had been raped. Yet even then he could not bring himself to admit that the attacker had been her own uncle. He never saw a reason to share that bit of his remorse from which his own heart could never heal.

"The coach is late," Rydek observed as he spied at his pocket watch, "but fret not, *mon ami*, as Warsaw is a far way off."

The coach was indeed over an hour late, causing Marek much angst. Just then a fine black carriage entered the square and headed directly toward their mounts.

Marek felt in his stomach a queasiness when he guessed at how Maya might look after a full decade's separation. Would she be as strikingly beautiful as he had remembered her from when they as children shared her lessons in French from a tutor upon the *folwark*? Or would motherhood have fattened her into a plump and rounded woman who only cared for her son Władek and nothing of herself and her appearance? Only seconds now stood between the burden of his wondering and the certainty of his knowing.

As the carriage came to a stop before them, Marek dismounted from his steed. Rydek remained in his saddle. Marek straightened himself into a militaristic pose, upright and rigid, as the coachman opened the door and a figure slowly emerged.

At first his heart dropped, seeing it to be the image of an adult male that emerged. Of course, Maya would not have been sent unescorted over such a great distance, but would it not have been appropriate to have him disembark before the coach entered the square to spare Marek the pain of spying her with another man?

Then, Marek's heart exploded with joy as he recognized that masculine figure to be his old friend and rescuer, Tolo. So, Magdalena had entrusted Maya in the very capable hands of this, his "newfound brother." Marek could think of no one better.

Marek broke his rigid stance and rushed forward to embrace his old friend. Tolo ran toward him also, covering the short distance in leaping, joyful strides. The two men collided chest to chest, their arms wrapping around each other in embraces so warm and sincere they could not have been artificially affected.

"Tolo, you scoundrel," Marek said into his ear, "how wonderful it is to see you again."

"I don't know," laughed Tolo, "the boy I left off at the banks of the *Wisła* near Maciejowice only seemed to play at being an Austrian Uhlan. You my friend seem to fill out this Legionnaire's uniform quite convincingly."

"Tolo, my friend, my brother…" Marek stammered.

"If not your brother by birth," Tolo joked, "then certainly by rebirth. Have you learned yet to swim, Marek, or are you counting on all the rivers of Europe to continue to spit you out?"

"Yes, Tolo here once brought me back to life," Marek said, turning to Rydek, "by fetching my drowning soul from the *Wisła* near Kraków. Tolo, this is my fellow Legionnaire, Rydek, from Toruń."

"*Cześć*, Rydek from Toruń," Marek's long lost friend said. "It is a pleasure to meet you. Yes, I brought him back to life then. And today, Marek, today, I bring you back to the rest of your life. Two anxious souls await you inside that carriage."

In all his excitement, Marek had almost forgotten about Maya and young Władek.

"The last time I saw Maya come out of such a carriage she was round, bulging with child, like the casing of an overstuffed *kielbasa*," Marek confessed, laughing slightly as he said these words. Yet inside him the acidity rendered by that memory etched away at the walls of a lonely cavity formed long ago.

"Well, my friend," Tolo smirked, "you look so dangerous in that uniform with your sabre hanging there. Please remember that this time if Maya is showing, that I have been with her for only the last few weeks, eh!" A devilish smirk exploded across Tolo's face, which somehow eased Marek in his internal distress.

Marek could not help but laugh aloud, and jabbed his elbow into Tolo's side while he did so. Rydek looked down from his mount upon the two friends engaging in the joyful embrace of camaraderie forged by the significant life events they had shared.

Tolo then called to the carriage, "Maya, my lovely traveling companion, someone is here to greet you, and he is tired of being teased with the anticipation of your appearance."

Tolo stepped to the coach to assist this passenger when suddenly another bounding form squeezed out before her. The boy jumped in a single leap to the ground and then exploded from his squat into a full sprint. He ran towards Marek, screaming all the way, *"Tata, Tata, Tata…"*

The child crashed headfirst into Marek, and wrapped his arms around the soldier's waist. Marek had instinctively pulled back his shoulders, not sure how exactly to respond to the child's gleeful outburst.

"My name is Marek Zaczek also, *Tata,*" the boy said, his eyes beaming up at his namesake.

"Władek, how nice it is to meet you," Marek said, tentatively placing his hands on the young boy's shoulders.

"No, *Tata,* call me Marek, just like you," the boy squealed, "I want to be a man just as you are. A brave soldier like you, *Tata.*"

Marek was caught completely off guard. He had told himself he would play along with the fiction, but the child's exuberance was too much for him to honestly accept.

"Just how old are you, my son?" he asked despite already knowing the answer. The boy's eyes alighted on the last two words spoken, even though Marek had intended the phrase in a manner just as he might speak to any other child. But clearly, Maya's son had interpreted the phrase more paternally.

"I am nine, *Tata*," the child answered, "but soon I will be ten, and then only a few years away from joining the army."

"So I see," said Marek.

"Who is the other soldier, *Tata*?"

"He is my colleague, Władek. His name is Rydek."

"No, please father," the child pleaded, "call me Marek. Please call me Marek!"

"Well, Władek," Marek said sternly, "it is true that Marek is most certainly a man's name. Until you prove to me that you are a man, no longer a mere boy and have earned the honor of that name, I will call you by the child's name given to you by your mother."

"Yes, *Tata*," the child dejectedly said.

Marek could physically feel the disappointment in the boy, who had until then tightly hugged his waist. First the child's python-like grip slumped, then released its embrace altogether before the boy backed off a step.

"Władek," a familiar voice called out from the coach, "I told you not to overwhelm your *Tata*. Come to *Matka*."

"Allow me, Madame," said Rydek, understanding the boy's dejection as well as the need to remove him from the moment of Marek and Maya's reacquaintance, "but I feel this child is in dire need of a ride around the square upon a Legionnaire's mount. After all, he shall soon enough be a soldier, will he not?"

With having said this, Rydek moved his horse forward and scooped up the boy in an effortless movement from the saddle. All could hear the child laugh aloud as Rydek broke his horse into a trot, and then, at Władek's urging, a faster pacing around the empty square. The empty space soon echoed with the child's glee.

"Careful, Władek!" The voice, despite being stern as intended for the child, carried to Marek as softly as the gentle cooing of a morning dove. It affected him greatly to hear it, and brought back a rush of memories. Even the smell of her childhood scent flooded his nostrils and evoked his emotions. All of these recollections were initially welcome and readily accepted, but in a split second they became interspersed with an element of caution.

Marek raised his head to look over at Tolo who assisted Maya down from the carriage. When his friend did so and stepped away from her, Marek had his first unencumbered look at his childhood love. Despite his wishing it not, his heart raced, all caution swept clean of him like a winter's wind. She was radiant, in both face and form. Marek was instantly transformed to a child no older than Władek, who even then had known he loved this girl.

"Maya," he said, taking steps toward her, "I did not mean to be so stern with your son…"

She reached out her hand for him to take. He did so, and bowed to kiss it when she pulled it from him and wrapped her arms around him.

"Our son, Marek, I fear our child has been too long without his father, that needs to be corrected," she said as they embraced. Then she whispered in his ear softly, *"Dziękuję, moja Marek. I will not forget this."*

Then she kissed his cheek, just in front of the ear she had whispered into. She then pressed her eyes against the vulnerability of his temple and cried softly, a mix of sorrow and joy.

Marek's head was spinning. He thought instantly of all the women he had bedded, here in Paris, away in Italy, and everywhere in between. All grouped together meant but only the smallest fraction of this sweet moment as his Maya had returned to him. His only concern now was how to sooth her tears.

"I missed you so terribly," she said to him, her voice quaking as if it might snap. "Your smile, your arms, your presence. I could not bear to think of you still hating me. I feared you would die in battle having never forgiven me."

"It is all right now, *moja Maya Manusca,*" Marek said tenderly, "I could never hate you. Now, here we are, all together in Paris. There is nothing to forgive. You were but a child yourself, abused by your own family. We are all together now, and will soon be the family just as you sought."

She pressed her head harder against his. Her tears did not abate, instead they increased until he could feel their shedding shaking throughout her.

"What is it, Maya?" he asked. "I thought this news would make you happy. It is what you want, is it not? It is what was asked for in my *matka's* letter…"

"That is exactly why I shed these tears, my Marek," she whispered between sobs. "I already dread the day, the very hour when Władek and I must leave this place and you behind once more. Especially now that you have agreed to allow me the use of your name, and for Władek to know you as his father."

"And, most importantly, for you to cherish as your husband," he said, overcome by the moment, surprised that the words flowed so freely from his heart after years of anger and hurt.

Marek had not decided to accept his mother's request even up to the coach's arrival, but the pain he felt in Maya's tears ripped though him and extolled him to do the right thing, there and then.

"Do not cry, *moja Maya Manusca,*" he whispered after he kissed her forehead, "I have decided to leave with you, to return to Poland and live out our lives there together. The family that we are here, we shall be together again in Warsaw. We have been re-united only an instant, but I already know I can never leave you again."

"But under Napoleon, you fight for the re-establishment of our country, free and sovereign," she said. "I cannot ask you to forego that. I know how committed you are to that noble goal."

He grasped her gently by the shoulders, then held her at the length of his arms to take in the full sight of her. "Let my eyes wander over you, to complement the fullness of your scent that already intoxicates me. There is no perfume in Paris as sweet. I will always carry Poland in my heart, so long as I can carry you in my arms."

Her entire demeanor instantly became infected with a joyous, nervous energy. "You mean it, Marek? You do not tease me? Please assure me you do not. Please do not let this be a trick of some sort, only to be pulled away in revenge."

"I would never tease you with a lie," he said. "Perhaps by withholding the full measure of the truth, but never a lie. No, I jest. We will leave in a week, right after the Emperor's coronation. I am committed to stay until then. After that, I will seek my release from General Dąbrowski, but Magdalena has already written to assure me that he has all but agreed to this."

Maya excitedly kissed him, overjoyed that all had been decided. As she did so, he could feel her bouncing on the balls of her feet. It was as if she could not contain herself. He knew that she surely had dreaded hearing him explain all the reasons why he must stay; why she and Władek could never claim his name. But here, so quickly, in only minutes, he had agreed to everything that her heart desired.

"Marek," she said, "I have a letter for you from Magdalena. Here, take it, read it, lest its contents change this joyous moment."

"Please explain exactly why my mother did not join you on this trip," he demanded as he took the letter. Like all notes he received, he ran his thumb over its seal, which was undisturbed.

"Magdalena is assisting a family as it prepares for a very important society wedding. She tutors a young girl, Marie Łączyńska, who is preparing to marry Count Athenasius Walewski, the *starosta* of the Warka district."

"You mean the same man who was long ago chamberlain to the last king of Poland, Stanisław August Poniatowski?"

"Yes, precisely."

"And this Marie is how old?" asked Marek.

"Marie is eighteen," Maya explained. "She and I have become close friends, even though I am a dozen years older than her. She has taken a great liking to Władek. She calls him her little soldier, which of course he loves."

"The poor girl," Marek said, "only eighteen years old. Count Walewski must be at least four times that by now."

"Nearly, but he is a very wealthy man, a great landowner," said Maya. "Surely it is an arranged marriage."

"Poor Marie," Marek repeated, "to be forced to marry such an old wart of a man. Please tell me she is not pretty."

"In fact," Maya answered, "she is perhaps the most beautiful young woman I have ever met."

"So he gets to enjoy his last years," Marek thought aloud, "only to deny her the joy of her own youth. And my *matka*, out of the kindness of her heart, prepares this Marie for such a betrayal?"

"No, Marek," Maya explained, "your *matka* does this because she needs the *zlotys*. She has been retained by the Łączyński family as a governess for young Marie. It is her job, her responsibility, the work from which she now must earn a living."

Marek opened and read the letter carried to him by Maya:

Dearest Marek,

Thank you for the return letter carried back to me by the Princess Czartoryska. I was most delighted at your reply to my request to receive Maya and Władek. I say thank you, as both are with you by the time of this letter's reading. I also appreciate your willingness to consider complying with my other request, which you so mockingly write of as "The Great Fiction." Of course, going along with this is a decision that you alone must make, and I will leave it to you to inform Maya of your choice over the course of her stay with you.

I write to you to explain that if you accept, even though you and Maya will be presented to everyone as man and wife, it is most important that you take no liberties with her while in Paris. I cannot possibly begin to specify why in this brief letter. Trust me that should you arrive in Warsaw with Maya, I will explain everything. It is something that I should have shared with you so very long ago, but somehow I could never muster enough courage to do so. I will explain everything when I next look into your beautiful eyes again, my son.

By now you will have met Władek. The child was absolutely bursting with enthusiasm to meet "his father." He will make you happy all your life, if only you can bring yourself to accept that God has blessed us all with his birth, even if he is not truly of your seed. Remember the proverb, "Only the shoe need know that the stocking is torn." In any case, he so greatly longs to soon be a fierce warrior just like his Tata.

Please tell Maya that your answer is yes, as I look forward very much to seeing you, my son. Aunt Ewelina asks that I say hello on her behalf. She is still so bitter that Uncle Jacek and their two sons have been away so long at war in the Austrian army. I pray each day that they all return safely, and she finds peace once again in her soul.

I look forward to hold you in my embrace.

With a Mother's Love,

Magdalena

Chapter 12: London
The Three-Sided Affair

Where goes a heart that has known true love? Wherever it must to again taste that irresistible nectar! In the case of Horatio Nelson, so adored by the thronging crowds awaiting him across England, the man was willing to undermine this adulating sentiment with the risk of ridicule. He openly lived with the Ambassador William Hamilton and Lady Emma after having abandoned his own lawful wife. Despite this, the public was not aware in late 1801 of the birth of Nelson's and Lady Emma's daughter, Horatia, who was still under the secretive care of the widow Gibson in Marylebone.

As mentioned, Nelson, upon returning from Copenhagen, resided in Piccadilly with the Hamiltons. He delighted in his time spent each day with his beloved Emma, and visited regularly with his daughter at the Gibson house in Marylebone. He would play with her with all the patience and love of a new father. This was a sentiment he had never truly known with his stepson, Josiah. For that matter, neither had he ever held a flame for his wife, Fanny, such as he did for Lady Hamilton.

In fact, Admiral Nelson had written to his Lady Emma many times from sea in great earnestness. Their letters would one day expose the depths of the love between them. These letters would be seen as scandalous if published. Nelson wrote to Emma regarding his poor spirits upon being away from her and Horatia:

***"Our separation is terrible, my heart is ready to flow out of my eyes. I am not unwell, but I am very low. I can only account for it by my absence from all I hold dear in this world."*[19]**

Emma had, in fact, desired for them all, herself, her husband and Nelson, to live together openly, albeit farther away from the public's ever probing eyes. To this end she persuaded Nelson to purchase an estate called Merton Place, just outside London in Surrey. This quickly became known in the family vernacular as *"the farm."* Emma and Nelson went on to live there, while Sir Hamilton retained his 23 Piccadilly townhome, although the Ambassador frequently stayed at *the farm* as a guest. There were also regular visits by Mrs. Gibson and Horatia.

Publicly, the child was falsely attributed as having been born in Naples to Vice Admiral Charles Thompson. Horatia was explained as being the goddaughter of Admiral Nelson and Lady Hamilton. Admiral Thompson had willingly agreed to this ruse in order to assist his friend Nelson.

Merton Place quickly became somewhat crowded. Not only did Emma's mother also live there, but when Emma finally divulged to Nelson the existence of her daughter Emma Carew (having since become known as Emma Hartley), Nelson was all too happy to have the oft rejected first daughter of his Lady Emma join them all at *the farm.*

Nelson's father, Edmund, had grown seriously ill in April 1802. Nelson did not visit him during his infirmity, instead stayed with Emma to celebrate her thirty-seventh birthday. Neither did the Admiral travel to Norfolk to attend his father's funeral when he succumbed. Perhaps he did not wish to encounter Fanny, sure to be present. Nelson's life appeared to revolve solely around Emma and Horatia in the insulated solace of their home at Merton Place.

---

[19] *"The Life of Nelson"*, Captain A.T. Mahan, Easton Press Edition of 1897 text, Vol. II, p. 139

The year 1802 was a time of peace between England and France that had kept Nelson home from the sea. Nelson embraced it by touring England with the Hamiltons. Huge crowds came out, town after town, not only to see the naval hero, but also to gawk at the woman who had been the subject of so much scandalous gossip. The woman who had captured their hero's heart, but also steeped him, they thought, in marital shame.

The following year brought even more tragedy. Emma's legal husband, Sir William Hamilton, collapsed at his home at 23 Piccadilly. On the sixth of April 1803, the former Ambassador died in Emma's arms. Despite their long time together, Emma was not treated with particular favor in his Last Will and Testament. The ambassador's surviving family soon had little need for her.

By this time, peace with France was already unraveling and quickly the hounds of war returned. Fearing the threat of a Napoleonic invasion of their island nation, Nelson was given outright command by the Admiralty of the Mediterranean fleet. He was seen as the only man, despite all his faults, aggressive enough and possessing the required strategic capability to take on the combined French and Spanish fleets.

Days before his departure, Nelson and Emma had their daughter baptized in the Marylebone Parish Church as Horatia Nelson Thompson. They changed her date of birth from 29 January 1801 to 29 October 1800 and its place from London to Naples in order to support the ruse that she was the goddaughter left to their care by Admiral Charles Thompson. It is important to remember that on this fictitious date when Horatia was supposedly born in Naples, Nelson and the Hamiltons were already *en route* returning to England. They thought this clever, as the many aristocrats they visited along the way would likely be willing to attest that Emma had definitely not been with child, let alone given birth along their extended coach journey across the Continent.

Chapter 13:
Notre Dame de Paris
The Emperor's Coronation

Illusions of grandeur are not merely illusions when one can hear, smell and reach out to touch their manifestations. The week leading up to the freezing cold Sunday morning of the second of December in 1804 was marked with Imperial Pre-Coronation Balls and Galas anticipating the upcoming crowning of the Emperor. When the morning itself arrived, it did so with solemnity and ceremony, although it was devoid of the dignity of silence.

At eight that morning, a cannonade was fired outside the Tuileries Palace that was reported to have awakened Napoleon. That frigid morning found Marek in the uniform of the Emperor's *Vieille Garde*, one of many soldiers honored to form a protective ring outside the palace on horseback. The *Vieille Garde, or Old Guard,* were an outgrowth of the earlier *Consular Guard* consisting of both infantry and cavalry regiments. The infantry consisted of regiments of both the *Grenadiers de la Garde Impériale* and of the *Chasseurs-à-Pied de la Garde Impériale.* The cavalry was formed of regiments including the *Horse Grenadiers* and the *Chasseurs-à-Cheval de la Garde Impériale.* The latter regiment contained the unit to which Marek Zaczek's battalion of Polish Lancers was assigned. Also offering protection to the Emperor that day were the traditional palace guard, the *Gendarmes d'élite de la Garde Impériale.* While they were independent of the *Old Guard,* this palace guard unit finished out the protective ring.

At eleven o'clock that frigid morning, leaders of the Senate convened in the palace to address the soon to be coronated Emperor. Napoleon was warmly addressed as the *"Father of France."* That title could have been a reference to the first great Continental leader, Charlemagne, who had been revered as *"Pater Europae,"* Latin for *"Father of Europe."* Surely, even then, in Bonaparte's mind, he was already contemplating adding all the lands of Europe beyond those already included in France's Empire.

To that end, Napoleon had assured that a medieval looking crown was fashioned which he would misleadingly name *"the Crown of Charlemagne."* Charlemagne had been crowned Emperor on Christmas Day 800 AD by Pope Leo III in Rome. That date is often referred to as the founding of the Holy Roman Empire, which still existed in 1804 under the control of the Habsburg dynasty of Austria. To compare himself to that first great European and Carolingian leader, Napoleon demanded that Pope Pius VII attend his coronation. Napoleon would not travel to Rome, instead he insisted that the Pope come to Paris.

Despite the indignity of the slight, Pope Pius VII consented. He had departed from Rome on November the fifth, and arrived at Fontainebleau nearly three weeks later. He was kept isolated there until the day of the ceremony. If Pius VII's forced travel was not degrading enough, Napoleon had the Pope transported to the Cathedral de Notre Dame at nine in the morning. The Pope arrived at the cathedral, only to punitively await the arrival of Napoleon and his bride Joséphine several hours later.

When Napoleon departed from the Tuileries Palace, he traveled in a grand procession along a route crossing the Seine symbolically upon the *Pont Neuf,* the oldest bridge in Paris, onto the *Île de la Cité.* The day was gray with clouds, and chilled by freezing temperatures, but even this could not dissuade the throngs of Parisians from enthusiastically lining the streets of the route. They hoped only to be rewarded with even the slightest glimpse of their beloved Emperor Napoleon or his Empress Joséphine.

Marek rode in the protective formation that flanked the Emperor's carriage fore and aft, as well as along each side. While their uniforms were the ornate full parade dress, their sabres and pistols were battle-ready in case of any threats of misadventure. Thankfully, there were none that day.

Napoleon arrived at Notre Dame at a specially constructed pavilion, artistically painted to blend into the cathedral's exterior. There the Emperor and the Empress would don their ceremonial garb. Napoleon would then change from his white satin tunic into the velvet robe lined with white ermine, upon which a recurring motif of Imperial Bees was stitched in golden thread. The bee insignia was adopted as an *"homage"* to France's ancient Merovingian kings, who long ago had selected it to represent their industrious style of leadership.

The Imperial Bee motif replaced that of the traditional *fleur-de-lis*. Surely the Emperor desired a symbol not already so closely tied to the Bourbon kings of France. For even then, the intent of Napoleon's Empire was to slash across the Rhine, spreading to eventually encompass all of Europe, and beyond.

Joséphine was adorned similarly in a great train of ermine lined velvet, again embroidered with the Imperial Bee motif. Her train was attended to by Napoleon's three sisters. Napoleon had been adamant that Joséphine be coronated as "Empress" during the ceremony along with himself, although this brought out great discussion from his family.

Marek was hand-picked by the Emperor as one of those members of the *Vieille Garde* assigned as the Cathedral's Interior Honor Guard. It was a duty someone as new as he to this prestigious unit might be viewed as not deserving, but the other members of the *Vieille Garde* knew he carried the favor of the Emperor. Marek's friend, Rydek, had been selected for the exterior perimeter duty that day.

Rydek and Marek had conspired between them to smuggle Maya into the cathedral. To that end, she was given a pass, stolen in advance by Marek. She was told to enter near Rydek's position. If she faced any resistance upon approaching the church's great doors, Rydek was to vouch for her. This turned out to be unnecessary, as the theft of the pass had gone unnoticed.

Inside the cathedral, after an extensive visual search, Marek was able to find her standing in the shadows of a side altar alcove along the *Rive Gauche (Left Bank)* wall.

The ceremony within Notre Dame was meticulously planned. Hundreds of musicians were stationed throughout the vaulting arches of the building. A choir of four hundred voices sang the *Te Deum* and other traditional Catholic hymns, giving the ceremony a sacred intonation.

The combined effect on Maya was overwhelming, as she awaited the arrival of Napoleon and Joséphine. She had always thought, even from her great distance away in Warsaw, how romantic was the love that spanned between them. Little would she realize that one day she would witness firsthand the Emperor's other great love affair, but from a much closer vantage point.

Next the Emperor's family arrived, with the exceptions of both Napoleon's brother, Joseph, (with whom the Emperor had been quarreling) and his mother, Letizia, known throughout France as *"Madame Mère,"* who wished not to take sides between her two feuding sons. Then, the heart of the coronation ceremony began. Napoleon entered the cathedral, his head already adorned with a golden wreath of laurels beckoning back to the days of Julius Caesar's Rome. He and his bride Joséphine processed toward the High Altar, as they paced their steps to the solemn accompaniment of the musicians' orchestration. Napoleon came to stand on the altar before the Pope. Joséphine took her place seated on a throne behind it at her husband's feet.

As the ceremony continued on, Pope Pius VII stood and with both hands elevated the so-called *"Crown of Charlemagne."* The Pontiff was prepared to place it upon the Emperor's head, when Napoleon audaciously stepped forward and took the crown from the Pope's outstretched arms. Napoleon had leveled one final indignity at the Pope, refusing the Pontiff even the slightest sense of dominion over him. It was said that Napoleon rested the medieval-looking crown upon his own head, but as his head still was adorned with the golden laurels, the Emperor merely symbolically held it closely above those.

Despite this humiliation by the Emperor's symbolic self-coronation, the Pope would nonetheless go on to profess,

"May God confirm you on this throne and may
Christ give you to rule with him in his eternal kingdom."

before offering the traditional Imperial Latin blessing,

"Vivat imperator in aeternum!
("May the Emperor live forever!") [20]

After this bold display, Napoleon set aside the *"Crown of Charlemagne"* and took up the crown of his Empress. Turning his back to the Pope, who was by then seated on the high alter, Bonaparte stepped toward his wife. As Joséphine knelt before Napoleon, he placed the Empress' crown over her head. Maya, along with so many others present, broke into tears as she witnessed this great display of love and mutual respect.

After the Papal Mass was concluded, the Emperor and Empress processed to the other end of the cathedral, signifying the separation of the religious and secular portions of the ceremony. Ermine lined trains trailed them like shadows of the monarchy.

---

[20] *Mémoires de Constant, premier valet de chambre de l'empereur, sur la vie privée de Napoléon, sa famille et sa cour.* ("Memories of Constant, valet of the emperor; about his private life, his family and his court,") by Louis Constant Wairy, 1895.

The Pope receded to Notre Dame's sacristy, not wishing to partake in the civil ceremony in any way. Napoleon placed his hand over the Holy Bible and took his Imperial Oath:

"I swear to maintain the integrity of the territory of the Republic, to respect and enforce respect for the Concordat and freedom of religion, equality of rights, political and civil liberty, the irrevocability of the sale of national lands; not to raise any tax except in virtue of the law; to maintain the institution of Legion of Honour and to govern in the sole interest, happiness and glory of the French people." [21]

To thunderous applause, Napoleon and Joséphine then left the Cathedral of Notre Dame de Paris. The ceremony was over and Paris was soon ablaze with illuminations of self-congratulatory celebration. An unmanned balloon had been tethered from the cathedral during the ceremony, candlelight outlining the other new imperial insignia - a large letter "N" surrounded by laurel leafs. Across the capital, more Coronation Balls were held, and lesser *fêtes* broke out in the salons of the elite.

General Dąbrowski had arranged for Marek to be released from service immediately after the ceremony concluded to spend the evening with his visiting Maya. After the Emperor processed out of the cathedral, Marek's responsibilities were satisfied, so he collected his love to celebrate into the night. They were comforted knowing that their faithful Tolo was watching over young Władek at the hotel like a father goose over a newly hatched gosling.

[21] *Napoleon: A Political Life*, Steven Englund, Harvard University Press 2005

Marek proudly escorted the girl he loved from his youth, so joyously returned to him, to several balls. They indulged in the festivities at *soirée* after *soirée* and became more than slightly inebriated. It was under this influence of alcohol, coupled with a giddy enthusiasm, that Marek decided to escort Maya and join the revelry surely to be found at Madame Larouche's salon.

Marek arrived with Maya after both had partaken excessively in champagne and cognac at the other venues. It goes without saying that this contributed to his poor decision and lack of discretion. Marek boldly had the servant at Madame Larouche's residence announce their arrival as "The Polish Legionnaire, *Capitaine* Marek Zaczek, and his wife, the lovely *Pani* Maya Zaczek." Marek insisted it be proclaimed in exactly those words.

"No, Marek," Maya pleaded. "I am not going along with this. It is insane…"

"What? It is simply time we began practicing this fiction you wish me so badly to accept," Marek replied with more than a hint of sarcasm in his words. "This is as good as any place to begin. After all, how will we deceive the Poles of Warsaw if we can't convince a few Parisians we are husband and wife?"

With this, the announcement was made, and more than a few audible gasps were heard from those gathered. Marek knew these to be from the friends of Baroness Larouche, aghast to learn that her highly regarded Polish lover had all along been secretly married. The insult was all the more stinging when Maya, herself highly besotted on the unaccustomed quantity of champagne imbibed, playfully and most audibly giggled as it was made.

Marek took Maya by the hand and strode directly toward their host, the Baron Larouche, to thank him for having opened his home to them. Of course, the Polish Capitaine knew they had not actually been invited. They were intercepted by the Baroness, a crimson flush of irritation already rising in her cheeks.

"*Pani* Zaczek," she said through gritted teeth, "what an honor to have you here in our home on this remarkable occasion."

"And *Capitaine* Zaczek, what a pleasant surprise," she added curtly turning to Marek, her face by then all but enflamed. "We were not expecting you here this evening. I would have thought you would be required in your posting to the *Old Guard* to protect our beloved Emperor. Have they dismissed you from that responsibility so quickly?"

The Baroness' husband noticed the effort of his wife to intercede and retaliate against the couple for having humiliated her in front of her guests. The Baron decided to join them after all, knowing full well, of course, of his wife's liaisons with this handsome officer. Baron Larouche thought it to be a terribly amusing situation.

"Well, *Capitaine* Zaczek," he said, as he came over to feast upon his wife's embarrassment. "Little did we know your lovely bride from Poland would be visiting for the coronation celebrations, or we would have put you up here, would we have not, my wife?"

"Yes," Baroness Larouche seethed, "for you yourself have always said, *'Whatever I have, I am always willing to share with those soldiers who defend the ideals of our French Republic.'* Have you not, my dear?"

"And share I indeed have!" the Baron declared loudly, enough so that many in the crowd around them turned their heads. Laughing gently at the irony of his wife's remarks, he continued to amuse himself by adding, "I could not have said it any more graciously myself, and since you insist those are my own very words, I suppose I did. But, *mon cherie,* the term French Republic is now ever so *passé!* It is from this day forward to be known as the French Empire. *La République de France est morte! Vivre L'Empire! Vivre L'Emperor!*"

"Be careful not to revel too long in your pleasures, my darling," Madame Larouche said angrily to her husband, as her temper began to flare at his enjoying her mortification far too much. She then turned to her Polish guests, "I am sorry to not have known you were in town, *Pani* Zaczek. I would have loved to have spent some time with you. Despite our being from different cultures, I feel we must still have shared many similar experiences as women in this world."

Marek could see his mistress intently examining the face of her competition - his new, if only fictional, wife. He could almost hear the Baroness think to herself, *You may be younger and more beautiful, but I am rich! By that measure alone, I am entitled to so much more than you will never be...*

"I would have loved to have attended the coronation with you, Madame Baroness," Maya said, "as it would have been nice to have another woman to share the event with."

"Oh, darling Maya," Baroness Larouche laughed gently as she began to lecture her unexpected guest, "it was impossible to get inside that cathedral today. Even my husband, as valued as he is by His Imperial Highness, could not get us access into that highly coveted setting. He tried desperately. Only the most elite of French society were afforded that privilege."

"You see, *moja Maya Manusca*," Marek then intoned for no other reason than to irritate Madame Larouche, "did I not tell you the Emperor held you in the highest esteem? Did he not invite you personally to attend today's ceremonies?"

"You were at the coronation?" an amazed Baroness Larouche gasped, not able to hold back either the surprise or the bitterness of her tongue. "You were actually inside Notre Dame de Paris this day? You were there to see the Emperor crowned by the Pope? How was this even possible? *Mon Dieu!*"

Other heads in the crowd turned at the Baroness' harsh exclamations. Those women slowly began to drift toward Maya. "*Who* was at the coronation today?" they asked with great interest.

"Well, Madame," Maya answered the Baroness, "it was actually the Emperor who held the crown over his own head, having taken it from the hands of the Pope. Marek only jests about the Emperor's invitation, but he was able to secure a pass for me."

"I cannot believe what I am hearing!" the Baroness stammered. She stared daggers at Marek, "And yet no one could secure a pass for me?"

"How wonderful for you, my dear," said the Baron to Maya as he chuckled aloud. "This is all too wonderful, too fitting, and so justly perverse." He then walked away, smirking with delight.

"You were at the coronation?" said an elegantly adorned woman, the guest having overheard the gist of the conversation.

"Please, you must tell us all about it ," said another.

"Please do, and don't leave out even the simplest detail," said a third.

"I think I've heard that last line a time or two, somewhere else," Marek said somewhat flirtatiously to Baroness Larouche. She only became all the more infuriated as Maya unwittingly but quickly displaced her as the focal point of the Baroness' socialite friends. Maya tried her best to capture completely her day's experience utilizing the full range of her French language skills.

"Have I told you, Baroness, that it is thanks to Maya that I ever learned French? It became our secret language, you see?"

"Well, *Capitaine* Zaczek," she answered, "you are just full of secrets and surprises tonight, aren't you?"

"I told you she was coming to Paris," he defended himself.

"You merely left out that you and she have been married all along," she said. "You have broken my heart, Marek! We were true lovers, I could have spent a lifetime listening to your every word."

"True lovers? *Non!*" Marek said, *"Nos mots n'étaient que les mots doux des tourtereaux!"* (Our words were but the sweet nothings of lovebirds.)

"We will never be the same after tonight," Madame Larouche said with a sadness in her voice.

"I believe you are right," Marek said cruelly to her, "as I will be returning to Warsaw with Maya in two days time."

The blush drained from the Baroness' cheeks. Her skin became pale and taunt around her mouth which had dropped open.

"You are giving up your service to the Emperor?" she said getting over her shock. "After he has honored you with this appointment to the *Old Guard* no less?"

"After Lido, the Emperor has always thought of me as something of a good luck charm, nothing more."

"You saved his beloved white charger there in Italy," she said flatly, as if retelling the story one last time of her lover's rise might somehow convince him to stay in Paris.

"Yes, that was eight years ago," Marek said, "But even now he has Marengo…"

The Baroness was stunned by the comment, it made no sense. "You mean his great victory over the Austrians in Italy? How does that battle replace his most beloved mount?"

"I mean the grey Arabian he brought back from Egypt and named after that battle. He loves that horse even more than the white charger I saved at Lodi, so much that he even brought back Egyptian Mameluke handlers just to care after the beast."

"My point is, Madame Baroness," Marek smirked, "just like our Emperor, you will find another mount, one who pleases you much more than the one you've been saddled to all this time!"

"What I would give to strip that uniform from you one last time," she said, "and release this anger trapped inside my body into one last delightful stream of pure pleasure."

"That might be one evening even I could not survive." Marek was enticed by the idea. He looked at the wicked flame that was alight in her eyes, and knew that if her pent fury were spent on him in that way, it would be worth remembering by them both. Then he looked over at sweet Maya, proudly retelling the story of her glorious day in the Cathedral of Notre Dame de Paris.

"In any case, without the trappings of my uniform," he said to the Baroness, "I fear you would soon find me not so becoming, after all. Maya loves me for who I might be, while you do only for the salacious stories I tell within the walls of your *boudoir.*"

Maya was surrounded by then by a half dozen women hanging on her every word. Her recalling the day's exploits had become the sensation of the *soirée*. Madame Larouche glared at Marek's love as a viciously sinister sneer stretched across the Baroness' face.

"Look at her," Madame Larouche said. "She has no idea of how many times you've been inside me, does she? And does she know all the while you were telling me those, how did you say, oh yes, *salacious* tales of your rescuing her."

"And she will never know," Marek said, "of the delightfully beast-like ways in which you always responded to those words."

"So much for those sweet nothings of lovebirds…" Baroness Larouche said sadly. "Perhaps you can visit me in the left bank apartment again when you are next in town, Marek."

Marek raised his glass of champagne to hers. With the clink of their touching, he said these words: *"Qui court deux lievres a la fois, n'en prend aucun"* which translates to *"When one runs after two hares, he catches none."*

Later that evening, Marek and Maya rode huddled together holding hands under a plush woolen blanket in a hired carriage on this frigid December night. The clip-clop of hooves striking the cobblestones sounded as constant as the ticks of a clock counting away the last few minutes of a truly exceptional evening. Maya's hopes to rein back the sweep of that timepiece's hands failed, and the carriage persisted its ploughing its way back to the hotel on the *Place de Grand Louis.* They had just passed the *Place de l'Hôtel-de-Ville* and headed in the direction toward the *Place de la Revolution.*

"Marek," Maya said, "I wish this night could go on forever. It is so perfect, I wish that it never had to never end."

With her saying this, a wicked idea struck Marek. He reached in his pocket to feel the steely hardness of his set of two skeleton keys, which he had long since taken to always carrying.

"Moja Maya Manusca," he replied, "this night need not yet end. Tolo watches over Władek, and so we are in no hurry to get back to them too soon. By now, both are likely lost deep in sleep."

Then, Marek rattled off an address in French to the coachman which Maya heard and understood, for her French was equal to Marek's own; yet still it meant nothing to her, for her knowledge of the city did not match his. The driver turned his team onto the *Pont Neuf.* As they crossed the Seine on to the *Île de la Cité,* Maya could not suppress her curiosity.

"Where are you taking me at this very late hour?" she asked. The coach quickly traversed the narrow tip of the isle and was over the Seine once more. Maya glanced out the window to watch the moon's glow slip along the surface of the river's frigid waters, almost like a free floating pack of pale ice.

"As much as I don't want it all to end," she said, "I don't think I can survive another celebration this night."

Marek took her in his arms and kissed her passionately, then pulled back abruptly as the coach entered the Latin Quarter.

"Not even a celebration of our love, Maya?" he asked with a playfully impish grin.

The carriage soon pulled up to the address, and Marek tried to pay the fare, but the coachman refused him. "Not today, for the owner of this coach instructs us that no soldier who fights for France should pay out even a *sou* on the day of the Emperor's coronation."

Marek then gave an expressive look of gratitude, in which both angelic and devilish thoughts occurred to him.

"Then, my friend, this is all for you and your family," Marek said, slapping several Franc notes into the driver's palm as he descended from the carriage. After helping Maya down, he said to the driver, "Now, be sure to be back here no later this morning than seven o'clock. I can't keep this beautiful woman out all night, *and* morning, or people will begin fashioning rumors, won't they?"

"Oui, monsieur," came the answer from the man, stuffing the gracious tip into his britches, *"je reviendrai à sept heures."*

The horse carriage pulled away, leaving the two of them on the *Rue Vanguard* near the *Place de l' Odéon*. Marek then retrieved the two skeleton keys from his pocket. The first gained him access to the door from the street. They entered into the central hall's stairway, dim and silent at that hour, and began to climb.

After the third landing, Maya said, "This does not appear to be leading to another *soirée*. Where exactly are you taking me?"

Marek turned back and held his finger upright across his tightly stretched lips. "Hush," he then whispered, "or you'll awaken the students. They need their rest, even those who live only to protest endlessly against the Emperor."

Maya giggled at Marek's joke like a schoolgirl herself. "They must be students from very wealthy families to be living in such a lovely building as this."

Marek and Maya then worked their way up to the top floor, where Marek used the second skeleton key to allow him access into a darkened room.

"What is this place?" Maya whispered, "And why might you have keys to it?"

"Just a little bit of Paris belonging to a friend of mine," Marek answered, his voice no longer suppressed, "kept because of its close proximity to the old Luxembourg Palace and its gardens. We would meet here for walks there, when it was warm."

He fumbled to light the oil lamp on the vanity by only the glow of the moon, which had risen high over the rooftops across the dormer windows. Maya moved to one of the windows to take in the nocturnal serenity of the city, finally at rest, after so festive a day and so raucous an evening of celebration.

The lamp slowly came alive with a warm arc of light and the pleasant smell of the burning oil. Its flickering beams revealed the sparse, but luxurious contents of the single room: a woman's vanity covered with bottles of expensive perfume and fine cognac, two small upholstered chairs and a hand carved mahogany sleigh bed covered in satin sheets. The draperies framing the dormers were as fine as any she had ever seen, certainly surpassing those she knew in the manor houses on her father's *folwark* growing up.

"Marek," Maya said aghast at the sight of the illuminated room before her, "what exactly is this place?"

"I told you," he said, "just an apartment my friend owns. I must admit he is something of a libertine."

"Marek, we must leave immediately," Maya said. "this is not right. It is not proper for me to be here alone with you."

Marek sat on one of the chairs and grasped her wrist gently, intending to pull her onto his lap. She resisted and came to sit with her *derrière* upon the vanity's surface.

"Maya," he began, "do you remember all those years ago when you thought me drowned in the waters of the *Wisła,* just before Tolo had brought me back to you?"

Maya relived the day when he had called out to her as she walked along the *folwark's* gravel road. How her heart leapt!

"Of course," she admitted, "it was a moment of great joy that I thought I would never again enjoy… I thought I would never see you again after my father caught and banished you."

"Until now," Marek finished her thought. "For now Tolo has once more brought our lives together. The only thing I long to find out is whether your kiss will still be as sweet as the one I stole from you under those trees that lined the gravel road."

He then tugged at her wrists delicately, but it was enough as her resistance was softening. She slowly twirled until she was sitting fully upon his lap. She could feel his breath upon her face.

"Oh, Marek," she said just as he pressed his lips upon hers. His hands found her waist and pulled her tightly to him. Her breath quickened, as she pushed her lips firmly back against his. She knew what he expected to follow. She wanted it too, but could not release herself fully to the reality of it, especially here in this obvious *nid d'amour (lover's nest).*

Still sitting in his lap, Maya arched her back and pulled away from his embrace. "Marek, this is not proper. We must stop."

"It is…" he said, with a pensive and most reflective look upon his face as his voice trailed off. He did not finish the thought. His mind seemed to her to be focused on some faraway place.

"So, then, you agree it is not proper?" she asked, almost dejectedly. In that instant she cursed herself for having talked him out of the moment. It was one she had so desperately wanted for such a long time. But in her disappointment, she realized it was perhaps best. Even then, she feared pursuing a physical union with him, as it might dredge up the unwelcome horrors from her past.

"It is…" Marek answered as if he hadn't heard her, "… it truly is as sweet as that day long ago… your kiss I mean. No, I am surely wrong. Your kiss is sweeter even than I remember it then." He pulled her close to partake deeply of the honey of her lips. His tongue traced the contours of their luscious, sensitive skin.

Maya's disappointment dissolved. She pressed herself hard against him, and allowed his tongue to explore her mouth. She felt all the worries of her life melt away as Marek then slowly drew her lower lip in between both of his own. In that moment, she forgot completely about the fiction conjured for Władek's benefit. All else escaped her as her life's only true love bit gently, playfully upon her lip. She forgot completely about her earlier fear, that which antagonized her all along the never-ending journey from Warsaw: that Marek, still angry over what her uncle had taken from her, might reject both her and Władek here in Paris. Instead, his hands then hungrily roamed up from her waist and across her bodice. She released her cares as one of his palms placed itself in the small of her back, while the other found the fullness of her breasts.

"Oh, Marek," she confessed in a soft voice, her lip still pinched playfully between his teeth, "I so feared you would turn me away, that I would have to live my entire life without you."

She felt him ever so gently part his teeth to release her lip. He then whispered, "Maya, all the furies of fate are not strong enough to keep us apart."

His hands then pulled her even closer for another deep kiss. Maya lingered in that dreamlike moment. As luxurious as it was fleeting, she clung to it, wishing it never to pass. That golden second was free of all the worries that had so cruelly plagued her life - worries of being permanently stained having been taken against her will; worries of having broken Marek's heart in his finding her pregnant; worries of carrying that child which she feared she might never truly love. But this moment was perfect, as had been the instant of Władek's birth, when all her doubts were erased. Although even then, a chronic guilt soon crept in for having ever harbored such vile thoughts.

In that golden moment, with all her burdens swept away, she thought only of herself, here in the strong arms of her protector, her love. His hands exploring more and more of her, producing a feeling in her as she had never before felt. A ravaging desire grew within her. It licked within her bosom like the onset of a thousand raging flames, on the precipice of overcoming her.

"We must stop," she forced herself to say, as she stood upright, just after his hands had found the lowest hem of her gown.

"Mais mon ange, tu as vole mon coeur," he whispered. "But my angel, you have stolen my heart."

Marek stood up, and used his boot to kick away the chair. He took her firmly in his arms and forced the embrace to continue.

"We must never stop," he said, so closely to her that his breath fell upon the skin of her face with the softness of the sweep of a bride's veil. "Not so long as we love each other. And I wish you to know that I have never stopped loving you, Maya."

Maya felt his hands release her as her emotions exploded.

Marek's hands slid lower and found her hips, the very cradle of her womanhood. Marek pulled her so close that even through their clothes she could feel the swelling of his desire. She could not deny, even to herself, that she craved what was to come.

Her own arms tentatively dropped to search his waist. Her right hand found the hilt of his sabre.

"I will never forget," she whispered into his ear, "the way you fought for me. How you saved me. You gave near all to do so."

"*Mon trésor*, I would face all the demons of hell itself if needed to protect you," he said. Marek then pulled her tenderly down on to the bed. She did not resist, except in the weakness of her spoken words.

"We cannot," she said with little conviction. The inferno of desire in her eyes betrayed her words. She knew, as she thought he did, there was no stopping what was to follow. It was too late for that. Passion had replaced logic, and want had driven off caution.

"We are man and wife, my love," Marek breathed hard as he kissed her neck, "and we have a lovely son to prove it."

With her then on her back beneath him, his hands moved to explore the most tender, most sensitive skin beneath her gown.

Her heart raced when she heard him say the words *"we have a lovely son."* All she ever wanted was for him to accept Władek, for them to be a family together. Now, all was coming true. Yet, the false flow of her words continued.

"We must control ourselves," she said, panting at the initial strokes and probing of his wandering fingers. Her words had become ever more detached from every deep breath she drew. She had never known this moment, saturated with need, full of want. The quavering of her voice urged him to take her despite her insincere pleadings. It trembled as it spoke the truest of words, "Marek, you must control yourself, for I fear that I cannot."

"Control? I cannot control this unquenchable desire I have for you, Maya," Marek said, as he kissed the exposed skin just above her bosom. "How can I control my heart beating so hard that I think it will explode? And only because it is so close to your own, the very font of your tenderness! If I had the will of a thousand men and pulled myself away, I would forever bemoan it. If we do not take this moment, here and now, then it will become our life's greatest regret."

Having said this, he rested his head upon the expanse of the gown spanning her breasts. His hands were quickly gone from her, and Maya could feel him freeing himself with them. Her body burned as the fire within her heart had broken free, energized by the furious expectation budding in the cold breath of night air. A craving had raced across her, from head to heel, her skin tingling with anticipation. She became speckled with gooseflesh, and upon it she could sense every profligate urge that threatened the sanctuary of what she knew to be proper. What they were about to do was wrong, but she knew not the full form of why it was so.

Maya took both her hands and caressed Marek's temples. She drew his head tight against her bosom, then cocked her neck to whisper in his ear, *"Take me, Marek. Take me now."*

He raised himself to again press his lips against hers. His face was moist with a nervous sweat. She could smell it, feel it on her own cheek. *Is he as anxious as I am?* she wondered.

Then she felt him, as he pressed hard upon the tender petals of the flower of her femininity. Her panting had given way to rasps of sordid breaths deeply filling her lungs as her swell of desire overwhelmed the protective defense of her nerves.

She had worried for so long how she might handle this moment with Marek, should it ever come to occur in anything other than her fantasies. Given the prior outrages forced upon her, would sinister memories and their dark emotions overwhelm her?

Maya was glad to learn they were indeed driven off by the love she had always felt for her Marek, and his for her in return. This moment was as perfect as any she had ever imagined.

"Tell me, *moja Maya Manusca*," she heard him whisper in her ear as he pressed himself harder, more firmly against her, "tell me that you want this as much as I do…"

Her entire being craved him. It was right, it was proper, she told herself. She wanted terribly to believe it was so.

"I only want you and I to be together forever, Marek."

"As do I, *moja Maya*," he replied

She arched her back and in doing so opened herself fully to him. He pressed hard against her, and she could feel him ever so tenderly part her. The bliss of expectation, which just before that moment she had been in, gave way to another feeling altogether. As he slowly began to move ever so lovingly within her, she felt as though the two of them had finally merged into one. A union of spirits - the singular satisfaction of their separate lifelong desires.

His head now raised from her chest, his eyes hunted in the dim morning light for hers. Searching her face, they found the red hot embers of hers, tender but burning with hunger. Their mouths merged together once more. She felt the bliss of their total union, of being fully overtaken by him, and wanting it never to end. It was a melding of mind, body and soul; its elation she had never before in her life experienced, and its sweetness she would never forget. It was the ultimate fullness of being, a loving unity of a shared existence. She realized in this, the precise moment of the ecstasy which they shared together, that anything even the slightest bit less intimate would never have fulfilled her.

Outside their window, a distant spire's clock chimed three times. In the hooded shroud of their intimacy, neither Maya nor Marek heard the bell's strike announcing the witching hour.

Figure 16: External Apse View of Notre Dame de Paris

Part Two:

The

Three

Emperors

"Victory belongs to the most persevering."

Napoleon Bonaparte

Chapter 14: Boulonge
The Imminent Invasion

Even the plans of Emperors are subject to the will and whim of the Divine. In January of 1805, Napoleon collected 180,000 troops on the French shore of what the British had always so audaciously called the English Channel. To the French, that waterway was known simply as *la Manche, "The Sleeve,"* given its arm-like shape connecting the Atlantic Ocean to the North Sea. Along its coast Napoleon had arrayed his troops, awaiting the strength of the combined French and Spanish fleets from the ports of Brest, Toulon and Cádiz to drive off the formidable English fleet that had for too long been the muscled arm rippling within that watery sleeve.

Napoleon had undertaken the building of thousands of transport barges, and all were nearly completed. He had even commissioned a study of tunneling under the Channel, and of ballooning troops over it, but these means proved infeasible. With nearly every tradesman in the north of France engaged in the massive campaign of barge-building, the pending invasion was a secret that was impossible to keep hidden from English spies.

The British had taken the threat very seriously, and resumed their blockades of all French ports. They believed Napoleon when he had so famously said,

> *"Let us be masters of La Manche for six hours*
> *and we are masters of the world."* [22]

---

[22] Oxford Dictionary of Quotes, Sixth Edition, p. 556, attributed to
History of the English People by J. R. Green (1880)

Yet finding those six hours would prove to be the Imperial conqueror's greatest challenge. When Napoleon ordered a test of troop-laden barges in the choppy waters of the Channel, the results were disastrous. Rescue efforts had to be deployed immediately, yet still many of the soldiers thrown overboard from the ill-designed barges were lost at sea. Despite this catastrophe, Napoleon pressed on with his intent of using the inadequate vessels to take his troops across the Channel and invade England.

May 1803 had proved to be a month of great consequence between the English and French as war resumed. Although hostilities had ended in October of 1801, the actual signing of the treaty between the two powers, the Peace of Amiens, was not signed until late March 1802. Thus, in only fourteen months, Britain was again at war with France. Hostilities between the two nations had ceased for just over twenty months. This would prove to be the only span, less than two years, in which France and England did not engage in direct conflict from 1792 to 1815.

And so, in May 1803, the English fleet put again to sea with a singular intention: to destroy the combined French and Spanish fleet before it could attempt to take control of the Channel and facilitate Napoleon's planned invasion of their isles. In fact, England had not been invaded *en masse* for nearly three quarters of a millennium when the Normans last did so in 1066.

The Emperor had funded his invasion's massive preparatory efforts by selling nearly all French possessions in North America to the United States for a price of fifty-million francs - then near eleven and a quarter million dollars. James Monroe, the envoy for President Thomas Jefferson was in Paris for the signing of the Louisiana Purchase in May 1803, the very month when Britain resumed its war against Napoleon. In fact, it is thought that the American negotiating team drove the deal to closure by suggesting a thawing of relations with England. This surely was something that Napoleon could not allow to occur.

While the British most certainly detested the deal doubling the size of its former colony in America, this negotiation was not the reason for their declaring war on France. Napoleon had sent troops in 1802 to Haiti (then the island of Saint-Domingue) to attempt to quell a slave uprising there. British Prime Minister William Pitt the Younger saw this, along with the Louisiana Purchase negotiations, as France meddling against their interests in North America. But even more antagonistically, the French had enraged the British by refusing to remove their troops from Egypt and Malta as agreed in the 1802 Amiens peace treaty.

So, in 1803 the war was re-engaged. British Prime Minister William Pitt worked feverishly to draw other European powers into alliance against the French. His efforts resulted in the Third Coalition, consisting primarily of England, the Holy Roman Empire (led by Austria) and Russia, but also including Sweden, Naples and Sicily. These countries were arrayed against the French forces, as well as the co-opted Spanish fleet. The Prussians, despite their hatred for the French and the exhortations of Russia and Austria, found it in their best interests to remain neutral.

In fact, Russian Tsar Alexander I would eventually visit Berlin in a failed attempt to lure the Prussians into battle, ignoring the advice of his Foreign Minister Adam Czartoryski not to do so.

The English had long feared an invasion by Bonaparte. Even before the turn of the century, the idea had caused a mass hysteria among the British. By 1801, the delirium had grown to such a feverish pitch that upon his return from the Battle of Copenhagen, none other than Lord Admiral Nelson was assigned the task of devising the plan to protect the country from a French invasion. Nelson, in 1801, quickly observed the poor condition of the Boulogne and other Channel harbors, and knew the French could not possibly launch any sizable landing force from these ports. But by 1805, so much had changed. With the funds from the Louisiana Purchase, the French then appeared ready to strike.

In January of 1805, Marek Zaczek found himself in the frigid winter climes of Boulogne amongst the *"Vieille Garde"* protecting the Emperor. He had planned to set off with Maya, Władek and Tolo two days after the Emperor's coronation for Warsaw. He longed to spend Christmas with them alongside his mother, Magdalena, and Aunt Ewelina. Instead, his request for permanent leave was denied by none other than Napoleon himself, who had overridden General Dąbrowski and demonstratively told the Polish leader he was appalled.

"Does Zaczek not recognize the great honor that this promotion bestows upon him?" the Emperor asked in an incredibly irritated voice.

"But, Sire, he is a man in love," said Dąbrowski, "he desires only to be reunited with his wife and child. They leave for Warsaw soon, he only wishes to join them on that journey."

To which the Emperor responded philosophically:

"Ah, Love! Love is merely the occupation of the idle, the distraction of the soldier, the danger of the sovereign." [23]

Marek was denied his request and with it the ability to depart to Warsaw with Maya. He promised to join his "wife and their child" in Warsaw as soon as he could secure his release, but admitted he knew not when that might occur. If the invasion came to pass, he feared that lonesome time would be measured in years.

The day after Maya, Władek and Tolo had departed, the heartbroken Marek received yet another high honor from the Emperor by being chosen to receive the Imperial Standard for his new lancer company from the hands of Napoleon himself during a ceremony held on the *Champs de Mars*. Marek suspected it was an honor given to ease the sting of his release being denied.

---

[23] Generally accepted but unattributed quotation of Napoleon Bonaparte

Even though the Polish Lancers were not, at that point, a complete regiment of their own, their incorporation into the light cavalry of the Old Guard was significant. Even more astounding was it for the Emperor to designate a mere *Capitaine* of these *Lanciers Polonais* to accept the entire regiment's colors and standard from his hand, in lieu of the regiment's colonel. All could see just how highly the Emperor regarded this lancer.

The standards were designed to resemble those of the Roman Legions, with the regiment's colors draped from a staff atop which was perched a warlike Imperial Eagle. Napoleon was building his new *Grande Armée* in the likeness of those great conquerors of history - the Greeks under Alexander and the Romans under Caesar.

The net effect of all this was that instead of leaving with Maya two days after the coronation, Marek ended up departing two days after Christmas to protect the Emperor as he headed to Boulogne to personally oversee the final preparations for the invasion of England. Napoleon had dredged the harbors at Boulonge and other Channel ports to accommodate the boarding of the invasion barges. All that was left in January 1805 was for France to achieve control of the Channel.

To assure that this did not come to pass, the British placed their Channel fleet in the hands of their Royal Navy's Mediterranean fleet commander. It then came under the control of their most capable naval warrior, Admiral Lord Horatio Nelson.

Nelson's strategy was to blockade the joint Franco-Spanish fleets in their respective ports, be they at Cádiz, Brest or Toulon, and should they depart those safe harbors, he intended to destroy each and every enemy Ship-of-the-Line. For only in that way, by removing from Napoleon the ability to take command of the Channel, could the *"Corsican Ogre"* be denied his objective of conquering England.

That plan would prove an elusive task for Nelson. One that would consume the war efforts of his nation, pursuing the French and Spanish fleet throughout the years of 1803, 1804 and 1805. The deciding battle for the final control of the seas would not occur until late October 1805.

In the months following his coronation, Napoleon had become increasingly agitated by the exploits of Nelson in preventing the French from taking control of the Channel. The Emperor himself would devise an intricate plan that would lure the British admiral to chase his fleet across an ocean. Once Nelson did so, he would be out of the way, allowing for the French and Spanish joint fleets to race back and seize control of *la Manche*.

Chapter 15: Nelson's Pursuit of The French

Loneliness is oft the most dire affliction of duty, when soldiers are separated from their loved ones by distances far greater than the bounds of their imaginations. Under these conditions one must consider the magnifying effect of time itself, for the longer the endurance of any separation, the greater grows the associated anxiety in those who are parted.

Lord Nelson and Lady Hamilton greatly enjoyed the twenty months of the Peace of Amiens, the bulk of which was spent at their home at Merton Place. Then, just after Emma's legal husband, Lord William Hamilton, died in April 1803, Lord Nelson and Lady Hamilton tearfully bade farewell to the Ambassador. Still they were finally free of all encumbrances keeping them from happily living out their life together. Then, the war weary admiral was recalled to take up the most decisive task in the renewed conflict with their old French rivals. Lord Nelson would be tasked with nothing less than the immobilization and ultimately the complete destruction of the combined French and Spanish fleets.

Nelson would immediately leave in 1803 to ply the distant waters of the Atlantic Ocean and Mediterranean Sea, keeping him from seeing and holding his beloved Emma for more than the next two years.

Nelson left England in May 1803 upon the warship *HMS Amphion*. In the Mediterranean Sea at Malta, he transferred to his flagship *HMS Victory* in June. He would not so much as step off that vessel again for another twenty-five months, when in July 1805 he would finally come ashore at Gibraltar.

Complicating the initial months of that separation was the fact that Lady Hamilton was carrying within her Nelson's second daughter. She was to be named Emma after her mother. Nelson wrote to his beloved Emma,

"I have not a thought except on you and the French fleet.
All my thoughts, plans and toils tend to those two objects.
Don't laugh at my putting you and the French fleet together,
but you cannot be separated." [24]

Shortly after her birth in January 1804, the child named after her mother would die, devastating both parents. Nelson had never laid his sight upon her. Yet, even before this tragedy, he was already feeling the effects of the separation from his family. In early December 1803, he wrote:

"Next Christmas, please God, I shall be at Merton;
for, by that time, with all the anxiety on such a command as this,
I shall be done up. The mind and body both wear out." [25]

Sadly, he would never again visit Merton at Christmas. Christmas of 1804 would pass with his being still at sea. He would not return to Merton until August of 1805, when he would at last see and hold his beloved Emma again. Even this would be but a brief respite of only four weeks. Then, Lord Nelson would be off for one final engagement of his enemy. Nelson was destined to spend twenty-six of the last thirty months of his life chasing enemy fleets at sea, away from the life he so dearly wanted with Emma.

---

24 *"The Life of Nelson"*, Captain A.T. Mahan, Easton Press Edition of 1897 text, Vol. II, p.222.

25 *"The Life of Nelson"*, Captain A.T. Mahan, Easton Press Edition of 1897 text, Vol. II, pp.209-210.

Initially, Nelson played a deadly game with his French rivals near Toulon. He had set up command of his fleet off the north shore of the massive island of Sardinia. Napoleon's home island of Corsica was between his fleet and the French.

Nelson wished to remain hidden there, far from the French fleet harbored in Toulon, some 200 miles away. He dispatched smaller, swifter frigates to watch the French fleet's movements. Nelson desired that his enemy would exit the harbor. Once in the open sea, he would lead his fleet to engage and destroy the enemy.

This strategy of luring out the French fleet was one he advocated with the Admiralty. Lord Nelson wrote;

"It is not my intention to close-watch Toulon, even with frigates… My system is the very contrary of blockading… Every opportunity has been offered the enemy to put to sea for it is there we hope to realize the hopes and expectations of our Country." [26]

The French admiral in Toulon, Latouche Tréville, quickly recognized that Nelson was attempting to lure his fleet out into battle. Tréville released one or two of his battle ready warships to sail just outside of the harbor to bait Nelson, but never allowing those vessels to travel too far from the safety of Toulon's berths. A very frustrated Nelson wrote in the spring of 1804:

"My friend Monsieur La Touche sometimes plays bo-peep in and out of Toulon, like a mouse at the edge of her hole." [27]

This would be the beginning of a much more expansive game of cat and mouse played by Nelson and the combined French and Spanish fleets while he was aboard the *HMS Victory*.

---

[26] *"The Life of Nelson"*, Captain A.T. Mahan, Easton Press Edition of 1897 text, Vol. II, p.202.

[27] *"The Life of Nelson"*, Captain A.T. Mahan, Easton Press Edition of 1897 text, Vol. II, p.214.

Nelson knew his duty to the British people was to keep those enemy ships from ever taking command of the waters of the Channel. For the British admiral knew that if they ever did, Napoleon's invasion of England would quickly launch from Boulogne and other French ports along the Channel.

Lord Nelson would spend all of 1804 and most of 1805 chasing the enemy fleets throughout the Mediterranean Sea, and eventually even across the Atlantic Ocean, ever frustrated that they would not engage directly with him. Meanwhile, he could only think fondly of his beloved Emma while the pangs of his imagination's jealousies reared themselves once more.

While he was away, the widowed Lady Hamilton was receiving marriage proposals from several gentlemen of very prosperous means. She could have readily secured her future in accepting any one of these, but instead she stayed true to Nelson. She sought only his return so they could spend their later years peacefully together at their home at Merton Place.

Chapter 16: Boulogne
La Grande Attente

oredom is the stealthy serpent that slithers into the garden of time spent idly waiting for an upcoming event to occur. *"The Great Wait"* erodes an army's heightened anticipation, and the longer the passage of time, the more likely are the inactive parties to take notice of the local distractions. And in Boulogne, *"La Grande Attente"* for the much delayed French and Spanish fleets to take control of the Channel was taking its toll.

It was a frigidly cold night in early March of 1805 when Rydek came to visit his friend, Marek. Both had been issued orders of leave. Marek sat outdoors around the campfire, wasting away his free time by practicing his mark in the sand with the tip of his sword. *MZ. MZ. MZ.* he scrawled over and over again.

"Come with me," said Rydek, "we both need the company of the local ladies now more than ever. Boulogne is not Paris, but even this town must have hidden some beauties for us to find."

"I cannot," Marek said cryptically.

"Why not? You are off duty, I know that to be a fact. What is it then? Did the Emperor force all of his *Vieille Garde* to take a vow of chastity? Maybe that is why all the other troops refer to you openly as *Les Grognards."*

Rydek then laughed at his cleverness. The French term *"Les Grognards"* translates to *"The Grumblers."* That nickname was appropriate, because unlike any other forces under the Emperor's command, *the Old Guard* were allowed to complain, even within the earshot of Napoleon himself.

The Emperor allowed this, because in this way, he could come to understand the complaints of his entire army. Through the grumblings of the *"Les Grognards,"* Napoleon could devise corrections to be made, and dictate these orders to his marshals.

The night was particularly cold, and the idea of Marek's friend indeed sounded so very enticing. But the newly minted *Capitaine* was still enthralled with his renewed love of Maya.

"Rydek, you, above all others, must know why I have given up the *putain*," Marek said.

"Of course, your lovely Maya," Rydek said. "Then to hell with the whores, we'll find ourselves a pair of respectable young ladies and use our charms to convince them to become otherwise."

"Again, my thoughts and desires are only of Maya," Marek said simply. "I cannot do this to her. She has captured my heart again. Perhaps more forcefully than ever before. I have been given a wonderful second chance to strike out upon my future alongside her. All I wish is to be with her."

"Surely, she does not expect you to behave yourself until this entire war is over, Marek."

"I am afraid it is exactly what she expects after our few days of unbridled passion together. More importantly, it is what I now expect of myself."

"Hoisted on your own *petard,* you are," said Rydek. The saying was particularly French and common among the military. It referred to a soldier being blown up while setting an explosive charge. "You lit a fuse in that girl, except that the longer it burns, *nothing* goes off. Certainly not for you, my friend. And who knows, perhaps your lovely Maya is sampling all the pleasures of Warsaw? After all, you did give her a taste of what the ecstasy of unforced passion can be all about. In any case, there is no need to save yourself, as I will never say a word to her, even if I was lucky enough to survive this war and see her again."

Rydek looked slyly at his friend, and then winked.

"It is not important whether she will know or not," Marek said, "I will know."

"Wait!" Rydek cried out. "Could this be the very same stallion that raced through a quarter of the wives of all the aristocrats in Paris? Nothing has changed, Marek. Let your horse run free among the mares in these meadows here. They may not be fenced off, well kept paddocks like those married baronesses you are accustomed to, but open green grounds sprawl before us here just the same."

The equestrian references only reminded Marek all the more of being raised on the *folwark* along with the only girl he had ever really loved.

"Leave me be," Marek said. "I choose to stay out of town. You go and enjoy yourself. You deserve it. I am confident that Maya waits patiently for me, just as I shall do in return for her."

"As you wish," Rydek said as he turned and walked briskly away from the fire. "You keep practicing your initials in the sand, perhaps you'll eventually get them right one day."

Marek laughed, and then said, "Yes, perhaps, one day." When Rydek disappeared again into the darkness, Marek blotted out his initials with a broad sweep of his boot. Then, with the great dexterity of his wrist, scrawled them again and again as the tip of his sword scribed into the sand. This sequence he repeated, over and over again, as he long had over many years to while away the incessant hours of boredom.

Chapter 17:
Nelson and Villeneuve
The Great Chase

Strategy without tactics is the slowest route to victory, so said
the great Chinese warlord, General Sun Tze. There can be
little doubt that Napoleon Bonaparte had read Sun Tze's
treatise, "*The Art of War*," as it was first translated outside China in
1782 into the French language. *Strategy without tactics* was one
particular line of advice very close to the Emperor's heart.
However, it becomes very clear that in developing the tactics to
make an overall strategy succeed, even Napoleon could become
oblivious to the domain in which those tactics were to be deployed.

A case in point was Napoleon's failure to understand that
the same tactics he had so successfully deployed on land, could not
be readily transferred to the unpredictable seas. For instance, rapid
coordinated movement of troops, often over inhospitable terrain
and under the foulest of weather, could almost always still be
effected, though difficultly, on *terra firma*. But upon the open sea,
the coordinated movement of ships was far too dependent upon
God's will, in the form of the winds and the waves. Despite this,
the Emperor devised just such a naval plan to clear *la Manche* of
its defending British warships. The Channel thus being opened
would then allow his long idle army to cross on their ready and
waiting flotilla of invasion barges.

Napoleon's great mistake was in believing that he could accurately control the movements of the fleets under his command. He would find out the error of this assumption in his boldest naval gambit to date which was to commence in early 1805.

The plan was for his fleet to break free from the French port of Toulon, exit the Mediterranean Sea, and linger off the Strait of Gibraltar long enough to be spotted. Then they would get under sail across the Atlantic to the Caribbean British Leeward Isles. Napoleon assumed that the Royal Navy would follow *en masse*, not wishing to have their Caribbean possessions threatened. Once the British Ships-of-the-Line arrived there in force, the French fleet would make haste back to Europe, rendezvous with additional French and Spanish warships, and fight for command of the Channel. This would allow his invasion forces to cross in the mayhem that would surely ensue. In this way, Napoleon would take England, and with it, effectively, the world.

It is likely that Napoleon had devised the broadest strokes of this plan well before his coronation. At that time, he had as his most experienced admiral, the highly capable Latouche Tréville, the man who had played the game of cat and mouse frustrating Nelson. Unfortunately, while Nelson had him hemmed in at Toulon, Latouche Tréville died of a relapse of a disease he had contracted years earlier on the island of Saint-Domingue. When Nelson learned of Tréville's death in August of 1804, he wrote:

> ***"The French papers say he died of walking so often up to the signal-post to watch us: I always pronounced that would be his death."*** [28]

In this way, God's will, although neither by the winds nor by the waves, had interceded in favor of the British Navy. The untimely death of Admiral Latouche Tréville would prove critical.

---

[28] *"The Life of Nelson"*, Capt. A.T. Mahan, Easton Press Edition of 1897 text, Vol. II, p. 257.

Latouche Tréville was succeeded by Vice-Admiral Pierre-Charles Villeneuve. Villeneuve was a respected leader and capable strategist in his own right, but was considered not quite up to the standards of Admiral Latouche Tréville in either category. Fate would prove Villeneuve far too cautious in this most critical stage of engaging his foe, Admiral Nelson and the British naval forces.

So in January of 1805, the recently coronated Emperor of the French launched his ambitious plan with Admiral Villeneuve at the helm. The French fleet's escape that month from Toulon was quickly aborted when they sailed into a gale, doing great damage to the topsails of many of the French Ships-of-the-Line.

After the fleet's return to Toulon and after all repairs were effected, Villeneuve's fleet finally escaped Nelson's watching frigates. They slipped out to sea at the end of March. The frigates who had been the Admiral's *"eyes"* failed to spot the enemy and Nelson was soon again off in search of the French. He knew from intelligence that they carried between 5,000 and 7,000 troops aboard. He searched in vane throughout the Mediterranean, until on the fourth of May, off the coast of Gibraltar, he stopped for provisions and was told the French fleet had earlier passed through the Strait, headed in the direction of the West Indies.

What happened next worked against Napoleon's plan. Ships from the British Channel fleet had been dispatched to Nelson's colleague, Admiral Culberth Collingwood. Having not yet arrived, Nelson decided he no longer wait for their arrival and set sail across the Atlantic. When Collingwood learned that his old friend was in pursuit of the French to the Caribbean, he decided to wait off the coast of Europe and thus was not be drawn across the ocean. The net effect was that Nelson's Mediterranean fleet would take up chase, but not the ships of the Channel fleet. This meant that even if Admiral Villeneuve's ploy was successful in evading Nelson's pursuit, he would still have a British fleet to deal with upon his Atlantic return crossing.

Nelson pursued Villeneuve's fleet of eighteen Ships-of-the-Line across the ocean with his own fleet of eleven. He made up ten days on the French, but even with this, Villeneuve's fleet arrived in the West Indies three weeks before Nelson. When Nelson finally arrived at Barbados on June 4th, he could not find Villeneuve.

The French had only lightly skirmished in attacking British possessions in the Leeward Islands during the intervening three weeks. Even then, Napoleon felt his plan was working as he had intended. The Emperor would later say:

"What a game had Villeneuve to play!" [29]

The English public had caught news of the great pursuit and was in a general panic. They waited in terror to hear what havoc the French had caused in their West Indies possessions, as well as the crescendo of fear rising in regard to the ever-pending invasion of their homeland from across the Channel.

Napoleon had dispatched another fourteen French and Spanish Ships-of-the-Line to rendezvous with Villeneuve in the Caribbean, bring their total number to thirty-two. Once this was achieved, Villeneuve set sail for Europe, fearing Nelson's having arrived with as many of twenty warships, unaware that in reality the British admiral possessed only eleven.

When word arrived to Nelson of Villeneuve's departure and return to Europe, he immediately set sail, continuing his pursuit. Nelson's fleet was only five days behind the French and Spanish, at that point, but given the winds and waves they faced, they could not catch the enemy force. Despite this, the Caribbean Governors of the British Empire were already crediting Admiral Nelson with having driven off the invading French. Word to this effect quickly reached England by fast frigate, where the populace would once again hail him as a great national hero.

---

[29] *"The Life of Nelson"*, Captain A.T. Mahan, Easton Press Edition of 1897 text, Vol. II p. 307.

Despite the close pursuit, Nelson failed to catch Villeneuve on the open sea, but he was successful in driving the combined French and Spanish fleet into a battle with other waiting British forces off the coast of Spain at Cape Finisterre. That engagement was a confused and indecisive battle, and while the British fleet did take two of their enemy's Ships-of-the-Line, the bulk of Villeneuve's joint French/Spanish fleet made their escape.

Nelson finally arrived at Gibraltar on June 12th, 1805. It was there that he disembarked his flagship, the *HMS Victory,* for the first time since July of 1803, just shy ot two full years. He was distraught for not having caught and engaged Villeneuve at sea, unaware he was again being hailed as a hero in England.

In fact, after resting briefly and resupplying at Gibraltar, Nelson took his ships to join the Channel fleet off Brest. There he awaited Villeneuve. Then, a most curious pair of events transpired over the course of the next few weeks. Admiral Nelson was awarded his long overdue leave to return to England on the 18th of August. Two days later, on the 20th of August 1805, Villeneuve decided to forego a direct order from Napoleon to confront and engage Britain's Channel fleet off Brest. Instead, he sought safe harbor for his combined fleet at the Spanish port of Cádiz.

Thus, Lord Admiral Nelson was given one final, fateful, albeit abbreviated, respite as his good friend Admiral Collingwood stood guard at sea, eventually finding and trapping the elusive enemy joint fleet at Cádiz. There Collingwood would patiently await the return of his mentor Nelson to join him in their final engagement with the enemy's combined fleet.

So, just as Nelson arrived one last time upon the green grass of England on the 18th of August, Napoleon still expected the invasion of England would be imminent. He had earlier sent orders for Villeneuve to engage and destroy the British fleet off the coast of Brest, thus clearing *"la Manche,"* the Channel.

Even by this date, Napoleon still believed the attack would open the *pas de Calais*, or Straits of Dover, if you prefer, to allow for the invasion from Boulogne.

Napoleon was not aware that, by this time, the British Admiral Collingwood's combined fleet was had already besieged Villeneuve at Cádiz. This is clearly evident in his letter bearing the Imperial seal sent to the Admiral and dated 22 August 1805, which read:

"Monsieur le vice-admiral Villeneuve,

I hope you have arrived at Brest. Set out, don't lose a moment, and with a squadron assembled, enter into la Manche. England is ours; we are completely ready; everything is on board. Appear in twenty-four hours and all is complete. Whereupon I pray to God that he have you in his holy and worthy keeping...

Napoleon" [30]

Little known to the Emperor, Villeneuve had already sealed his fate when he opted to not venture any closer to Brest than to idly ply the waters of the Atlantic far from the coast of France. He had feared that more British firepower resided near that Bay of Biscay port than actually was present. Perhaps had he attacked per his Emperor's plan, Napoleon's invasion would have succeeded. This cannot be known. But what is known is that due to Villeneuve's overly cautious nature, his fleet had taken premature refuge at Cádiz, where it quickly came under seige by the British Admiral Collingwood. There, Villeneuve could await three things: the wrath of his Emperor, the certain return of Nelson, and his combined fleet's ultimate fate.

---

[30] Correspondence of Napoleon Bonaparte to Admiral Villeneuve, August 22, 1805

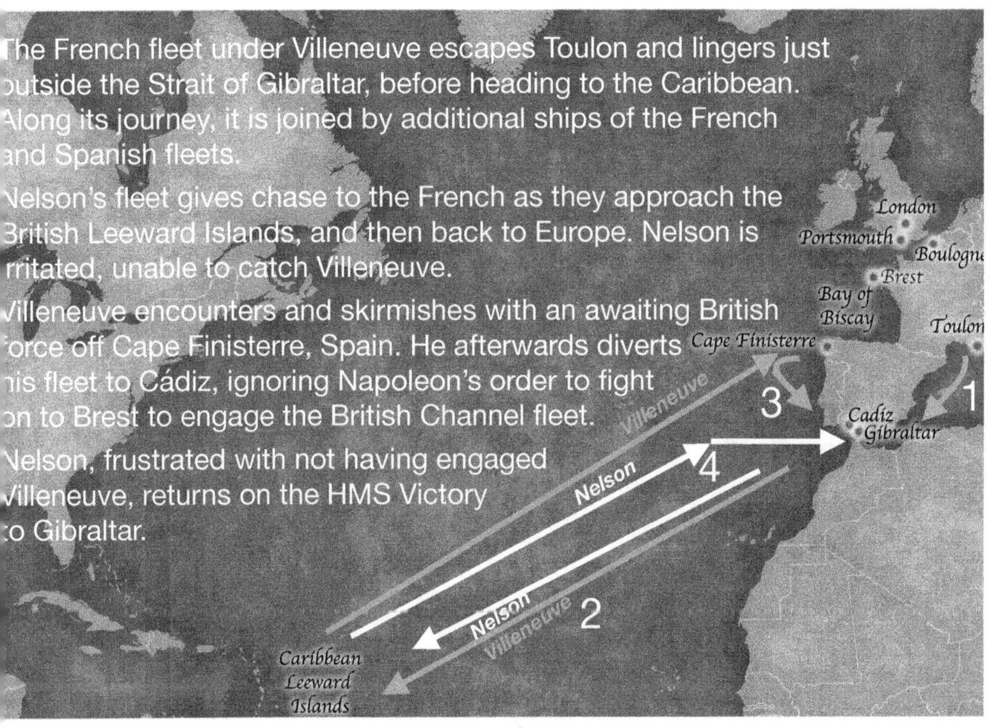

Figure 17: The Great Chase between Nelson and Villeneuve (1805)

Chapter 18: Boulogne
March of the Grande Armée

Agility is the most valued and least anticipated attribute of a fighting force. The Americans had made this clear in winning their independence from the British in the few decades that had recently passed. Napoleon Bonaparte had learned this lesson as well, when he utilized his artillery's mobility at Toulon in 1793, to rain shot down upon the British ships in the harbor. He would utilize it again in leading his army, crossing the Alps in May of 1800 to again surprise his enemy. He waged battle after battle and ultimately defeated the Austrians, driving them from Italy once more, culminating in the French victory at the Battle of Marengo on 14 June 1800.

But more than four years later, by the end of 1804, the Emperor had perfected the concept in what he boastfully renamed as *"La Grande Armée."* This force was designed to optimize the advantage of mobility and independence of movement of its eventual mass of nearly one million soldiers. Agility meant speed, but without sacrificing power.

The armies of the day were concentrated into one large unified mass, for reasons such as safety of numbers, the simplification of supply lines and the streamlining of transmitting orders. These armies were slow moving, lethargic giants that left behind them a bloated trail of evidence for their enemy's spies.

And it was information from his spies in Austria that reached Emperor Bonaparte while he and his vast army were collected on the shores of the English Channel in the late summer of 1805, where they prepared their invasion of England.

The Austrian and Russian armies were on the move, hoping to join up and surprise the French forces as they waited for their navy under Villeneuve to break free from the British blockade of the port of Cádiz. What could tempt Napoleon's enemies more than trapping his army up against the waters of the Channel as he was focused so intently on the invasion of England?

The General Karl Mack von Leiberich had decided to move his large army towards the Rhine while Napoleon and his 180,000 troops were consumed with the invasion along the Channel shores. The trap proved too tempting to the Austrian General Mack, who had made the fateful decision to begin marching his own troops westward in advance of the arrival of the troops from Russia.

The Russians had already begun to move their army westward under the highly seasoned General Mikhail Kutuzov, but they were several weeks behind the impatient Austrian General Mack. By the end of August, it was clear to Napoleon that Villeneuve had failed him, and he began mobilizing his troops southward to intercept General Mack before the Russians could arrive to reinforce the Austrians. And this is where the Emperor's radical redesign of the *Grande Armée* paid such high dividends in agility and speed of movement.

Napoleon had divided his army into smaller units, designated as corps. Each of his corps was in itself a small army that was commanded by a Marshal of the Empire. These smaller units could move independently, without the burden of waiting for the other corps. Each could forage for food from the countryside villages as they marched, traveling separate routes for this reason.

Yet, with the lines of communication assured by Napoleon's insistence on highly mobile cavalry units, messages could be couriered between the Emperor and his various corps. In this way, the corps could be rapidly reformed into one massive army, and act with the greatest of force when ordered to do so.

The key to this concept was the leadership of the Marshals of the Empire. Initially there were fourteen selected from generals and others who had distinguished themselves during the French Revolutionary Wars against the First and Second Coalitions of the Allies. The Marshals of the Empire were hand-picked by Napoleon, and represented a broad sweep of temperaments and personalities. The Emperor valued in his marshals the traits of loyalty, aggression, and courage. The mix of these three factors resulted in a variety of distinct and broad-ranging personas.

First and foremost was Marshal Joachim Murat. He had been at Napoleon's side a decade earlier at the *"Whiff of Grapeshot"* rebellion where the rioting mobs of loyalists were fired upon in Paris. Murat had also married one of the Emperor's sisters and was present at Napoleon's coronation at Notre Dame de Paris the previous December. He was loyal and steadfast to his brother-in-law, the Emperor, and as a reward, Napoleon would later name award him with the title King of Naples.

Murat was contrasted by Marshal Michel Ney, who Napoleon would much later proclaim *"The Bravest of the Brave."* Marshal Ney, an excellent cavalry rider in his own right, was aggressive and loyal, but would often impetuously act on his own beyond the Emperor's orders. Often this would result in great victories, while at other times it would put the soldiers of his corps in great peril. He would stay with Napoleon through Waterloo, only abandoning him along with the other marshals just before the Emperor's first exile to Elba. But notably, it would be Ney sent to capture Napoleon after his escape from Elba, who instead would throw down his weapons to rejoin the Emperor.

One of the most trusted of the Marshals of the French Empire was Louis-Alexandre Berthier, a highly regarded veteran of the Expeditionary Force to the War of American Independence. Berthier would later become the Emperor's Chief of Staff.

Another, Marshal André Masséna, was given the monicker of *l'Enfant chéri de la Victoire* (*the Dear Child of Victory*). He was rewarded with the title of the Duke of Rivoli. Marshal Masséna's right hand man during the French Revolutionary Wars was also amongst the initial fourteen Marshals of the Empire. Jean-de-Dieu Soult was named the Duke of Dalmatia in reward for his services to the Emperor. Marshal Soult was a great organizer and a strong leader. Soult would command the French forces along the Adriatic.

Perhaps the most overall effective Marshal of the Empire was Louis-Nicholas Davout. Marshal Davout had served with Napoleon with honor during the Egyptian Expedition, and was considered to be among the Emperor's most trusted leaders.

In addition to the fourteen initial Marshals of the Empire, four generals from France's Revolutionary Wars were given the title honoring their past service, but under Napoleon's assessment their advanced ages precluded them from active command.

The historian William M. Sloan documents that when Napoleon learned the Austrians were marching along the Danube, he wrote in an August letter to his minister Talleyrand that:

> *"...if the fleet appeared in the Channel there was still time, and he would be master of England; if not he would start for Germany."*

adding that if he could not be in London in a few days, then would be in Vienna by November. Napoleon further wrote:

> *"The Austrians have no idea how quickly my two hundred thousand will pirouette."* [31]

---

[31] "The Life of Napoleon Bonaparte," William M. Sloane, 1896, Vol. II, p.232.

Napoleon, in the last days of August, ordered his troops all along the Channel ports to concentrate all invasion barges at Boulogne, giving the impression of an imminent launch.

Then on the second of September, he quietly left the Channel coast with the bulk of his army. When his separate marshals' corps independently moved south from Boulogne to intercept the Austrian General Mack, they did so with great agility. They covered roughly five hundred miles with unanticipated, tremendous speed. In this way, Napoleon's forces were able to maneuver, recombine and surround the Austrian forces under Mack in mid-October along the Danube near the Bavarian town of Ulm, just to the west of Augsburg, a town which itself was just to the west of Munich. This came after several small but decisive battles, fought notably by two marshals, the ever impetuous Marshal Ney and the Emperor's loyal brother-in-law, Marshal Murat.

The Austrian General Mack had seriously miscalculated how rapidly Napoleon's army could cover great distances. Mack incorrectly calculated that by the time Napoleon arrived, the Austrian army would have been reinforced by the Russian troops.

In fact, Kutusov's Russian forces were still hundreds of miles to the east. This is often attributed to the fact that the Austrians followed the Gregorian calendar, while their Russian counterparts followed the older Julian calendar, as the Eastern Orthodox countries had no desire to adhere to that alternate calendar instituted by Pope Gregory. It is doubtful that this simple reason was the root cause of the timing disconnect, but in any case, the Russians were much further east than was necessary to assist General Mack. General Kutusov's army traveled among a route through the Austrian province of formerly Polish lands in Galicia, on through the town of Olmütz (present day Olomouc in the eastern Czech Republic) and then on to Vienna. They were in no position to reinforce General Mack, who, on the 20th of October, found himself completely surrounded at by the French at Ulm.

General Mack had no other option than to surrender his entire force to Napoleon. In a complete loss of face, General Mack handed the Emperor his sword, as was the custom of the time when surrendering to a superior force. The Austrians had lost four thousand soldiers killed in battle, with another six thousand wounded. The rest of the Mack's Austrian forces were taken prisoners of war. General Mack was disgraced and was subsequently court-martialed for his failure. He would later spend two years in prison for his gross incompetence of leadership in the field.

But the failure of General Mack did not end the Austrian army's participation in the war. Another large portion of that country's soldiers remained to the east, where they did, in fact, join up with the Russian forces under General Kutusov. The lure of these two great armies proved an irresistible draw to Emperor Bonaparte.

Napoleon's *Grande Armée* had itself a great victory at Ulm, losing only fifteen hundred dead or wounded. It was true that it had been pulled away from the Channel, but by then Emperor Bonaparte had realized there remained only the slightest of hope of the joint Franco-Spanish fleet escaping from Cádiz and clearing the Channel for him. To Napoleon, Admiral Villeneuve had committed the unforgivable sin of not being aggressive in fighting his way to Brest. Instead, his massive joint fleet was trapped in the port at Cádiz. If there still remained any hope of invading England, it would die upon the events of the next twenty-four hours in an epic British naval victory led by none other than Admiral Horatio Nelson off the Spanish Cape of Trafalgar.

Chapter 19: London
Nelson's Farewell to Emma

Tender is the endearment of an embrace after a great and prolonged absence. Tragic is that embrace when it is overshadowed by the threat of imminent dangers awaiting those departing. This was the swing of emotion, from most tender to most tragic, that Lady Emma was to transpire over the little over three weeks of Lord Admiral Nelson's return to London.

Nelson was surprised at the reception he received upon his arrival. *HMS Victory* sailed into Portsmouth on the 18th of August, and after a much abbreviated quarantine, Nelson came ashore the next day at 9 pm. Even at that hour, he was met by a throng of heartily cheering well-wishers, all ever so grateful for the Admiral's keeping the French fleet on the run, and thus Napoleon's invasion of their homeland at bay.

Nelson then headed directly for Merton Place and his awaiting Emma. In the capital, Londoners also received him as a conquering hero. He was mobbed in Piccadilly and throughout London was greeted with *"Huzzas"* wherever he was recognized. One of his contemporaries, Lord Minton, commented:

> *"It is really quite affecting to see the wonder and admiration and love and respect of the whole world; and the genuine expression of all these at once, from the gentle and simple, the moment he is seen. It is beyond anything represented in a play or in a poem of fame."* [32]

---

[32] *"The Life of Nelson"*, Captain A.T. Mahan, Easton Press Edition of 1897 text, Vol. II, p. 257.

The widowed Lady Emma Hamilton clutched Lord Nelson in her arms once again at Merton Place during his brief return to England after serving two-and-a-quarter years at sea. The Admiral was clearly frustrated and aggravated after having let the enemy fleet under French Villeneuve cross the Atlantic Ocean to the Caribbean and back, never catching or engaging his foe in battle. He had blockaded them, had pursued them, but never decisively engaged the combined French and Spanish fleets. His command had not destroyed or captured a single of their number.

Perhaps what Nelson feared most was that another admiral, during his own absence for rest, would lead the British to one final and glorious victory over the foe Villeneuve who he viewed as his own personal nemesis.

Nelson must have been somewhat reluctant to return to London with the destruction of the enemy fleet left unfinished. But he most assuredly needed the rest after being aboard his flagship *HMS Victory* for such an extended period of time.

Nelson spent the rest of August 1805 receiving and entertaining friends with Lady Emma at Merton Place, spending only four days of his leave engaged in London at the Admiralty or other offices of His Majesty's Government. Great feasts were planned with family and friends at *"The Farm."* Nelson turned down numerous invitations to be *fêted* at dinners by the richest and highest-bred of London's elite, with only one notable exception - an invitation to dinner from the Duke of Wales - the future King George IV.

Instead Nelson spent the bulk of his limited number of days with his beloved Emma. One can only imagine how distraught Emma must have been with her Nelson so distracted with his unfinished business at sea. She had desired only to be with him for so long, yet he was was preoccupied with what awaited at Cádiz.

Lady Hamilton still mourned the loss of her namesake second daughter, Emma, whose birth had come after Nelson had put to sea two years and three months earlier. Emma had spent the intervening chasm of time turning Merton Place into a fine home for which her returning love could retire. By some accounts it became a museum to the man, decorated with artifacts and souvenirs of his many conquests, which surely would have appealed to the Admiral's unabashed vanity.

One of the souvenirs Lord Nelson had held on to was a rather large recovered section of the mast of *L'Orient*, the enemy flagship that had so devastatingly exploded at the Battle of the Nile only seven years earlier. It was the battle just before Nelson became attached to Emma. Before his departure more than two years earlier Nelson had ordered that his coffin should be fashioned from its wood. In doing so, Nelson assured this wreckage of *L'Orient* would symbolically encapsulate their entire romance as well as eventually his mortal remains.

Emma had created a fine garden for her returning love's tranquil repose. They both took to calling it the *"quarterdeck."* Nelson spent much time in it as he recovered his health, spirit and ambitions during that stay. She must have been overjoyed to see her admiral restored so, but Emma must have known that his recovered spirits would be but the fuel to light the lamps aboard the *HMS Victory* as it returned to sea.

How Emma must have dreaded that second of September when Captain Blackwood arrived from the Admiralty with news from Admiral Collingwood's fleet. Collingwood commanded Nelson's force temporarily during his friend's respite and had Villeneuve and the combined Franco-Spanish fleets trapped at the port of Cádiz. That harbor was a small strip of Spanish soil that jutted out into the Atlantic above Gibraltar, with not much else than Cape Trafalgar between the two. Who could know then how famous the seas off this part of the Spanish coast would become?

Just over two hundred miles to the northwest of Cádiz, as the crow flies, lies the Portuguese harbor of Lisbon. In the future, Lisbon would become the arrival port on the Iberian Peninsula of the man who would become the Duke of Wellington, Sir Arthur Wellesley. These two most famous combatants of Napoleon - Nelson at sea and Wellesley, Duke of Wellington on land - would meet only once in their overlapping lifetime. That most insightful meeting took place during Nelson's last visit to London.

Wellesley had recently returned from his assignment in India, arriving in London on the 10th of September, 1805. He went to receive his next assignment from the Secretary of State for War. In the waiting room of the Secretary's office, Wellesley recognized the one armed Admiral from his likeness commonly shown throughout the British Empire. The two men struck up a conversation, although Wellesley thought it one-sided by Nelson, and found the Admiral to be incredibly self-absorbed. Wellesley later wrote to a friend:

"… [it was] really a style so vain and so silly as to surprise and almost disgust me. I suppose something that I happened to say may have made him guess that I was somebody, and he went out of the room for a moment, I have no doubt to ask the office-keeper who I was, for when he came back he was an all together different man, both in manner and matter. All that I had thought a charlatan style had vanished, and he talked of the state of this country and of the aspects and probabilities of affairs on the Continent with a good sense and knowledge of subjects both at home and abroad, that surprised me equally and more agreeably than the first part of our interview had done; in fact he talked like an officer and a statesman… I saw enough to be satisfied that he was a very superior man, but certainly a more sudden and complete metamorphosis I never saw." [33]

---

[33] *"The Life of Nelson"*, Captain A.T. Mahan, Easton Press Edition of 1897 text, Vol. II, p. 322

And in this brief encounter, the future Duke of Wellington saw both sides of the man who preceded him as Bonaparte's primary opponent, what Napoleon might call his *Bête Noire*. Nelson could be fleeting and vain in dealing with those he considered not to be his equal, but in a split second he could be engaging and impressive in dealing with those he found to be able to comprehend the depths of his knowledge.

All the while during his return to Merton Place, Nelson used his extensive command of that knowledge to devise his plan of attack upon his immediate foe, the French Admiral Villeneuve. He would lure the French and Spanish fleet out into the open sea and break its line of battle into three pieces forcing a *mêlée* of assault upon his enemy's scattered forces. It was a strategy not unlike the tactic employed years past at the Battle of Cape St. Vincent, but even more daring in its sheer audacity.

Emma knew she could not keep her Nelson at Merton Place so long as Villeneuve's fleet was bottled up at Cádiz. She urged him to return to the sea, no matter how much the very thought pained her. In response to her, Nelson was to have said:

> ***"Brave Emma! Good Emma! If there were more Emmas, there would be more Nelsons."*** [34]

On the twelfth of September, Nelson and Lady Hamilton were called on by an urgent Prince of Wales, who demanded to see the Admiral before his departure. It was the one invitation that Nelson would not turn down during his last days at Merton Place. By the time of the dinner, Emma was so distraught, she neither ate nor drank, knowing that the next evening her Nelson would ride the overnight coach to Portsmouth.

---

[34] *"The Life of Nelson"*, Captain A.T. Mahan, Easton Press Edition of 1897 text, Vol. II, p. 331

Somehow, it was fitting, and ominously so, that Lord Admiral Horatio Nelson would spend his last day with his beloved Emma on Friday the thirteenth.

They both must have been mindful of the gypsy who had foretold Nelson's fortune in the West Indies as a much younger man. She had told Nelson he would be the pre-eminent man of his profession by the time he was forty, and indeed his fortieth birthday party was thrown by Emma in Naples just after the Battle of the Nile. When young Nelson asked what was to follow, the gypsy elusively said that she could tell him no more, saying only that *"... the book is closed."*

Before leaving that night, Nelson ordered that the finishing touches be made to the coffin carved from the wood of the *L'Orient's* mast. He recorded in his private diary the following entry:

"At half past ten drove from dear dear Merton, where I left all I hold dear in this world, to go to serve my King and Country. May the great God whom I adore enable me to fulfill the expectations of my country; and if it is His good pleasure that I should return, my thanks will never cease being offered up to the Throne of His Mercy. If it is His good Providence to cut short my days upon earth, I bow with the greatest submission, relying that He will protect those so dear to me, that I may leave behind.

His will be done:
Amen, Amen, Amen." [35]

---

[35] *"The Life of Nelson"*, Captain A.T. Mahan, Easton Press Edition of 1897 text, Vol. II, p. 355

Chapter 20: Augsburg
Marek's Prisoners

Fate laughs at and often teasingly plays with those caught in its tenacious grasp. Marek would find this to be ever so true. At Ulm, just hours before the surrender of General Mack to Napoleon, Marek was called to ride to an encampment by a message sent by his friend and trusted confidant, Rydek.

"My good friend, Captain Marek," the couriered note read, "I have in my possession here at Augsburg the bodies of two Austrian infantry that I need you to identify as soon as possible. It was reported that they claimed to have been your cousins. Please come to the camp at Augsburg as soon as your duties permit."

Marek waited until he was relieved that evening by another members of the Old Guard. A cold, heavy rain had begun to pour as he rushed on horseback to the outpost along the outskirts of the town of Augsburg. Its waters drenched him throughout his night ride, but did not permeate as deeply into him as the fear of what he would find upon his arrival. He feared the ride's end throughout his journey, when he would be forced to lay his eyes upon the bloodied bodies of his cousins, Andrzej and Bartek.

How would his *Ciotka* Ewelina take the news of her two boys having been butchered by Napoleon's *Grande Armée*, the current version of the same army that Marek had so enthusiastically defected to? He knew from his mother of his aunt's detesting his defection at Lodi as if it were an unforgivable sin.

After his exhausting ride, Marek was taken immediately to Rydek. His friend told him of the two captured Austrian soldiers who spoke no French, but kept repeating their cousin's name.

"Marek Zaczek! Marek Zaczek! Marek Zaczek!" Rydek said, imitating their pleas. "The French guards did not know what to do with them, so they brought them to me. When I spoke to these brothers in Polish, they said they knew you were one of Napoleon's personal guards. "

"What do you mean, *When you spoke to them?*" asked Marek. "You mean to tell me they were still alive when they were brought before you as prisoners?"

"Precisely," Rydek said simply, ignoring the obvious question. "It would be hard to speak to them otherwise."

"Then they must have been terribly wounded during the battle?" Marek wondered. "When exactly did they die? Was it from their wounds? If not, under whose command were they executed? If that was the case, then I want to know who murdered them! I will have the bastard shot upon the Emperor's very command!"

Marek's blood was seething. To think his two cousins had been ordered to be killed as prisoners of war infuriated him. It was then that Rydek burst out laughing. His whole being heaved with the one-sided mirth of a great joke having been played on his friend. "Who on earth said that your cousins were dead?"

"You did! I have your communiqué here in my pocket," Marek said angrily. "It clearly states that you have in your possession the bodies of two men thought to be my cousins."

"And I do, *Capitaine* Zaczek," Rydek said, still laughing heartily, "but I never wrote that they were *dead* bodies."

"Dupek!" Marek cursed him in Polish. *"Gówniarz!"*

Marek was infuriated. Such a joke was immature, not to mention insensitive. He should have expected it from Rydek, who had always been the Polish Legion's worst practical joker.

"Yes," Rydek said, his rolling laughter slowly coming to a stop. "You can call me an ass, even a little shit, but would your superiors in the Old Guard have released you to come here if I said I am holding two prisoners that you could see later at any time? I think not. I did this as a courtesy to you my friend. I knew you would want to speak to them."

"Take me to them already," Marek snared. "How the devil did they know I was in the Old Guard of the Emperor?"

"They said they'd received the news in a letter from their mother," Rydek said as they walked. "They don't understand how many thousands of soldiers there are in the Old Guard. They thought you were the Emperor's sole personal protector. It was only then that they told me they were your cousins."

Marek was still recovering from his night's ride in the cold, drenching rain, as well as the mental torment that saturated throughout him, having assumed his two cousins killed in action.

Rydek led Marek to a building down the main street that had been the town's jail before it was commandeered. He explained to Marek that the brothers had been separated from the other prisoners of war, and held there until his arrival. He wanted to assure his friend the privacy needed in dealing with these close relatives from his youth.

"Who knows," Rydek said, "perhaps we can convince them to join the ranks of the Polish Legions under Dąbrowski? They can take up the fight to free our homeland from the usurpers. Surely riding as Polish cavalry for us would be the safest fate for them."

Marek's brow became troubled at the suggestion. "The truth of the matter is, my friend, that even though their father, my Uncle Jacek, was the Duke's stable master, neither of his sons ever learned to ride. It was forbidden for any peasant child to mount the Duke's horses. The one time when the Duke was away, Uncle Jacek snuck them atop a steed, just for the overall experience, both Andrzej and Bartek were terrified of the animal."

"So then, my friend," Rydek asked, "how did you ever learn to ride like a ghost on the wind?"

"For some reason," Marek admitted, "I was always the exception. Not only would I be allowed to exercise the Duke's various mounts, but often he would take a break from his affairs to come out and watch me run them. Some of my best memories as a child were galloping through the paddock while the Duke and his beautiful daughter, Maya, watched. I never understood why that nobleman not only trusted me atop his mounts, but seemed to revel so in my riding them."

"All right," Rydek reacted, "so your cousins are not the horsemen that Marek Zaczek is. Indeed, few are. They can still be drafted into the French infantry, can they not?"

"That is exactly the offer I hope they have sense enough to accept." Marek said as they entered the jail house and dismissed the guards inside. Rydek stayed with Marek as he unlocked the iron cell, then rushed inside to embrace his kin.

"Andrzej! Bartek! My cousins! I am so glad to see you," Marek said as the three men formed a triangle of enwrapped arms. "I always feared that you might have been lost to the battlefield cannons somewhere in Italy. Now, here I stand in your embrace. Praise be to the Lord Jesus Christ!"

"Forever and ever!" the brothers responded. "Marek, it is so wonderful to see you again, to be with you once more."

Marek stepped back to look upon the two soldiers, dressed in the all white Austrian uniforms with brilliant blue piping. That color was offset by the stains of mud they both bore, but Marek was relieved to see neither of his cousins bore any bloodstains that would indicate they had been wounded.

"So tell me, how are your parents? My mother writes that Aunt Ewelina lives with her now in Warsaw," Marek said.

"Did she bother to tell you just how bitter our mother has become, with the both of us, along with our father stolen from her by the war?" Bartek asked. "Her letters drip with bile."

"I do know she misses all three of you terribly," Marek answered diplomatically. "And how is Uncle Jacek?"

"Still in the stables of the Imperial Riding School in Vienna," stated Andrzej. "We saw him during the last year of the so-called peace between Austria and France. Our father is a broken man, after years under the thumb of a procession of Austrian stable masters, all of whom could ride no better than himself. Yet, father was never considered for the post because he is only a lowly Pole. Instead he lives out the last years of his life humbled, mucking stalls and setting out tack for the student riders."

"Psia krew!" Marek spat, using the expletive that translates literally to *Blood of a Dog!* "It is all the fault of that damned Austrian Count Von Arndt, for he was the one who prodded the Duke to send us all off to serve in the Austrian army. For that and what he has done to drive our mothers back into near poverty, I swear I will return one day to make the Count pay for his misdeeds. I will bleed the dog's blood from his veins, so help me!"

A strange look came over the faces of the two captured soldiers. Marek looked at Rydek, who stood by his side and returned a glance that confirmed something was amiss.

"What is it that you both have not the courage to say to *Capitaine* Zaczek?" barked Rydek.

"It is true," Andrzej said, his voice as wobbly as a cart's wheel on a rutted road, "that our mother is impoverished. She lives in Warsaw only off the generosity of your mother, and certainly they are much better off than when they were peasants, but she detests being so dependent on *Ciocia* Magdalena who still lives in that grand townhome in Warsaw."

Marek spoke not, he only let the words sink deeply into him. Was it possible that his mother had somehow managed to keep from Ewelina that she was also dependent on another's charity, that being from the Princess Czartoryska?

"Why do you both still wear those boastful white uniforms of the Austrian Empire - that which invaded Poland and seized the very lands upon which we were all born and raised?"

Andrzej and Bartek looked at each other, startled. "What option do we have otherwise?"

Marek smiled warmly. "I am here to make another option available to you, my cousins. I will see that you are enlisted and dressed out in the fine uniforms of the French infantry. Napoleon knows and respects the pride that beats in the hearts of all Poles. For he knows that all Poles detest the three empires that stripped away our nation from the map of Europe. Damn all Russians, Prussians and Austrians!"

Once again a queer look passed among the cousins. It became apparent that they had anticipated Marek's offer and discussed it during their captivity.

"We cannot accept this option, my cousin," Bartek spoke. "The fact of the matter is we would dishonor all Poles who fought for the Austrians if we defected. We are prepared for whatever fate the French have in store for us."

Marek was astounded. "You fools! The honor of your fellow Poles who also mistakenly fight for our country's Austrian invaders means more to you than your own lives?"

It was Andrzej who next spoke. "Cousin Marek, men can live without a country, and even without honor. But what Bartek and I will not do is live without our family."

"Why should you ever have to?" Marek asked.

"Because our mother has written to us many times," Andrzej replied, "that if we ever defected to the French like our shameful cousin Marek, she would forever disown us."

Marek was shocked. "*Ciocia* Ewelina actually used those words? Shameful?"

"Actually," Bartek corrected, "she referred to you as our *cowardly* cousin Marek." With this, his brother's arm shot up and shoved him as if to say, *you idiot, I left that out intentionally.*

Marek then whispered an order into Rydek's ear. His friend quickly left the jailhouse to carry it out. Alone with his cousins, Marek then continued to press them again with the offer his heart yearned for them to accept.

"Once more I offer you the chance to fight for the Emperor of France who will restore the Poland we all love."

"While we truly do love our native Poland," Andrzej said, "we love more our family! So no, we cannot accept your offer."

Marek shook his head in disbelief. Many minutes passed with Marek continuing to try but unable to persuade them to fight for the French. Then Rydek returned. In his arms was a cloth sack of clothes. It appeared to hold not military uniforms, but the rags of peasants. Rydek nodded to Marek that he had successfully followed his instruction.

"My cousins," Marek said, "as you so steadfastly refuse my offer, then you leave me only one last choice. Remove your uniforms. Go ahead, strip now!"

The cousins were unaccustomed to hear Marek speak to them for the first time in the commanding voice of a captor.

Bartek began to unbutton his tunic when Andrzej reached up to grasp his hand and pull it down. "If you intend to put us in front of a firing squad, cousin, then we have every right to die with dignity in the uniforms in which we served when captured."

Rydek broke out in a guffaw that filled the close air of the small jailhouse. "I have always known your cousin Marek to be a true bastard, but even he would never possess the moral decadence needed to line you up in front of French riflemen."

This being said, Rydek emptied the contents of the cloth sack and out tumbled two sets of clothes, each stripped from a local peasant who had fallen during the battles of the past days.

"Now, off with your uniforms," Marek ordered. "You will dress out in these peasant clothes and make your way back to be with your mother. Neither France nor Austria are at war with Prussia at this time, so once you escape the Austrian provinces, you can travel freely through Prussia all the way to Warsaw. Do not dare to dress out again in the white uniform of the Austrians. If I were to come across you on the battlefield, and unknowingly kill either of you by my own hand, I would never forgive myself. Instead I give you your freedom. Go home. Do not force me or any other member of the *Grande Armée* to take it away in battle."

"But then why do you take our uniforms," Bartek asked, "what need have you of them?"

Marek responded to his cousin's question only by drawing his sabre and raising it to Bartek's chest.

Marek flipped his wrist and his cousin's first tunic button fell to the floor, then the second and third. He then worked the sabre's tip beneath its surface, and with the gentlest movement of his hand, drew a profuse stream of blood from his cousin's chest. Bartek grimaced, but otherwise stood as still as a stubborn mule throughout this minor assault.

"Brother, do you not see?" Andrzej said knowingly. "They intend to dress out the two peasant corpses in our uniforms to explain our disappearance, and in order to make it appear honest, there is need for some of our blood to stain the muddy but otherwise pristine white tunics of these uniforms."

Andrzej then unbuttoned his uniform and tore at his undergarment to reveal the flesh of his chest. Marek then inflicted the same wound upon him as on his brother, producing a great quantity of blood, but in such a superficial way that he expected it to quickly heal in a few days.

Both cousins bore Marek's mark, a single sword-scribbled motion he had practiced over many years in his boredom. But always in the dirt or sand, or upon the discarded hides of animals, even the bark of logs. This was the first time he had ever imparted his mark upon soft swells of human flesh. It would heal to a scar, he hoped, looking somewhat like his initials:

"Each of you now bear my mark," Marek said. "Should you be foolish enough to rejoin the Austrian army, well, then I will know your mangled bodies when they are dragged, perhaps otherwise unrecognizable, from the battlefield. I implore you not to return to the fight, for I wish only to see the scars from these wounds again after they are long healed, that is, when the war is over and we are all reunited safely in Warsaw."

The two brothers said nothing in response. They merely used their hands to smear the free-flowing blood from their freshly gashed skin over the white uniforms. Then, after several minutes, the flow had stemmed to just a trickle. It was then that the brothers stripped themselves of the blood-stained Austrian uniforms and cast them to the floor, looking somewhat like surrendered red and white Polish flags.

The brothers each dressed out in the peasant's clothes. Both their outfits were ill fitting, which only made them look all the more the part of poor villagers.

"I am afraid I have no boots for you," Rydek said, "you will have to scavenge those in your travels, but do not take a dead soldiers' boots, as that will give away the ruse."

Marek then walked over to the door in the rear of the small jailhouse. He opened it and sheets of rain in the darkness blotted out all but the outline of a thicket of woods not far off.

"Lieutenant Rydek has sent away the guards. You are both now free to egress. Safe travels to you both, my cousins."

"You know if the Austrians find us dressed like this, we will be shot as deserters," Andrzej stated coldly.

"That is your concern," answered Marek, colder still. "You need only to make it to the Prussia border. I have offered you another possible future, one which you simply flittered away. You both must now answer to the idiocy of that decision."

With this, each cousin said simply, *"do zobaczenia, Marek"* and lurched out into the darkness of the cold, wet October night. Marek prayed they would make their way to Warsaw unharmed.

Chapter 21: Trafalgar
Nelson's Final Naval Battle

The sun rose timidly, almost as if it could not bear to illuminate the morning sky under which Lord Admiral Nelson traveled on September 14th, 1805. Beneath it, he approached the English Channel harbor town of Portsmouth. Great crowds formed awaiting his coach's arrival. Nelson's procession to his flagship *HMS Victory* became an intensely remarkable scene as members of the public knelt in reverence as the Admiral passed by them. Men broke into tears at the anticipation of Lord Admiral Nelson's returning to battle with the enemy upon the high seas, so soon after his return to the green lawns of England just weeks before.

Nelson dined that evening with members of Prime Minister Pitt's staff and personal friends on board *HMS Victory*. Certainly their discussions must have ebbed and flowed from the Franco-Spanish fleet bottled up at Cádiz to Napoleon's still pending invasion of England. None around the table could possibly have known at that point that the French Emperor had already begun moving his troops to Ulm twelve days earlier.

In any case, Nelson, was eager to set sail. He had previously said he would not board the flagship until one of its two anchors had been weighed, meaning raised. *HMS Victory* was imminently ready to set sail. In the *morning,* so would so depart.

Another twelve days later, on the 27th of September, the *HMS Victory* reunited with the fleet off the port of Cádiz, Spain. Two days after Nelson's arrival there, the officers of the fleet converged upon *Victory* to celebrate their Admiral's forty-seventh birthday. It must have been hard for them to realize it had been only seven years since his great victory at the Nile, even those who had sailed with him into Aboukir Bay that day of 1 August 1798.

Less than two weeks after that birthday celebration, on the very day after Napoleon's great victory over the Austrians at Ulm, Nelson would deliver to the Emperor another most crippling defeat at sea. This attack off the Cape of Trafalgar and would be even more devastating to the Emperor than that at the Nile or of any of Nelson's other battles.

Lord Admiral Nelson, having upon his return retaken overall command from his longtime friend and subordinate, Admiral Collingwood, had implemented a two pronged strategy. The large Franco-Spanish fleet of thirty-three Ships-of-the-Line (eighteen French and fifteen Spanish) cluttered and choked the small harbor of Cádiz. The besieged fleet rapidly drained that town's ability to support so many sailors with food and other necessary resources. Each day the fleet was in that Spanish harbor, the overall strain of the situation increased for his counterpart, the French Admiral Villeneuve. Nelson knew his opponent would soon be forced out into the open, even if he was not prescient enough to foresee exactly what the final impetus might be.

Nelson implemented his first strategy and moved his fleet some fifty miles out to sea, beyond the horizon, inviting his enemy to make a break from its entrapment. Believing that Villeneuve's move would be toward the Strait of Gibraltar, Nelson positioned his fleet to intercept the enemy. It was not unlike the cat and mouse game he had played with Villeneuve's predecessor, Admiral Latouche Tréville, tempting his foe to come out to sea from Toulon. When Admiral Villeneuve decided to do so from Cádiz, there would be Nelson, waiting to engage and crush his enemy's line of warships. He only needed for Villeneuve to decide to move.

Villeneuve had stayed in port for so long that he had refused yet another direct order from Napoleon. This time Napoleon directed that he should move the joint fleet to the Mediterranean, to support operations near Naples.

It was only later when Villeneuve learned that the Emperor had drafted orders which were en route to relieve him of command that the Admiral finally decided to move the fleet. On the 19th of October, Villeneuve began to move his ships at Cádiz to sea. It took two full days for all thirty-three warships to exit the port and position themselves in two parallel lines before proceeding south along the Spanish coast. Villeneuve intentionally had departed Cádiz before Napoleon's orders could arrive.

With his fleet of large warships hidden out of Villeneuve's view, Nelson used the smaller and much faster network of frigates under Captain Blackwood's command to stay aware of the enemy's movements. Their position was relayed to Nelson's awaiting fleet, which the Lord Admiral then moved to intercept.

This is where the second bit of Nelson's strategy played into the overall battle. Instead of following the conventional tactic of aligning his ships parallel to the enemy's line and trading broadside volleys of cannon fire, Nelson ordered his fleet to form into two columns to attack perpendicularly to the enemy's line. He commanded the northernmost column of attack; Admiral Collingwood upon the *HMS Royal Sovereign* commanded the southernmost column. This twin assault took place south of Cádiz, just off the dangerous shoals of Spain's Cape Trafalgar.

The days preceding the battle had been full of gale winds and battering waves. This day, the waters remained calm and the winds faint from the northwest. This was only a temporary lull as another gale was expected later in the advance of evening. The clam was both a relief and a curse, as while they avoided the gale, the lack of wind hampered Nelson's own maneuverability. The attack that was to play out would do so in seemingly slow motion.

Nelson ordered his fleet to move in on its prey. The slack winds advanced them slowly. Upon seeing the size of Nelson's formation of twenty-seven warships, Villeneuve ordered his fleet to *wear* (turn around) and return to harbor at Cádiz, but it was too late. The British ships approached the Franco-Spanish line lazily, perhaps at speeds as slow as one and a half knots, allowing Nelson time to send the famous flagged message to each of his warships,

"England expects that every man will do his duty." [36]

Nelson's two columns intersected the crescent-shaped lines of the enemy's joint fleet, dissecting it into thirds.

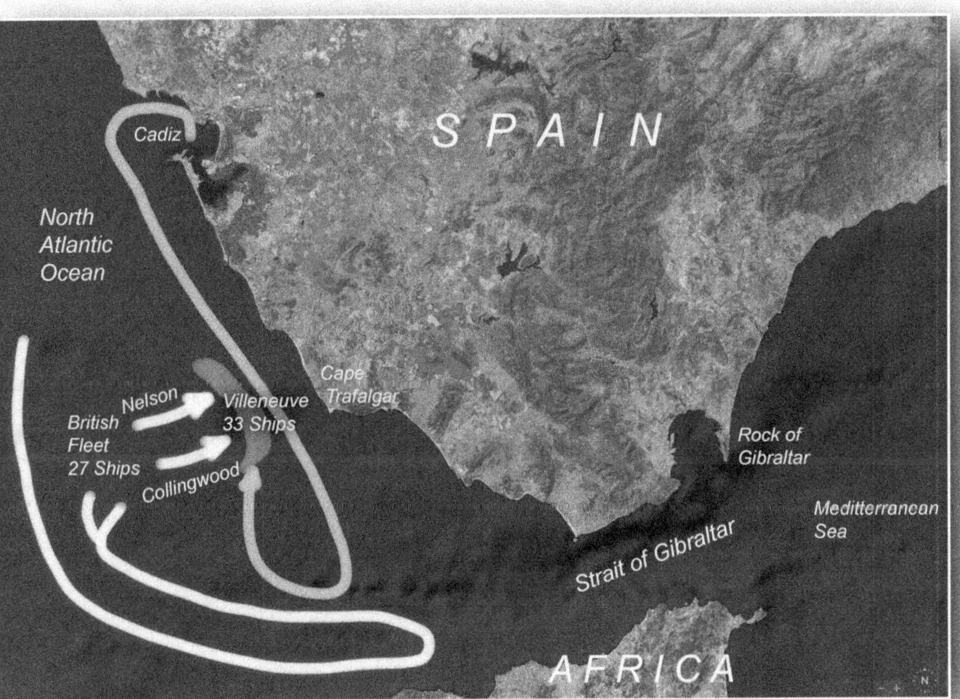

Figure 18: Map of the Battle of Trafalgar
(Sea Battle Positioning Scale Exaggerated)

---

[36] *"The Life of Nelson"*, Captain A.T. Mahan, Easton Press Edition of 1897 text, Vol. II, p. 382

Nelson's flagship *HMS Victory*, took direct aim upon Villeneuve's flagship *Bucentaure*. Nelson was on deck as the engagement began, wearing his admiral's frock coat complete with four large star-shaped naval decorations, one representing each Order that had awarded it. His longtime captain of the *Victory*, Thomas Hardy requested the Admiral to stay below deck. When Nelson refused, Hardy suggested that the star-like medallions would make perfect targets for sharpshooters sure to be lurking in the French ships' overhead rigging during the impending close quarters engagement. Nelson would not hear of removing them.

The two British columns moved at a crawl toward the enemy line. At noon, Villeneuve ordered for his warships to open fire on them. Collingwood's southern column was already closing upon the enemy line, but Nelson's column led by *HMS Victory*, one to two miles northward, was slightly further out. Neither column returned a single shot to the enemy's withering onslaught, showing great discipline. Nelson's personal secretary, a man named Mr. Scott, was swept away by an enemy cannon blast. In all, twenty men were killed and thirty more wounded before Lord Nelson signaled *Victory's* guns to be fired in anger.

Hardy and Nelson walked along deck when a fragment of the ship's splintered structure fell upon and bruised the Captain's foot, causing Nelson to say,

"This is too warm work, Hardy, to last long." [37]

A few minutes after one in the afternoon, the two fleets closed within feet of each other, resulting in nothing short of an all out *mêlée*. Captain Hardy skillfully steered his craft, Nelson's flagship *Victory*, just aft of Villeneuve's flagship *Bucentaure's* stern. This was after *Victory* had already taken extensive damage from volley after volley of heavy French cannon fire.

---

[37] *"The Life of Nelson"*, Captain A.T. Mahan, Easton Press Edition of 1897 text, Vol. II, p. 386"

Figure 19 : The Battle of Trafalgar (William C. Stanfield)

Another half an hour had passed, when under Nelson's order, Captain Hardy rounded the *Bucentaure* astern, during which *Victory* fired twenty cannon rounds through the very length of the French flagship. That volley alone was later attributed to having killed some four hundred enemy sailors and gunners.

Nelson then ordered that,

> *"… every effort must be made to capture*
>
> *the hostile commander-in-chief."* [38]

Hardy pulled the *Victory* tightly around and along the French flagship. The maneuver brought the *Victory* between the *Bucentaure* and the French seventy-four gun warship *Redoutable*. As the *Victory* fired upon both ships from its port and starboard cannons, taking on tremendous damage of its own, Admiral Nelson strode alongside Captain Hardy. It was then when the Admiral was felled by a French sniper's ball. It was fired from the rigging of the *Redoutable,* only some fifty feet above the *Victory's* deck.

---

[38] *"The Life of Nelson"*, Captain A.T. Mahan, Easton Press Edition of 1897 text, Vol. II, p. 387

Figure 20: Nelson lays mortally wounded upon the deck

Nelson fell in the exact same spot along that deck where his secretary Mr. Scott had earlier been swept away. During this incredible moment, with the battle raging on either side of the flagship, Captain Hardy attended to Nelson, who had collapsed onto the deck's planking knowing that the shot was most certainly fatal. When Captain Hardy expressed his hope that he was all right, Nelson replied,

"They have done for me at last."

When Hardy again asked if he was badly wounded, Nelson simply said,

"Yes, my backbone is shot through." [39]

The shot had indeed entered Nelson's left shoulder, punctured his lung, severed an artery and passed through his spine before becoming embedded in the muscles of his back. Nelson was carried below deck, his face covered to keep his tremendous pain from distracting the men as the battle raged on.

---

[39] *"The Life of Nelson"*, Captain A.T. Mahan, Easton Press Edition of 1897 text, Vol. II, p. 388

of the Flagship HMS Victory during the Battle of Trafalgar.

Hardy remained on deck to lead the men, as the French were attempting to board *Victory* from both sides. The *Bucentaure* was on one side of *Victory* and the *Redoutable was* on the other. Miraculously, these boarding attempts were repulsed under the command of Captain Hardy. Below deck Nelson would tell the ship's surgeon, Dr. William Beatty,

> *"You can do nothing fore me, Beatty,*
> *I have but a short time to live."* [40]

Nelson, throughout his excruciatingly slow death, called again and again for Captain Hardy, at times fearing him lost in the battle above. By two in the afternoon, the *Victory* had forced the flagship *Bucentaure* to surrender. but only after Villeneuve had signaled for other French vessels to rally and attack the *Victory.*

It was at this point that Captain Hardy freed himself to go below deck and look in on his dying admiral. Nelson was relieved to see his captain unharmed. Despite the *Bucentaure's* surrender, the battle continued to rage on all around them.

---

[40] *"The Life of Nelson"*, Captain A.T. Mahan, Easton Press Edition of 1897 text,
Vol. II, p. 389

Nelson then asked,

"Hardy, how goes the battle?
How goes the day with us?" [41]

To which Hardy replied that fourteen or fifteen enemy vessels had struck their colors (surrendered), and none of their own were lost. The actual number, after the haze of battle cleared, would be determined to be eighteen. Nelson replied,

"That is well, I bargained for twenty." [42]

Captain Hardy hovered nearby his fallen admiral, when he heard him say,

"Take care of poor Lady Hamilton. Kiss me, Hardy." [43]

Hardy then leaned forward to kiss Nelson on the cheek. The Captain would later kiss him again, that time on the forehead, drawing forth from Nelson the response, **"Bless you, Hardy."** [44]

As blood filled Nelson's wounded lung, and his thirst intensified, he pleaded with the surgeon, saying,

"Drink, drink; Fan, fan; Rub, rub." [45]

The last request was for the surgeon, Dr. Beatty, to continue to rub his breast. The touch of another human comforted him as the noose of mortality tightened around him.

---

[41] *"The Life of Nelson"*, Captain A.T. Mahan, Easton Press Edition of 1897 text, Vol. II, p. 392

[42] *"The Life of Nelson"*, Captain A.T. Mahan, Easton Press Edition of 1897 text, Vol. II, p. 394

[43] *"The Life of Nelson"*, Captain A.T. Mahan, Easton Press Edition of 1897 text, Vol. II, p. 395

[44] *"The Life of Nelson"*, Captain A.T. Mahan, Easton Press Edition of 1897 text, Vol. II, p. 395

[45] *"The Life of Nelson"*, Captain A.T. Mahan, Easton Press Edition of 1897 text, Vol. II, p. 395

**Figure 21: Nelson's Last Moments Belowdeck
Aboard the HMS Victory**

Beatty's touch was Nelson's last link to the brotherhood of those who sailed the perils of the sea with him. As Nelson drifted into his final moments, he repeated these words on a fragile ebbing breath,

"Thank God I have done my duty!" [46]

He repeated this over and over again until his voice became so soft that Dr. Beatty had to lean over, his ear close to the Admiral's mouth, to hear the last words escape upon Nelson's final breath,

"God and my Country..." [47]

---

[46] *"The Life of Nelson"*, Capt. A.T. Mahan, Easton Press Edition of 1897 text, Vol. II, p. 396

[47] *"The Life of Nelson"*, Capt. A.T. Mahan, Easton Press Edition of 1897 text, Vol. II, p. 396

By the time of the death of Nelson at half past four in the afternoon, some three hours after his being shot, the battle had been far beyond any doubt of being won. Their admiral, gone in spirit, lived just long enough to know how resoundingly complete the victory had been.

Nelson's simple but elegant plan, even given the slight winds that forestalled maneuvering, exacted precisely what he had imagined while drafting it. All that was left for the British fleet to do was to drop anchor, as even in the throes of death, Nelson had repeatedly demanded of Hardy. This prevented the victorious British fleet from being driven into the disastrously shallow waters of Trafalgar's treacherous shoals by the gale that approached immediately after the fighting.

Captain Hardy then began to prepare Nelson's corpse for its return voyage to England. There was no thought of committing his remains to the depths of the sea. To retard the process of decomposition, his body was placed in a cask of brandy mixed with camphor and myrrh. The cask containing those remains was then lashed to the main mast and put under armed guard.

The victory at the Battle of Trafalgar gave Britain control of the seas for the next hundred years. Napoleon's dream of invading England had been snuffed out forever. Yet, it cost the British Empire its greatest seaman and naval warrior.

When King George III received news of the tremendous naval victory and of Nelson's sorrowful death, he reportedly uttered the words, *"We have lost more than we have gained."* [48]

---

[48] "Nelson: A Personal History," Christopher Hibbert, 1994, Da Capo Press

Chapter 22: Austerlitz

Battle of the Three Emperors

It is the temptation of glory that draws great men to their reckoning. For some, it is claimed on a battlefield where the trap of their ego is sprung, their ruination insured for all time. More cruelly for other men fate is deferred, luring them on with the immediate sweet taste of victory only to eventually draw them into a later more disastrous collapse. Finally, a rare few men escape the field after a crushing and immediate failure, hardened with resolve to face still more challenges, stiffening the spine of their being until it bears the crippling weight of ultimate victory. The Battle of Austerlitz would prove all three of these three manifestations to be accurate, one for each of the three Emperors present there - Austrian and Holy Roman Emperor Phillip, Emperor Napoleon Bonaparte and Russian Tsar and Emperor Alexander.

On 2 December 1805, exactly upon the one year anniversary of his coronation, the Emperor of the French, Napoleon Bonaparte would face off on a battlefield against the joint forces of the Austrians and Russians. Emperors Francis of Austria and Alexander of Russia would lead their armies that day. This epic battle would commence that morning among the rolling hills roughly between Vienna and Prague, just east of the town of Brunn. This was a land of pastural beauty and bucolic peace in the fields and hills to the west of a small village whose name would soon become famous across the globe - Austerlitz.

Over these fields, the sun would rise over a lingering heavy morning mist as the three emperors pondered their destinies. Yet, before the battle itself is addressed, one must understand exactly what lured each of those three emperors to that battlefield. Austerlitz would be transformed from its God-given tranquility to being the site of that young century's most severe butchery of human life. The bodies of soldiers of all sides were so wantonly strewn across this, our Deity's paradise, by His more imperfect creation, man. In short, Austerlitz would disfigure a heaven on earth into a blazing hell that would forever infest the minds of all those unfortunate enough to survive.

In the year 800 AD, Charlemagne was crowned Emperor of the Francs on Christmas Day. This is widely regarded as the genesis of what would become the Holy Roman Empire. On this day, the second of December, over a thousand years later to the very month, the leader of that Holy Roman Empire was Emperor Phillip II, who also served (somewhat confusingly) as Emperor Phillip I of Austria. His General Karl Mack, had two months earlier walked into Napoleon's ambush at Ulm and surrendered all the troops under his command. With this, Phillip put all remaining Austrian troops under the command of his brother, the Archduke Charles. - only fitting as Charles had been the most vigorous voice in the Habsburg Kingdom demanding war with France. When Napoleon overran Vienna in mid-November of 1805, Phillip II and Archduke Charles had already fled the capital. They headed to the eastern town of Olmütz where they linked up with the Russian army under General Kutusov. Kutusov was then joined there by his Tsar Alexander I, and the Tsar's adviser, the Pole, Adam Czartoryski.

The brothers Habsburg, driven out of Vienna ahead of Napoleon's arrival there in mid-November, did not expect to be exiled for long from their capital. At Olmütz, they thought, the Tsar's Russian forces combined with those Austrian forces that remained in battle would easily defeat Napoleon's over-extended *Grande Armée* and regain control of Vienna. In fact, they saw this as the last chance for the Habsburgs to salvage a victory for their empire in this war of the Third Coalition.

At the time of the Battle of Austerlitz, Russian Tsar Alexander I, was still a few weeks shy of his twenty-eighth birthday. He was the grandson of Catherine the Great, who had murdered her own husband, Tsar Peter, (Alexander's grandfather) in order to rise to power as Tsarina. Her son (Alexander's father), Tsar Paul I, succeeded Catherine upon her death in 1796. Tsar Paul quickly emptied her jails which were full of political prisoners. He freed the wounded Polish patriot, Tadeusz Kościuszko, along with the Czartoryski brothers, Adam Jerzy and Konstanty Adam. Tsar Paul allowed his son, Tsarevich Alexander to strike up a relationship with the highly learned and much traveled Adam Jerzy as his mentor. The two developed a very close friendship. Adam Jerzy was granted soon allowed to visit the Czartoryski holdings that had been restored to his family, including the Palace at Puławy.

After reigning for only five years, Tsar Paul was murdered by elements within the Russian Court that resisted his desire to align their country more closely with the Prussians to their west. When Alexander I succeeded Paul as Tsar in 1801, he undid many of his father's unfavorable policies.

As Napoleon grew in power over the years, Tsar Alexander's resolve against the French stiffened. The young Russian Emperor would go so far as to call Napoleon the *"oppressor of Europe and the disturber of the world's peace."* [49] He saw the defeat of Napoleon as his personal cross to bear, although initially he would not attempt to do so alone.

Alexander had taken on his friend and intellectual mentor, Adam Jerzy Czartoryski, as his Foreign Minister. Czartoryski had long before traveled to England, and was impressed by the strength of their people, the resolve of their leaders and dominance of their Royal Navy upon the seas. He urged Tsar Alexander to more closely align the Russians with the British. The Tsar did so, wishing to benefit from that union. Alexander thought with the British upon the seas and his troops strengthening the Austrian army on land, they could prevail in their war against Napoleon. That left the remaining power, the Prussians, as neutrals in the war.

However, Tsar Alexander did not always heed the advice of his highly regarded foreign minister. Against Czartoryski's pleadings, Tsar Alexander I spent the summer of 1805 in Berlin, attempting to stir up support of the Prussians against Napoleon. In fact, Foreign Minister Czartoryski was forced to accompany his Tsar in that Prussian capital attempting to implement this very strategy that he himself had argued against.

Tsar Alexander soon developed a close relationship with the thirty-five year old Prussian King Frederick Wilhelm III and his beautiful young wife, Queen Louise of Mecklenburg-Strelitz. Tsar Alexander had found a kindred spirit in the Queen. She urged her own husband to forego Prussia's neutrality and join the Austro-Russian armies in the war of the Third Coalition against Napoleon. All to no avail, however, as King Frederick Wilhelm stayed the course with Prussia's neutrality.

---

49 Quote Attributed to Tsar Alexander I of Russia

The Prussians did not join the Third Coalition, and as such, did not participate in the Battle of Austerlitz, but that did not mean Alexander's pleadings had fallen on completely deaf ears.

Queen Louise was not only listening, but she took Tsar Alexander's requests to heart and continued to wear away at her husband over the coming year. Napoleon had great admiration for the Queen, referring to her as *"the only real man in Prussia."* [50]

As the day of the battle, that second day of December 1805, drew near, Adam Jerzy Czartoryski found himself huddled alongside Tsar Alexander at Olmütz as they reviewed General Kutusov's troops. That city was then part of the Austrian Empire, just over the mountain pass from the lands of Galicia to the east. Those lands had been, only a few decades before, stolen from Poland by Austria in the times of the Partitions. One must wonder what thoughts passed through Adam Jerzy's mind, as his own father had been one of the drafters of the 3 May 1791 Polish Constitution that had precipitated two wars that would be lost to the Russians and their Prussian allies, opening the way for the last two Partitions of their beloved homeland.

If Napoleon was drawn to Austerlitz by destiny, then Marek Zaczek was dragged along by his Emperor's firm grasp on the Polish cavalier's career. Napoleon was an ardent believer in fate and omens, despite his claim to the opposite. He refused to release Marek from the *Grande Armée*'s Imperial Guard. This young Polish officer had brought him good luck ever since Lodi in 1796.

---

[50] *The Napoleonic Wars: The Rise and Fall of an Empire, Todd Fisher, Gregory Fremont-Barnes, and Bernhard Cornwell (2004)* Oxford, England: Osprey Publishing.

To Marek's benefit, after leaving Boulonge, they were continually headed east. This pleased Zaczek immensely, and when Vienna fell to Napoleon on November 14th, Marek felt as close to home as he ever had been since the Duke Sdanowicz had committed himself, his uncle, and his cousins to the Austrian army. Marek had trained here in Vienna as an Austrian Uhlan on horseback, and later, after he was relieved of that honor, spent many months retraining in Vienna for the Austrian infantry.

One particular evening in late November of 1805, Marek found himself called to Schönbrunn Palace at the Emperor's request. He soon found himself alone in a room with the Emperor who studiously leaned over an unfurled map of the lands that surrounded Vienna. A fire crackled in the hearth, and a frost fogged the windows looking out over the expansive gardens.

The Schönbrunn Palace was not inside the walls of the city itself, as was the Winter Palace. The Schönbrunn had always been the Habsburgs' summer residence. Napoleon had no desire to bottle himself up inside the walls of the capital. He had always lived with his troops encamped around him, and here outside the city walls there was ample room for that. At the Schönbrunn Palace, south of the city's walls and ramparts, Napoleon was already planning his next great battle. He knew it would take place to the north, across the Danube River, and along the eastern edge of the route to Prague. Napoleon knew then that definitive battle would be fought near the town of Austerlitz.

"Do you know why I have asked specifically for you, Zaczek?" asked the Emperor. He did not look up, instead his nose hung suspended over the map like a beak of a hawk surveying the same countryside from its winged loft.

"No, Sire," Marek stated, "I only know it is a great honor."

"You were trained as an Austrian Uhlan, were you not?"

"Yes, Sire, until that was stripped of me."

"Yes, yes. The Austrians are fools. To take away the saddle from a man who makes it fly on the very wind. There are many ways to straighten a damaged arrow without forever removing it from the quiver."

"I am sorry, Sire," Marek answered. "I do not understand."

"The Austrians were idiots to take a cavalryman of your skill and instincts and force you to become infantry for whatever reason. Now, Zaczek, you have ridden these lands between Vienna and Prague many times, no?"

"Many times. Yes, Sire."

"Good. Tell me about this area here. I need to know every detail about the land that lies around it."

He stabbed his finger on the map.

"The Pratzen Heights, Sire?" Marek spent the next few hours describing the terrain surrounding the heights in great detail, including the approximate elevations of the hills, depths of its valleys and the course of those streams running through them, as well as the locations of the surrounding lakes.

"...It has already been a very cold November, Sire. I believe those lakes will be frozen solid enough to allow the transit of troops across them without fear of the ice breaking, but you may wish to have them tested," Marek said as he finished his discourse.

Napoleon had listened attentively to the young officer, interrupting him only sporadically with questions probing Marek's knowledge of the sight lines from those heights. The answers from the cavalryman pleased the Emperor. He seemed very satisfied with Marek's depth of knowledge of the area, as well as with his keen recollections of the terrain.

"Very good, Captain Zaczek," Napoleon said. "Tomorrow I will take you and a contingent of your Imperial Guardsmen along with myself and my marshals. We will reconnoitre these lands.

Even with your detailed descriptions bringing life to the lines of this map, this battle will be so momentous I must first see the grounds it is to be fought upon with my own eyes. The lay of the land will dictate the battle plan, although with your help, I already have a strong idea of how this will play out. *À demain*, Zaczek, you served me well this night."

Marek hesitated as the Emperor caught sight of his face upon looking up.

"What is it that troubles you, Zaczek?" Napoleon asked, having read the angst in his *capitaine* of the Imperial Guard.

"It is only a trifle, Sire," Marek said, "surely not important enough to raise to your attention, Emperor."

"Yet you hesitate long enough that I might ask," Napoleon said sharply, "so ask if you have something to ask. I have no time to waste!"

"There is an Austrian stableman, Sire," Marek began, "assigned to the Imperial Riding School here in Vienna."

"A countryman? A Pole?" asked the Emperor.

"Yes, Sire," Marek responded.

"Could this man be family to you?"

"Yes, Sire," Marek admitted, "the man is my uncle."

"And you, Zaczek, plan to release him as you did the two Austrian infantrymen at Augsburg."

"You know of this, Sire?"

"Your Emperor knows all, Zaczek."

Marek was stunned. His action was cause enough for court-martial. Yet until his request, Napoleon had failed to raise it with him, or he supposed any of the chain of leadership between them. Marek now regretted initiating this request from his Emperor.

"Worry not," the Emperor said. "I did not see fit to interrupt your plans. The two soldiers you released remain free. I am told they too were kin to you, Zaczek?"

"Yes, Sire," said Marek, lowering his head in shame. "They are my cousins."

"I can only hope you have a small family, Zaczek." Napoleon said, "or I will soon find myself fighting the Austrians and Russians alone."

Marek tried to suppress his laughter, but the joke was too quick upon him and his mirth escaped him. The Emperor did not laugh with him, but seemed not to be offended either.

"I am concerned, though, Zaczek, that when you lead your unit into the heat of battle with the enemy, among the ranks of both the Russians and Austrians many Poles will be forced to fight. I dread that when the sabres are raised in fury, you might hesitate, even for a second, in killing any Polish brethren fighting for the enemy that you can identify by feature or insignia."

"I am sure that I will not, Sire," Marek responded. "Anyone, even a Pole, who raises his arms against France, raises his arms against you. I would first rather give my own in battle life than fail you, Emperor."

"That is exactly my point, Zaczek," Napoleon said. "Any hesitation on the battlefield, even the slightest, could well claim from you your last breath. You are too well trained a cavalier to see flittered away by emotional indecision. Too natural a leader in battle to be wasted so. Even more, any hesitation on your behalf could imperil the men fighting under your command."

"Yes, Sire," Marek answered, his head still hung low.

"Look upon the eyes of your Emperor, Zaczek," Napoleon said. "You are a fearless warrior. This, I know. Never avert your eyes, it shows weakness."

Marek raised his head until he looked directly into the steely gaze of his Emperor. It seemed to sear through him, but he dared not look away. Napoleon then swept his gaze down over the map of the surrounding countryside.

"This man, your uncle, he is yours to do as you see fit," the Emperor said with a wave of his arm. "Leave his name with Roustam as you depart from me. He will be assigned to your ranks with the rise of the morning's light."

Raza Roustam was Napoleon's Mameluke man-servant and personal bodyguard. Bonaparte had brought him back from the campaign in Egypt, along with various units of captured Mameluke warriors. Roustam cut a towering figure, and no single man was closer to the Emperor. Rarely was Roustam more than a few steps away from his side, and at present stood guard outside the room's door to assure that Napoleon and Marek were not interrupted. He traveled with Bonaparte on every campaign, attending his every need, from overseeing the preparation of his meals, arranging his clothes, attending to his weapons, anticipating the books he would wish to read, laying out the maps he might wish to pore over, and even dousing Napoleon with his ritualistic *eau de cologne* each morning.

At the coronation ceremony, Roustam was very conspicuous among the throngs of onlookers inside Notre Dame de Paris Cathedral. He was dressed out in his most formal *"Oriental"* Mameluke trappings, including the turban wrapped loosely around his head. But Roustam was not Egyptian as everyone there assumed. His true nation of birth was Georgia in the Caucasus, although by bloodline he was said to be Armenian.

"*Merci*, Sire," Marek said as he moved to depart the room. The Emperor did not raise his head. Marek opened the door, took one last glimpse of the man over the map, and readied to step out.

"You will not release this man, Zaczek," his Emperor said at exactly the last second. "Should you ever again be caught releasing prisoners, you will be severely dealt with. You will train your uncle to fight for France, for the Empire, for me."

"Yes, Sire. But the man is not a soldier, just a lowly stableman." Marek was frozen in place, three-quarters shielded by the gilded wood of the massive oaken door.

"And does my army not have cannons that are in need of horses to pull them? A stableman *is* a soldier, Zaczek. Every man in an army is a soldier, necessitated with a given task. Otherwise he is superfluous and redundant, and is merely a dead weight that must be discarded. You personally are to make sure whatever task your stableman uncle is assigned, that he is indeed trained and capable of doing."

"Yes, Sire. *Merci beaucoup,* my Emperor."

"*À demain*, Zaczek," Napoleon repeated, as he rarely ever did, his thoughts already sunk into his imagined order of the coming battle.

Marek left, knowing he had come so very close to wallowing in catastrophe, but then thought over the outcome of his request. He was satisfied that he had secured the future for his Uncle Jacek. Just as he had his cousins, Andrzej and Bartek, by releasing them.

My Ciocia Ewelina will be ever so pleased, he thought.

On the morning of the second of December 1805, a chill permeated the wet mist that hung in the air like indecision. Marek was already risen by four in the morning, when his unit's cavalry riders were awakened.

The freezing temperatures reminded Marek of exactly one year ago, as he processed from the Tuilleries Palace to the Cathedral of Notre Dame de Paris for the Imperial Coronation. He thought of his Maya, later that day spotting her lovely excited face within Notre Dame, and then his thoughts raced ahead to that night in the apartment. That night with her consumed him, as did the next as well. She had seemingly come from nowhere to regain the hold on his heart. As he stood enveloped in the dark morning fog, he wondered if he would ever see her beautiful face again.

He had left his uncle the night before with an artillery unit on a hillside overlooking the town of Telnitz. He thought about the instruction he had given to Uncle Jacek. *Tend to the horses needed to pull and rapidly reposition the cannons. Follow the commands of the corporal in charge. Stay out of the artillerymen's way.*

Then Marek's thoughts departed that hillside artillery unit and shifted to his responsibilities in the Cavalry of the Imperial Guard. Marek was confident that Emperor Bonaparte's strategy would be successful. Napoleon had set an elaborate trap for the Russians and Austrians along the French right flank, its southernmost line.

Combined, the Austro-Russian armies numbered just over 90,000 troops. They believed the French to have less than 60,000, giving the Allies confidence they possessed a tremendous numerical advantage. They did not know that Napoleon had significantly more reserves hidden out of view, below the mist that lingered in the valley before the Pratzen Heights, as well as two more divisions coming up from Vienna. These "surprises" would bring the numbers between the two sides closer to parity.

The lay of the land was exactly as Marek had described it to the Emperor inside the Schönbrunn Palace. The day after he did so, Marek had joined the Emperor on horseback as they had reconnoitered the site. Napoleon carefully took in the rolling hills, the deep valleys and glistening lakes. He glanced at Marek, smiled tightly, as if acknowledging his recollections were indeed correct. Satisfied with the land's topography, the Emperor boasted to his marshals,

> ***"Gentlemen, examine this ground carefully, it is going to be a battlefield; you will have a part to play upon it."*** [51]

Napoleon had also extended a psychological ruse for his enemy. He had his troops take the superior position high upon the Pratzen Heights, only to cede it without a fight in the days before the battle. This unnecessary yielding of the high ground led the Russian and Austrian leadership to believe Napoleon did not have adequate troops for the battle.

This wove seamlessly into the fiction that Napoleon had fabricated to seduce his opponents into overconfidence. The Emperor had sent an envoy to Olmütz, the town headquartering Tsar Alexander and Austrian Emperor Phillip, with a message that Napoleon desired an armistice in lieu of a battle. Napoleon knew this would be perceived as the French not having equal numbers to effectively engage the Allies. In fact, Bonaparte had "hidden" 26,000 troops behind a great rise on the battlefield the day before the engagement. Under the cover of darkness, they filled the valley below the heights.

As the sun rose on the morning of the battle, these troops were obscured by a very dense low hanging mist. Napoleon took this natural veil covering his hidden troops as a beneficial omen.

---

[51] *"The Campaigns of Napoleon"*, David Chandler, Folio Society Edition, Vol. II, p. 36.
Sourced to *"Histoire et Mémoires"*, Philippe Paul, Comte de Ségur,
Volume 2, p. 279 Paris 1837

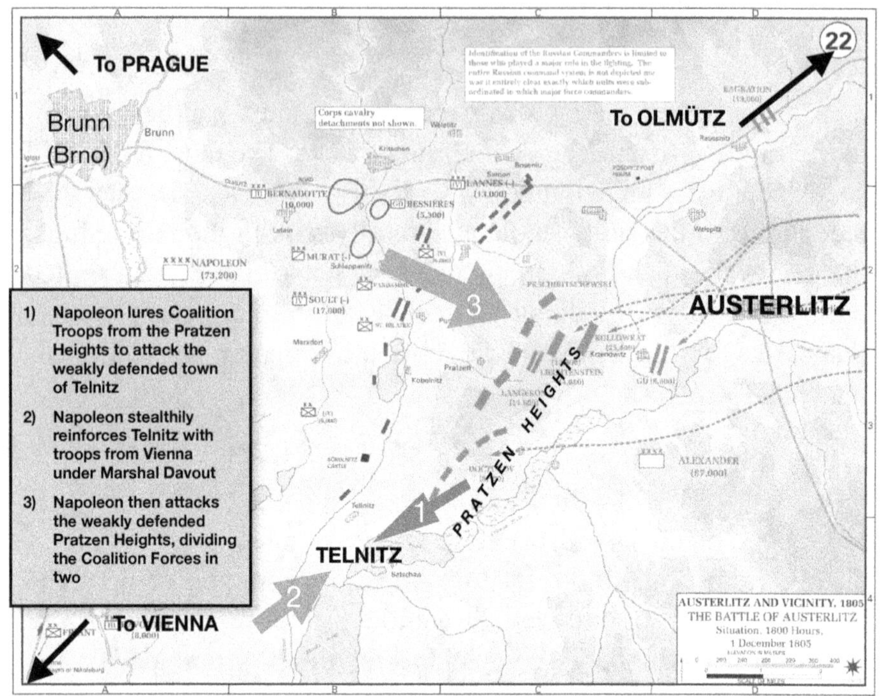

Figure 22: Map of the Order of Battle at Austerlitz

So instead of the 91,000 soldiers of the combined army of the Austrians/Russians going up against Napoleon's army of 57,000 as they thought, they faced instead a French force of 83,000. And this did not include the 6,600 coming in relief of Telnitz from Vienna under Marshal Davout. When those troops arrived, Napoleon would be in approximate parity with his enemy.

The dense mist lingered throughout the morning of the battle. But as the high ground was clear, Napoleon could see that the Austrian and Russian leadership and their troops had taken the Pratzen Heights, just as he had planned.

The Coalition allies noticed immediately the weakness of the forces on the French right flank near the southern village of Telnitz. Surely this must be due to the French shortage of troops, they thought. In assuming this, they had fallen right into the trap that Napoleon had set for them. All that remained was whether they would decide to move their forces to attack Telnitz.

A war council was called on the heights. The Austrians, beaten so often and so soundly by Napoleon in the field, cautioned restraint. Russian General Kutusov was particularly leery of such a weak flank being exposed so temptingly before him, as the Russian general was an experienced warrior. He expressed his concern to his Tsar. Yet, all were to be overruled.

Young Tsar Alexander, on the battlefield that morning, sought his first taste of glory in warfare. He ordered Kutusov to attack the French at Telnitz. He reasoned that by defeating the French in this undermanned southernmost flank, the Russians could force through the village and cut the French off from retreating back to Vienna. This was exactly what Napoleon had wished for his enemies to think. This was the trap he would lure them blindly into, and Alexander fell prey to Napoleon's bait.

Napoleon waited and watched as the Coalition forces drained from its center lines atop the Pratzen Heights and readied for an attack at Telnitz. When the bulk of the troops had significantly moved from the heights, they had played directly into Napoleon's plan. Napoleon waited until nearly 40,000 troops engaged his "weak" right flank at Telnitz. But the French forces there held, and would continue to hold, as Marshal Davout and his 6,600 reinforcements arrived from Vienna just in time to join the Emperor's troops at the town of Telnitz and assist in repelling the massive Coalition assault.

As if on cue, the morning mist burned away as the sun rose high in the sky. The worst of the fighting was already ongoing at Telnitz, but as the visibility cleared, the Coalition commanders that remained on the Pratzen Heights were shocked to then see the full magnitude of French forces aligned against them. Napoleon released his troops to attack the Coalition's nearly vacated center lines on the Heights. When the French indeed took that high ground and split the Coalition forces in two, they then had the Austro-Russian army near Telnitz trapped in a pincer movement.

Throughout the day heavy fighting would occur upon the Pratzen Heights as the Coalition forces attempted to regain them, but the French would end up securing this crucial position, and would thus command the entire battlefield until day's end.

Marek's Imperial Guard Cavalry unit was held in reserve throughout the battle, but when the Russians mustered a massive cavalry charge late in the day to the north of the Pratzen Heights, Napoleon released his Imperial Guard Cavalry to engage them. What ensued was perhaps one of the greatest cavalry battles of the entire length of the Napoleonic Wars.

Marek led his unit to meet the Russian charge. First, he had his cavalry carbineers dismount and fire a volley into the on-charging Russians. Then he released his brigade of Polish Lancers to attack. These horsemen he had trained himself, and perhaps were the most dangerous in all of Europe. They galloped without fear or reluctance directly into the charging Russian line of horsemen, softened but not stopped by the carbine volleys.

Their mounts drummed out a thunderous beat. The Polish horsemen rode first with lances upright, the red and white pennons dangling beneath the tips of their lances boldly decrying the colors of their homeland. As they had done for hundreds of years, they neared the Russians, lowered their weapons and engaged the onslaught. Soon they skillfully speared the lead Russian cavaliers in their chests, driving them from their saddles, snapping the shafts of their lances with the impact. In doing so, these lancers also broke the formations of the attacking tsarist horsemen.

This being done, the battle then degraded into an urgent struggle for life, to be won or lost by those most skilled in saddle and sabre. The lancers discarded their then useless weapons, most often with an impaled Russian upon it. These Poles surged deeply into the Russian line of forces, and continued to battle deadly with the furious strikes of their slicing sabres.

Once the Russian line was broken, the second wave of French Imperial cavaliers, their own sabres drawn high, furiously drove their steeds into the gaps in the Russian formation opened by the lancers. They fought valiantly to meet up with their ingested countrymen. Marek soon found himself immersed in a torrent of horsemen, as if his mount had been thrown into the waters of a raging river racing down an increasingly steep embankment.

The crash of cavalier upon cavalier, French and Polish upon Russian, created a lethal disruption to the Russian charge. Its impetus was arrested like the torrid waters of a deluge, white with frenzy, breaking against a wall of massive immovable boulders. The onslaught resulted in thrashing eddies - deadly swirls of frantic skirmishes of opposed horsemen fighting for their lives.

Marek's horse, trained for exactly this type of engagement, performed magnificently as its master slashed and thrust his sabre at any dark green image on horseback he could reach. Dark green was the color worn by the Russian cavalry and greatly distinguished them from the uniforms of his own unit.

Men from both sides dropped from their saddles, bleeding extensively from gaping wounds that pulled open slowly after the enemy sabre's initial slicing pass. Soon the floor of the battle was saturated in crimson, draining out in mournful agony as the battle raged above the dying. But Marek Zaczek, a masterful horseman ever since his peasant childhood, and a skilled warrior on horseback since his Uhlan training days, was not among the wounded.

Marek remained in his saddle, which danced in perfect unison with the warhorse beneath him. Any fear the *Capitaine* had was suppressed into a space so deep within him that he would only open it days later in his reflective solitude. But in the moment of battle, the young Imperial Guard *capitaine* had no time to think of his next sabre stroke or even who to select as his next victim.

Marek's actions were instinctual, impulsive, as if his sword pulled along his hand, and not the opposite. He had driven many Russians from their mounts, while taking not the slightest wound.

After what seemed an eternity of mayhem, with a carpet of death rolled out all around him, a Muscovite bugle sounded, and all green uniforms still erect in battle fought to disengage and recede to its call. Marek's unit had held the field and had blunted the massive Russian charge. He directed a portion of his unit to pursue the fleeing Russian cavaliers, not intending to re-engage them unless the Russians attempted to regroup, which they did not.

It was then that he realized he never thought as to whether any of the enemy horsemen might have been conscripted Poles. If they wore the dark green tunics, they simply died at his sword.

Having broken the Tsar's final onslaught, Marek led his surviving *chevaliers* back to their position atop the Pratzen Heights. Upon returning, a horseman relayed the message that the Emperor himself wished to congratulate him on his victory.

The day of the battle had all but passed, and it was nearing half past five in the afternoon. An early darkness had begun to descend over the battlefield. It seemed to blanket all the soldiers slain, and to concentrate the awful stench of death already in the air. It was not Marek's first battle by far, but it was perhaps one, more so than all others, that had been less a field of engagement than a staged butchery. Marek thought only of the French word *abattoir*, the place where cattle were taken to slaughter.

Marek found Napoleon, surrounded by an array of officers as the Emperor scanned over the frantic battlefields before him.

The Emperor barked out orders, never ceasing, but glowing with the aura of a great victory taken. He had achieved his original intention, to break the Coalition armies of the Austrians and Russians, yet the commander in him would not yield to his attack until all of his enemy's forces had surrendered or withdrawn.

Marek, still sweating profusely atop his mount, his heart beating wildly in his chest, was met by a crowd which parted in respect as he sidled up to the Emperor.

"Magnifique, mon Capitaine Polonais des Chevau-léger!" The Emperor praised him. "Your Lancers are the best in all of Europe, but of course, they had the very best horseman in Europe to train them, no? Here, you have earned this. Deliver this order to the artillery unit there." He pointed to the south, perhaps a mile off. "The battle is at its end. See how the Austrians flee? Give that unit this day's last bit of glory. They will one day tell their children and grandchildren of it."

Marek took the folded order and looked off in the direction of the battlefield. It was the artillery unit where Marek had stationed his Uncle Jacek. *With all that was going on across the battlefield, how could the Emperor possibly know this? Am I being rewarded for my courage in leading my cavaliers against the Russians with this trip to that particular artillery unit?*

Marek thought it as so he could check on the fate of his uncle. It was the only possible explanation. It was entirely consistent with who Napoleon was.

"I am so honored, Sire," Marek said, and not reading the order, set off on its delivery. As he rode along the battlefield, he avoided the strewn, dismembered bodies of infantrymen, more Austrians than French, who had given their all for their country. Marek looked up to see the white masses of surviving Austrian infantry scurrying in disarray across the frozen lakes below like packs of terrified dogs seeking refuge.

Marek reached the unit and passed the order to the corporal in charge. He read it and shrugged his shoulders at Marek, as if to say, *Pourquoi?* (*Why? For What Reason?*)

Marek, having not read the order, simply replied, "It is the order of your Emperor. Waste not a second in executing it."

Marek then looked over to his Uncle Jacek, who appeared shocked and disoriented by his first day ever in battle, and in having spent it in such close proximity to the roar of the cannons.

"I had hoped we were done. The Austrians are fleeing in a panic," Jacek said in a tremulous voice.

Marek did not respond, but instead thought only of his own first day of cannon fire. The difference being, as infantry, Marek had been shot at, while his uncle was assisting those firing.

The corporal gave a command to Jacek in French, which his uncle did not appear to understand.

"He says to help him reposition the cannon," Marek interpreted. "There is not enough time to fetch the horse."

Marek decided the two men alone could reposition the cannon and did not dismount to assist them.

"Where is your other artilleryman?" Marek asked the officer.

"Struck down in battle," said the corporal, "when we were hailed with fragments from an enemy round. This man here handled the shock of nearly being killed much better than many of my trained gunners. He did his duty and much more. Good thing you left him with us," continued the corporal as he and Jacek grunted to move the iron beast, "I gave him a course in loading the cannon by hand signals. Despite his not speaking French, he took to it very quickly. As I said, he did very well."

Jacek and the corporal repositioned the cannon so its muzzle pointed out over the frozen lakes. Ahead of them, the Austrian forces continued to flee in retreat across the expanses of white ice. The corporal and Uncle Jacek then retreated to behind the weapon, preparing to load it to fire in that direction. Marek could not understand why they were doing so. *Why would Emperor Bonaparte order them to ...*

Figure 23: The Battle of Austerlitz 2 December 1805
by François Gérard

"Allons, Allons!" *(Let's go! Let's go!)* the corporal said to the Pole, while making a movement with his fist forcing it through his other hand's half-open palm. Jacek immediately began the loading process.

"Bon, Bon!" said the corporal, his message learned earlier by Jacek as meaning *good, now step away as I light the fuse.*

No, no no! Marek thought as his stomach soured. He looked out upon the frozen lake, where the nearly indiscernible figures in white uniforms scurried across its pale, snow covered ice to safety, fleeing from the French forces. Then the cannon thundered, belching fire and smoke as it lurched back violently.

"Encore, encore!" yelled out the corporal. Jacek began the loading process even while the first ball was still in flight.

This can't be, Marek thought as the first cannonball roared and flew through its ballistic arc. It crashed down savagely piercing the ice of the frozen lake. Marek watched as a spider-like web raced across the surface. What must have been fifty men became trapped as the ice shattered and they fell through. Weighed heavy with the vestiges of war, they were soon fighting for their lives in the icy waters which they had moments before been fleeing over to safety.

Those poor bastards survived a day of horrible but honorable warfare only to be drowned in a pond like barn rats thrown in by mischievous peasant boys, Marek thought. After all the killing he had witnessed and even participated in this day, it was this unnecessary tragedy that brought tears to his eyes.

BOOM! Another cannon ball flew free from the shuddering, smoke-belching mass of iron that guaranteed another section of the lake would be taken out from the frantically retreating infantry.

"Allez, Allez!" The corporal yelled once more and the process repeated anew. Before the next shot could be fired, another round came from the cannon on the next hill, and then a third. Soon, more than twenty cannons took aim upon the perilous ice.

Marek saw no need for this inhumane treatment of the retreating enemy. It was as cowardly as shooting a fleeing soldier in the back. Marek watched as the entire lake was swept clear of its icy cover, and filled with the panicked flailing of drowning Austrian soldiers.

Then the next lake became the center of aim for the gunners. In all, hundreds of Austrian soldiers died attempting to escape across those placid lakes when they came under the deadly artillery fire. It sickened Marek, watching those men thrash about for their lives in the icy waters until its surface finally became as still and silent as when the ice was intact.

Chapter 23:
Lost Embers Of Love

Love, in that variety being the truest and deepest of all passions, is often appropriately described as a lightening strike. It can come from seemingly nowhere, blind those it encompasses, and fade away just as elusively. Yet the echo of its rare strike can ring in the mind and the heart forever.

Nelson returned home, at least in the dormant flesh, one last time. His flagship *HMS Victory* had to be towed back to England, as its battle damage was so extensive. At the mouth of the Thames, the Admiral's remains were transferred to a private yacht, and taken upriver to Greenwich, where they were carefully removed from the barrel of rum, placed in a lead container, which was then itself placed inside the coffin carved from the mast of the French flagship, *L'Orient*, as Nelson had earlier directed.

Nelson was to lie in state at Greenwich for three days, after which his coffin and remains were barged upriver, to the Admiralty. They were under the escort of none other than the Prince of Wales. At the Admiralty, they would rest in peace for the night awaiting their final journey.

Nelson was finally home.

The next morning, January 9th, 1806, Lord Horatio Nelson's remains undertook their last movement upon this earth. The funeral procession from the Admiralty to Saint Paul's Cathedral included over ten thousand members of the service, including admirals, captains, all the way to able seamen and soldiers. After a four hour service in Saint Paul's, his body was lowered through the floor of the transept to the crypt below.

To this day Nelson rests there. His remains, those of the greatest naval commander in Britain's illustrious history at sea, decay slowly to dust, forever entombed in that coffin made from the wooden mast of his French enemy.

All England mourned the loss of Lord Admiral Horatio Nelson. For every man, woman, and child, from the highest bred to the least privileged, were quick to give gratitude up to him that their island home was by the time of his funeral, and at the cost of his life, then safe from the peril of a Napoleonic military invasion.

In the decades that followed his death, a column bearing his statue would be erected in the space that would later become Trafalgar Square. In the century that followed, the Admiralty Arch would be constructed spanning the opening that lay between Nelson's Column and the Mall leading to Buckingham Palace. From up above his column, Nelson would forever look down upon the arch and beyond it to the palace. No greater tribute could be given him than to keep an eternal watch over his only superiors during his life on earth, those being the Sea Lords of the Admiralty and the British Monarchy.

Nelson, on his last sea voyage, had written a codicil to his Last Will and Testament. It was intended to provide for Lady Hamilton and Horatia in the circumstance of his death. It was prepared on the 19th of October 1805, and signed two days later, only hours before the commencement of the fighting that would ultimately take his life.

The codicil addressed Horatia in the ruse as being his adopted daughter, Horatia Nelson Thompson. It included the Admiral's desire for her from that point on to solely use the name Nelson. It was never enacted, as after his funeral it was presented to the Courts who quietly dismissed it as being invalid.

Alongside the codicil was found his last letter to Emma. Also dated October 19th, 1805, it read:

"My dearest Emma, the dear friend of my bosom.
The signal has been made that the Enemy's Combined Fleet
are coming out of Port. We have very little wind, so that I have
no hopes of seeing them before to-morrow. May the God of
Battles crown my endeavors with success; at all events,
I will take care that my name shall ever be most dear to you
and Horatia, both of whom I love as much as my own life.
And as my last writing before the Battle will be to you,
so I hope in God that I shall live to finish my letter after the
Battle. May Heaven bless prays your Nelson." [52]

Nelson's every wish came to pass, except the last as he never lived to affix his signature. A letter to Horatio was found accompanying Emma's letter, also finished but unsigned. It ended with the line,

"Receive, my dearest Horatia, the affectionate
parental blessing of your Father, Nelson." [53]

Assuming Lord Nelson first wrote the letter to his Emma, it is interesting that his last written words were to acknowledge his being the parent of Horatia. How meaningful this must have been to her throughout her long life which was to follow.

---

[52] *"The Life of Nelson"*, Captain A.T. Mahan, Easton Press Edition of 1897 text, Vol. II, p.365

[53] *"The Life of Nelson"*, Captain A.T. Mahan, Easton Press Edition of 1897 text, Vol. II, p. 366

It is interesting to consider the relationship between Lord Nelson and Lady Hamilton. It is nearly certain that their affections spanned only the seven years, eventful as they may have been, between the Battles of the Nile and Trafalgar. Yet, her heart attached itself so strongly and so steadfastly to his own. Was it because of her youth that she was infatuated with him? Or was it because throughout her young adult years, she had been sought after by men only as an instrument of beauty and illicit pleasures? Was Nelson the first man to dedicate his interests in her to qualities far beyond these? Was he the only man in her life to truly love her?

Emma certainly had stroked the vanities of the admiral, just as he had stroked those of hers. Yet she had many opportunities for affection beyond those offered by Nelson. She had the comfort and elegance of having been the British Ambassador's wife, in which she apparently found great comfort but little solace. Emma instead treated that relationship with the ultimate humiliation by devoting her heart to another.

Widowed after Sir Hamilton's death, Emma had, with Nelson away at Copenhagen, received offers of marriage from several prosperous gentlemen and even drew the rather focused attention of the Prince of Wales. Yet, she disregarded all of these opportunities. Why? She certainly knew Nelson would never prove to be as extravagantly rich as any of these men, so only one answer logically remained.

Despite Emma's flirtatious and attention-seeking life, she had found in Nelson something no other man could deliver to her - in a word, love. After being handed over from one much older man to another, Nelson was much closer to her own age, being only some seven years her senior. His devotion to her was overwhelming, going so far as to jettison his own wife and endure the public ridicule which followed. He certainly knew of what was being openly written about them in the London newspapers.

Yet still, the hearts of Emma and Nelson burned bright with the flames of true love, leaning against each other like logs in a bonfire's stack, each bearing the other's support. And as they became consumed by the inferno which followed, they pressed harder into each other until they crumbled into a single, searing pile of red hot embers. Embers which would only grow cold and sooted with ash by the unexpected wash of a fresh wave of fate.

Emma was devastated by the news of Nelson's death which she received in private at Merton Place. Its impact would forever change the trajectory of her life. While alive at sea, Nelson left her tragically alone. In death, he left her disastrously crippled. Emma would write in her diary,

"They brought me word, Mr Whitby from the Admiralty. 'Show him in directly,' I said. He came in, and with a pale countenance and faint voice, said, 'We have gained a great Victory.' – 'Never mind your Victory,' I said. 'My letters – give me my letters' – Captain Whitby was unable to speak – tears in his eyes and a deathly paleness over his face made me comprehend him. I believe I gave a scream and fell back, and for ten hours I could neither speak nor shed a tear." [54]

Emma lay in bed grieving for weeks, and what few visitors she did receive, she did so in tears. She found herself increasingly isolated, neither invited to nor allowed to attend the funeral. No, Lady Emma Hamilton would not be extended this dignity, if only because she was the woman who had brought upon the Viscount Nelson his only perceived indignity in life - shame.

The codicil to Nelson's Will was ignored, and the bulk of Nelson's estate was awarded to his brother, William, who quickly distanced himself from Emma. She was awarded Merton Place, a sum of two thousand pounds, and a meager annual allowance of only five hundred pounds.

---

[54] *"Nelson: A Personal History,"* Christopher Hibbert, 1994, Da Capo Press

Emma soon found herself unable to keep up with the expenses of Merton Place. The stress of trying to do so drove her to drink in excess. She was a battered soul, lost in a typhoon of events beyond her control. For the first time since moving in with Charles Greville as a teen, she had no one to look after her affairs.

Perhaps, it was the affairs of her heart that needed the most attention. The tide had turned in her life, she found herself no longer the center of attention of any man. She was after Nelson's death only the recipient of her nation's resentment. This thrust her deeper in to a maelstrom of debt and despair, her dependencies on drink and drug (laudnum) ever increasing.

Emma Hamilton leveraged every line of credit she possibly could. Her woes were ignored by Nelson's family, until finally she had but a single recourse. On the first day of July 1814, she crossed the English Channel with Horatia on a private vessel in order to evade British law that would otherwise have had her arrested and quite possibly imprisoned for her debts. She had only fifty pounds sterling to her name. It is ironic that the very waterway which her love, Admiral Nelson, had given his life to keep open became her only route of escape, as if he had protected her passage to the land and people he so detested.

By the time Emma took up residence in Calais, France, Napoleon had already been exiled to Elba. Emma would die in that French port town on the 15th of January 1815, two full months before her love's *bête noire,* Bonaparte, would escape Elba and begin his infamous Hundred Days to Waterloo.

Emma's daughter Horatia would go on to live a long and mostly quiet life. She returned not only to England, but to the shire of Norfolk, where her father had been born. There she married a small town clergyman, like her grandfather, in 1822. She died in 1881 at the age of eighty years, spanning from the Napoleonic Wars through forty-four years of the reign of Queen Victoria.

Love's embers, so suddenly quenched for Lady Hamilton upon the death of Nelson, were having a much more gradual remission between Emperor Napoleon and his Empress Joséphine. What was needed most to pacify the Emperor was an heir, and that most desired gift was not forthcoming from his bride. The Emperor did not know whether the problem originated in his own seed, or in the fertility of the Empress' womb. Due either either source, children were not forthcoming, and their romantic passions faded over the years.

This can readily be seen in the fading emotion for her in his letters. After the ferocious fighting at the Battle of Austerlitz was victoriously behind him, Napoleon penned only a brief, dry, factual letter to Joséphine:

"I have beaten the Austro-Russian army commanded by the two Emperors. I am a little weary. I have camped in the open for eight days and as many freezing nights. Tomorrow I shall be able to rest in the castle of Prince Kaunitz, and I should be able to snatch two or three hours of sleep there. The Russian army is not only beaten but destroyed. I embrace you.

- Napoleon." [55]

By the time of this letter's writing, Napoleon and Joséphine had been wed for over nine and a half years. It had been a near decade of incredible highs for their relationship, which seemed to be drawn from a fairy tale. Yet, this fabled marriage was to be undercut by astonishing acts of betrayal. And these appeared nearly as soon as the wedding celebration itself had been concluded.

---

[55] *"The Campaigns of Napoleon"*, David Chandler, Folio Society Edition, Vol. II, p. 55. Sourced to Letter to Joséphine, quoted by C. Manceron, *"Austerlitz"*, Paris, 1962

Famously, Napoleon had left their matrimonial bed in March of 1796 after their spending only two days together as man and wife. He departed for Milan, where he would take up command of the French *Armée d'Italie*. He would write passionate letters to Joséphine throughout his time away while on campaign and incessantly pleaded with her to join him there.

Joséphine always found convenient reasons to not accept her husband's invitations. She was enjoying the time she was spending with her lover, a much more junior army officer, during Napoleon's absence. Separated by the Alps, Joséphine was not as discreet as she should have been, for Napoleon's family was still residing at the capital. Initially, Bonaparte remained ignorant of Joséphine's infidelities, but word of her tryst would soon enough reach him, but before it did, Napoleon wrote to her with fervent love and emotion.

The following excerpt is taken from a letter written by Napoleon in Milan to Joséphine in Paris just after their separation:

"Since I left you, I have been constantly depressed. My happiness is to be near you. Incessantly I live over in my memory your caresses, your tears, your affectionate solicitude. The charms of the incomparable Joséphine kindle continually a burning and a glowing flame in my heart. When, free from all solicitude, all harassing care, shall I be able to pass all my time with you, having only to love you, and to think only of the happiness of so saying, and of proving it to you? ... I hope you will soon join me. I thought that I loved you months ago, but since my separation from you I feel that I love you a thousand fold more. Each day since I knew you, have I adored you yet more and more. This proved the maxim ... that 'love comes all of a sudden,' to be false." [56]

---

[56] Letter from Napoleon Bonaparte to his wife Joséphine, 1796.

Napoleon began to hear stories of her infidelities in Paris during that campaign, though he still could not bring himself to believe them. One can clearly read his concerns which accusingly bleed through in his letters:

"I write you, my beloved one, very often, and you write very little. You are wicked and naughty, very naughty, as much as you are fickle. It is unfaithful so to deceive a poor husband, a tender lover! Ought he to lose all his enjoyments because he is so far away, borne down with toil, fatigue, and hardship? Without his Joséphine, without the assurance of her love, what is left him upon earth? What can he do? Adieu, adorable Joséphine; one of these nights your door will open with a great noise; as a jealous person, and you will find me on your arms.
A thousand loving kisses." [57]

Finally, Joséphine conceded in November 1796 to join Napoleon at Milan. The first night they spent together in Italy was only their third together as husband and wife. He once again immediately abandoned her in that city to attend to military affairs in the nearby countryside. He was away for six days. In that span of time, he wrote to her often. Here is an excerpt from his first letter since departing from her:

"My waking thoughts are all of thee. Your portrait and the remembrance of last night's delirium have robbed my senses of repose. Sweet and incomparable Joséphine, what an extraordinary influence you have over my heart." [58]

But when he returns to Milan he finds that Joséphine has left the city to escape to Genoa. Napoleon is outraged, assured that she has gone to meet her lover in the Italian seaport. He waits nine days before sending the following letter, but it is still full of rage:

[57] Letter from Napoleon Bonaparte to his wife Joséphine, 1796.

[58] Letter from Napoleon Bonaparte to his wife Joséphine, 1796.

"I don't love you anymore; on the contrary, I detest you. You are a vile, mean, beastly slut. You don't write to me at all; you don't love your husband; you know how happy your letters make him, and you don't write him six lines of nonsense…

***Soon, I hope, I will be holding you in my arms;
then I will cover you with a million hot kisses,
burning like the sun at the equator"*** [59]

Later, after hearing rumors about Joséphine's trysts from the lips of his own brother, Joseph, Napoleon finally confronted his wife. Joséphine initially and vehemently denied everything. She offered for him to pursue a divorce if he believed she has been unfaithful. Her ploy was successful.

Napoleon did not initiate a divorce, but decided instead to begin taking mistresses of his own. And in a very unexpected and unanticipated response, Joséphine abandoned all lovers other than Napoleon from that point on.

After having initiated his first affair with the wife of a subordinate officer in Italy, Napoleon wrote to his brother:

"The veil is torn … It is sad when one and the same heart is torn by such conflicting feelings for one person…I need to be alone. I am tired of grandeur, all my feelings have dried up. I no longer care about glory. By twenty nine I have exhausted everything." [60]

That letter to his brother was never delivered. It was among the possessions of a French courier captured by the British. Soon, it was printed in the London papers. All of France thereafter knew of the infidelities of Napoleon and Joséphine. The couple that had been thought to be so deeply committed to each other proved to be as susceptible to temptation as any other union of man and wife.

---

[59] Letter from Napoleon Bonaparte to his wife Joséphine, 1796.

[60] Letter from Napoleon Bonaparte to his brother Joseph, 1798.

Later, on becoming First Consul, Napoleon would profess,

"I am not a man like others, and moral laws or the laws that govern conventional behavior do not apply to me. My mistresses do not in the least engage my feelings. Power is my mistress." [61]

Over the following years their passions would cool considerably, although their marriage remained amicable. When Napoleon informed his family he intended to crown Joséphine as Empress, there was great consternation from his siblings. His brother Joseph refused to attend the ceremony and his mother, not wishing to take sides, also abstained. Napoleon claimed that his love for Joséphine required him to crown her Empress of France.

And so their marriage would continue, with Napoleon infatuated only by his conquests of war. Joséphine increasingly isolated herself at their country home named *Malmaison*, for the most part forgoing the regal palaces, châteaux and estates at their disposal. *Malmaison*, by comparison to the Tuileries or Fountainebleu, was quite modest. At *Malmaison*, she would tend to the gardens, and immerse herself in the house's upkeep, as her husband conquered most of Continental Europe.

It would be late in 1806, when Napoleon was far off in Eastern Europe, that he would take up with a Polish mistress, one that would fall deeply in love with the Emperor. In doing so, she would bring his troubled marriage to Joséphine to a fateful conclusion.

The woman known throughout France as Joséphine de Beauharnais (after her first husband), and later the Empress Joséphine Bonaparte, was actually named at birth Marie-Josèphe-Rose Tascher de la Pagerie. She would be the first of three Maries that would so fatefully impact Napoleon's life. The second Marie, the Countess Marie Walewska of Poland, Napoleon would soon come to meet him as he pressed east in the closing months of 1806.

---

61 PBS. Documentary: *"Napoleon"* written, and produced by David Grubin, 2000

Part Three:

Lovers

And

Conquests

"Amor vincit omnia,

et nos cedamus amori"

A Latin Proverb, meaning,

"Love conquers all things,

so we too shall yield to love.)"

Chapter 24: The March to Berlin

November 1806

Anticipation hollows out both the heart and soul of a soldier who hungers for the sweet comfort of his lover's embrace. In the case of Marek Zaczek, *Captaine* of Napoleon's Imperial Guard Lancers, the physical lapse between he and Maya had, by then, been a full two years. And a very consequential two years they were, with nearly all of Marek's time spent away from Paris while at war with the various powers of Europe.

Marek and Maya had last parted in December of 1804, only days after the Emperor's coronation. What a whirlwind of emotion those precious days had been, ever since her arrival in Paris. Marek had been thunderstruck once more by her sheer beauty as she stepped off the carriage in the *Place de Grand Louis,* undiminished by the ravages of childbearing, and untouched by the passing of time. That day his heart, which had become weeded with an overgrowth of bitterness, was swept clean as if by the pass of a mystical scythe. It soon raced anew with a beat metered out by an uncontrollable flash of desire. It replaced the empty lust which had until then consumed him, but which was never fully satisfied.

Marek's heart reawakened as he watched Maya walk toward him in that Parisian square, reminding him of how their souls had melded together as children on the *folwark.* It produced a state of bliss in him that no number of sexual conquests could ever achieve. In that moment, the fleshy escapadess of his past clung to him coldly like the lifeless dirt of an awaiting vacant grave.

It was after the coronation, the grand balls and the receptions had been attended, after all the champagne and *foie-gras* had been consumed, that Marek came to realize how wastefully he had squandered his most precious gift - the limited time with his love, Maya. For only hours after the consummation of their love, the Emperor himself had denied their joint dream of returning together to Warsaw. Only then did the two lovers fully realize the fragility that threatened the tenderness of their reunited embraces. They spent their last night together consuming the bodies, dreams and souls of each other, yet even that ecstasy was tempered by their knowing that Maya would begin her sojourn home the next morning without him. The trek of over a thousand kilometers might as well have been to the other end of the earth. For each league that Maya travelled tore away painful strands of Marek's soul. It was as if the sins of Marek's lustful past were a cat-of-nine-tails that with each bounce and sway of her carriage flailed away at his tortured spirit.

Over the two years since being so cruelly separated from her, Marek stayed true. He could think of no one but her, desired no body but hers. Unlike the purely carnal desires which consumed him before Maya arrived in Paris, Marek longed not only to immerse himself in her physically, but more so to take solace in her beauty, her kindness, and the sweet lure of her companionship. He knew she would reciprocate in kind by staying true to him, and that upon their reuniting, their two spirits would soulfully diffuse into one. Then there would be no Marek, no Maya, only their joint existence - only "them."

Marek's anticipation to see her again gnawed at his gut as they neared what had been the border of Poland. They were but days away from Warsaw and the freezing chill of December had descended upon them from an overhead canopy of heavy gray skies. The Emperor, protected by Marek's guard unit, demanded to continue eastward from Berlin in pursuit of what remained of the Prussian forces, before they were fully strengthened by the armies of their Coalition allies, the Russians.

The Prussian King Frederick Wilhelm III and his Queen Louise had fled the capital of Berlin to take refuge in Königsberg, East Prussia. These were the Prussian lands that dated back to the days of the Teutonic Knights, the lands that Marek knew from his father's tales had been stolen from Poland centuries before even the first partition. *Now to win them back,* he dared to think.

A year earlier, after the battle of Austerlitz had been won so decisively by Napoleon on December 2nd, 1805, peace seemed to settle over the continent. The very next day, the Austrian and Holy Roman Emperor, Phillip, begged Napoleon in person for a cessation of hostilities. The price he agreed to was an onerous one, as he surrendered to the French Emperor the Netherlands, and various states along the Rhine, along with committing to a crushing sum for reparations. But having done so, the War of the Third Coalition was then over.

There was of course, still England and Russia who remained at war with Napoleon. After Austerlitz, the badly routed Russian army had escaped eastward into their pilfered Polish provinces to regroup. The battle had been such a complete thrashing that when English Prime Minister William Pitt the Younger was shown a map of Europe after Austerlitz, he was quoted as having declared prophetically:

"Roll up that map; it will not be wanted these ten years." [62]

By the end of the very next month, January 1806, Prime Minister Pitt was dead. But just as Austerlitz had been Napoleon's consummate victory, the crushing of the French and Spanish fleets by Nelson at Trafalgar was equally devastating. England was safely delivered from the threat of a Channel invasion, but Britain still could not rival Napoleon's land forces. England controlled the seas, and France the lands of the European Continent.

---

[62] Stanhope, Philip Henry [5th Earl Stanhope] (1862). *Life of the Right Honourable William Pitt, Vol. IV*. John Murray. p. 369.

This period would come to be known as the *"Time of the Whale and the Elephant,"* with England and France each being invincible upon their own domains.

After the Battle of Austerlitz, with Russia withdrawn and Britain held at bay, the only other major military force to concern Napoleon was the once highly revered Prussian army. Prior to Austerlitz, Tsar Alexander had spent much of the summer in Berlin attempting to persuade the indecisive Prussian ruler Frederick Wilhelm III to join the war against the French, over the objections of the Russian Foreign Minister, Adam Czartoryski.

While the King of Prussia demurred, there was a strong faction building in his court that favored war. It was led by his own wife, the beautiful and strong-willed Queen Louise of Mecklenburg. She reportedly used every influence she had over her husband, including withholding the privileges of the royal matrimonial bed. But after the trouncing of the Austrian and Russian armies at Austerlitz, Frederick Wilhelm was convinced more than ever that he was correct to maintain Prussia's neutrality.

But by late 1806, the King of Prussia was finally persuaded to declare war on France by an arousing of the populace. Despite their country being neutral, Napoleon demanded the Prussians cease all trade with Britain. The British then boarded Prussian ships and confiscated cargo. Outraged, the militaristic young men that made up the Prussian *Noble Guard* incited the citizenry by defiantly sharpening their sabres on the steps of the French Embassy in Berlin. This insult did not go unnoticed by Napoleon.

In August, Napoleon dissolved the Holy Roman Empire, which had stood for over a thousand years, since Charlemagne's founding of it on Christmas Day 800 AD. The Empire's dissolution was quite possibly one insult too many for Frederick Wilhelm to ignore. Among his many titles was being named the Elector of Brandenburg to the Holy Roman Empire.

In October 1806, the King of Prussia sent a letter of ultimatum to Napoleon, demanding his answer by the 8th of October. The Emperor responded not in writing, nor by envoy, but by attacking Prussian forces on the very next day. Then, a few days later, on October 14th, the twin battles of Jena and Auerstädt were won decisively by the French under Napoleon's command. The dual victories decimated the bulk of the fabled Prussian military, and soon led to the fall of the capital of Berlin.

During the battle of Jena that day, Marek would become forever intertwined with Marshal Michel Ney in a close relationship that would ultimately be severed only by death.

During the Battle of Jena, the impetuous Marshal Ney initially followed Napoleon's orders to the letter regarding the positioning of his troops. Yet, as the hours of the morning's battle passed by, Ney became impatient as they were continued to be held in reserve. Then, without any command to do so from the Emperor, Marshal Ney ordered his infantry to attack a stronghold held by the Prussian forces. Ney's troops were successful in that charge, but in their haste they had penetrated the enemy's ranks too deeply and soon found themselves entirely cut off from Napoleon's other forces. Surrounded by Prussians, Ney ordered his infantry into a defensive position known as *Le Carré, or the Square.*

During the time of the Napoleonic Wars , *"The Square"* was a drilled formation undertaken by infantry whenever one's forces were completely surrounded by the enemy. In that way, each of the four outward faces of the square could fire upon the attacking or circling enemy, while those soldiers on the square's interior were somewhat protected. However, the square's defensive protection would erode rapidly with time as the attrition of the attack took its toll. The square was intended as a last ditch measure of survival until help could break through and rescue the surrounded unit. With his forces enveloped amongst the Prussians, Ney needed to be rescued and for it to happen quickly.

On the battlefield that day, Napoleon recognized the dire position in which Marshal Ney's ill-fated charge had placed his troops. He ordered another of his marshals, Marshal Lannes, to fight through the surrounding Prussian forces to rescue Ney's Corp. Marshal Lannes immediately requested the support of *Capitaine* Zaczek's Polish Lancers from the Imperial Guard and was granted their support. The remainder of the Imperial Guard was then moved to the center of Napoleon's line, to sure up the position from which Lannes' troops were vacated.

Marek led his Lancers through the swarm of Prussian cavalry surrounding Marshal Ney's imperiled troops. The charge of the Poles in its v-shaped line came as quite a surprise to the Prussians, many of whom turned in their saddles just in time to be run through by the razor sharp tips of the Polish lances. As they were driven from their saddles, it was not uncommon for the shafts of the lances to snap, ripping a final searing flash of agony for those already mortally impaled. The Prussian cavalry could not flatten the wedged line of Poles attacking on horseback. The precision of the lancer's attack opened a corridor through the Prussians for the forces of Marshal Lannes to initially reach and then extract Marshal Ney's troops from the deadly *mêlée*.

During the course of this extraction, Marshal Ney mounted his horse only to have it quickly shot out from under him. As Ney rose from the dirt, stunned but unharmed, a Prussian Dragoon spotted the Marshal and immediately drew his sabre as he reined his horse about to close in on the French officer from behind.

Marek recognized the Dragoon's intention and raced his horse to intercept the Prussian. Marshal Ney was flailing his arms to signal Zaczek as he neared, oblivious to the risk from the Prussian horseman closing on him from behind. It was at that point that Marek realized he was too late to intercept the Dragoon, who had raised his sabre high, intent on decapitating the Marshal.

Both Marek and the Dragoon advanced such that they would each arrive upon Marshal Ney at nearly the same time, but with the Dragoon being just ahead of Zaczek. Marek thought, *if only I had another lance I could save him,* but Marek had already broken off his weapon in the chest of another Prussian rider.

Just as the Dragoon leaned forward in his saddle for the fatal strike, Marek screamed to Ney in French, *"tomber au sol!"*

Marshal Ney heeded Marek's instruction without any hesitation and dropped immediately to the ground, just as the Dragoon's sabre laterally swept the air inches above the Marshal's head. Had the Dragoon aimed for the chest and not the neck, Marek thought, Ney would surely have received a mortal blow. Instead, he lay on the ground as the Prussian's steed raced overhead.

Marek had already drawn his own sabre. The swing of the Dragoon's weapon, having missed, left the Prussian in an exposed position, after his arm had swept across his own chest. As the Prussians fielded no body armor at that time such as the metal breastplates worn by the French *Cuirassiers*, Marek's sabre struck the Dragoon across the exposed upper right shoulder and high in his chest. Marek failed to unseat the Dragoon, but knew from the resultant force upon the weapon in his hand that the sabre's bite had sliced deeply into the chest of the enemy.

The wounded Dragoon proved unable to raise his right arm after the strike. His face was white with disbelief. He turned his horse back to Zaczek, who had already wheeled and was again charging. The Dragoon fumbled with his left hand for his pistol.

The Prussian raised his gun, but the pain searing through him caused his left hand to shake violently. Marek swung his sabre at the enemy as the pistol shot rang out. Its ball found Marek's right arm, but went cleanly through the Pole's upper limb.

The burn in Marek's upper extremity was intense, unlike any other wound he had ever had. Yet, because the ball struck no bone, Marek's thrust, already in progress, was true. His sabre again slashed deeply, slicing the Dragoon's chest open in the other direction. The result was to mark the Prussian cavalier with a heaving "X"-shaped chest wound. The Dragoon looked down incredulously as blood gushed in crimson spurts from his chest. The warrior then dropped the pistol, as it was useless after having fired its one shot. He then slumped over in his saddle using both arms in a futile attempt to stem the wound's immense flow of his blood, and thus his life.

The stunned Dragoon was violently pulled from his mount by Marshal Ney, who then climbed into the enemy's saddle to commandeer the Prussian's horse.

"You saved my life, *Capitaine* Zaczek," Ney shouted as he reined in the animal, "a debt I hope one day to repay. But for now, let us return to the Emperor's line in haste."

As one might imagine, from that point on, Marshal Ney was always partial to Marek Zaczek. They would fight on together until the very last of the Emperor's battles at Waterloo.

As Napoleon commanded the action throughout the Battle of Jena, the Emperor thought he had engaged the main body of the Prussian forces. It was not until that battle was over that Napoleon learned he was fighting only a massive flank of the Prussian forces, and that his Marshal Davout had in fact engaged the main body of the Prussians ten miles away at Auerstädt. That battle pitted the outnumbered Davout against none other than King Frederick Wilhelm III, who proved more indecisive than usual. The Prussian king thought he was on the battlefield facing Napoleon himself, and feared making a mistake that might cost him his life. It was that very fear of Napoleon that allowed Davout and his forces to claim victory at the Battle of Auerstädt.

At the end of that day, at both Jena and Auerstädt, the Prussian forces could not match the agility of the French *Grande Armée*. This was very admirably demonstrated in the charge of Zaczek's cavalry against the Prussian Dragoons. Yet agility of its forces was not the only issue affecting the Prussian army. The Prussian military command was desperately outdated, as was its leadership. Their Generals were most often in their seventies and eighties in age, and even their newest ascending military leader, General Gebhard Leberecht von Blücher, was already in his sixties. They proved no match for Napoleon, then only thirty-seven years old, in terms of energy, planning or strategy. The Prussian army, under the inept leadership of Frederick Wilhelm III, proved to be but a shell of what it had once been under Frederick the Great.

After the dual victories of Jena-Auerstädt, the road to Berlin was essentially open. As he approached the capital, Napoleon made a point to stop and visit the tomb of Frederick the Great. Upon arriving at the town of Potsdam, the French Emperor went to *Sanssouci Palace*, expecting to find Frederick the Great's remains buried in the graveyard of the home where he had lived. Rumors had reached Paris that this Prussian king had desired to be buried there with his beloved greyhounds. As it had turned out, his successor had discounted this provision of his Last Will and Testament, and instead had the Prussian king buried in Potsdam's Garrison Church graveyard. Years later, Frederick the Great's remains would be exhumed, and his request would be honored.

Napoleon went to the Church Graveyard and spent a full ten minutes standing in reverence over the Prussian king's grave. Frederick the Great, after all, had been a man he had studied and truly respected for his military leadership. Marek stood nearby, his battalion standing guard as the Emperor paid his respects. Marek wondered if Bonaparte secretly wished he could have faced Frederick the Great in battle as a worthy adversary, instead of his timorous great-nephew, Frederick Wilhelm III.

In any case, as he departed the gravesite, the Emperor ordered the confiscation of the monarch's military awards, including Frederick the Great's sword, medals and even his general's uniform sash. They were to be boxed up and sent to Paris. Napoleon considered this petty larceny in itself to be a form of reverence.

Less than two weeks after the Battles of Jena–Auerstädt, on October 27th, 1806, Napoleon entered Berlin victoriously. He led his forces in a parade through the Brandenburg Gate. It had been constructed only a little over a decade earlier by the current king's father, Frederick Wilhelm II, and was already one of the best known landmarks of all the European capitals. It was dedicated in honor of Frederick the Great's many military victories. Emperor Napoleon was so impressed by it that he ordered the statue which adorned the top of the Brandenburg Gate to be dismantled and shipped to back to Paris. *The Quadriga,* as the statue was known, was of the goddess of victory driving a chariot pulled by four war horses racing abreast. In Paris, it would join a similar sculpture absconded from Venice, the fabled *Four Horsemen of Saint Mark.*

If the French occupation of Berlin that followed was not insulting enough, Emperor Napoleon ordered the captured Prussian *Noble Guard* be paraded in shame through the capital to the French Embassy's steps where they had so audaciously sharpened their sabres before the war. There, they were left in chains, as if to warn the Prussian populace of ever again giving the support of their armies to bring war against France.

Even the presentation of the key to Berlin to the conquering Napoleon came as a shock to the Prussian leadership remaining in the capital. Napoleon had the Prussian Prince of Hatzfeld arrested for spying immediately after accepting the city's key from him. Though the prince was later released, this along with the vengeful treatment of the *Noble Guard* convinced Berliners that Bonaparte was not a conqueror who should be insulted in any manner.

King Frederick Wilhelm III, his lovely Queen Louise, and their court, as well as all their remaining armies, had by that point, fled eastward to Königsberg in East Prussia. That land safely adjoined the lands of Russia, and from there the Prussians could reunite with the forces of the Tsar's army to prepare for meeting Napoleon again in battle. Both the Russian Tsar Alexander and the Prussian King Frederick Wilhelm III were confident that Napoleon could not resist pursuing them there.

Before chasing the Prussians further eastward, while still residing in the Prussian capital, Napoleon famously issued his Berlin Decree on the 21st of November 1806. It instituted his Continental System, forbidding any European state, even those proclaiming to be neutral, from engaging in trade with Great Britain. Napoleon changed tactics in that if he could not invade that *"nation of shopkeepers,"* [63] than he would assure their financial ruin by isolating them from trade with all of Europe. In this way, he hoped that their desperate pleas to His Majesty's Government would result in the Crown seeking a settlement with the Emperor. This blockade would, in the end, prove an overreach that would later draw Napoleon into disastrous campaigns in both the Iberian Peninsula and his attack upon Russia itself.

In Berlin, Marek's wounded arm was cared for. It was a clean penetration through the muscle, just below the shoulder. Luckily, it missed any major arteries. The wound healed quickly, but the pain lingered, first in his body, and then much longer in his mind. It had been the first time since his joining in fighting for Napoleon and France that Marek had felt vulnerable. It brought back the spectre of death he had come so close to succumbing to after rescuing Maya from the attack of the Cossacks a dozen years earlier. For the first time since then, he feared he might die in battle before ever seeing her lovely face again.

----

[63] Oxford Dictionary of Quotes, Sixth Edition, p. 556, attributed to
Napoleon in Exile by Barry E. O'Meara (1822(

Having spent nearly a full month in Berlin, Napoleon was anxious to gain control of the Prussian lands between the Oder and Vistula Rivers. This was territory that had once belonged to the Polish State prior to the Partitions. Napoleon had taken two actions prior to leaving Berlin. First, he had dispatched forces under General Dąbrowski to raise an insurrection against the Prussian forces still scattered throughout those lands. Second, he ordered several of his marshals with their corps to advance to, but not beyond, the banks of the Vistula. This they would do by various routes, so they were not competing with each other for food and shelter to be foraged along the way.

Marek had healed barely enough from his wounds by the last days of November to return to the command of his battalion of Polish Lancers within the Imperial Guard. He had been advised to recuperate longer in Berlin, which he refused. Instead, he demanded to accompany the Emperor on his travel eastward into the lands that had once been Poland, but were still then under Prussian control. They departed Berlin at 3 AM on the morning of the 25th of November. With each fall of his horse's hooves, pain seared throughout Marek. Still, he was honored that Napoleon ordered him to be retained close at hand, so that the Emperor could readily query his Polish *Capitaine* on the landscape of his home territory's soil, as well as utilize his services as an interpreter.

Of course, in the months ahead there would be other Poles that the Emperor would consult, especially Dezydery Chłapowski, the famous Polish cavalry rider who had recently served as a Prussian Dragoon under General Scharnhorst. Chłapowski awaited the Emperor's arrival in Poznań, the city that was the approximate halfway mark between Berlin and Warsaw.

The month of November had indeed been a remarkable and hectic period in the Polish territories. General Dąbrowski had been sent ahead of the main French forces not only to raise an insurrection against the Prussian forces stationed between Berlin and Warsaw, but also to register as many Poles as he could to fight on behalf of the French *Grande Armée*. Both tasks he completed admirably, significantly softening the advance of the corps of Napoleon's Marshals of the Empire and adding to their numbers tens of thousands. These Poles were eager to recover their lost lands from the Prussians and earnestly desired to make war against the Russians to their east.

As they neared the city of Poznań, or *Posen* in German, the Emperor's Mameluke manservant, Roustam, rode postillion (meaning on the back of one of the horses in the team pulling Napoleon's carriage). The turbaned Mameluke signaled for Marek to approach, which he did. Roustam then directed *Capitaine* Zaczek to ride up to the carriage window. When he did so, the Emperor asked Marek for a recommendation for a Polish rider to accompany the courier team carrying his Imperial messages forward to Marshal Murat, who was already nearing Warsaw.

Marek immediately volunteered his own services, but Napoleon rejected this, claiming he could not spare the Pole's leadership to the guard. He then suggested his friend Rydek, a cavalryman familiar with the terrain to be traveled, and who had been reared in the nearby city of Toruń, or *Thorn* in German. Napoleon accepted Marek's choice, and ordered for Rydek to report to the courier party as an escort, guide and interpreter.

Marek took advantage of the situation and hastily wrote out a note and sealed it for Rydek to carry. When his friend reported, Marek told him it was essential that this message be hand-delivered, without delay, to Maya at the Czartoryski townhouse in Warsaw. Rydek was to accept no denials, to entrust the letter to no one else but her, and was to personally deliver the note from his hand to hers. He was further told to wait for a response from Maya before returning.

The Emperor approached the city of Poznań late in the night of the 27th of November. A Polish Honor Guard, trained by General Dąbrowski, awaited Napoleon's arrival. Behind him and other military leaders were throngs of Polish citizens patiently waiting to greet the Emperor. All peered off into the dark night. Soon only a bobbing white object became visible.

"That would be Roustam's turban," Dąbrowski announced to an aide, who then spread the word to the guard and the awaiting crowd. Great volleys of cheers arose as Dąbrowski rode forth in the darkness to welcome the Emperor and ride astride his carriage.

"My Emperor, welcome to our homeland," Dąbrowski said, "and listen as the hearts of my countrymen beat wildly for you, Sire. I have news from Warsaw. Marshal Murat is just outside the city. The remaining Prussians are fleeing north to Königsberg. The Prussian Governer has already abandoned Warsaw and was said to have had rocks thrown at his carriage as he departed. Murat will enter the city tomorrow. And word from the city's fathers is that he will be welcome as a liberator."

"That is most welcome news, General. And what of the Russians?"

"They appear to be holding up just across the Vistula River in the village of Praga, Sire."

Napoleon thought on the news for a moment. "They will retreat when they see the numbers I have moving against them."

"Sire, you will have no problem inspiring the Poles themselves to drive them out of Praga after the massacre of the villagers there only a decade ago by the Russians during General Kościuszko's uprising." Dąbrowski said.

"Tell your countrymen, General, that there will be more than enough Russian heads to claim in retribution, but for now, allow Murat to secure the city peacefully. Any other news?"

"Yes, Sire," Dąbrowski said. "It is reported that Marshal Duroc was injured when his carriage overturned and he broke his collarbone."

General Duroc had been appointed Grand Marshal of the Palace and was the single officer most responsible for the Emperor's personal residences while on campaign. He was as close to the Emperor as any other officer, and one that Napoleon considered a loyal friend. Duroc had been sent forward to secure Napoleon's quarters in Warsaw, where the Emperor had decided that he and his forces would spend the winter.

"It is no wonder," said an aghast Napoleon, "given that these Polish roads are nothing but rivers of mud. My carriage alone has at times seemed pressed for stability. If these damn rains keep up and the freeze comes, I will have no choice but to travel from Posen to Warsaw in the saddle."

The Emperor was welcomed that night to great fanfare in the square of Poznań as the liberator of Poland. It was impossible to measure the full depths of the joy of the Poles, as their hearts had already been stoked by General Dąbrowski. And everywhere along the route of their procession, the loudest cheers arose for the Polish Lancers of the Imperial Guard.

"It appears that your countrymen are very proud of *Capitaine* Zaczek and his Lancers," Napoleon said to Dąbrowski.

"We are a proud people, Sire," Dąbrowski responded, "and we are most proud to see our youth serve you so admirably."

Chapter 26: Napoleon's Polish Problem
November 1806

Smoke in one's own country is purer than any fire in a foreign land, or so says an old Lithuanian proverb. And with Lithuania and Poland having formed a Commonwealth that lasted centuries until the final Partition of that state in 1795, it is appropriate here. For within the lands of Poland between the Oder and the Vistula, there was not only the smoldering of nostalgia, but a blazing passion for war with the Partitioners. Napoleon was offering the Poles an opportunity to fight for their lands, to take them back from the Prussians and the Russians. Surely, they thought, Napoleon has the restoration of our country in his heart.

Marek himself had heard then General Bonaparte profess openly in Verona in 1797 during the Italian campaign,

"The Partition of Poland was an iniquitous deed that cannot stand. When I have finished the war in Italy I will lead the French myself and will force the Russians to re-establish Poland." [64]

Marek remembered that moment and the excitement that it stirred within his soul. But he, like all other Poles, had never heard the quote of the Emperor's Foreign Minister, Talleyrand,

"Speech was given to man to disguise his thoughts." [65]

---

[64] Exhibition at the Czartoryski Museum, Kraków: October 23rd, 2004 - January 15th, 2005

[65] "Charles Maurice de Talleyrand Quotes." BrainyQuote.com. BrainyMedia Inc, 2023.

Figure 24: Napoleon's Movements Across Prussia, 1806

Talleyrand was the same minister who had advised Napoleon that the cause of the Poles was not worth the shedding of a single drop of French blood.

Whether or not Napoleon agreed with his advisor is debatable. One thing is not, that the Emperor used the cause of undoing the Partitions of Poland to swell the ranks of his armies. Polish recruits were drawn by Napoleon's championing their homeland's reinstatement as a sovereign nation. He had first used this to swell Dąbrowski's Legions in the *Armée d'Italie*, and of late to inflate the ranks of the *Grande Armée* with fresh Polish soldiers.

But there is evidence that Napoleon merely used the cause as a wedge to rally the enemies of the Partitioners. The Emperor certainly knew that his true options in the matter were much more limited and forged by the convergence of war and politics. Bonaparte was quoted, in private, as having said the following about the Poles:

"They have allowed themselves to be partitioned. They are no longer a nation - they have no public spirit. The nobles are too much; the people too little. It is a dead body to which life must be restored before anything can be made of it. I will make officers and soldiers of them first; afterwards I shall see. I shall take Prussia's portion; I shall have Posen and Warsaw, but I will not touch Cracow (Kraków), Galicia (Austrian Southern Poland) or Vilna (Today's Vilnius, Lithuania)." [66]

Why not take all of Poland in one fell swoop? First, it would enrage the conquered Austrians and bring them into conflict on his southern flank just as he was battling with the Prussians to the north and the Russians to the east. The *Grande Armée* was already a thousand kilometers away from France, and being surrounded on three sides could prove disastrous.

And regarding the Russians? Napoleon's real objective with the Russians was never to annex their lands, not even those partitioned from Poland. Instead, Napoleon desired only to secure Russia as an ally, one with whom he would share control of Eastern Europe. Then, and only then, would Napoleon have the ability to effectively blockade the English from all commerce with Continental Europe and drive *"Perfidious Albion,"* as he referred to the Brits, to their knees. Napoleon was also to have said in correspondence that:

"I should like to make Poland independent, but that is a difficult matter. Austria, Russia and Prussia have all had a slice of the cake; when the match is kindled, who knows where the conflagration may stop... We must refer this matter to the sovereign of all things - time." [67]

---

66 *"The Campaigns of Napoleon"*, David Chandler, Folio Society Edition, Vol. II, p. 137
Sourced to *"Souvenirs des guerres d'Allemagne"*, Baron de Comeau, 1900, p. 281

67 *"The Campaigns of Napoleon"*, David Chandler, Folio Society Edition, Vol. II, p. 137.
Sourced to *"Mémoires of Napoleon Bonaparte"*, M. De Bourrienne, 1836,
Vol. II, p.3

Chapter 27: Rydek Returns to Poznań

December 1806

Marek awaited in Poznań for the return of Rydek. It was two days since his departure to the troops advancing on Warsaw. Rydek was expected back imminently as part of the courier group returning with reports and correspondence to the Emperor from Marshals Duroc and Murat. Napoleon, by then headquartered safely within the city of Poznań, also awaited. The Emperor spent his days learning the geography of the country and developing the strategies and tactics that would result in overtaking his enemies alongside General Dąbrowski.

Dąbrowski had several other Polish generals in tow, among them Kosinski, Sokolnicki, Serawski, and Gedrowski. These men were all veterans who had led forces during the Italian campaigns under him. All were highly trusted and were in Poznań for planning the expected engagements with the Russian and Prussian armies. In addition, rumor also had it that they had been consulted by the Emperor on questions regarding the restoration of the homeland. Marek had no access to these discussions, but like the rest of the Polish troops who were abuzz with excitement, he was mesmerized with the idea of his Polish homeland once more becoming a sovereign state.

The Emperor impatiently awaited the return of the couriers. He must have their reports before he would press forward on to Warsaw. Napoleon had to be sure the city was secure, that no Russian or Prussians troops could encircle it after his arrival.

The courier group, accompanied by Rydek, finally arrived the next morning. They were one of many such groups, with multiple couriers arriving daily. Yet, this particular group carried the most important news from Marshal Murat; Warsaw was now secure, and expected the Emperor's arrival in the coming days. After their release, Rydek rode up to his friend, carrying a return note from his love.

"So, Rydek from Toruń," Marek taunted him, "I see you were successful in finding my Maya?"

"Yes," Rydek said hesitantly, "and she is as beautiful as I remember her from Paris two Decembers ago."

"She read my note?" Marek asked excitedly.

"Of course," Rydek said flatly, and his manner showed traces of being somewhat withdrawn.

He is holding something back, Marek thought. He could not understand his friend's lack of excitement for him. The note Rydek had carried to Maya had only told her to expect his arrival shortly in Warsaw, along with, of course, a professing of his love for her.

"Well, where is my response?" Marek asked, a hint of exasperation in his voice.

Rydek reached into his saddlebag to produce the return letter from Maya. He began to hand it to Marek, then suddenly pulled it back from his colleague's outreached hand.

"My friend," Rydek said, his voice strained, "I know not what words which grace this letter, as you can see it is sealed. But before you read it there is something you must know."

"Rydek," Marek said, his arm still outstretched, "this is no time for one of your jests. I am eager to read my Maya's words. Give her letter to me."

Rydek ignored him, and continued to hold the letter close to his chest, away from Marek.

"This is no jest, my friend," he said. "When I went to the townhouse you instructed, I was told that your Maya was in the garden, as it was unseasonably warm that day. I asked to see her, but was told simply to leave the letter. I refused and demanded that it was necessary that I personally hand the note to her. After much discussion, I was shown to the garden, where Maya was caught by surprise. I don't know how else to tell you this, but imagine my shock to find her nursing an infant at her breast."

"You are not amusing," chided Marek to his friend.

"Nor do I intend to be," Rydek replied immediately. "My first thought was that the child was yours, Marek, but this young one was only a few months old, not two years on, so I knew you could not have fathered it."

"And how exactly did Maya react?" asked Marek, still in disbelief of his friend's story having any veracity to it.

"She was of course slightly embarrassed at my unannounced arrival, and pulled the nursing blanket over the infant's head," Rydek went on. "Of course I apologized for interrupting her. She did remember me from Paris, and was quick to ask about you and your health. I passed her your letter, which she read immediately. It was touching to watch as her eyes teared up as they flew across your words. Upon having read it, she asked if I was headed to see you again, to which I replied that I was just about to do so. She asked that I wait for her to quickly draft a reply, which I intended to do, in any case, per your instruction."

Rydek held the reply letter in his hand. Marek reached for it a second time, but his friend still refused to hand it over just yet.

"Your story is too fantastic, my friend," Marek said, his voice by then edged with the onset of anger. "First of all, why would Maya even have the milk in her breast needed to feed the young one? Władek is by now nearly eleven years old. It makes no sense at all."

"There is more," Rydek said, ignoring the answer to Marek's question that was obvious. "I am sorry to have to be the one to tell you so."

"Go on, Rydek," Marek said dismissively, "finish your wild and fanciful tale."

Marek watched closely, but Rydek did not flinch at the sting of his friend's disbelief. Had he expected Marek to respond so, given the litany of jokes he had played upon him in the past?

"The tale is true, my friend. I assure you so. After I agreed to wait, your Maya called out to one inside the house. She called out the name 'Bohun,' followed by some words I did not understand, but I took to be in the Ukrainian tongue. Quickly, a man appeared, a very strong young man, indeed, perhaps five years younger than ourselves. This 'Bohun' then spoke to her in that language and took the child from her. As he did, he kissed your Maya, not on the cheek mind you, but fully on the lips. True, it was not a deep, romantic kiss, but still it shocked me to see her so readily allow it. Afterwards, she glanced at me with a look of concern, as if I might share with you what I had just witnessed. Then she said she would be brief in drafting your letter, and asked if I would mind waiting in the garden, which I did. When she came out a few minutes later, I took her response, kissed her hand and again apologized for my interruption."

Marek was unimpressed. His anger grew at this friend's persistence in pursuing this cruel joke.

"I can see you had a long ride from Warsaw to concoct such a story," Marek said, obviously disturbed. "I only hope you did not share it with the other courier riders to whittle away the time."

Marek was very surprised to see his friend's face instantly go pale upon hearing these words.

"What is it, Rydek?" asked Marek, troubled by his dismay.

"It is just those were her very words," Rydek answered. "Before I left she asked for me not to tell you what I had seen, that she would explain it all when you arrived in Warsaw. She said that it would be a nice way to *whittle away* at any awkward moments that might arise between you both, given so much had happened in the past two years."

The words struck Marek with the blunt force of a stone falling from an overhead ledge.

"I don't believe you," he said to Rydek bravely.

"I think you do," Rydek responded, "and you should. I am sorry, but this is indeed what I saw. I could not possibly keep it from you, my brother-at-arms. We are too close to do that."

Rydek then took from him the letter, customarily folded such that its edges formed an "X" sealed at its center in wax. Marek stroked over the seal with the fleshy pad of his thumb, unsure if he should even bother to break it open.

"I will leave you with her words, my friend," Rydek said. He reined his horse and began to trot off slowly.

"Wait, Rydek," Marek called out, "what did this Bohun even look like?"

Rydek turned in his saddle, and over his shoulder said, "I intended to spare you this, but as I said, he was a young man, strongly built, like a warrior. His bushy mustache nearly black, his hair dark, though that was hard to tell as there was not much of it."

"What do you mean not much of it?" Marek asked.

"His head was shaved on either side, down to the skin," Rydek added, "only the center line along the top of it was long enough to see any real color. It was long enough to be tied off in a knot at the back of the crest."

"You mean that he was…" Marek's next words faded off as he fumbled with his emotions.

"Yes, my friend," Rydek said solemnly. "That is why I have had so much trouble telling you this. He was dressed as a Cossack. A Zaporozhian Cossack, by my eye. It appears your Maya has given birth to his infant child."

"You truly don't expect me to believe that," the stunned Marek scoffed.

"I do, with regret. It is indeed my great sorrow to share this with you." Having said this, Rydek sauntered off atop his mount.

Marek was stung by the vision in his head. It was of Maya's assault at the hands of her Ukrainian uncle. It had reinvaded his mind, from which he had worked so hard to expunge the vile thought over the past two years. Yet, this image rapidly morphed to one even worse. He imagined his Maya freely giving herself to a Cossack from those lands. Not just giving herself to him, but willing to bear his child. An infant she would lovingly nurture at her own breast, to suckle it full of her warm milk, and then so naturally hand it over to her "Bohun."

Marek held the letter in his hand and stared at it. He noticed something about it that differed from his mother's earlier letters. They had been sealed also, but unlike those, this one was wrapped taut with string. Why had his Maya taken the time for this additional safeguard? Why was she especially fearful of it being tampered with? In any case, both the string and wax seal bearing the Czartoryski crest in which the string had been set were undisturbed. If it truly was a letter from his Maya, Rydek would have had a very difficult time tampering with it. But what secret from Maya could necessitate this level of precaution.

Marek felt a fury building within him. He decided he need not know any more, then pitched the letter off into road in the distance. He then cursed Maya aloud as his anger for her crested. Yet, he never took his eyes off that letter, which had come to land slanted upright, its edge buried in a pile of manure.

After a few minutes, Marek's rage abated. He convinced himself that this could all be nothing more than one of Rydek's elaborate farces. Marek assured himself that he would open the letter only to find a note, not from Maya, but in his friend's hand delighting in how gullible he was. Rydek was likely watching him, and might return laughing aloud carrying Maya's real correspondence. Marek dismounted and walked over to the letter and carefully extracted it from the manure. He smiled to himself.

Rydek surely had convinced me this time, Marek thought, before recalling the proverb, *In a game it's difficult to know when to stop.*

Marek carefully broke the seal with his thumb, and ripped away the string, only to immediately feel the veil of his self-deception lifted as he recognized Maya's handwriting. His heart plummeted on seeing the cursive script, knowing that this was not one of Rydek's fooleries after all, as he had hoped. Instead he found the same fine woven paper and regal purple ink as had been used in his mother's earlier letters.

He forced himself to read the words, even though he feared they would scrape and tear against the flesh of his own heart. He read these words written in Maya's hand:

Figure 25: Maya's Letter

My Dearest Marek,

How excited I am to hear you are so near! That you are in Poznań with the Emperor himself! Everyone here is so excited for Napoleon's arrival, as we all await you. I must see you as soon as you reach Warsaw. So much has occurred, but I must tell you all that in person. Come directly to me, as I wish you not to hear this news from any other than my own lips.

There is an especially important young man who has entered my life that I must introduce to you. Wladek is already very taken with by him, but do not worry, the child will still be overjoyed to see his warrior Tata once more.

I can only hope you will not be too upset with all that has occurred in your absence. Magdalena believes you will understand and accept all that has transpired. Rydek tells us that Uncle Jacek is safe and travels with the Emperor's army also. This will delight Ewelina, of course, who has endured so much loneliness over these many years. I am sure you understand.

Your Maya

Marek read the note, and the rancor of his heart spilled over increasing the turbidity of his stomach. It was not a cold note by any means, but neither was it as warm as he had hoped it to be. He read it again, and then a third time. Each reading only resulted in seeding more questions that would swirl through his mind like a cyclone of evil spirits.

What "especially important young man" does Maya need to introduce me to? If it be Bohun the Cossack, how could she be so cruel to do so?

How could she ever explain bearing his child to me?

How could this have been allowed to come to pass when the Church had already sanctioned "our secret marriage?"

What other acts have been condoned in the name of saving the family that Magdalena thought I would quickly accept?

What great loneliness has been inflicted on Aunt Ewelina? Did I not release her sons back to her? and finally, most troubling to him, *Why sign the letter merely, "Your Maya?" Why not "Your Love, Maya?" Why not "Your Loving Wife, Maya?"*

The queasy sickness in his gut spread like a flame through kindling, overtaking him. He soon became extremely depressed. Yet, he could not turn off his mind. It raced like a thoroughbred, one that even his mastery of the reins could not subdue.

What a fool I have been for these past two years! How could she do this to me? To make love to a Cossack, no less? To bear him a child? To feed it the milk of life drawn from her own bosom? All the while I have been chaste, thinking only of her! Waiting to taste the honey of her lips again, only to realize in them hides the sour kiss of a traitor, a cheat, a betrayer. He had so easily remained true to her, and yet she could not do the same? Had she forgotten him so soon? Had she doubted the love that he carried in his heart for her?

Marek climbed back into the saddle. He decided he would go on to Warsaw, listen to her explanation, and no matter how well she made excuses for her actions, he would kill the Cossack, Bohun, and do so as she watched.

This was to be the terrible price she would pay for her infidelity to him. She would forever be forced to live with the knowledge that her unforgivable tryst had through his vengeance robbed her in eternity of her new lover's embrace.

Then Marek decided he would leave her, never to speak her name again, never even to allow her to enter into his sight. He would return to Paris, or wherever the *Grande Armée* took him, and so help him God, he would do so alone.

Chapter 28: The Meeting at Blonie

December 1806

Rains fell in a deluge with the onset of the Polish winter. Even the most ordinary of man's travels become trapped in the oozing slurries of mud that mired the rough dirt roads. Every inch forward proved a tremendous struggle, as if against the very will of God, as every muscle of man and beast became saturated with fatigue.

So too, it seemed, became the pondering of Marek's mind as he rode along the road to Warsaw. He was accustomed to assessing even the most complex situations clearly and quickly, and then taking whatever decisive action was needed. But the news of Maya, her Cossack lover and their child became the very downpour within him. It saturated with contempt the hardened earth within him under which Marek had buried his most painful memories. He thought these vile recollections would remain underfoot and forgotten forever. Instead, the tormenting relics of the past crawled free and were swept up into a fetid whirlpool of confusion and indecision that hid from him the path forward. Its vortex dredged up the bitterness suppressed for the past two years. He had assured himself he'd never have to endure its taste again.

Betrayal - the most vile of all embarrassments. The same feeling that had pierced him upon seeing Maya emerge from the carriage so full with child all those years ago. Now, there was a greater and more crippling image haunting him: Maya and Bohun. A Cossack? Marek could not reconcile how this ever came to pass.

His thoughts were broken by the Emperor's mount losing its footing and sliding sideways in the slippery swill that had once been a road. The conditions were truly treacherous. Only weeks earlier, Marshal Duroc's coach had flipped over along these same rutted tracts which had frozen solid. The Marshal's shoulder blade was broken in the accident, but he was indeed fortunate that the crash had not proved to be fatal. For this reason, the Emperor rejected the use of a carriage, and instead rode on horseback, centered in a loosely formed pack of eight lancers.

Only the mount of Roustam, Napoleon's Mameluke manservant, was allowed inside the protective bubble. Each rider, including both Marek and Roustam, were reminded by the fall and muddied splash of each hoove of their respective mounts that they had pledged their very lives to this detail. Under no circumstances could any attack be allowed to penetrate this shield. The Emperor could not fall! Of course, fore and aft of the interior ring of lancers were waves of other horsemen and foot soldiers, thousands in all, and the likelihood of any attack was miniscule. This day, the Polish Lancers under *Capitaine* Zaczek had been given the honor of being the Emperor's last and ultimate guards. They were on their final leg to Warsaw.

Napoleon was dressed out in furs to protect him from the precariously dropping temperatures and the pelt of freezing rain. His famous bicorne hat had given way to a warm fur head-dressing that rivaled Roustam's turban in looking out of place.

"Zaczek," the Emperor called out.

"Yes, Sire," Marek replied.

"Your country is such a cold and unforgiving place. This road is nothing more than a *mer de merde!* The temperature threatens to soon freeze it solid. When is our next stop?"

"In about an hour, Sire, we will change horses in the town of Blonie," Marek answered, "and then it is on to Warsaw itself. The weather may be inhospitable, but you'll find the hearts of my countrymen to be anything but. They will deny you nothing, Sire."

"Except, it would seem, good roads. These rivers of mud become so menacing that they are more threatening than the Russians. You have Marengo ready for me to enter Warsaw upon?"

"Certainly, Sire. Marengo has been kept fresh for that final ride." He knew the Emperor always wished to be seen upon his beloved grey Arabian - named after his greatest Italian victory. "Soon enough we'll be arriving in Blonie. And, Sire, be aware I have sent a rider ahead to warm a coach in which you may conduct your affairs there while our saddles and bridles are transferred to the fresh mounts. It is too unsafe to enter any taverns or houses there that we have not secured. It will be only a brief stop."

"Ah, Zaczek," Napoleon reacted, "I thought your countrymen were so hospitable? Yet you worry they might pose a threat to my safety?"

"Please remember, Sire," Marek said, "that Warsaw and all the lands along the way are formally Prussian territory. It would not take much for a Prussian provocateur to play the Pole just to get within harm's reach of you."

The entourage pressed on to the poor, rural town of Blonie, to the west of Warsaw. Napoleon took his place in the coach which had been heated by bed-warmers in the old style. There he reviewed correspondence that awaited him from Marshal Duroc by the light of an oil lamp. In typical Napoleonic fashion, the Emperor wasted not a second in consuming the material as Marengo and the other rider's mounts were readied.

During this time, Marek and the other Polish Lancers ringed the coach on foot, with only Roustam allowed inside their protective circle. As Marek scanned over the faces of a curious crowd that had begun to form, he saw one that was familiar to him, but could not immediately place it. *Was this onlooker a threat?*

"Bring me that man," he said, pointing into the crowd, to one of his lancers.

The soldier plucked the man coarsely from the throng and brought him over to *Capitaine* Zaczek, who felt ashamed for not having instantly recognized the Pole's face.

"What on earth brings you here?" Marek asked the man.

"Another mission from your *matka*, Marek," Tolo answered. He appeared pleased to have been dragged through the thickening crowd and directly before his old companion. "The lovely Magdalena has asked me to escort a beautiful woman here in the hope of glimpsing the Emperor. Alas, word of his arrival has leaked, I fear half of Warsaw will be arriving in Blonie soon."

"I am sorry, my friend. I have no time nor do I care to see Maya just now," Marek said sharply.

"Nor will you, my brother, as Maya is still in Warsaw," Tolo responded. "She is not the beauty I have been tasked to bring forth. I have brought along the woman who employs your mother."

"You mean the girl, Marie Łączyńska, that Maya had spoken of in Paris?" Marek asked. "The young maiden who was to be married off to the decrepit old Count?"

"Yes, but that old decrepit Count turns out to be richer than King Solomon. And that girl is now a Countess. Since Marie Łączyńska married Count Walewski, she has already bestowed him with a son. Your mother, who had been her governess, now serves her as the infant's nanny. All that Countess Walewska speaks of is meeting the Emperor! Magdalena thought you might be able to make that happen for her, even if only for a minute or two. The Countess is so terribly excited."

Marek knew this was strictly against protocol and that the safety of the Emperor must be beyond any threat of being compromised. It mattered not how remote that risk might be.

"I am sorry," Marek said, "it is impossible, even as a favor for you, my friend. Or for that matter even on behalf of my *matka*."

"I suspected so," Tolo replied, "but even now as I speak to you, I am able to glimpse the Emperor in the coach over your shoulder. The Countess Walewska would be very happy with that, I am sure. May I bring her here, just to gaze over your shoulder?"

Marek rolled the idea around in his mind for a second. He thought that there would be little risk in allowing the Countess to look. The only way she could do any harm would be to carry a pistol, which he felt was extremely unlikely. Even in the off chance she turned out to be an enemy agent, Marek was confident that he could disarm her easily enough. He decided to at least try to make his *matka* happy that day.

"I can't imagine what harm that could cause," Marek said, "but tell her to do so in haste as the Emperor will be mounting up shortly for the final leg of our ride into Warsaw. I do not like the size of this growing throng."

Saying nothing, Tolo turned and rushed into the amassing crowd. Moments later, he emerged from it leading a figure enshrouded in a full length coat made of the finest furs, including a deep lined hood that clung protectively around her face. It cast shadows obstructing his view of her. Even beneath the warmth of the bulky fur outerwear, Marek could discern her slender and feminine contours.

"*Capitaine* Zaczek, allow me to introduce to you the Countess Marie Walewska. I have instructed her, as you have asked, that she is only to look over your shoulder into the Emperor's coach. She will do nothing to draw his attention."

With the grace that was befitting a monarch, the Countess reached slowly to grasp the hood enshrouding her face. When she lowered it, the full impact of her beauty exploded into view. Only days before turning twenty years old, her porcelain skin was vibrant with youth. Her features were remarkably proportioned. Her blonde hair cascaded in an elegant fall upon her shoulders.

The contours of her mouth welcomed Marek's gaze with a sweet smile before she ever said a word. Her nose was small and delicate, and from its top softly spread two of the most expressive brows that Marek had ever seen. They arched wide as she wasted no time peering past him into the coach, struggling to get even a passing glimpse of Napoleon.

"*Pani* Walewska," Marek said, reaching for and taking her hand which he kissed, bowing with respect. "It is my great honor."

Marek stood upright quickly, not desiring for the others to see his focus waning from the Emperor's protection.

"*Dziękuję, Pan* Zaczek," the Countess said. "Tolo has told me so much about you, I feel as if I already know you. And of course, I am very indebted to your mother, Magdalena, and my good friend, your wife, Maya. They both have filled me with many stories from the great love they share for you. I appreciate your making this opportunity occur on my behalf."

"I am sorry I am unable to arrange an introduction, Countess," Marek said. As the words left his lips, he saw her eyes catch on some detail just behind him.

"Ah, but it appears you may have already done so," the Countess said continuing to peer over Marek's shoulder.

At that moment, Roustam put his massive hand on Marek's shoulder. "His Imperial Highness wishes for you to introduce the Emperor to your countrywoman, *Capitaine.*"

Marek was shocked, but knew he should not have been. He was aware the Emperor had a keen eye for beauty.

"You are honored, Countess," Marek said with surprise. "I can tell you that few women have drawn the Emperor's attention away from his reports. Come, I will introduce you."

"It is more than I could have hoped for!" Marie replied nervously, placing her hand in his as Marek led her to the coach.

Napoleon exited from the carriage just as they approached. "Sire," Marek said, "allow me to introduce Countess Marie Walewska who has ridden out from Warsaw and risked the crush of this crowd with the sole intention of seeing you."

The Countess gave her hand to Napoleon who had reached out for it. Instead of kissing it, he held it as he took in the depths of her beauty. His eyes wandered over her features, sparking with delight upon what they observed.

"Zaczek," Napoleon said, "I wish you to translate my every word into Polish to this beautiful woman."

"There is no need, your Imperial Highness," Marie said in French. "I apologize in advance for the pronunciation of your language, but I assure you I understand your every word."

Marek then stepped away, behind the Countess Walewska.

"Ah, Countess," Napoleon responded, "your French appears to be excellent. And if all the women of Poland are as incredibly lovely as yourself, then I am doomed. How could I possibly read my field reports with your star shining so brightly outside my coach? But you need not have come so far in the cold, as I will be in Warsaw soon enough!"

"My apologies, Sire. I just couldn't stand to wait!" the Countess said, before adding:

"Be welcome, a thousand times welcome to our land! Nothing that we can do will ever express strongly enough either our admiration for you personally or the pleasure we have seeing you set foot in this land. We have been waiting for you to save us." [68]

She smiled at him, not seductively, but earnestly. An energy radiated from her joyous countenance. She knew she was staring at the man who would soon enough liberate Poland from the grips of the Austrians, Prussians and most especially, the ruthless Russians.

---

[68] *"Diary of Marie Walewska"*, Family Archives, 2006 by Alexandre Christian Walewski

It was obvious that the Emperor could not get enough of her to sate his eyes. They feasted on her, but still hungered only for more. He bowed and most gently kissed her hand.

"I plan to arrive in Warsaw and have my army make Winter Quarters nearby. While I am there, I would be honored if you would show me all of what your homeland has to offer, Countess. But for now, my lovely Marie, I am most disappointed to tell you that circumstances sadly require that I make haste and bid you *adieu*." Then he gave her a bouquet of flowers which Roustam had taken from the coach's interior.

> *"Keep these as a pledge of my good intentions.*
> *I hope we shall meet again in Warsaw and that*
> *I shall receive a thank you from your beautiful lips."* [69]

Marie took the bouquet of fresh flowers from his hands and raised them to her nose. She inhaled their delicate scent, that fragrance which would linger in her memory for a lifetime.

Napoleon excused himself with a bow and walked off to mount his gray charger, Marengo. Then, in coordination with his protective detail, he rode off to the east, that is, in the direction of Warsaw.

Marek had retaken his position as *capitaine* of the Imperial Guard Polish Lancer unit riding directly astride the Emperor. He glanced over his shoulder to see the Countess Walewska rejoin his old friend Tolo before they both melded back into the crowd.

Napoleon then signaled for Marek to draw close. When Marek did, the Emperor demanded, "Zaczek, you must ascertain and tell Roustam exactly where Marshal Duroc can find the Countess Walewska in Warsaw. She is truly a delight. Having now but a taste, my soul craves only to feast at her table. Your Emperor's happiness is counting on you, *Capitaine* Zaczek."

------

[69] *"Diary Marie Walewska"*, Family Archives, 2006 by Alexandre Christian Walewski

Napoleon rode into Warsaw to a thunderous reception. He was greeted at the city's walls by crowds of everyday citizens thronged atop the grass laden ramparts, all wishing to get an unobstructed view of the approaching Emperor. Below them was a distinguished group of noblemen, first among them was none other than Prince Józef Poniatowski, the nephew of the last king of Poland. King Stanisław August Poniatowski had died in the last years of the decade before. His nephew Józef was a highly regarded warrior and Polish general who had fought in the Kościuszko Uprising against the Russians just before the third and final Partition that robbed Poland, and his uncle, the King, from their sovereignty. In addition to being a military general, Prince Józef Poniatowski was still one of the foremost patriots calling for the restoration of the sovereignty of Poland.

The Emperor was greeted and soon was led by Prince Józef and the entourage through the double gates of the medieval brick and mortar barbican, and entered the *Stare Miasto*, or the Old Town. Napoleon rode astride Poniatowski through the narrow streets as the Polish Prince engaged the Emperor in conversation. They emerged from the Old Town in the plaza where the column of *Zygmunt III Waza* was raised. Prince Józef explained that King Zygmunt had been beloved by the Poles.

"King Zygmunt moved the capital from Kraków in the south to Warsaw in 1596," Prince Poniatowski explained.

"*Waza?* Is that not The Royal House of Vasa," Napoleon interjected, eager to display his knowledge, "was that not a lineage from Sweden?"

"Very good, Sire," Poniatowski used the title for the first time. "Indeed, King Zygmunt III was originally Swedish, but he so loved his Polish Kingdom, and the Poles so loved him, that he gave up his claim to the Swedish throne."

"So, Prince Józef, you have brought me by this route, past this very column in the hopes that I would deduce that the Poles do not mind being led by a foreigner, eh?" Napoleon paused to watch the reaction of surprise on the Prince's face. "But you have bent the facts of history to your purpose, no? King Zygmunt did not abdicate his Swedish throne, as you say. Is it not true he moved your capital to Warsaw so he could be closer to Sweden which he also ruled at that time and which was undergoing a Protestant Revolt? In fact, only a few years later the Swedish throne was taken from him by his brother, Charles. A half century later Sweden invaded deeply into Poland. So, be warned my Prince, that allegiance to foreigners can also have its inherent risks."

Napoleon had impressed the prince with his knowledge of the local history, but Prince Poniatowski was quick to reply, "But, Sire, we have never been led by a foreigner such as yourself, who has never been defeated in battle."

A smile flashed across the Emperor's face. "No, it is true you have not. But you have also never been led by a greater champion of freedom than myself. I have come to your country not to annex it, but to restore it to its legitimate status as one of the great sovereign states of Europe!"

The assemblage of Polish riders, nobles and lancers alike, joined Marek Zaczek in applause upon hearing the Emperor profess his intentions. Bonaparte allowed it to go on for a long minute before he finally raised his hand for it to stop.

"But that is still somewhat off in the future," the Emperor added after the clapping subsided, "we still have the remaining Prussians and Russians to defeat first. Lead me now to the palace so that I may settle and engage Marshal Duroc along with my fighting Marshals of the French Empire."

"Yes, Emperor," Prince Poniatowski answered, it is just behind us. Let me show you to the entrance."

As they guided their mounts in procession to the Royal Castle, Napoleon caught sight of the river behind it.

"That is the Vistula?" he asked, pointing in the wide river's direction.

"Yes, Emperor," Prince Poniatowski replied, "in our language we call the river *Wisła*."

"Then those lands just beyond it are Russia itself?" Napoleon asked, knowing the answer to be true in his mind.

"No, Emperor," Poniatowski said defiantly, "those are the lands that Russia has stolen from Poland. The true border with Russia is the River *Niemen*, much further east." Poniatowski to that day refused to acknowledge the reality that was imposed by the neighboring powers after the Partitions were completed over a decade beforehand.

"And the Austrians?" Napoleon asked.

"They have unjustly claimed all the lands on the opposite bank of the *Wisła* below Warsaw."

"Well, when we have driven the last of the Prussians from the Polish soil they have unjustly taken, and after we chase the Russians beyond the Niemen, then we will correct the Austrian incursion. But first, to the castle."

The procession entered the courtyard of the Royal Castle, which was even then much more of a palace than a castle. Grand Marshal Duroc, his arm still in a sling, awaited the Emperor, after having overseen the preparations made for the his stay.

"Ah, Duroc," Napoleon said just before dismounting, "it is good to see you in one piece. These Polish roads can be a little treacherous, no? More dangerous than engaging in battle, yes?"

"Thank you, but I am fine, Sire," Marshal Duroc replied. "You'll find the Royal Palace (Duroc refused to address it as a castle) has been made very comfortable for your stay. Just this morning we received and installed your field library for the winter's visit. All the marshals have picked out their bivouac locations and identified their foraging areas."

"I would like to review all those selections, Duroc," Napoleon said, "for *Les Grognards* are grumbling. They do not like being so far from home, the women are too chaste here, and the food does not please their palates. In all, they are not happy spending Winter Quarters here in Poland. It is the reason, after all, why I allow the Old Guard, that is *Les Grognards* to grumble so openly. It allows me to understand exactly what all the soldiers of the infantry and artillery are thinking."

"Yes, Sire," Duroc answered. "Also, the locals are enthralled with your spending the winter in Warsaw. They wish to throw you a gala, that is, a ball in your honor. Would you consider that, Sire?"

"I see no trouble in it, but no sooner than after the New Year," Napoleon chided, "we have far too much to do and far too many Russians still nearby. Eh?"

"Yes, Sire," Marshal Duroc answered, "I will plan it for the week after the New Year. Is there anything else?"

"Only that I will refuse to attend that ball, or any other function being scheduled in my honor or not, unless the Countess Walewska attends. *Capitaine* Zaczek of the Imperial Guard Lancers has been tasked to give Roustam the particulars. She must be present. Make it so."

Napoleon spent his first full day in Warsaw, not in the city at all, but on horseback, protected by the cavalry of the Imperial Guard, reconnoitering the surrounding countryside. Then, two days before Christmas, the Emperor prepared to engage the nearby Russians in a series of skirmishes just to the north of the city, intending to crush them altogether. Marshal Davout had already cleared them from the eastern village of Praga, just across the Vistula. Napoleon knew that his troops, planning to camp in Winter Quarters on the outskirts of Warsaw, needed to be assured they would not be attacked by marauding units of the Tsar's army. The Prussians were less of a threat, as they had already retreated further north into East Prussia near the fortress city of Königsberg, where the Prussia King Frederick Wilhelm and his Queen Louise had taken refuge.

But as the forces of the French marched out of the city, they did so without two figures that would otherwise be expected to be within their ranks. Napoleon himself had decreed that Marek and his Uncle Jacek were to be granted leave to reunite them for a week with their family in Warsaw. The two soldiers would be expected to report back the day after New Year's Day.

Neither Marek nor Jacek had been to Warsaw before this trip. They had to stop several times to get directions from the locals to the Czartoryski townhouse where his mother lived.

Marek and Jacek found and approached that same townhouse to which Rydek had earlier been sent. They were greeted by a solitary figure, Marek's *matka,* Magdalena. It was the first time Marek had laid eyes upon her since over a decade earlier in Milan, when she had come to that city while the Austrian army was encamped there. It was before Marek's defection to the French at Lodi. She had come to tell her son of her plan to marry the Austrian Count Von Arndt. He was thankful it never came to pass.

In Warsaw, she stood before him like a vision, elevated on the high steps of the townhouse, with great joy beaming from her smile and radiating from her tired, slightly haggard eyes.

"Marek, joy of my life," she exclaimed from the marble steps which rose like an opaque white pillar from the street level. "How wonderful that you are home to celebrate Christmas with us all. Oh, and Jacek, how happy Ewelina will be to see you when she returns tomorrow night for *Wigilia.*"

The welcome of his mother's smile warmed him. But behind its exuberance, Marek thought she looked older, more frail than he remembered. Magdalena had only recently turned fifty, but the wrinkles of a hard life had begun to settle in upon the smooth skin of her face that he remembered. Her hair was still the same color that Marek recalled. There was no hint of gray, but somehow it seemed more coarse, more flaxen. In a strange way she reminded him of a hare that had just outrun a fox, nervous and uncertain but once again safe in its burrow. He feared to think in what condition he would have found her had Princess Czartoryska not rescued her from the attempts of Count Von Arndt to drive her back into poverty, and thus under his clutches once more. Thank God that she had escaped Austrian Kraków for Prussian Warsaw when she did, escaping away from the Austrian Count's villainous grasp.

In Warsaw, watching safely from the raised steps of the town home, he thought her the exhausted hare venturing just to the edge of that berm protecting entry into the Princess' burrow haven.

"Where is everyone else?" Marek asked.

"And why is my Ewelina not here to greet me?" Jacek scowled. "I have marched halfway across Europe. I am offended!"

Magdalena's eyes darted between the two of them, unsure as to which to answer first. She decided to address the sting of the perceived insult by her sister-in-law's husband.

"Ewelina left two nights ago to travel to meet Doctor Olszewski in Kraków. You surely remember the good doctor from the *folwark,* Jacek. His letter to her stated he had something urgent to discuss with her. I arranged a carriage and Tolo agreed to escort her. There is no war there, as Austria and France have been at peace since Austerlitz, so she is quite safe. Everyone else is waiting inside in the parlor. I believe they wished me to have the honor of greeting you both alone."

"And who exactly is counted among everyone else?" Marek asked.

"My son, my son, my Marek," Magdalena said as she floated down the steps to him and wrapped her arms around him, the joy of her life. "The war has made you so strong!" She kissed his cheek. "Give the reins of your horses to Ignacy, our coach house attendant, he will take them round back and care for them. Come inside, both of you, it is bitterly cold out here."

Marek and Jacek dismounted, but his uncle could not resist giving the stableboy detailed instructions on exactly how to care for the animals. After playing the role himself so long for the Austrians, the care of the horses had become a second nature to him. He knew he was welcome inside, but truthfully would have felt more comfortable in the stable tending to the mounts.

"Come Uncle Jacek," Marek finally interrupted, "I am eager to meet and engage *everyone.*" Of course, the reference was a veiled threat to the Cossack, Bohun, if he should be among those collected inside.

"Ignacy is a good name," Jacek said to the stable boy, patting him dismissively on the head, "it is one of the names I considered for my own sons, Andrzej and Bartek, who are great infantry soldiers for the Austrians."

"Come now, Uncle Jacek," Marek said with more urgency in his voice. As the two men climbed the steps behind Magdalena, Marek said softly to him, "Uncle, you are not even sure they still serve the Austrians. Remember, I gave them their freedom at Augsburg. That was over a year ago. They could be anywhere in Europe by now."

"I know my boys," Jacek bragged. "They went straight back to their units once you released them. Had they not, they would have made their way here, to reunite with their mother. They are not like those who abandon their families only to chase their personal ambitions."

The criticism came out of nowhere, and wounded Marek.

"Well," he replied casually, not wishing to acknowledge the bite of the words from his uncle, for whom he had personally interceded, "the Emperor's war with Austria was over only a few weeks after they were released. If they are still in the Austrian infantry, as you believe, they are indeed very safe. For as my mother has said, Austria is at peace with Napoleon."

"For now," Jacek muttered. "Austria and France are at peace just for now. It cannot last."

Marek had avoided saying the obvious which he knew must remain unspoken; the boys had not been reported lost in war, so they must still be alive somewhere. Marek knew this because he had scoured the published Austrian casualty reports and never found their names.

Magdalena guided Marek and Jacek into the interior of the home, splendidly decorated in white walls gilded with gold trim and ornate *plaster of Paris* ceiling moldings.

"*Matka,* what a refined home you live in," Marek said aloud, "but I am confused. I thought you were living in poverty, forced to take on work as a governess just to make ends meet. These are indeed some very elaborate ends that meet my eye. You have redefined what it is to be poor."

"Later tonight, my son, I will explain everything to you, as we sit by a warm fire. But let it suffice to say that we all reside here only out of the most generous charity of the Princess Czartoryska. I work as a governess to the Countess Walewska, because I need to pay for our food, the clothes on our backs, and firewood to warm us, although the Princess has also offered an allowance for these needs. That courtesy I politely refused because I enjoy working for the Walewski family. The Count can be quite rude and overly demanding at times, but the Countess Marie is a delight. She told me you were so wonderful in arranging for her to speak briefly to the Emperor. You know, other than Maya, she is the only other woman I would be happy to see you marry."

"*Matka,* Countess Marie is almost half my age," Marek said in a shocked voice, "and she is already married."

"Yes," Magdalena said, "to a man fifty years her senior. Nothing is so sad as to think of the blossoming of her youth being wasted in the shadow of his old age."

"What is still more sad to think is her flower being defiled by the touch of his icy fingers," Marek answered. "And yes, before you even ask, Emperor Bonaparte seemed quite taken with her. He has asked that I tell him precisely how he can contact her here in Warsaw. I had to tell him I did not know, but would soon find out."

"What on earth could the Emperor expect of Countess Marie? She is a happily married woman," Magdalena said.

"Mother, you yourself just said in so many words that any woman who is twenty years old and was forced to wed a man in his seventies, rich or not, can not truly be *happily* married."

"Well, my Marek, we will have that discussion later," Magdalena said as she led them both through the house and down a wide central hallway. "*Proszę,* follow me into the parlor."

As they walked, Marek spied an ornate set of glass doors leading out into a garden blanketed white by an overnight snow. He thought to himself that must be where Rydek found Maya nursing the infant. Instantly, his blood thickened within him, as anger's drum measured out the beat of war that instantly pulsed throughout him.

Magdalena turned through a wide doorway, and as she did she began to say, "It is so wonderful you both could join us while we have our houseguest for Christmas…"

Marek turned the corner, still anguished at the idea of Maya nursing another man's child, when he saw her sitting by the fireplace. Maya sat on a sofa holding an infant, next to her sat a man clearly dressed in the robes of a Zaporozhian Cossack.

"Bohun!" Marek seemingly spat out the name.

The Cossack stood sharply. He was as Rydek described, young, strongly muscled and darkly complected.

"Well, you must be the famous Marek, savior of runaway horses," he said with a chortle, although not intending to give any particular offense to the soldier.

"And killer of Cossacks," Marek added in a rage.

As he said these last words, Marek drew out his sabre, quickly bringing its tip under the chin of Bohun. He applied enough pressure that the Cossack felt its point sink into the soft flesh an inch or so behind his chin. Bohun seemed surprised at first, but also determined not to show any concern. Instead, the man held at the end of Marek's sword stood perfectly still and responded only with a wry smile as his blood began trickling down the sabre's shaft before dripping onto the floor.

"Marek!" Magdalena cried out, "Stop immediately! Have you lost all composure? Bohun is our visitor. He will join us in the seat of the unexpected guest at *Wigilia* tomorrow night. How dare you treat him with such disrespect!"

Uncle Jacek reached up and put his hand on the forearm of Marek that threatened Bohun with the sword. "My nephew, what are you doing? This man is unarmed. Collect yourself. What has he ever done to you?"

"Yes, he is unarmed," Marek agreed, "and he may be the guest of this house, but this Cossack has come to help himself to take liberties with my *wife*." As he said these words, he glanced at Maya, sitting still on the sofa with the infant child.

"Marek," she said with a smirk, "are you suffering from the fatigue of battle? Allow me to explain."

"Yes, *moja zona*, I know from your letter. This is the young man to whom you could not wait for me to meet. The man who has taken advantage of my prolonged absence to give you another child to take to your breast!"

Marek then heard and felt the laughter coming from the Cossack. He heard it roll through the air like not so distant thunder, thick and voluminous in its mockery. He felt the echoes of the raucous guffaws in his weapon hand, for every quiver of the Cossack's jaw forced the tip of the sabre to cut slightly deeper into the underside of his chin. Still, the Cossack did not flinch, he merely continued to laugh loudly.

"Marek Zaczek, savior of horses," he bellowed, "cuckolded by Cossacks!" Bohun then laughed even more freely, and blood began to run faster, more voluminously down Marek's blade.

Maya having had enough of her husband's misplaced jealousy, rose to her feet, and holding the infant in one arm, placed the nursing blanket under the blade of the sword to catch the rivulets of Bohun's blood as they dropped.

"Magdalena," Maya said in an irritated voice, "would you mind collecting the other children and bringing them in? And Marek, don't be so ridiculous! My bearing the child of another man! How could you ever have such a ridiculous thought?"

Uncle Jacek slowly floated his hand over the sabre's grip, then forward along its blade to just before the tip, where he gently pulled it down. Marek, now realizing that something was sadly amiss, allowed the blade to be lowered.

"Marek, you have absolutely ruined our plans for your homecoming," Maya said, still holding the blood stained nursing blanket under the Cossack's chin. "You are a fool. This young man is my cousin, Bohun."

Bohun continued to laugh aloud in a deeper and more rolling, more insulting, manner.

"Then who is the infant that you hold?" Marek asked.

"This is Bohun's newborn son, Orest." Maya said. "I am wet nursing this infant child for him as Bohun's wife, Anastasia, died during Orest's birth. How could I possibly have said no to either he or his son in their urgent need of my help?"

Bohun had stopped laughing at the mention of his wife's death. He then pried the nursing blanket, stained scarlet with his blood, away from Maya's grasp and after looking down at it, he said, "Now, Marek Zaczek, you can boast that you truly have spilled the blood of three Cossacks."

Marek in that second felt the fool. He pulled away his bloodied sabre after which Bohun placed the bloody cloth tightly back against the underside of his chin.

"But you told me you had a young man for me to meet?" Marek said. "Is it this infant, Orest? How were you even able to produce the milk this child needs? And why did you just moments ago ask my *matka* to bring in the *other children?*"

Marek wiped his weapon's blade on the last clean portion of the nursing cloth that dangled from Bohun's hand as the Cossack continued to hold it to the pierced skin under his chin. Marek slowly returned his weapon to its scabbard.

Just then, from behind, Marek heard the ear splitting, high pitched squeal of a young boy's voice. "*Tata* Marek! *Tata* Marek!"

Marek turned to see Władek, the eleven year old, running across the parlor floor towards him. The child slammed in to him, exactly as he had done in Paris two years ago, and on impact wrapped his arms around the soldier.

Marek laid his arms, somewhat uncomfortably, on the boy's shoulders. "Władek, how nice to see you again," he said.

"No, *Tata,* call me Marek!" The boy played with the sabre's hilt, which by then had been safely returned, resting in Marek's scabbard. The child pulled it out the few inches his little hands could manage, oblivious to the danger of its slicing sharp edge.

"Call me Marek Zaczek," Władek begged, "a Polish soldier just like you, *Tata!*"

"That sabre is not a toy, Władek," Marek replied stiffly, pulling the boy's hands away from the razored blade. "That blade is sharp enough to slice off your tiny little fingers. When you are old enough to wield it, then I will call you 'Marek.' But for now, you are merely a child, and you must bear a child's name."

"And this is the young man I was so eager to introduce you to, Marek," said Maya, as she handed the infant Orest to Bohun before walking over to the doorway in which Magdalena stood. She reached behind the fall of her mother-in-law's dress to produce a very young, very small, and most shy child. The young boy stood awkwardly, as standing was still somewhat new to him. He was dressed in plain brown clothing. He was clutching something tightly in his hands.

Marek extracted himself, almost forcibly, from Władek's embrace. "And who is this fine boy?" he asked, not yet appreciating the delicacy of the situation.

"This fine boy," Maya answered, "is Czesław, *our* son. He is only a year and a half old. He is the reason I still had milk to offer for the infant Orest."

Marek was astounded. "I have a son?" he asked aloud in disbelief. *A son. I have son,* he kept repeating in his mind to himself. *Can this really be true?*

"Why did you not tell me?" Marek asked after regaining his composure. He walked over to the boy, who cautiously pulled back behind the hem of his mother's skirt. It was as if Marek, so quick to push Władek aside, was being punished by Czesław's avoiding him. Marek stared upon the toddler, and a fresh breath of pride filled his lungs.

"Maya," Marek said, "how is it that you kept the news of my son's birth from me?"

"After Paris," Maya answered, casting a glance at Władek, "I was unsure as to how you might react. I feared the news might drive you away. Also, I wanted to wait until the child was born, so you would not be worried about me during my term of carrying him. After he was born, I drafted many letters to send to you in Paris, but I was told by Tolo that by then you would have already gone to war with the Emperor's army. So I never sent them. My thinking was I did not wish to distract you from your many important responsibilities."

"But you and he are my most precious responsibility," Marek said. As he did the math of months in his head, he realized he most likely was just leaving the beaches of Boulogne on the English Channel for the march to Ulm when Czesław was born.

"Czesław," Marek reached out, "come to me. I am your *Tata…*"

The boy reached up for his mother to lift him. In his right hand still dangled something familiar.

"Does my son not yet talk?" Marek asked, "and what is in his hand?"

Maya lifted the boy, who snuggled to her bosom.

"My brother Czesław does not talk yet, *Tata,*" interrupted Władek. "I could speak plainly when I was his age, couldn't I, *Matka?*"

"Yes, Marek, you could, but your brother is more slow to take to it." She used the name her child Władek preferred, as she had become prone to do because it reminded her of her missing husband.

"And may I ask again what is in the boy's hand?" the older Marek repeated.

"It is his rosary. The one Sister Maryja Elizabeth gave to me for him at his birth."

"And you allow him to play with something so holy?" Marek said.

"…Asks the man who kills and maims for the butcher of France…" interjected Bohun sarcastically.

"He does not play with it," Maya replied, "it comforts him. Even at his age, he treats it with the respect and reverence it deserves. He never leaves it laying about, always he has it with him. We have had to repeatedly keep him from putting it over his little head. I fear he might strangle with it around his neck."

Marek stepped closer to her as she held him. He reached out and grasped the rosary's crucifix as it swayed from the boy's grasp. He bowed before his son, and kissed the cross as the boy clutched the rosary to which it was affixed. A smile unfurled upon the child's chubby face.

Marek then leaned in slowly to kiss the delicate soft flesh of the child's feet.

"You have given me a gift I could never have thought myself to be worthy of," he said to Maya as he then closed in to kiss her on the lips.

While he did so, his *matka,* Magdalena, spoke. "Marek, I have only one request while you stay with us in this house. I wish for you to leave your military uniform in your room for the days you are here. Napoleon has stolen enough of your time from us. I have brought along a *zupan* that was once your father's."

She handed him the richly embroidered blue garment, with fine mother of pearl buttons up its center front. It was longer than a shirt but too short to be called a robe. Its length dropped just above the knees of its wearer, and often was cinched with a sash. It was the traditional attire of the Polish noble classes - the *szlachta.*

Marek released the rosary's crucifix and took the silken *zupan* from his mother's hand. It seemed so foreign to him.

"You will find additional garments in your room laid out upon the bed," Magdalena said. "Jacek, Ewelina has left some clothes for you as well."

"I don't remember my father ever owning anything as fine as this, or for that matter ever having seen him in this garment," Marek said rubbing the *zupan's* silken cloth between his fingers. "Bronisław was a miner of salt, a simple man. He himself was the very salt of the earth. Are you sure in your remembering that this elegant *zupan* belonged to my father?"

"Well, my son, that is something I wish to discuss with you further while you are here."

Chapter 31: A Requiem
23-24 December 1806

Anxiety crawled along the spine of Marek Zaczek. He had expected the worse during his stay at the townhome regarding Maya and Bohun, but that had turned out to be nothing but a great misunderstanding. He should then be feeling relaxed after being reunited with those he loved, but instead he felt agitated. Initially, he assumed it to be from being separated from his unit while they were out skirmishing with the Russians. Yet, that wasn't quite it. There was something unsettling in this household, with his *matka* hinting at a discussion they needed to have, but then making excuses to pull away every time he tried to engage her in it. Her display of conflicting feelings set him on edge, as if he was being lulled into a past that never was, an elegant but fictitious veil of nostalgia.

The first night after he arrived was festive. While the women worked away in the kitchen preparing for the next night's Christmas Eve *Wigilia* meal, the men gathered round the fireplace sharing stories of war to young Władek. Each man, in turn, felt compelled to trump the story told before his own. First the tales came from Marek, then Bohun the Cossack, then finally from Uncle Jacek. At the end of the telling of each tale, the men would toast each other from a bottle of local vodka.

Young Władek anticipated with excitement the telling of each story. His infant brother Czesław had long been laid down to sleep, and as such was not lingering about to draw attention to himself. Władek had these mighty warriors all to himself.

With Maya assisting Magdalena in the kitchen, there was also no one there to insist the men hold back on the details, no matter how grisly or dark they became. And as toast after toast of vodka warmed the bellies of the competing storytellers, the tales incrementally became more gory, more somber, as if the men in their increasingly drunken state forgot the young boy's presence among them. They merely went on competing in outdoing each other when their turn came.

Władek had noticed a strange truce had been forged between his *Tata* and his "Uncle Bohun." Whereas earlier in the day, his *Tata* Marek had held his uncle at the tip of his sabre, the anger between the two men was now seemingly gone completely. Władek did not understand how men could go from being enemies to friends so quickly, but was glad they had settled their bloody dispute in the parlor just as he arrived.

Marek had begun the night's competition by telling a simple story as the men settled by the roaring fire. He told of how he had escorted the Emperor, with a whole battalion of lancers, from the English Channel town of Boulogne all the way through France and across the Alps to go on to Milan in the springtime of 1805. He explained to Władek that Napoleon had been named Emperor by the Senate almost exactly a year earlier in May of 1804, although he was not coronated until that December.

"That was when you came to Paris to see me, my son. When the Emperor was to be crowned," Marek said.

"Yes, Tata, I remember. It was so very far away," he said.

"Remember the big cathedral we took you to see, Notre Dame de Paris? That was where Napoleon officially became the Emperor while you were visiting. Your mother and I were both there."

"I just remember being in that hotel room with Uncle Tolo far too much," the boy said.

"Well, Władek, that next May we did the same thing in Milan where they have another beautiful church called the Duomo. There, the Emperor was crowned the King of Italy."

"Wow. You mean the King of all Italy?"

"Well, mostly Northern Italy, which in the years earlier we had taken from the Austrians in battle. The Pope controls the papal states around Rome, and the King of Naples rules all the lands below that. But earlier this year, Napoleon has taken even those lands from them also."

"So the Emperor controls all of Europe now, Tata?"

"He will once we have driven the last of the Prussians and their Russian allies off the lands of Poland."

"You may well defeat the Prussians, I grant you this," scoffed Bohun, "but even the mighty Napoleon will never take control of Mother Russia."

"Władek," Marek went on, ignoring the Cossack, "you should have seen all the people there in Milan and how beautifully they were dressed. It makes this look like a rag." Marek held the silky weave of the blue *zupan's* collar he then wore between his fingers. "All the princes and noblemen came out to pay tribute to the Emperor. And you know what? He was crowned with the Iron Crown of Lombardy."

"But Tata, I thought he was crowned with King Charlemagne's crown?"

"That was in Paris, Władek," his Tata said.

"It was no more than a cheap imitation," sneered Bohun.

"But in Milan," Marek went on, "they used the Iron Crown of Lombardy. It is a very special crown, even more important than Charlemagne's Crown. It has a band of iron in its rim that is said to be made from the nails that bound Our Lord Jesus Christ to his Holy Cross!"

"Wow," Władek said, as Marek cast a glare, warning Bohun not to interrupt any further. Marek answered Władek's questions, which seemed to be endless.

Then, Bohun offered the first vodka toast. They filled a glass for Władek of apple juice, so he could join the men.

"Now, let me tell you a real warrior's story, Władek. Not one of fine clothes and magnificent cathedrals, for a Cossack is proud to dress in the rags of the peasants, and the great outdoors that the good Lord created are our only church. Now, I will tell a tale of conquest and adventure, when the Cossacks rode alongside the Poles."

"But Uncle Bohun," Władek said, "I am confused. I thought the Cossacks are Russians and Napoleon is here to drive off the Russians."

"Ah, my young one," Bohun answered, "Cossacks are neither Polish nor Russian. We are the proud sons of the Steppes and the Wild Lands that lie between the two nations. Over the years we have fought with and against both sides, whenever our interests align with or oppose their own. But the story I will now tell is of when they rode alongside the Poles at Vienna to drive off the invading Turks."

"They were merely paid mercenaries," Marek chided, but was ignored just as he had ignored Bohun's comments before.

Bohun told the tale of the Cossacks riding astride Polish King Jan III Sobieski and his Winged Hussars as they charged down from the Kahlenberg Hill to rout the unsuspecting Turks. He went into great detail how they set powder charges in and blew up the Red Tent of the Turkish Grand Vizier. Then he detailed the precious booty looted from the Turks, including gold and jewel encrusted daggers and sabres, but the most valued being the fine Arabian horses the Ottomans had ridden upon.

The men downed another round of vodka, the boy his juice.

After downing that celebratory toast, Marek said to Bohun, "I am glad you did not decide to tell tales of the Cossacks during the Chmielnicki Uprising only thirty years before that attack on Vienna." He winked at Bohun, thanking him for leaving out the terrible carnage and atrocities on both sides of that nine year long Polish-Cossack war.

Then Jacek took up the speakers role and struggled to compete with the others, offering a story of his own experience in Vienna. His tale was amusing enough, and was of an Austrian officer who had belittled him at the Imperial Riding School. When time came for Jacek to prepare his mount, he intentionally did not cinch his saddle tight enough.

That Austrian officer ended up falling as his saddle loosened during drills that day. Jacek knew his little ploy had worked when he saw the mud splattered across the riding uniform of the officer on his return. All the others partaking in that day's drills were spotless. Jacek embellished the story by telling Władek that the officer who had so rudely and unnecessarily called him out the day before never uttered another cross word towards him again.

"Now it is your turn again, *Tata*," Władek said excitedly.

"Hold on, Władek," first we have to drink to Uncle Jacek's story. Then the three shots of vodka, as well as Władek's apple juice, were once more slammed back.

As the night advanced, each round was unbalanced, with exciting stories of valor and conquest being told before the fire by Marek and Bohun, followed always by a lesser story from Uncle Jacek. But as the evening wore on, Jacek began to succumb to the effects of the alcohol in his system. He wished to compete with the two younger men. At the end of what turned out to be the final round, he decided that he had saved his best for last. He was intent on giving young Władek at least one truly exceptional story of warfare to take to bed with him.

"Young man," Jacek said, "This is my last story, but one that is perhaps the most interesting of the night…"

"Do you mind if we join you men before the fire for a few moments?" Magdalena asked on behalf of herself and Maya who had finished their preparations in the kitchen.

"Please do," Jacek said with a wave of his arm to the empty sofa, as by now all three men were sitting cross-legged on the floor before the fireplace. "I have a most interesting story to share with everyone."

"*Dobrze,* but let this be the last," Magdalena said, "for in the morning I need Marek to go into the *Stare Miasto* market to buy our carp for the *Wigilia* meal tomorrow night. If you men stay up all night, he'll not wake early enough to get one of the best fish."

"And this one needs to get himself to bed as well," said Maya as she pointed to a yawning Władek at her feet.

"Well," Jacek said, conceding that his would be the last fireside tale for the night, "this final story begins with my nephew, Marek, having saved me from being rounded up with the rest of the remaining Austrian soldiers when the Emperor overtook the city of Vienna. Keep in mind most of the Viennese fighting forces had been led out of the city by the Archduke Charles, brother of the Austrian and Holy Roman Emperor Phillip. They waited with the Russians at Olmütz, near the old Polish border."

"Marek had me," Jacek continued, "a simple stable hand, assigned to an artillery unit, to look after the horses that pulled and positioned the cannon. I joined the two officers who aimed, loaded and fired the massive weapons. Have you ever seen a cannon up close, Władek?"

"Yes, Uncle Jacek. The Prussian cannons pointing out across the Vistula. *Matka* has taken me many times. They are a favorite place of mine to visit."

"Have you ever heard one fired up close?" came the next question from Jacek.

"No, only from far away, Uncle. But even then they are so loud!" Władek's tiring eyes were now stretched wide open with the anticipation of a truly captive listener.

"Well, up close, they are incredibly thunderous. I learned during the Battle of Austerlitz, or the Battle of the Three Emperors as it has come to be called, that you can feel the ground shake beneath you as every round is fired. Each blast makes you feel the bones inside your body rattle and loosen away from the flesh. And not only are you firing from your position, but along the ridgeline you are surrounded by many other of your fellow cannon installations also firing. That day we killed many of the enemy."

"Jacek!" Magdalena said, "The boy needs not hear this!"

"But yes, *Babcia,* I do," protested Władek. "I really want to hear the rest of Uncle Jacek's story…"

The child's plea warmed Jacek's heart, as he finally felt his story to be worthy to stand alongside those of Marek and Bohun.

"Well, my nephew," Jacek said, taking up the tale once more, "as devastating a weapon as our cannon was, it was sure to draw fire from the enemy cannons. One of the two artillery officers I was with was then killed when an Austrian cannonball exploded near us. Guess who had to take his place - Great-Uncle Jacek."

"How did you know what to do?" asked Maya, already showing a great interest in Jacek's story. "You had never fired a cannon before!"

"I had been watching them clean, load and fire that beast of a weapon all day. Until the man was blown away, I merely tended the horse to move and reposition the cannon. Luckily, the officer who survived did the aiming and firing. He quickly taught me how to clean and load between firings."

"Were you not afraid another cannonball from the enemy would strike you?" asked Władek.

"Yes, my boy, of course I was, but luckily another of our cannons had destroyed the Austrian weapon that had fired on us, so I had a little time to learn to load the cannon. But after you do it once, it is merely repetition. That is, so long as your nerves hold out."

"And were you successful, Uncle Jacek? Did your nerves hold out?" asked Władek, completely consumed by the story.

"They did not fail me," Jacek boasted. "Not only did we rout the Austrian army, but at the end of the day when our cavalry and infantry moved in on them, the enemy fled like wild dogs scurrying across the frozen lakes to try and get to safety."

"That is an incredible story, Uncle Jacek! You are a hero!" For the first time that evening, Władek beamed with pride and drew closer and closer to his great-uncle.

"All right, Władek," Maya said, "now its time for bed. You have already stayed up far too late."

"We have not yet toasted Uncle Jacek, *Matka,*" the child objected.

"But wait," Jacek interrupted, "you have not yet even heard the most interesting part of the story. As the Austrians fled across the ice, we received an order from Napoleon hand carried by your own *Tata* to fire upon the enemy. Soon all the cannons along the ridge line did so, breaking up the ice and casting the retreating soldiers into the frigid waters where thousands drowned."

"Well," Marek for the first time interrupted his uncle's moment of glory, "that is what the Emperor's bulletin said. In reality, it was several hundred Austrians that drowned, but that is still very many. You know these bulletins of war tend to exaggerate the facts a bit…"

"They are rags full of lies," said an outraged Bohun. "Why does the great Emperor of the French need to fire on retreating foes? It is like running your sabre through the back of a fleeing enemy! It is disgraceful."

"We were ordered to fire because these soldiers would live only to come back and make war again," said Jacek. "How many times must our Emperor defeat the Austrians? Each time they settle for peace only long enough to regroup and come back far too soon to attack the French armies. Despite what you say, I am proud of what we did that day."

"And we are proud of you, Uncle Jacek," Władek said in defense of his Great-Uncle. "You are a hero, just like *Tata* Marek and Bohun."

"All right, enough already," Maya insisted, "make your last toast and its off to bed."

The four of them did so, after which Jacek said, "I only wish Ewelina was here to hear my tale. Well, it will be wonderful to finally see her tomorrow. I will tell it to her then."

That night Marek waited for a half hour or so after Maya took Władek to bed. He drank alone in front of the fire, anticipating the renewal of his acquaintance with his Maya.

Marek had embarrassed himself with his incriminations against her regarding her cousin Bohun. Yet somehow, she seemed flattered by his jealousy. She was kind to him all night, even after he had been so quick to accuse her of infidelity. Now, he decided, we will see just how forgiving she is.

Marek climbed the staircase to the room at the top of the steps. He entered to find Maya already in bed, then searched the darkened room for Władek.

"Both he and Czesław are sleeping with Magdalena tonight," Maya said coyly.

"You mean we are alone?" Marek asked.

"Well, not exactly," Maya said softly, tilting her head to the corner of the room nearest her. "I hope you don't mind that Orest sleeps nearby in case he awakes and I need to feed my Cossack infant." Maya's face lit up with a smile that seemed to cut through the darkness like a beacon.

"Ah, you mock my jealousy," Marek said as he undressed, "at least you know I still have the ability to make quite an ass of myself. I should never give in to my envious thoughts so."

"I thought it was sweet," she said, "but I also thought it strange that your friend Rydek never told you that Bohun was my cousin."

"You mean he knew all along?" Marek said.

"Shhh! Not so loud, you'll wake the child," Maya said as the fully naked man she called husband slipped into bed next to her. "Yes, of course. He saw me nursing the infant in the garden. I had to explain."

"That bastard and his jokes," exclaimed Marek. "I could have run Bohun through tonight."

Marek's eyes adjusted to the darkness in time to watch her face stretch ever wider to accommodate the pleasure of her joy.

"I know that you would never kill an unarmed man," she said, "but I must admit you made me feel like a storybook princess in the way you defended me. It was so chivalrous of you." She then flowed over him like a mist, and rested her head upon his strong chest. "Of course I have remained faithful to you, my love."

He pulled her up to his lips and kissed her passionately. The scent of her wafted through his nostrils like waves of pleasure itself. He had waited so long for this moment, once again glad he had saved himself in every respect, that he had to force himself to hold back his desire to immediately take her. Instead, he lavished his attentions on her. He kissed her mouth, then slowly down to the tender skin at the top of her full breasts.

"My Maya," he breathed heavily, "the fullness of motherhood looks so wonderful painted upon your slender frame."

"Well," she answered, "you mean the afterglow of pregnancy. Remember that you did not think such when you first saw me full with Władek."

"But he was not my child," Marek said, "I was crazed, taunted by thinking you had been with another man."

"Not of my own doing, Marek…"

"But I did not know that, then…" he said. "Emotions flooded me on seeing you that way, my heart dropped into my stomach, just as it had thinking of you and Bohun together…"

"Now, everything is new," Maya said. "Remember I am your wife, and Władek is our child. Can you please treat him as such. Shower him with the kindness and love that you do me."

"Yes, my love," he said. "I will. But there is something I must tell you. I want you also to know that I have been completely faithful to you since we last parted."

"Even after you thought I had been with another man?" she asked.

"Especially then," Marek said, "I couldn't give up the high ground."

"You and your high ground. So you remain a soldier even in love. Well, in that regard only, I lay here as your enemy before you, waiting only for you to invade."

And that night they reignited a most tender love. All jealousies washed away, all fears of the other having shared themselves with strangers calmed, they enjoyed each other throughout the night.

When they were fatigued from satisfying their pent-up hungers for pleasure, Marek kissed her cheek and said simply, "I did not think it was possible."

Maya said softly, "Whatever are you talking about, my love?"

"I never imagined I could conquer an enemy only to still find myself held captive."

The next morning Marek took Władek with him into the market square of the *Stare Miasto* to pick out the best carp they could find for that night's Wigilia dinner. They went first to the stall selling the fish on ice, but then decided to splurge to purchase a live fish swimming in a wooden bucket.

"You couldn't get a fish any fresher if you caught it in the *Wisła* yourself," Marek said Władek. He was slowly warming to the child, but still somehow could not fully embrace the boy. Well, he decided, that was not Władek's fault. But still it changed little in how he felt.

"I enjoyed the stories last night, *Tata*," Władek said. "When I grow up in a few years, I want to become a warrior like you and Uncle Jacek. I will have many tales to tell."

"And you will," Marek replied as they walked back to the townhouse, "I am sure you will. Soldiering is all you speak of."

When they reached the house, it was late in the morning. A coach hitched to a team of horses was out front. It appeared that Tolo had brought Aunt Ewelina home in time for them both to attend the Wigilia meal that night.

They walked into the house and headed directly for the kitchen. Before he could see anyone, Marek called out, "*Matka*, do you have a wooden bathing tub? This beast of a carp needs to swim, he is too confined in this wooden pail."

But Marek heard nothing. Worse than nothing. The emptiness of the house was laced with a solemn heaviness. As they neared the kitchen, Marek could hear the soft sobbing of not one woman, but several. Ewelina was indeed back from Kraków, and she brought with her an unbearable sadness.

"Then, Dr. Olszewski offered to take Tolo and I out of the city and on to our old *folwark* in Wieliczka," his Aunt said through tears, which flowed uninterrupted on her face. Her voice was unsteady, stilted with grief. "There the Count Von Arndt joined us and showed us to their graves."

"That man is a bastard," said Magdalena. "He stripped me of everything but my dignity."

"Władek," why don't you go find Tolo and Ignacy to take the horses round back to the carriage house to be looked after. They have had a long journey."

The boy ran out of the room, leaving only Marek, his mother Magdalena, Maya and the distraught Ewelina.

"I know he has been a terrible person to you in the past," Ewelina said, "but the man was like a saint to me that day. He told me how he had searched and searched for the bodies of my sons. They eventually were found, but were unrecognizable from being under the waters of that lake for so long...My poor boys, drowned...Our poor boys...I have no idea how I will ever tell Jacek."

Ewelina then heaved with a sorrow so pervasive that one is lucky to never feel it in their lifetime. Her delicate frame trembled with anguish. Marek and Maya looked at each other while Magdalena wrapped herself around her wailing sister-in-law.

"Where?" Marek asked. "What lake do you refer to?"

"Austerlitz," Maya responded tersely, having heard Ewelina's tale of woe from the beginning.

"But that was long ago," Marek said, "over a year ago."

"Their bodies were not found after the battle," Maya explained as quietly as she could. "They remained under the lake after it froze again. They remained there until the lake thawed in the spring. Only then, their bloated bodies were unrecognizable."

"Then how can the Count be sure he received the bodies of Bartek and Andrzej?" Marek asked. He thought of his last night with them in Augsburg, when he had set them free.

"No one recognized them at first," Ewelina said, fighting to contain her own grief. "Doctor Olszewski said each boy's body bore no wounds…" Then Ewelina lost control again and sobbed to the point that her own body became racked with crippling pain.

Maya finished the retelling of Ewelina's tale. "Their bodies each only had the same nick of a sabre's tip in their chest, nearly identical, as if someone had intended to mark them. So from these the authorities knew these two bodies were somehow tied together, likely brothers. When word finally reached the Count, he sent Doctor Olszewski to examine the bodies. He arrived just before they were to be committed to a mass grave. The bodies were bloated beyond recognition, but the doctor was able to identify them from some scar tissue on each boy that he had treated from their childhood injuries on the *folwark*. He had been authorized by the Count to take control of the bodies. The Count paid for them to be shipped back to the Wieliczka *folwark* for burial in the cemetery there as Austrian war dead." Her voice cracked with sorrow.

"This is horribly tragic news," was all that Marek could think to say.

"NO! NO!" Ewelina exploded, *"NO, MAREK! THIS WAS MY LIFE!* These boys were my sons, the joy of my life!"

"Of course they were, *Ciocia* Ewelina," he said meekly.

"NO, DON'T YOU DARE SAY THAT TO ME! I know you were the one who marked them when you released them from being the prisoners of the French! Jacek wrote me so! You knew they would go back to their units! That's why you defiled the skin of your cousins with your own initials, like they were nothing more than cattle! Marek Zaczek, your cousins' deaths are on your head! If the French still held my children they would be alive this morning! May the almighty forever curse you, as I have since the day you left the *folwark!* At least they were not sniveling deserters like you!" Her fury had increased with each word. Her face filled with rage, then became as bright as a beet.

Ewelina then swooned and collapsed just as Marek moved in close to catch her. Magdalena attended to her as Marek held her in his arms. At that point, Jacek came into the room and helped his nephew carry his wife to a bedroom.

Magdalena had followed them into the bedroom and sat on the chair next to the bed where Ewelina was laid. She said, "Tolo told me she was in a daze the entire trip back, but refused to speak of her sons. It appears talking of all this has overcome her."

"What exactly happened?" Jacek asked Marek, his wife laid out on the bed, completely unconscious, no longer able to bear the strain of the moment.

"Take Jacek out and tell him all of it," Magdalena said to Marek. "He must know everything." So Marek took his uncle out of the room and went through the horrendous chain of events with Jacek, who crumpled into a ball of pity with each sentence. The reality of his sons' deaths struck him incredibly hard.

"Fate has treated me most cruelly for taking pride last night in telling the story of how I turned the guns of France on the retreating Austrians. God has punished me, as it turns out that I had fired upon my own two boys… I can only hope that the Lord *Jezus Chrystus* will forgive me. I know my Ewelina never will."

You don't know that your cannon fire killed them, Marek began to say, but stopped himself realizing it really didn't matter. Before Marek could console him, Jacek walked way from his nephew, swatting away Marek's outreached arms. He said nothing more and wandered out of the house, away from all the horror of the loss of his beloved Andrzej and Bartek and to the carriage house where be could be amidst those who seemed to understand him best. Jacek wished only to be alone with the longtime companions of all stablehands - the horses they cared for.

Marek wanted to give Jacek some time to collect himself, so he did not follow his uncle. Instead he had to deal with his own conflicting emotions to the news of their loss that had so tragically transpired. He had set his cousins free, that was true, but only after they refused to join the French infantry. Then they ignored his instruction to return home and instead returned to the Austrian army. Why had they ignored his pleas? Instead, they survived the worst of that horrendous Battle of Austerlitz only to have the ice they scurried across in retreat shot out from under them. And among the artillerymen firing upon them was their own father.

Twenty minutes later, he went out to console his uncle. As he walked through the coach house and stables, he was distracted by the neighing and restlessness of the animals. Then, as he came to the tack station, he found the reason for the horses' agitation. His uncle's lifeless body swung from a rafter, a leather bridle cutting into his neck. Marek paused in shock for a second, then raced to grab his uncle's legs and lift him. He was able to bring his uncle down, but in the process of doing so he knew from its dead weight response that there was no life left in Jacek's body.

As Marek laid his uncle's corpse on the stable floor, Marek looked sorrowfully at Jacek's lifeless body. His thoughts instantly took him to the forest pond where they had collected swan feathers for Marek's childhood project of making Hussar wings. How Jacek had laughed when a swan attacked the unsuspecting child he was.

It was then that Marek noticed a note scratched on some paper kept at the tack station. Marek stared at it curiously, and at first did not make the connection. Instead, he thought of those Hussar wings that were mounted on the walls of Władek's room.

Under the weight of this, one of his most pleasant memories, that brave soldier broke down and cried like a child. He cried for what seemed an hour but physically felt like an eternity. The tears rained from him like the fat drops of a sudden summer thunderstorm. Each tear seemed to pull shreds of himself up through his throat. Shedding these left his heart and soul feeling devastatingly empty, and the muscles and sinew of his body feeling raw, but still weighed down by the entire world.

When he finally stopped sobbing, he once again spotted and reached for the note. It was scrawled in a legible cursive script.

"Forgive me, my Ewelina, for not being able to bear any longer what I have done without knowing, even to have openly bragged about my role in it. I cannot bear to face you with the truth. When you kneel to pray for the innocent souls of our sons, please remember my ever-cursed spirit…"

The note seared Marek's bleeding heart. It made him realize how little he really knew about his uncle. When Jacek was conscripted in Vienna over a decade ago, Marek had to read his aunt's letters to him. Somewhere over the years since then Jacek had learned to read and write. It occurred to Marek at that moment, that since being reunited with Jacek, he had never even noticed it. And Jacek had never mentioned it. Marek broke down again as shame and guilt overcame him in equal measures .

Chapter 32: The Foretelling
Christmas Eve and Morning, 1806

Wigilia was abandoned that night given the horrific nature of the circumstances. The live carp and all the prepared foods were given to a family in need.

At least some good could come from the ghastly triple tragedy. No one could be expected to eat. Ewelina had to be given opium from the nearby apothecary, which Marek visited just before their early closing for the Holy Night. He had to plead with the chemist for the sedative on her behalf by sharing the horror of his aunt's devastating disasters. What he received was a sleeve of crushed opium, fresh from the head chemist's mortar and pestle.

Marek had been trained in administering the drug for the battlefield. Earlier that year a German pharmacist had isolated a new compound from the raw opium, and named his drug after Morpheus, the god of dreams. But morphine was heavily sought after by all the militaries of Europe, and was not available to the public. It would not be long before it was discovered just how truly addicting that new compound was.

After sedating his Aunt Ewelina with the crushed opium, Marek went for a long walk through the town, during which he decided he would return to his unit the next day. He had shown Magdalena how to administer the sedative, for even then he knew he could not bear another week of being under the same roof as his aunt. He would only serve to be a visual reminder to her of those tragic circumstances. It was clear from the night before she blamed him for every disaster that had descended upon her family.

If returning early to his unit meant being separated from his wife and their child, Czesław, he knew Maya would certainly understand. He would miss them both terribly. He decided he would even miss Władek, to whom he felt himself slowly warming in affection.

Marek would, of course, also miss his mother. Magdalena was distraught not only with the unexpected deaths of her brother-in-law and nephews, but also she worried as to how this might affect Ewelina in the future. The separation of more than a decade from Jacek and their boys had made her sister-in-law intensely bitter. Ewelina had already become, even before their deaths, unbearable to live with. Whether it was just or not, her rage seemed to have been triggered by a single event - Marek's desertion from the Austrian army to the French. It got to the point that Magdalena would not speak of Marek whenever Ewelina was present, lest she go off on another of her acerbic rants.

Magdalena had long thought the seed of it all was jealousy - her son had escaped the Austrian army, while Ewelina's sons and husband remained trapped, seemingly forever, within it. With the finality of their three deaths, that *"forever "* had hardened into a cruel cell of tormented reality.

Magdalena had also decided that on Christmas Day she would find time to be alone with her son and reveal to Marek the secret of his father's identity. Yet given the descent of darkness on this house, once more the time was not right to share with Marek this truth. It was too much for her son to bear.

The morning of Christmas Day, Marek came down from his room hoping to leave before anyone else awakened. He had said his goodbyes to Maya and his *matka* the night before, but told them since the *Grande Armée* was in its Winter Quarters around Warsaw, he could still stop by to see them regularly over the next few months. He had come down the main staircase in his Lancers Uniform, his rucksack in hand, and headed for the door when he heard an unexpected voice from behind.

"Good! I no longer have to see you in that ridiculous blue *zupan* of your father's," his Aunt Ewelina said.

They were alone. No one else had stirred.

"No, you do not, *Ciocia*," he said.

"Of course," she went on, still clearly groggy and under the lingering effects of the opium, "the *zupan* is still less offensive than that garish uniform you could not wait to crawl back into."

"Yes, *Ciocia*, now I must leave you," Marek said, hoping to end the discussion.

"Leave me with what?" she bit back, her voice filling with venom. "You are leaving me with nothing - no sons, no husband, no future and no hope."

"You do not know what you are saying," Marek replied. "I could never bring harm to any of them knowingly. If you believe otherwise, then you do not know me at all."

"Ah, but beloved Marek," she said, her voice becoming flatter, less sharp, "I know more about you than you even know yourself. Recall that it was I who was there when you were brought into this world. I was your mother's confidant. I know things that she has not even revealed to you."

"You are still at the mercy of the opium," he said, "I am paying you no mind."

"Yes, Marek," his aunt hissed at him. "No mind, pay me no mind at all. I suggest you think long and hard on what I am about to tell you. Remember that it was your actions that took my sons and my husband away from me. It is only right that I now take your cherished father away from you in return."

"You can never take away my memories of Bronisław, for he was and is a saint to me. I have always and will always revere him. Nothing you can say will affect the fondness with which I hold him. Remember, of the dead speak well or not at all."

A sly look slithered across his aunt's face. She was enjoying this discussion of riddles. "I will never speak ill of my brother, Bronisław. He was a good man, better than your family deserved. But tell me, do you ever recall seeing him dressed in that ridiculous blue *zupan?*"

"As I have already told my mother, no," Marek confessed, "he would never have worn anything that fanciful."

"Recall I said it was your *father's* garment?" she spat the words at him.

"As did my mother. What is your point?" Despite his sympathy for his aunt, Marek was tiring of her.

"Marek - here is the truth. The truth that your own mother has kept from you since your birth and will never find the right time to reveal to you. That blue *zupan* was worn often by your father. Not Bronisław, but rather the man who raped your mother and placed the evil seed in her that became you. Your father was not Bronisław the miner as you were raised to believe, but was actually the Duke Sdanowicz. How do you think you were ever allowed such leeway in riding any mount from his stable, when my husband, his own stable-master, was not allowed that privilege?"

"You mind is still affected by the sedative powder, *Ciocia,*" he said truly believing so.

"Yes, it is, but it only gives me the courage to finally speak the truth to you. I am not your mother, who creates fictions to hide truths! Why do you think the Duke went to such great lengths to keep you and Maya from running off? Because he knew you were both from his loins - a half-sister and half-brother. And now you have broken God's law and created another. Do you not wonder why your child Czesław is so slow? Shows little interest in other people? Why he only clutches onto that rosary and crucifix? His soul prays for salvation from the fate that you and Maya have so sinfully delivered him into."

"You are mad with grief," Marek said as he grabbed his rucksack and stormed out the door. Ewelina, still in her bedclothes, followed after him and yelled from atop the steps.

"YOU CANNOT RUN FROM WHO YOU ARE, YOU BASTARD!" she screamed at the top of her lungs, splitting the hush of the chilled Christmas morning's air. "It is time for you to erase my brother from your memories. Bronisław was too pure a soul to bear you as a son. Remember Duke Sdanowicz wearing that damned blue *zupan*. That jackal was your real father!"

Marek walked away defiantly, around to the coachhouse in the rear. Ewelina turned to race through the house so as to continue to confront Marek as he saddled his mount. She was intercepted by Magdalena, who stood with a lamp behind her in her nightclothes.

"What is all this shouting? You will wake the dead!"

"Then let every corpse stir, Magda," Ewelina sneered, using the peasant form of her sister-in-law's name. "I have now done what you what you in your weakness never could!" Ewelina then tried to push past Magdalena, who moved instinctively to cut her off, protecting Marek from further abuse.

"You need to return to bed, Ewelina. You need your rest," Magdalena said forcibly, blocking the hall, but not the staircase.

Ewelina sneered in return. "There will be no more rest in this house. Not for me, ever, but neither for you. For the secret you could not bring yourself to tell your son, I now have. I did it to strike back at you, as much as him. You both have taken away all that I ever loved in this life. I hope I have done the same to you."

Magdalena realized what her sister-in-law had done and began to collapse into a wounded ball onto a hall bench behind her. Ewelina raced through the opening beyond her, but by the time she made her way across the small yard to the coachhouse, she could only hear the hooves of Marek's horse galloping away.

Chapter 33: The Savior's Day
Christmas Day 1806

Marek Zaczek returned on Christmas morning to his unit camped out on the grounds along the Vistula surrounding the Royal Castle. He tried desperately to forget all that had occurred, and the haunting feeling that shadowed him. The only problem was that the refuge he ran to was a vacated one, devoid of any companions to distract him from his troubles. The Polish Lancer Battalion of the Imperial Guards was out on maneuvers with the Emperor.

However, the few souls left behind to tend to the untaken horses in the stables quickly spread the word of *Capitaine* Zaczek's return with their counterparts serving within the castle. Word soon came that Marek was invited that Christmas Day to dine with the Grand Marshal of the Palace, General Géraud Christophe Michel Duroc. Marshal Duroc was still recovering from the broken collarbone he suffered when his coach flipped on its way to Warsaw. For that reason, Duroc did not join the Emperor in the pursuit of the Russians. To bounce in a saddle with his injury would have been a torture Marshal Duroc could not possibly have endured.

They were treated, along with a few others of high rank still in Warsaw, to a fabulous holiday feast. Local women were brought in to prepare it alongside the traveling army chefs. It was a high honor for these *pani*, as they prepared local dishes. Poles traditionally feasted from meat dishes on this Holy Day after having eaten only fish during the *Wigilia* meal late the night before.

So the women prepared plates of meat-laden dishes of *gołąbki* (stuffed cabbage) and *bigos* (hunter's stew), along with a spread of many meatless dishes, including *śledź pod pierzynką* (a layered herring salad), followed by *kutia* (wheat pudding), *buraczki* (beet salad), *barszcz z uszkami* (the Polish version of borscht only with mushroom dumplings), *kluski z makiem* (egg noodles and poppyseeds), mushroom soup and, of course, mushroom and sauerkraut filled *pierogi*.

Marek, given his depressed state, did not partake of anything. The few French officers he ate alongside noticed their companion's distraction. Marek soon found himself, at their requests, describing and commenting on the cultural significance of each dish.

"In all, twelve dishes were prepared for the *Wigilia*, the Christmas Eve feast," Marek explained, "to represent the twelve Apostles. A typical Polish Christmas Day meal would be made from those dishes left over from the *Wigilia*, as well as anything else the women of the house had freshly prepared."

Providing this commentary took his mind temporarily off all the accusations his Aunt Ewelina had weighed upon him that morning. He fought the temptation to dwell on her words and sink into that morass of black thoughts. He focused on his commentary. After all the main dishes were sampled, Marek moved over to the separate dessert table.

"Ah, Marshal Duroc," he said, "we have a real treat here today. The ladies have outdone themselves. First, we have *kołaczki*, Polish butter cookies filled with farmer's cheese and fruit preserves. These delicious delights I would have expected at this hardy meal, but alongside them is a special treat reserved only for Christmas, and sometimes the last day of Lent before the Easter holiday. They are *chruściki, or faworki*, lighter than the angel wings they are fashioned after. As a child, these were the rarest of treats, offered only by the Duke to us peasants on these holidays."

As the word's slipped his tongue, Marek could not help but think of his aunt's horrific ramblings.

Marshal Duroc's gaze seemed to be fixed upon the delicate pastry treats, which were piled high with powdered sugar - a rarity in that time. Marek was not surprised to discover that Duroc had it carted all the way from Paris, just for the Emperor's enjoyment.

"They look delicious," Marshal Duroc said, "I can't recall anything in French pastry quite resembling them."

"Go ahead, Marshal," Marek said, "try one. It is very rare, even now, to have the confectioner's sugar needed to make these properly. It will be quite a treat for you."

Marek then picked one up and demonstrated how to hold it such that the sugar would not fall all over the person eating it.

The Marshal reached with his good arm to take one, lifted it to his mouth and took a bite, smiled broadly, and said, "These are truly heavenly, Zaczek."

"Yes," Marek agreed, "we also have a little custom that my friends and I would do while eating them. Take another bite and I'll be happy to demonstrate…"

The Marshal was pleased to indulge Marek and took another bite of the feather light pastry piled high with white powder. Marek then quickly raised his hand, made a strained circle with his thumb and forefinger, and reached out to the Marshal's pastry. Duroc could not react as his own hand held the delight while the other was still immobilized in the sling. Marek then released his forefinger with a snap, just as the Marshal took his bite. The powdered sugar exploded in Duroc's face, and drifted down like a light winter's snow, falling in a meandering fashion upon this uniform and sling. As the white veil slowly settled from the air, an agitated Marshall Duroc was revealed. His cheeks became flush with rage at this mere *Capitaine* playing such a childish prank on someone so elevated as himself.

Marek initially laughed aloud, but became concerned when Marshal Duroc did not join him. Duroc's face looked stamped with anger, but the small crowd of officers began to clap, and called out in French, *"Bon Sport! Maréchal Duroc, Bon Sport!"*

Then slowly, Duroc's clenched-lipped countenance of embarrassment gave way to a slightly quivering chin, and afterwards a hearty laugh. "Yes, Zaczek, I can see how that would be hilarious to a group of children. Now, take a plate of these delights and let you and I retire to my private office for coffee."

When they arrived there, after using a napkin to clean the powder from his uniform jacket, Marshal Duroc and Marek sat across from each other around a small table. Coffee was served in fine china, and each man took a hearty sip.

"As we sit here enjoying these fineries, Zaczek, I was made aware by courier earlier that the Emperor plans to attack the Russians, some 50,000 strong at Pułtusk. Do you know this town?"

"I believe so. About fifty kilometers north of here, on the River Narew. But that is much more of a battle than the skirmishing that I was led to believe would be happening. I should ride to join them."

"No, Zaczek, I need you to remain here. If there are problems, then I myself will give the order to send you there, either as a courier or to retake command of your battalion of lancers."

"Yes, General," Marek replied, "but may I inquire which Russian leader the Emperor is up against?"

"It appears to be General Bennigsen, but the Emperor has Marshal Lannes' V Corps with him and Marshals Davout, Murat and Augereau and their corps are nearby. The conditions are apparently horrendous, a blizzard of mixed sleet, snow and rain over swampy grounds. What roads there are have become a morass of mud. We will know for sure by the end of tomorrow the results of the battle, but I am confident that even in those elements, our Emperor will prevail."

Marek truly felt the need to mount up in the morning and ride out to the sound of the guns. Nothing would clear his mind of the revelations from his aunt then to be forced to concentrate upon the battle at Pułtusk. But to do so after the Marshal's direct order to stay put would be grounds for his court-martial. His face must have shown his regret, for Marshal Duroc then changed the tone of the conversation entirely.

"Now, Zaczek," Duroc said, "we have another pressing concern. I understand you were present when the Countess Walewska exchanged pleasantries with the Emperor at Blonie?"

"Yes," Zaczek said, "I was there." He left out that it was his doing that resulted in the two coming together.

"Well, Zaczek," the Marshal continued, "she is all that he has been talking about. Our Emperor has become infatuated with her. I have served him for many years, and in many lands, and have never seen him as focused on any one particular woman."

"I can surely understand," Marek said, "that night was the first time laying my own eyes on her, she was quite striking in her beauty. Is the Emperor aware that she is not only married to a rather respected nobleman, but also recently became a mother to her first child?"

"That was shared with the Emperor," Duroc admitted, "but somehow he has found out that the woman's husband is four times her age. He seems to feel the need to rescue her from that horrid situation. He says her beauty is not to be wasted on the seventy year old count. The Emperor knows the price she will pay, being trapped in a loveless marriage. He is, of course, married to Joséphine, but between us, I dare to share with you, and for no others' ears, their love has long ago dimmed out. I say all this, as I have said, I have never seen him as mesmerized by a woman before as he is with the Countess Walewska. He said you would provide me with the information needed to contact her..."

"Well, as it turns out," Marek then said, "my own mother is well acquainted with the family. She has given me the address of the Countess while she is here in Warsaw."

"You say, *'while she is here in Warsaw'* ?" Duroc asked. "Where is her and the Count's primary residence?"

Marek noticed an unfurled map of Poland on the desk and moved to it.

"They have a beautiful estate here, in the town of Walewice, not far from the city of Łódź," Marek said, "or so I am told. My mother has spent much time there. She describes it as quite a magnificent palace in its own right."

"This Count that the young Madame is married to must be as rich as he is old…" Duroc said, "to have a town named after his family, and a palace there no less. Do you suspect he will make trouble for the Emperor if he decides to pursue his wife?"

"The man is very important, and thus very proud," Marek said. "He was Chamberlain to the last king of Poland, Prince Poniatowski's uncle. If he thinks the Emperor only wishes to use his wife during his stay in Warsaw throughout the winter, then who can say what the Count might say or do."

"Thank you, Marek," Duroc said, "you have given me a great idea. I speak to Prince Józef Poniatowski and explain that this is in the best interest of Poland. Then he can feel out the old Count. See what he thinks. Is the revival of his country more important than his sharing his wife with the Emperor a bit?"

"I am sorry, General, but it all sounds so seedy to me," Marek said, "to procure the Countess like a mare for the Emperor."

"But is the Emperor before all else not a man?" Duroc asked aloud, then used the Emperor's name for the first time. "Does Napoleon Bonaparte, the man, not have the same needs as do all of us?"

"But even Poland is not so pure we do not have some women of lesser virtues who could attend to the Emperor's needs," Marek argued. "Why must it be a married woman? A mother? The young Countess, no less?"

"Because this is exactly who the Emperor desires."

Marshal Duroc then took another cup of coffee and rang a service bell for his attendant.

"Would you like a brandy?" Duroc asked Marek.

"Perhaps a vodka," Marek replied.

Marek needed that drink. He could not help but feel as though they were negotiating the acquisition of the Countess as one might a sale of cattle, or some other commodity to be consumed, and whatever was left of it was to be thrown aside like an empty carcass.

"Zaczek, I have one other request," Duroc said. "Prince Poniatowski and the elders of Warsaw wish to honor the Emperor for liberating Poland with a ball soon. I am scheduling it for January 17th. The Magnate Stanisław Potocki has agreed to hold it at his Wilanów Palace here in Warsaw. However, the Emperor refuses to attend unless the Countess is there. Would it be possible to request your mother to assure the Countess Walewska will still be in Warsaw and will plan to attend? In return, I will be happy to set aside an invitation for your mother and her escort."

"Only if my wife may join her," Marek said, "assuming, of course that I will be in Sire's Polish Honor Guard?"

"Of course, of course," Duroc said. "I can explain their attendance away as the Emperor extending an honor to his favorite Polish cavalry officer. Just beware that may this may make General Dąbrowski and Prince Poniatowski quite envious."

The two men laughed at the General's joke as their drinks arrived.

"Marek, just remember," Duroc then said seriously, "the Emperor could be the very savior of your Poland."

Marek paused, gave the comment great consideration, then said, "Marshal Duroc, Poland, this day, holds glory for only one Savior. And he is neither French nor Corsican. Today, all glory goes to the God that I happen to know our Emperor does not believe in."

Marshal Duroc looked at Marek with a hint of dismay.

"While the Emperor may not hold the reverence you do with regard to the dogma of religion, he certainly holds with its traditions. I believe that the giving of gifts is still appropriate with Christmas, no? So be aware, my young *capitaine*, that the Emperor has decided to expand your Lancers *Polonais* unit from a single battalion to a full regiment in strength a few months from now. I also want you to be aware that the regiment will come under the control of Count Wincenty Krasiński as its colonel, but do not despair as you will be promoted to lieutenant colonel as his second in command. Congratulations and Merry Christmas, Zaczek."

The news crushed Marek, who responded merely by saying, "So you are telling me, Marshal Duroc, that the unit I have created is to gain a regimental standing, but in the course of it being so elevated I will lose direct control over it. I am not sure I can be as appreciative as you might expect me to be."

With his sarcasm being heaped atop his words, Marek swallowed the rest of his vodka in a single gulp, rose and bowed to the seated Duroc. He then rushed to leave the Royal Castle.

Chapter 34: The Confrontation
New Years Day, 1807

The Battle of Pułtusk, fought on the day after Christmas, 1806 proved to be an inconclusive engagement. Napoleon's 27,000 man army took on a superior 45,000 man combined Russian and Prussian force in the snow. Neither side gained an all out victory, but with Count Bennigsen withdrawing his troops after the fall of darkness, Napoleon would, the next morning, take the town the Russians had abandoned. He could thus declare the engagement a French victory before heading south to the comforts of Warsaw.

Upon their return, Marek was pleased to be reunited with his unit, which for the first time had gone into battle without him. Yet, even with this comfort, *Capitaine* Zaczek could not ease his mind enough to forget the acrimonious words of his Aunt Ewelina. Could it be that they were just a venom spewed in anger without any veracity whatsoever, or were they seeds of a bitter, hidden truth hurled at him in despair?

Marek could not face Magdalena directly. He had sent her a message by courier, asking her to seek out whether the Countess Walewska would attend the ball honoring the Emperor. Now he awaited her reply.

Could it really be true, he wondered, *that the late Duke Sdanowicz, the man he had long grown to despise, was actually his father? The very man who committed him to the Austrian army?*

Marek refused to accept it. Bronisław the miner who had toiled all his life for the Duke was his father, he was sure. He could feel it in his bones. Yet still, something gnawed at him.

Marek remembered his last encounter with the Duke, when they both stood over Bronisław's grave in the *folwark* cemetery. *Why was Bronisław even given a spot in those grounds reserved for the Duke's family? Was it as a gift, an enticement of some form for his mother?*

The more Marek thought over the possibility, the more unfounded his adult life seemed to become. It was as if everything he held dear had been forcibly corrupted. His homeland had been stolen from him by the three greedy empires that neighbored it. The virtue of his love had been stolen by her own despicable uncle. And now, his own father was stolen from him by the lust of a rich and powerfully corrupt Duke? Even worse, *I am expected to believe that horrible man's blood pulses in my very veins?*

Rape. Rape. Rape. It appeared all that he cherished in life had been spoiled forever by the force of rape - that fleshy avarice. And worst of all, the man he admired most, the Emperor, was desirous only of raping the women of Warsaw. Or at least one in particular - the Countess Marie Walewska. Marek's entire world had become unfounded.

Word soon came that Magdalena refused to answer her son's request by courier. Instead, the return note read, she would meet him on New Year's Day in Castle Square, at the foot of the King Zygmunt III Waza column at one o'clock.

So, on that first day of 1807, mother and son met, upon the beginning of that thirteenth hour of the new year. A light snow was falling, slowly frosting over the previously corrupted snow-laden streets, thickly soiled from the wheels of wagons and horse dung. Marek thought that the nature of the questions he had for Magdalena will also defile the purity of the flakes freshly falling.

"Well, *Matka,* do you have an answer from Countess Walewska? Will she and the Count attend the ball at the Wilanów Palace on the 17th?"

Her eyes looked tired, weary of his direct manner. "Walk with me, my son. Before I give you the answer from Countess Marie, we have other, more urgent, matters to discuss."

She began walking, knowing her son would follow so long as the answers he sought remained not given. Magdalena headed into the narrow maze of streets of the *Stare Miasto,* the old town. They were mostly empty that frigid New Year's Day.

"Your Aunt Ewelina is in a truly desperate state of mind. She had been stripped of the love of Uncle Jacek and her two boys for so long, and had become so bitter, that now with them taken from her permanently, she only wishes to lash out."

"Yes, *Matka,* and I appear to be her preferred target," Marek said softly, as he could feel his mother tensing as the subject was broached.

"No my son, *we* appear to be her preferred target," she said. "What she blurted to you in her anger on Christmas morning was not meant only to wound you, but me in equal measures. She is using my inability to tell you this secret as a cudgel of revenge."

"Then you know?" Marek asked, "Those awful accusations? They are true?"

"I had begun dressing to come down and see you off," she admitted, "even though you had said your goodbyes the night before. I heard her awful rant from the top of the staircase. I am so sorry, my son."

Marek noticed tears forming in her eyes as they walked in a rigid forward line through the narrow streets. He wondered how she could walk so perfectly straight while at the same time dancing around the issues that lay like an expansive gulf between them. Yet she did not deny his Aunt Ewelina's accusation.

"So it is all true," he said, "the more I thought on it, the more I knew what she said had a ring of truth to it. But why did you never tell me of this? Not after Bronisław's death, not after I was nearly killed at Maciejowice? Not when you came to Milan to tell me of your intentions to marry that swine Count Von Arndt?"

Marek had to stop himself. His words were racing from his lips with an urgency assailing them like spears at Magdalena. She began to cry softly, and turned her face away from him in shame.

"The Duke Sdanowicz took me against my will," she finally whispered, although there was no one within earshot to have heard her even had she yelled it. "I swear to you I did not give myself willingly to him, that I never would. He threatened to kill Bronisław if I refused him. Bronisław, that man who was such a good husband to me."

"And a wonderful father to me," said Marek added, "but he was, in reality, not my father, was he? His blood, simple and pure, does not flow in my body, does it? No, instead in these veins flows the blood of my true father, the man who killed Bronisław. He trapped him forever in that damned salt mine. He stole him for days and weeks at a time from me. And then finally forever. Always I hated the Duke for that reason alone. Yet, that last time I saw him, standing with me over Bronisław's grave, he gave me permission to take Maya as my wife. Why would he do that? He knew we were half-brother and sister…"

"By then the Duke was a twisted, defeated man," Magdalena said. "The Count Von Arndt had not only stolen from him all he possessed, but had also elevated me over him. You see, even though the Duke forced himself on me, he still thought I was his property. He thought he owned all of us peasants. Yet he had a warped desire that I might one day give myself willingly to him, which I never did. So in his disgrace of having lost everything, his giving you Maya's hand was the last and only weapon he had to stab back at me."

"And Maya, his own daughter," Marek replied. "She was all I ever wanted, the only girl I ever really desired. Then, after I have finally won her heart, I learn that this is all just a farce! A folly that could have been avoided had you just told me years ago! A bastard child that need never to have been born…"

His words were becoming accusatory once more. It was then that his mother broke, and stopping on the steps of a church, a mixture of shame, embarrassment and regret poured forth from her.

"Marek!" she cried. "Never again speak of your son in that tone again in front of me. All life is precious. You too were a bastard, as you say. So many times I was on the very cusp of telling you but just as I worked up that last bit of courage needed, there was always a valid reason not to. In the end, I feared hurting you and driving you away forever, my Marek, for I knew from the very first instant that I looked upon your face, that you were the one thing I could not live without. Not riches, nor titles, and although it is sad to admit, not even my husband. I have myself been a Duke's daughter, then a peasant girl, then a Countess restored, and finally now just a mere old woman living on the charity of another, bless her soul. But along the way, I am above all else a mother. And no mother could ever live without those she bore. You, my son, are my very life, the spark of my existence. I cannot live without the promise of seeing you again. And this is exactly why your Aunt Ewelina is so very wretched in her agony."

Her tears were by then streaming down her face. Marek took out his handkerchief and wiped them away.

"There is nothing that I can do to change any of this," Marek said. "So the father I loved so much turned out to be a lie."

"No, Marek," Magdalena interrupted, "Bronisław never knew. He loved you as his own because to him you were his own. He knew no better. My most delightful years were my hardest, but softened by the love that good man had always for us both."

"And my Maya?" he said. "Surely, you must have told her after the birth of Czesław?"

"How could I possibly?" Magdalena protested. "It would very likely have killed her."

"Yet you came up with this intricate fiction?" he asked.

"Just to cover the shame of her being taken against her will, as I once was. To lift that disgrace from her, the stares of the other women in the markets and squares. At least I never had to endure that because everyone always assumed you were Bronisław's son. My *"fiction"* was developed to make her whole and keep Władek pure. But never did I tell her I had undergone the same disgrace at the hands of her own father. I never dreamed you and she would have a child together. Don't you recall how in my letter I begged you not to consummate this relationship?"

"Mother, you are so amusing," Marek scoffed. "You think you can create false worlds out of whole cloth, and then control them by decree? No, *Matka*, you only light a fuse to a powder keg, and when it flares out of control you are surprised? So, now, a half-brother and half-sister have given birth to a slow son. Is it a surprise that God would would punish us so?"

"Marek, do not say that," Magdalena replied. "All life is a gift from God, no matter how impure the circumstances under which it is created." Her hands raised to caress his handsome face. "There is no greater gift. As I just said, you, yourself are living proof of that, my son. Life is the answer to all prayers."

Then she allowed her hands to slide from his jaws, coming together in a prayerful and supplicate manner.

"And do not lose faith in young Czesław," she continued. "Yes, he is behind where I think he should be right now, but there is something special about that child. I can feel it. He reveres the Lord, even at his young age. I will work very hard to be sure he never loses that grace. Now, come inside, my son. Pray with me.

Just one rosary will lighten your mother's heart so. Pray to our Lord that all this will be reconciled to His will."

"The Countess Walewska," inquired Marek, "will she attend the Emperor's ball?"

"Yes," Magdalena said, "but only accompanied by her husband, the Count Walewski, of course."

I hardly think that will deter the Emperor, Marek thought.

"Now, you have your answer," Magdalena said, reaching in her purse for something. "Come inside, take shelter in the house of the Lord. Let us pray for your safety in all these dreadful battles and wars. Do this for your mother, Marek."

She pulled from her purse a rosary, with large black beads and a silver crucifix. Marek recognized it as the very rosary that his son, Czesław, had held so dearly.

"I am sorry, *moja Matka,*" he said. "I must return to the Royal Castle."

Magdalena's eyes unleashed torrents of remorse as he said his goodbye. She thought it might be the last words he would ever again speak to her.

Then Marek leaned forward and kissed her forehead in a prescribed, almost loveless manner, before turning and retracing his steps in the fresh fallen snow. He left his mother in a sobbing heap which slowly collapsed onto the landing of the steps of the church. Upon laying flat upon that surface, where vile earth held the promise to transition to heaven itself, a guttural groan of pure agony escaped from her.

Marek Zaczek heard her sorrowful wail as he walked away, but he did not turn back to her.

"I must be strong," he thought, "for the Lord only knows what other evils await us all in this world."

All the nobility of Warsaw turned out for Stanisław Potocki's ball given in honor of the Emperor Napoleon at the magnificent Wilanów Palace. Those attending were a collection of proud people bound together by a valiant history, and who shared a well defined and cherished culture. But they also all shared the pain of being without the legitimacy of a nation to call their own. They searched frantically for any enticement to serve up to their conquering Emperor which might induce Napoleon to deliver them from their unjust servitude.

After all, Napoleon had seemingly driven their Germanic overlords from their immediate area - the lands between Berlin and Warsaw - with little effort. Yet, the Prussians remained hunkered down just to the north in the lands where East Prussia adjoined Russia along the Baltic Sea. These were lands that once had historically belonged to the Poles as well, before being taken from them by the Teutonic Knights.

The Poles needed the Emperor to defeat their current Germanic neighbors once and for all. Then, they could drive the Russians back to the east, past the historical boundary that was the Niemen River. The Poles could recover their lands stolen by the Russians in the Partitions, which along with the lands recovered from Prussia would make up the core of the Polish nation. All that would be left afterward was to retake the Austrian lands of Galicia from the Habsburgs to the south. Then, when that was completed, Poland would, once again, be made whole.

But as all parties settled in for the harsh winter months with the *Grande Armée* quartered safely around them, the Poles searched for anything with which they could win Napoleon's favor.

They were encouraged by the fact that Emperor had been joined in Warsaw at this point by his Foreign Minister, the *duc de* Talleyrand, who Napoleon had recently elevated to the post of Grand Chamberlain of the Empire. Talleyrand was Napoleon's maker of treaties, and they hoped desperately that his next proclamation would result in the restoration of the nation of Poland. Still, the Poles were sure that something further was needed to convince the Emperor that this last step was necessary; something that would align Napoleon's heart so closely with the Polish people that he could never fail to deliver on his promise to right the horrid crime that was the Partitions of Poland.

The ball at the Wilanów Palace turned out to be a grand affair. Amidst its vast marbled halls, to the moving strings and reeds of the land's best musicians, a large crowd gathered, including the Count and Countess Walewski. They were placed in a receiving line of Polish dignitaries that the Emperor would, after his arrival, soon work his way through.

The crowd stirred with anticipation of the Emperor's entrance. The musician's strings and reeds soon gave way to the trumpeting of horns celebrating Emperor's entrance.

Marek stood among the ranks of the Polish Honor Guard that lined the room. In their Parade Dress uniforms, they were living reminders of the commitment Poland had already made to Napoleon. Dąbrowski's Legions had served the Emperor well for over a decade by then.

Marek Zaczek, known to be one of the Emperor's favorites, stood prominently amongst the honor guard. The hall was abuzz with the fact that his wife and mother had been invited to attend this grand affair, such was the high standing of *Capitaine* Zaczek with the Emperor.

It was Maya's second great occasion in the presence of Napoleon, the first being his coronation. Magdalena had never before had this honor. Yet in seeing all the grandeur and finery on display, in her mind she could only counterpose its civility to the cruel, barbaric order of the Emperor to shoot out the ice from under the fleeing Austrian soldiers at Austerlitz. She thought of Jacek, from whom Napoleon had stolen the lives of his sons and his own will to live. She then thought of the crippling anguish of her sister-in-law, Ewelina, whose heart had been crushed by this beast of a man. Magdalena was instantly regretful that she had ever agreed to attend this event.

Napoleon worked his way down the receiving line, accompanied by his host, the Magnate Stanisław Potocki and with Prince Józef Poniatowski following along. Napoleon graciously spent a few minutes with each couple of Polish nobility, attesting to the beauty of their country, or recalling some ingratiating fact about their family history as researched and supplied by Talleyrand. But upon coming to Count Athenasius Walewski and his young bride Marie, the Emperor lingered noticeably longer. Napoleon seemed to bow lower to her than all the other women; he seemed to hold her hand more tightly in his palm. His eyes wandered over her with an expressive yearning. At least, so must have thought his host the Magnate Potocki and Prince Poniatowski, both of whom had already heard the rumors of the Emperor's wanton desire for her.

"Count Walewski, you are quite a fortunate man to have found late in life a wife so rare in her beauty." Napoleon said.

"Indeed, I am, Sire," Count Walewski replied. "If I may be of any service to your Imperial Highness, as I have in years past to our own country's king, I would be honored if you would call upon me. My countrymen and I are willing to provide you whatever your Imperial Highness needs to defeat our common foes."

"Merci, monsieur," Napoleon said with a nod of his head, "one never knows where fate may place our needs, does one?"

"No, Sire," the aged Count replied, "one surely does not. Yet, wherever that may be, you are assured of my service."

"And you, Madame Countess Walewska," Napoleon said, "we finally meet again. I have not forgotten you since our brief interlude at Blonie before Christmas, and your thousand times welcoming me to Poland. Here in the softer light of this palace, I am blinded even more so than I was that night by your beauty."

The Countess, whose youthful appearance in her white evening gown became flushed with embarrassment at the level of the Emperor's attention. The Count could have been outraged by Napoleon's comments, but instead wore them merely like the pride of a man whose most prized possessions are coveted by others.

"I am quite honored that your Imperial Highness remembers me at all, given all the people of Poland you have surely met since then," she said, still blushing.

"Madame Countess," Napoleon responded, "on a battlefield, the victory goes to those who quickly sift through every detail to find those which matter most, then never let them stray from their awareness. Life is but one continual battle, and I could never allow your smile to wander from my attention. For whether it be wrapped in furs or fine velvet, it commands me."

With this said, Napoleon proceeded to the next couple in the receiving line, but took every opportunity to glance back at Marie. This was noticed by both Potocki and Poniatowski, virtually confirming all that had been rumored.

Later in the evening, Madame Walewska sought out her governess Magdalena, and her friend, the beautiful Maya Zaczek. She held them both in the highest regard, as they were among her truest friends, even though Magdalena was in her employ.

"I am so glad that I can share the majesty of this ball with each of you," the Countess said to them. "It is a truly special honor that you both were invited here tonight, a true testimony to the regard in which the Emperor holds your Marek."

"It appears that our Marek is not the only person that the Emperor holds in such high regard," Magdalena said. "Everyone is talking of how he fawns over you, Countess. It is exactly as our Marek described when you met him at Blonie."

"Yes," Maya added, "the tongue of every woman here is laced with jealousy as to how he looks upon you, even from across the room now as we speak. In fact, Countess, one of his entourage approaches behind you. An officer in a uniform with a sling."

Maya had met the Countess through her mother-in-law, and as their ages were closer, they had become close friends.

"A sling?" Marie repeated. "That would be General Duroc, Grand Marshal of the Palace."

Just then, she turned to see the Marshal click his heels, bow in front of her, and take her hand in his palm. "Madame, I would be honored if you might give me the honor of a dance."

"The honor would be mine, General," the Countess Walewska said, "if your infirmary does not preclude you from doing so."

"I would endure any pain necessary," he assured her, "for the pleasure of holding you, if not in my arms, then next to me for a few brief moments. Please excuse us, Madames."

Duroc escorted Countess Walewska to the dance floor. Magdalena and Maya watched as they began the steps of a *contredanse*.

"The French officers are so refined and elegant," Magdalena said to her daughter-in-law. "They must teach them that in officer's training."

"Well, if they did," Maya replied, "it must have been on a day when my Marek was absent. He would much rather be out in the field learning new ways to kill the enemy, I am sure."

They laughed together. The lightness of the moment contrasted with the weight of Magdalena's thoughts. She had assured Marek that she would not tell Maya the truth regarding the Duke, that she would leave that for him to disclose to his "wife".

The *contredanse* was only half way through when the Emperor approached Marshal Duroc and Marie on the dance floor. All eyes followed him on his approach.

"Ah, Duroc," Napoleon said, "you are needed by Prince Poniatowski at once. Alas, you should not be attempting to lead such a beauty as this with only one arm. Countess, do you mind if I relieve my Grand Marshal of the Palace?"

"I would be honored, Sire," she said, curtseying before him. Napoleon took her by her hand as he slipped his arm behind her back as Duroc retreated.

"I have the feeling that Marshal Duroc's offer to dance was merely a facade so that you might be spared any chance of my saying no to you, Sire."

"Countess," he replied, "one never commits to an engagement unless he is sure he will not be rebuffed. It is not the first time I have utilized a false charge to distract an adversary."

"I would be honored even more if you might call me by my name instead of my title, Sire," she said.

"So, my beautiful Marie, I am told you have rejected my early advances." stated Napoleon. "On the contrary, I lay my heart at your feet. I am your conquered subject, Marie."

"You draw all attention to us Sire," she replied, "Already every eye is upon us. You have made me the talk of the ball. Perhaps I should have held you even further at bay."

"Marie, you dance so delightfully," he whispered. "It has been far too long since I have had such a pleasant distraction ."

"Sire," she responded, "I am merely a distraction to you? I am quite sure your life has been full of a multitude of pleasures."

"I would like for you to join me for dinner tomorrow night, Marie. Can you help ease the loneliness of the man who fights on behalf of your country?"

"Sire," she said, "I am a married woman. I have a son. I could never dishonor my husband so."

"It is only dinner, Marie," he said to her. "There is no dishonor in sharing a meal together."

"Than you don't mind if I bring along the Count?"

"C'est impossible!" Napoleon said. "That would be unbearable for me to watch, the beauty of your youth on the leash to that wrinkled old dog of a man. Instead, allow me to set your beauty free, to revel in its delights."

"I cannot find the words in your language, Sire," Marie said as they had been conversing all along in French, "to tell you just how sad it makes me to even be asked this of you. I am a married woman, be my husband verile or *vieille*, he is still my husband."

"Ah, you see, your French is very good, Marie," Napoleon said, "but do not play the coquette with me too long. My heart cannot bear your refusals. My friend Duroc will make all the arrangements."

"I am sorry, Sire, you ask of me a gift not mine to give."

"Marie, never let anyone take from you what is yours alone," Napoleon said. "It is the same mistake your country has made. Do not allow a rich old man to lord over you so. Do not give in to his leverage. You are too fresh a flower to be cut and arranged in an antique vase. You must bloom, Marie, until your most vibrant colors are set ablaze for all the world to enjoy!"

"Sire," she replied, "I allow a rich old man to protect my honor because of vows I have taken before the Lord. And the Count respects my virtue, unlike the proposition you make before me."

"I wish, Marie, you could see yourself at this moment. Your beauty unfolds before me as my words rile your imagination. Vows are made for the nunnery. I offer you a love that you would be foolish to reject. Come to me, Marie - willingly - I will not take you by force, although I will have to fight every desire within me not to do so."

"Sire," she said at last, "I must retire from you now. I must return to the side of my husband, the Count. I will not mention this conversation to anyone, please be sure to know."

"I know only this Marie - Pursue! Pursue! Pursue! Until my objective yields to me, I will relentlessly pursue!"

"And how many objects of your desire have you abandoned in the morning's light, Sire?" Marie found the nerve to ask. "I think I respect myself too much to be counted among their number."

With this the Countess separated herself from her pursuer, curtseyed again for all the guests to witness, found her husband, the Count, and left the palace. Napoleon not long after retired from the festivities, and spent the rest of the evening sequestered with Marshal Duroc, Magnate Potocki and Prince Poniatowski. It was there in the Wilanów Palace's back chambers where the Emperor emphatically laid down his expectations as what exactly was needed to regain the sovereignty of Poland.

The next morning Marie Walewska awoke to emerge into her bedchamber's outer room, and found it full of fresh cut irises. Alongside them lay a handwritten note:

> *"Last night ,*
> *I had eyes for no one but you,*
> *I admired you alone.*
> *I desire no one but you.*
> *- N"* [70]

"The Emperor awaits your reply, Madame," said her attendant.

"There will be no reply," the Countess Marie said curtly. "This vulgarity deserves no reply."

Later that same day, the Walewskis were called upon by Prince Poniatowski and the magnate Stanisław Potocki. First they met together with the Count, and after about an hour, the Countess was allowed into the meeting room. Marshal Duroc had accompanied them, but he was asked to wait until the Poles finished their discussions.

When Marie entered the room, the Count's face was racked with a responsibility he never expected to have thrust upon him.

"My darling wife," Count Athenasius Walewski began, his demeanor heavy with angst, "What I am about to say may be very unsettling to you. It appears these august gentlemen believe that it is in the greatest interest regarding the restitution of our country for me to, *err… 'share'* you with the Emperor."

---

[70] *"Diary of Marie Walewska"*, Family Archives, 2006 by Alexandre Christian Walewski

She sat still before them, but was not shocked in the least at what she had heard. It was merely another of Napoleon's aggressive advances, to use the respected leaders of her country to approach her husband and soften his will.

"Yes," she said, finally breaking from her trance, "his Imperial Majesty made that most clear to me during our dance together last night and again this morning in his note. I assure you that I rebuffed his advances quite directly, my husband."

"Yes, so I am told," he said, "not by yourself, my love, but instead I only learned of it by way of these esteemed gentlemen." The Count, had the look of a man who had been greatly insulted but was too vain to admit it.

"I am sorry," the Countess said, "but I was too upset to discuss it in the carriage last night returning home."

"Countess Walewska," *Pan* Potocki began to say, "of course, that was the entirely proper way for a woman of your standing to react to the Emperor's suggestions. Normally, I would expect no other reply. But please keep in mind what this could mean to the restoration of our Polish nation. If you were to *appease* the Emperor, it could be very favorable to all of us."

Upon hearing the last sentence, the Countess Marie snapped up quite briskly. Her ears had been pricked by the magnate's selection of words.

"I think *Pan* Potocki misspoke," she said abruptly in reply. "He used the word *'appease'* when in earnest he meant to say *'please.'* If only I was to *please* the Emperor… I would suggest to these gentlemen that the latter word selection more appropriately carries the vulgar intentions of the Emperor."

She then added, ***"Ah, that is not the type of success to which I aspire…I am leaving it for others to be worthy of the honor to please him and occupy him!"*** [71]

---

[71] *"Diary of Marie Walewska"*, Family Archives, 2006 by Alexandre Christian Walewski

The Countess Marie Walewska's face was flushed crimson, not with embarrassment, but with anger. These well-respected men were asking her to surrender her virtue to this man who only weeks before she herself had seen as the savior of their nation. Now, she was finding out that there would be a very high price to pay for the Emperor's rescue. She apparently held the only currency that could satisfy the debt, with which it could be paid in full.

The two guests appeared to be flummoxed by her last statement. They looked upon her and measured the rage building within her. Then they cast glances at her husband, who had not a word of his own to add. It was as if he had told them in advance, *The Countess is a very pious woman and will never agree to such an outrage, but you have my approval to try to convince her otherwise.* Just the thought of him even possibly having said this enraged her all the more.

"Madame," Potocki said next, "Prince Poniatowski and I have come today of our own volition in hopes of cultivating the seed of patriotism that we know lives within you. All of Warsaw, in fact, all of Poland, knows you to be a virtuous, devout woman of the church. What we now ask of you is certainly unseemly and is in no way fair for us to have you even consider. It is your companionship that the Emperor seeks most intently. In fact, in personal conversation with him, he has directly tied it to any future consideration of restoring our national sovereignty. Yes, we are asking you to undertake a task that is disgraceful and despicable. But consider, please, that so long as the Polish people labor under Prussian and Russian overlords, how many of our innocent women will be plundered against their will? We have absolutely no recourse to protect them. We have no police, no courts, no prisons to arrest, convict and salt away these offenders. Your sacrifice in this matter can change all that. We will assure this relationship is kept as discreet as needed to fully protect your sterling reputation."

Pan Potocki's words were so transactional, she thought. *You give up this, the nation regains that. It's a disgrace.*

Marie looked at her husband, who continued to actively take no side in the matter. He did not shield her in the least from the onslaught. She thought to herself, *my brothers forced me to marry you and bear your child so that our family's debts could be expunged, and now you don't even have the civility to protect me from the ruinous sacrifice these men are asking of me?*

The indignity brewed within her, roiling in its rancor, and gaining strength. The magnitude of its abhorrence finally became uncontrollable. Marie's emotions exploded from within her and spewed like molten hot ash at the their guests. "I think that the level of corruption and infidelity that you ask of me even your efforts cannot keep secret for long. The walls of every palace, of every castle has ears. Tongues delight in passing on such scandalous intimacies. Just last night the women of Warsaw openly remarked to me as to how I was drawing the Emperor's attention. Imagine the lewd words that would drain from their mouths once this '*arrangement*' inevitably becomes known."

Then Prince Poniatowski knelt before her. "My most gracious Countess, I, like your own father, fought in General Kościuszko's uprising against the Russians and their allies, the Prussians. I was lucky enough to survive that war when my own uncle, King Stanisław Augustus, sold us out to the Tsarina. Your father was not so fortunate and died in the same battle at Maciejowice as Kościuszko wounded and taken prisoner. Your family has already given so much for Poland."

The Prince then took her hands in his and added, **"Madame! Small causes often have great effects! Women have always had a great deal of influence on world politics - men are most dominated by their passions."** [72]

---

[72] *"Diary of Marie Walewska"*, Family Archives, 2006 by Alexandre Christian Walewski

"Excuse me for interrupting, Prince Poniatowski," Marie said, "but I hope your point cannot possibly be that I should somehow give myself to this adulterer to avenge my family's loss. I know you would never so brazenly play on my sympathy as to suggest that *pleasing* the Emperor would somehow offset Father's tragic death, which cast our proud family into near destitution!"

She left out the next words which had already entered her head - *That very destitution which drove my family to force me to marry this rich old man who now refuses to fight for my honor.*

Then she continued, "My father was, after all, a very righteous man, my Prince. I doubt he would ever ask his daughter to sacrifice her virtue, only so his nation might prosper."

"Exactly," exclaimed Prince Jozef, "but we are no longer a nation, are we? That sovereignty has been stripped from us. We are now merely slaves. To the Russians in the East, to the Prussians in the West, the Austrians in the South. We are a people in need of assistance to throw off these shackles. And your father, being a man of faith, would have recalled from the good book the story of Queen Esther, who became submissive to King Ahasuerus of Persia to save all the enslaved Jewish people from being killed. Her people were so appreciative of her sacrifice that they would later come to lovingly call her *"Hadassah."* It is the Hebrew word for Myrtle, and they believed her personal sacrifice was as pleasing as the scent of Myrtle offered up to their God. In the end, her people were saved from destruction. Today, the culture of our Polish people is actively under attack from those who only want its total destruction. The Russians wish only to *Russify* us, the Prussians wish only to *Germanicise* us. Yet, this very day, we have in our midst the power of the Emperor's army, more powerful than any we ever have raised from Poland. It can defeat those who subjugate us! It is a most rare opportunity, I assure you, my Countess."

The Prince's argument tugged at Marie's heart, which at her tender age of twenty was filled with idealism and sentimentality. Yet, she still could not believe her own husband would permit this sacrifice to even be asked of her.

"I wish to hear the opinion of Count Walewski," she said after a few seconds of silence. "Athenasius, my husband, what is your advice in this matter. Your silence unsettles me."

The Count seemed surprised to have his wife make this demand of him in front of the others. He sat in a chair, physically removed from the others who had been positioned on the matching sofa facing his young wife. Marie faced *Pan* Potocki across a small table, with Prince Poniatowski still kneeling before her, as her husband reclined in a winged chair several feet away.

"My dearest," he said, "my silence is only because I wished not to interfere in your decision. This is a most invasive request that is made of us…"

WHAT! OF US! She screamed to herself. *YOU MERELY WOULD HAVE YOUR FAMILY'S REPUTATION VIOLATED, WHILE I AM ASKED TO SUBMIT MY VERY PERSON, MY FLESH AS WELL AS MY SOUL…*

"… but I can understand the benefit for our oppressed people. You, my dear, have lavished your love upon me…"

GIVEN MY OWN DESIRES IT WOULD NEVER HAVE BEEN SO!

"…and you have delivered to me a healthy child, a fine son…"

WHO THE VERY WOMEN OF YOUR FAMILY HAVE ALL BUT TAKEN FROM ME, CLAIMING I AM TOO YOUNG TO RAISE MY OWN CHILD PROPERLY! AND YET, YOU WOULD HAVE ME, A MERE CHILD MYSELF, ACT SO IMPROPERLY ONLY TO ADVANCE THE CAUSE OF THESE MEN!

"… but now, you can make our family the deliverer of Polish Independence. The Walewski name would then never be forgotten throughout our restored nation's history. Ever to be linked in glory to the Emperor himself."

SO THERE IT IS! I AM TO LAY MYSELF LOW MERELY TO RAISE UP THE WALEWSKI FAMILY NAME!

Later, Marie would write in her memoir the following:

"The sacrifice was complete. It was all about harvesting fruit now, achieving this one single equivalence [convincing Napoleon to support Polish independence movement], which could excuse my debased position. This was the thought that possessed me. Ruling over my will it did not allow me to fall under the weight of my bad consciousness and sadness." [73]

"So, Countess Marie," Stanisław Potocki said, "should we give you time for your consideration of this terrible but necessary request?"

Marie all but glared at her husband, and swore to herself that in some way, she would make him regret having placed her in a position to even have to answer the magnate's request. A sadness more pervasive than she had ever felt rippled through her like a wave. Not so much from having to give herself to the Emperor, but more so from not having a single person, her husband included, to even attempt to rescue her from this debacle.

"No," she said sorrowfully, "I am in no position to refuse your request, as distasteful as it may be."

"You are doing the proper thing, my dear," the Count said to his wife. She refused to look at him, to acknowledge his very presence. Instead she stared off into the distance.

---

[73] ""*Marie Walewska (Les Maîtresses de Napoléon)*" by Frédéric Masson, E. Guillium, 1897.

"I assure my husband that it is truly a most *improper* thing," Marie finally said aloud what she thought, " but I will satisfy this request without pleasure, and I can only hope that when the Emperor realizes the remorse it fills me with, he will not hold it against the Polish people, for I am not one to hide my emotions."

"As we have seen today in this room," Prince Poniatowski observed, "but most understandably so. The sacrifice we ask of you is truly despicable, and were it not for the good of the Polish people, we would not have the brought this dark request to your door. Let me be the first to thank you on behalf of our countrymen and women. *Dziękuję!*"

All three men stood and repeated in unison, "*Dziękuję bardzo!*"

"Let us bring Marshal Duroc in the room for the news."

"No," insisted Marie, "I demand to speak to the General alone. Stay here and I will go to him. I can not possibly debase myself in the company of men so distinguished as yourselves."

Her last statement was coiled with sarcasm. Marie left the parlor and went into the grand hall of the residence where Marshal Duroc waited. He stood, clicked his boot heels together, bowed and gently took her hand to kiss. His arm still in a sling, he offered her no embrace.

"Ah, Countess Marie," he said, "I am sorry that this occasion has been thrust upon you. Yet, I assure you that the Emperor has never been as infatuated with another woman than he is with your most precious self. I bring you this note from His Majesty."

Duroc handed Marie a third hand-written note from the Emperor. The second note she had initially refused to read and set aside. Only when asked by her husband about its contents had she mustered the nerve to read what was a rambling diatribe.

"Do you not find me to your liking, Madame? Nevertheless, I was entitled to hope the contrary. Was I mistaken? Your eagerness has abated, whereas mine is increasing. You are interfering with my rest! Give a bit of joy, happiness to a poor heart that is ready to adore you. Is it so difficult to get a response? You owe me two!"

- N" [74]

Marie was then forced by Marshal Duroc to open the third note, the one which he had carried with him, and to read it in his presence. She quickly sensed it continued in the progression toward the sublime:

"There are times when too much elevation is a heavy burden and that is how I feel. How can I satisfy the Imperial need of a smitten heart, which would like to throw itself at your feet and finds itself stopped by lofty considerations, paralyzing the sharpest of desires! Oh if you would!

You are the only one who can remove these obstacles that separate us! My friend, Duroc, will make this task easier for you!

Ah! Come, come, all your wishes will be my command! I will be more devoted to your homeland! When you take pity on my poor heart.

- N" [75]

Marshall Duroc then added, "He is smitten by your unmatched beauty, Madame!"

"My good Marshal Duroc," she answered, "there is no need for flattery. I have resigned myself to my duty. You may tell your Emperor that I will submit myself to his advances but only on behalf of our people. I will become his Polish companion in the absence of his beloved Joséphine."

---

[74] *"Diary of Marie Walewska"*, Family Archives, 2006 by Alexandre Christian Walewski

[75] *"Diary of Marie Walewska"*, Family Archives, 2006 by Alexandre Christian Walewski

"You do not understand, my Countess," Duroc said. "I handle all of the Sire's correspondence, and I am sure he would become angered at my telling you this, but the Empress has been writing to him requesting to come to his side here in Warsaw. Yet the Emperor writes to her that it is impossible given the condition of the winter roads and cites my own misfortune." The Marshal held out his slinged arm. "But I can clearly see what so many others already have. The Emperor is consumed by your beauty, by your grace, and by your purity. He desires only you, not Joséphine. Not any other woman of Europe, only you. You have enthralled him. You will bring him great joy. I will send a carriage tonight…"

"Not tonight," Marie said, "I am not available this night. Tomorrow evening, at the earliest, my Marshal Duroc."

"Tomorrow evening it is," Duroc said, "for dinner with the Emperor. How thrilled he will be, Madame."

"There is no need for that false civility," Marie said, "as I can promise you that I will have no appetite for a meal."

"You do not understand, Countess, the Emperor will have it no other way. He explicitly said he desires to engage you in conversation over candlelight in his quarters. He wishes to learn all about yourself. As I have said, you enthrall his Imperial Majesty. Tomorrow evening, at seven, the carriage will await you."

"À demain," she said to the Marshal. "Until tomorrow."

That night Countess Marie sought out a dear friend who also had attended the ball, one she respected above all others. The woman listened intently, then consoled Marie, saying:*"He only has eyes for you! He showed his passion for you! It was visible, you alone can convey the voices of an entire nation, influence destinies…and yet you hesitate? …twenty million Poles and your son will have a homeland! Sacrifices do not matter if they obtain such results!"* [76]

---

[76] *Diary of Marie Walewska"*, Family Archives, 2006 by Alexandre Christian Walewski

Chapter 36: The Revelation

January 1807

Preparation is the advocate of the war fighter. Know the land, every inch of it, before a battle is engaged. Anticipate your opponents' options to attack you, but more importantly their routes to flee. Determine how you will cut them off, and force them to finish the contest.

The day after Marie Walewska's capitulation found Marek accompanying Maya on a walk along the banks of the frigid but unfrozen Vistula.

"Why on earth would you bring me here, Marek?" she said through her heavy overcoat as the winds whipped across the waters with a penetrating chill. He could not tell her it was to cut off her routes of escape. He could only begin with the opening salvo of what might forever be their last engagement.

"Aunt Ewelina is so very distraught," he said, "and I needed to be far away from her. She holds me responsible for the deaths of her sons, and thus for the tragic loss of Uncle Jacek as well."

"You have been away so long, Marek," Maya said, "that you do not understand just how bitter Ewelina was in their being taken away. But even over that time, she clung to the hope that one day they would return to her. Now, with their deaths being so tragic, so final, I worry your Aunt Ewelina may never pull out of her despair. I can only hope and pray that she does."

"I would be very surprised if that ever should come to pass," Marek responded. "I fear what this great calamity might drive her to do in retribution. She has already struck out most viciously at me."

"How has she done so?" Maya asked, knowing nothing of the Christmas morning engagement between the two of them.

"She has shared a secret so devastating that I feel it threatens our very 'marriage' - fictitious as it may be."

Maya face soured at his use of the word *"fictitous."*

"Don't say that, Marek," she answered. "It is real to me. I have accepted it as such. You are my husband. I love you. I love our family. Nothing else matters. Nothing Ewelina can say will change that."

"Nothing?" he murmured as he took her hands into his. He wore his Lancers uniform, complete with his squared *Czapka* headgear, including its large white dress plume. "I only wish that could be true. You are likely not to feel that way once I share this heavy burden of a secret with you."

"Marek, you are worrying yourself for no reason," Maya wished to eliminate his fear. "Whatever you have to tell me changes nothing! I will still love you."

"I do not doubt your love, but what I have to say will change everything," he said. "You of course remember how my mother cared for you as you gave birth to Władek?"

"Yes, of course," she said, "had it not been for Magdalena's kindness, I would have never made it through that terrible time. Not only did I have my horrid uncle's injustice weighing on my mind, but you had been sent off to the Austrian infantry. I fear what I might have done without your mother's consolation, without her kindness, her love."

"Did you ever stop to wonder why she was so kind and tender with you?" he asked.

"Because she loves me," Maya snapped back, not letting any indecision creep into her words. She was unsure where Marek's words would take her, but felt ominous shadows arise within her for the first time that day.

"Magdalena has known me since I was a child," she continued, "even before, when I was still growing in my mother's womb. She loved me then, and she still loves me. She loves us, Marek, and she worked so hard to bring us together again."

"There is no doubt of her love, for you or me, or us both together being fictional man and wife."

"Stop saying that!" she rebuked him.

"Magdalena has also expressed great interest in our children, no?"

"Yes," Maya said. "She bears great happiness in Władek's energy, his enthusiasm, his love for you, his *Tata*."

"And what of our *real* child, Czesław?"

"I have grown to detest to your saying that also," she shot back. "They are both real children, and have had no say in who fathered them. They are both our boys now, Marek. The sooner you accept that, you'll become much happier."

His face was stoic. It's lack of emotion scared her.

"I can surely understand a boy not having any say in who his father is," Marek admitted, "but what does Magdalena say about Czesław?"

"She worries after him because he is somewhat slow. He seems to prefer being away from people, he is not an active child like those of his age should be. I also share her concerns, of course, but pretend otherwise. Nonetheless, I love Czesław as his *matka*."

Maya searched Marek's face for a key to the riddle that was hidden in his words. A sharp wind blew and she shuddered.

"Here, Maya, stand with your back to the river and the wind will no longer be in your face." He repositioned her. *Good,* he thought, *now you have no retreat from what I am about to tell you.*

"Will you please just tell me what this is all about, Marek?" she begged him.

"Magdalena has been harboring a great secret from both you and I for all of our lives," he said. "She only shared her disgrace with Ewelina, who in hatred for me belched out the black truth Christmas Day as I left the townhouse."

"What do you mean her disgrace?" Maya asked.

"I have learned from Ewelina that her brother, Bronisław the miner, was not my true father," he finally said, "and I have since confronted Magdalena who has confirmed this."

"What are you saying?" Maya asked, aghast at the revelation. "She gave herself to another?"

"Like yourself, not willingly," Marek corrected her. "Her honor was stolen from her. This was the very fount of her kindness for you after your misfortune at the hands of your uncle, for she had been through the exact same scenario when she was young."

Maya gasped at the revelation. "But at whose hands?" A thousand thoughts began to fuse and diffuse themselves in her mind, until they became ensnarled in each other like the tangled web of a spider's doing. "Who is your father, Marek?"

Marek could not bring the words to his lips. His pause caused her mind only to continue to clutter itself further. Her thinking became full of disabling emotion, rendering all logic useless. She felt herself the ensnarled creature in the strangling web, incapacitated, unable to think, only to fear the spider she now felt approaching.

"Tell me, Marek," she cried out. "Who is your father?"

"My father," he finally brought himself to say, pausing, almost choking on the words, "is your father." Then there was a universe of silence that enshrouded them both. Finally he felt compelled to add, "The Duke Sdanowicz raped my *matka*. I am so greatly ashamed to confess to you that he is my father."

Maya was struck by Marek's debilitating words. Yet, she recalled the corrupted nature of her father, long since departed from this world. She knew instantly in her heart that he was truly capable of what Marek had just revealed. Then she thought of Marek, of how tragic this news was to him. As she delved into sympathy for him, only then did the real absurdity strike her. *If my father was truly his also, then our union had been unnatural. It made he and I …* a great tension twisted within her as she realized why Marek asked about Magdalena's concern for Czesław's slowness…

"NO, NO, DON'T SAY THAT," she exploded at him. "IT CANNOT BE SO." She went to rush past him, but he merely embraced her sobbing frame. She buried her face into his chest.

"It is so, my love," he said as softly as he could into her ear. "I wished it not to be, but the more thought I gave it, the more I knew it to be true. It is why he picked me to be your partner in learning French. What other peasant boy had this courtesy extended to him? It explains why I was given free rein over his stallions and mares. It is also why he went to such great lengths to keep us apart from each other as we matured. It is why he eventually sent me off to the Austrian army, as far away from you as I could be kept."

She shuddered, heaving at each sentence he had said, as if they had been rendered by a black-robed magistrate, who passed judgement on her entire life. She was knocked violently from the safety and protection of the fictional world she and Magdalena had conspired to build. Overwhelmed, she finally conceded to Marek through a deluge of tears, "This indeed changes everything."

"Yes it does," he said without consolation, as if in shock himself at the future that awaited them both. "I have given it great thought, Maya, and there is only one thing we can do."

"I am listening," she said, trying to catch her gasping breath, to clear her abused mind.

"I will stay in the Emperor's army and continue to lead the Polish Lancers. This will surely keep us apart, but honorably so. If I should die in battle, it would only shower respect upon you and the boys. To everyone else, we will appear to be like so many other families across Europe today, separated by war. In doing this, we will place our future together in the hands of fate. Who knows what may come of her fickle nature?"

Maya merely cried, unable to bring herself further to any words.

That evening at seven o'clock, a carriage arrived to collect Marie Walewska from her residence. It contained none other than Marshal Duroc himself. He greeted her inside her home, carrying in his arms a large oversized black cloak. She thought fitting as it matched perfectly the black velvet gown she had selected for the occasion.

"Countess, please slip this over your outerwear," he said, helping her. He then carefully pulled up the hood over her face.

She was consumed completely by the garment, her face swallowed by its hood, which drooped down obstructing her sight.

"I feel like the grim reaper in this thing," Marie objected. "Do you not wish me to see where you take me?"

"It is not that, Countess," Duroc said. "I thought you would wish not to be seen in the Emperor's carriage as it is drawn through the streets of Warsaw."

Marie reached up and pulled down the cloak's hood from her head. "Let them see my face. Let them all know my disgrace."

"As you wish, Madame," Duroc said, "but there is no disgrace in being singled out by the Emperor."

"Singled out in what way?" she asked. "All he knows of me is what he sees. A smile? A smooth young face framed with soft blonde hair? A shapely silhouette? What he sees he likes, perhaps even lusts for. He is just another man, merely one who does not have to make any effort whatsoever to hide his desires."

"Ah. Countess," Duroc replied, "he desires you, of that there can be no doubt. But imagine how many smiles and silhouettes this man has seen across all of Europe. I have seen women of all ranks and privileges eagerly throw themselves at him. But I have never seen him so fixed on any woman as he is on you, Madame. It is more than your impressive beauty. It is your spirit. You see the Emperor has a knack for taking the measure of any man he meets in mere seconds. He is rarely wrong. And you, Countess, while you are certainly never to be confused for a man, Napoleon has taken the full measure of you and he remains very much intrigued."

Marie thought it unusual for Marshal Duroc to call the Emperor by name, and wondered if he did so to suggest that Napoleon was merely another man after all. If there was one thing that Marie was sure of, before this night was over, she was sure to know just how much of a man he was.

They arrived at the Royal Castle, it being more of a palace than a rough hewn castle of stone. Duroc escorted the Countess up to the rooms being used as the Emperor's private quarters. Outside its doors, she was introduced to a turbaned figure.

"Madame Countess, this is Roustam," Marshal Duroc introduced the Mameluke. "He is the Emperor's private and most faithful aide. No one enters these quarters without his permission, not even myself."

"Yes," Marie said nervously, "I had a brief encounter with Monsieur Roustam at Blonie."

"Just Roustam, Madame," the Mameluke's deep voice boomed. "No need for any title, Monsieur or otherwise."

"Well, Madame, I leave you in Roustam's very capable hands," the Marshal said. "If there is anything you might need, let Roustam know and I will procure it for you. I hope you will enjoy your evening with the Emperor. *À bientôt, Madame.*"

Marie gave a slight tilt of her head, as if disappointed.

"In Polish, Marshal Duroc, we say, *'do widzenia.'* You must learn this. Save your French for Paris, say farewell in Polish."

She said this with a slight smile. She had grown to look kindly on Marshal Duroc. Marie thought the man over the past few days had treated her with more tenderness and consideration than her own countrymen, even her husband.

"Of course, Countess," Duroc said, bowing this time, "*Do widzenia*, or more accurately perhaps, *Do zobaczenia później.*"

'Until I see you later'. The Marshal had thought of her enough to prepare to put her somewhat at ease. For the first time that evening, the flash of a full smile crossed her beautiful face.

Marshal Duroc departed and Roustam then said to Marie, "Madame, before we enter, I wish to inform you it is customary to address the Emperor as 'Your Imperial Highness' or more simply as 'Sire' until he invites you to address him otherwise."

"Yes, Roustam, I fully understand," she said, feeling nervous again but thankful for his courteous reminder.

"And should you need anything at all, Madame, merely call out Roustam's name loudly, and I will appear. Please be comforted to know that Roustam speaks to no one but the Emperor of his, and now your, doings. Not to generals, marshals, princes, or kings. You are in my care and confidence always, from this point on."

"Thank you, Roustam," she said earnestly.

"*Proszę bardzo*, Countess," he answered in Polish, resulting in another smile from her. "Now, let us begin your evening." With this, the massive door was swung open to the Emperor's private chambers. Her nervousness returned anew, but she found the courage to step inside. Even before she took that step, her first sensation, unexpected as it was, welcomed her - the delicate but sweet scent of flowers. It drew in her memory the bouquet of flowers the Emperor had given her in Blonie.

Marie remembered how surprised she was that this man of war would have a bouquet to hand her then. "Ah, the Emperor has brought in flowers on my account," she said to Roustam.

"No, Madame," Roustam answered, "he always has vases of fresh cut flowers brought in whenever he is not in the field. He is a man who enjoys the most beautiful gifts that life has to offer, as you shall soon see."

Marie walked in and Roustam pulled the door shut behind her, with the Mameluke standing guard outside it. Marie took in the elegantly appointed outer room. What appeared to be a fine hand-carved wooden table, set with fine French china and polished silverware, glistening under the fluttering glow of two candelabra. Then Marie recognized the pattern of the place settings and realized them not to be French at all, but the most exquisite Polish ceramics from the town of Bolesławiec in Silesia.

"Ah, Countess Walewska," Napoleon said upon entering from his bedchambers, "you are finally here! I feel as if I have been kept waiting half of my life!"

Napoleon moved briskly in her direction, bowed before her while taking her hand and kissed it tenderly.

"It has only been a few days since we danced, your Imperial Hi -Highness," she answered with a slight stutter.

"You see," he said, "that title is too much for such a delicate mouth as your own. Never call me by it again."

"As you wish, Sire," she answered.

"Better," he said, "but only when we are among others, all others except Roustam. When we are alone, which includes in front of the Mameluke, you shall call me simply by my name, Napoleon."

She was suspicious to be on such personal terms so fast, but even so was highly flattered. "Then, you must call me Marie."

"Ah, Marie, but I will call you by a thousand names, my dear, each one more descriptive of you than the next, only will I start with Marie. My beautiful Marie. I hope you are famished."

The Emperor led her over to the table. "I also hope you enjoy French cooking. Myself, I am quite simple. I prefer chicken and fried potatoes, but tonight we dine to impress your palate, my dear, not mine. We will have escargot first, to delight our taste buds, then a splendid green salad and for a main course, a rustic specialty that my chef calls *coq au vin.* It is chicken in burgundy wine with herbs and mushrooms. He says someday it will be known the world over, but as of now, it is not well known outside of France. Yet, the recipe is very old, reportedly it was a favorite of Julius Caesar while he was in Gaul."

"So, if it was fitting for one Emperor, then it must be fitting for another?" Marie joked. "Or are you still upset that Caesar conquered Gaul before you did?"

"I like a woman with a fast wit," Napoleon said, "and sharp as a razor also. At least I am not forcing you to eat Persian lamb just because Alexander conquered that land long ago."

The comment made her think of the Queen Esther reference made by Prince Poniatowski. "To be truthful, Sire…"

"Napoleon," he insisted.

"To be truthful, Napoleon, I do not have much of an appetite. Do we need to eat?"

"Marie - you have kept me waiting for this luxury of dining with you for days now. I am only a soldier, I like simple foods and tend to eat them far too quickly, as *ma mère* would tell you. But not tonight. I will force myself to slowly move them around my plate. Why? Because I intend to feast on the conversation we will have over the meal. So yes, we need to dine. You on the *coq au vin* and I on learning all all things in your life that led to your becoming the lovely *Marie Walewska.*"

He pulled back her chair and she seated herself. He then seated himself opposite her.

"I yearn to learn more about you, Countess," he said across the table, "and all the myriad of things that have occurred to make you who you are. So, I will pretend to be interested in the food and you can pretend to be famished. Is it a pact we can agree on, Marie?"

"Yes, Emperor. I agree," she said, for the first time beginning to lose her nervousness just a bit.

"Napoleon! Napoleon! Napoleon!" he reiterated. "I have men of the highest authorities call me *'Emperor,' 'Sire'* or *'Your Imperial Highness'* all day long. I desire most to hear my given name roll off your lips, Marie."

"I am sorry, but I have never dined with an Emperor before," she explained.

"Ah, but you have dined with a man before, have you not," said Napoleon. "Well, it may surprise you to learn that I'm just a man, my dear. Relax, and don't be so nervous. The *Corsican Ogre* promises not to attack you. Your lovely flanks are safe. I promise to make no sweeping motions, no false charges. Relax, my lovely Marie. Do not let my staring at your lovely face concern you."

"After only a few minutes with you," Marie found herself saying, "I can certainly see you are no ogre, and I do not understand how anyone could call you as such."

"Perfidious Albion!" Napoleon nearly spat.

"I do not understand," she admitted.

"The English have given me that hideous name! They have mocked me as the ogre! They scare their children with it. I gave them peace, but they wasted it and declared war on France again. But let's not allow politics to invade our night together. Ah, the dinner has arrived."

They remained seated as they were served in an elegant fashion. Napoleon wasted no time in discovering what riches his guest carried in her past. He uncorked a bottle of champagne to mark the occasion.

"So Marie, I am told you were born in a place not far from Warsaw. You were the firstborn to your family of seven. You still have four brothers who survived infancy. But your father was fatally wounded at a battle against the Russians in 1794?"

"Yes, Your Majest-, Napoleon," she caught herself. "It was at the Battle of Maciejowice where General Kościuszko was wounded and taken prisoner by the Russians."

"Ah, yes, your famous General Kościuszko. I met the man in Paris at the *duc de Talleyrand's* urging and offered for him to lead all the Polish troops in the *Armée Révolutionnaire Française,* but he refused me. He is your country's hero, I know, but he was not much more than a battle-weary old man by the time I met him."

"Then why did you bother to offer him to lead your Polish troops if you found him to be so *'battle-weary'* as you say?"

"It was Talleyrand's idea," the Emperor responded abruptly. "He thought it might curry favor with the Americans who thought so highly of the man, as well as your people, of course."

"And do you always do everything that the *duc de Talleyrand* suggests to you. Do you respect him that much?"

"The man is nothing more than a sack of *merde* in silk stockings," Napoleon snapped.

Marie laughed out loud. She never expected to hear him speak so. "Then why do you keep him so near to you?"

"To control him, of course," Napoleon answered. "And, I must admit, despite all his shortcomings, he is still the best minister in all of Europe. But of course they are all shit!"

Marie laughed again. She then pressed him further, "And your true thoughts on General Kościuszko? Other than being battle-wearied?"

"The man garnered great respect from President Jefferson and the Americans," Napoleon softened his take on the man. "Still, I concede he must at one time have been a great military mind."

Napoleon added the last sentence to appease his guest, although he did not necessarily believe the words as they left his mouth.

"By the way, Marie, your French is excellent. Where did you find such a fine tutor in all of Poland?"

"His name is Monsieur Nicolas Chopin," she answered, "he was from the Vosges Mountain region. He taught me for many years."

"Well, Monsieur Chopin is certainly very talented. Your pronunciation is exceptional."

"He is no longer my tutor, but I am fortunate to still see him occasionally. He has just married a Polish beauty this June past, and they live outside Warsaw in a small village, Żelazowa Wola. I am told she is now carrying their first child. Perhaps I owe my abilities in French in that I am able to speak your language often with good friend, Maya Zaczck. She is the daughter of my governess and the wife of your *capitaine* of the Polish lancers. "

"How wonderful, you know the family of our Polish Lancer Zaczek," Napoleon said. "All the more proof that Poland and France were meant to be in union. As are you and I, Marie."

The Emperor raised his glass. "A toast to Monsieur and Madame Chopin. May they have many beautiful offspring together. So, your father died in battle? With your family having no patriarch, I understand it came upon difficult times. Your tutors did not last for long after your father's death, did they?"

Marie was surprised just how much he seemed to know about her. She noticed he spoke very little of himself, which surprised her greatly.

"My, my, Napoleon, you have gone to great lengths to learn all this about my family and myself. I am flattered."

"But, my Marie, I always study hard those I face off against, whether it be across a battlefield or a dinner table, eh? But what I cannot understand is why a woman so young and voluptuous as yourself would marry such a fossil as Count Walewski."

"I am insulted to have you speak of my husband so," she replied to him, "but the answer is so very simple that you surely must have deduced it. The Count had need of a wife, and our family had need of erasing our growing debts. It was arranged by my mother and brothers, and as I was the first born daughter of the family, I was told the sacrifice rested on my shoulders."

"*Hmmph!* It is not unlike your people's patriarchs convincing you that it is your duty to give yourself to the Emperor, no?" Napoleon scoffed. "Poor little Marie, her duties to her family and her people assure she will never know real love in her life. Her beauty, her youth are treated as mere commodities to be traded."

Everything he said was true, she thought. But it saddened her to think that he was prepared to take her even knowing all this.

"Was it that fool Potocki who persuaded you to give yourself to me? Wretched man, when I met him, all he wanted to say was that he had his own portrait made by the same artist who captured my own spirit, Jacques-Louis David. I detest those who coddle and compliment me, only so they themselves might claim to be my acquaintance, as if the valor of my accomplishments might reflect somehow on them. So Potocki it was?"

Now the side of him emerged that she had expected to see, that mix of vanity and contempt for lesser mortals.

"Actually, Sire, it was Prince Poniatowski," she admitted. "His words moved me…"

"Napoleon, Marie!" he barked with a smile before dabbing the corners of his mouth with his napkin. "How often must I remind you? They see their Emperor, their Sire, but only you will see the true heart of Napoleon. You will relish to be in Napoleon's embrace, because the more he learns of you, the more he loves you. And now he knows why. The smile that so radiantly abounds from you is from the youth trapped within you that has never been allowed to enjoy the pleasures of life!"

Napoleon, who had risen from the table, took a few steps to kneel by her side. Taking her hand in his, he said:

"I already love you too much to do to you what your family and countrymen have already done. I will not ask, and certainly not force you to lay down beside me this night. No, you will find what my soul needs from you can not be satisfied merely in this physical way. What I desire as much as anything is to be loved by your heart. Of course, I would deceive you greatly if I said I do not desire both, but love must come before the fulfillment of need."

Marie Walewska knew that this was surely a line practiced by Napoleon for this occasion, but she was none-the-less still glad to hear the words.

"I am so happy to hear what you are saying, Napoleon," Marie replied. "I must tell you that although I had agreed to others to give myself to you, in the coach I convinced myself I could not go through with this indecency. It took all my nerve to tell you that I am a faithfully married woman, and would like to remain so."

Napoleon, still on his knees, took both her hands into his and kissed them. "I only want one thing from you, Marie Walewska. To see how bright that smile of yours could truly shine once you allowed yourself to experience the inexplicable lightness of a truly romantic love."

She was surprised that her eyes began to tear up at his expressing such a melodramatic and maudlin sentiment. Yet, the man somehow clearly seemed to understand her. While all others thought she had everything, this man recognized, perhaps instinctively, that she had never even come close to tasting the greatest joys of her youth. Marriage had been thrust on her before love, motherhood before ravishment.

They spoke for hours, becoming deeply acquainted with each other. Layer after layer of their personalities were slowly revealed. He asked about her life, her dreams, what she herself desired of life. He spoke often of her beauty, and how it had captured his heart. She slowly ceded to the sincerity of his compliments with each passing volley. She felt her inhibition being slowly overcome; her guard voluntarily lowered to the ambitions of the man.

It was then when he began to relentlessly press her on exactly why she had agreed to marry that decrepit old Count. Was it vanity, titles, wealth? Do you even love the man?

It was then that she broke down in tears.

"I have told you already it was forced on me by my family," she admitted through her profusion of emotion. "No, I don't love him in the way a wife should love her husband. You already sense this.

By then it was two o'clock and there came a knock at his chamber's door, Napoleon responded by saying:

"What already? Well, my sweet and plaintive dove, dry your tears, go and rest, and fear the eagle no longer. The only power he has over you is that of a passionate love - but a love that wants your heart above all else. You will end up loving him, because he will be everything to you! Everything! Do you understand?" [77]

---

[77] *Diary of Marie Walewska"*, Family Archives, 2006 by Alexandre Christian Walewski

As she rose to wish him farewell, the Emperor shot up before her. He took her mournful face in his hands and used his fingers to wipe away the tears. When his lips found hers, they were not forceful at all. They were tender, full of passion. His arms wrapped around her as had no man's ever before.

"Go, my love," he said as he pulled away from her, "return to your life knowing I love you too much to take you by sheer force, by merely the circumstance of our being alone together in this *chambre*. Yet, I wish you to know that it has taken every ounce of my willpower not to do so."

She then realized she did not wish to leave this man, the first in her life to ever truly show sincere consideration for her deepest feelings. Marie couldn't believe that the man so many had called the beast, the ogre, the butcher, had shown more compassion for her circumstances than any of her countrymen or even her family, not to mention her own husband.

Her face dried, he assisted her with her coat. He walked her to the door, but when she reached to go he threw up his hand over the latch, and said:

"Promise me you'll come back tomorrow, or I won't let you leave. I have you and anyway, what do I care what people say? You are the dearest thing to me, the most desired conquest."

"I promise," [78] she responded, yielding to her heart's new, but true desire.

He kissed her tenderly once more, and she kissed him back in return. Marie Walewska, still not assaulted by this man, as undefiled by the Emperor as when she had entered, felt a shiver of excitement mix with remorse as she pulled away from him and she slipped off into the night. Moments later, as her coach pulled away, she wondered if he watched from his window.

---

[78] *Diary of Marie Walewska"*, Family Archives, 2006 by Alexandre Christian Walewski

When the coach returned to the Warsaw home of Count Walewski, she had hoped to slip in unnoticed. But her husband had drifted off to sleep in the leather wing chair by the fireplace awaiting his young wife to walk though the door. When she did, the frigid morning's blast of an icy gust awoke him. When his eyes cleared to see her, she did not shiver once, in fact, not at all. Marie was instead glowing, giving off a warmth even the winter winds of Warsaw could not subdue. She seemed to glide, as if she skated on the frozen air itself beneath her feet.

"You are finally home, my dear," he said to her.

"It is done," she merely replied to him. "I have done exactly what you compelled me to do." She refused to explain to him that Napoleon had not demanded her to give herself to him.

"Tell me all about your evening," he inquired. "How did it progress? Was the Emperor forceful with you? Did he hurt you in any way? Remember, you are my wife. I have a right to know."

She stopped in her movements before him. "Come, husband, your old body must ache from being in that chair all night long."

"My mind aches from wondering about you all night long. Now tell me what occurred. I must know!"

Marie knew the Count would desire to hear the details of her night with the Emperor, expecting the most intimate, and it disgusted her. She had already concocted a way in which to refuse him his wicked delight.

"Husband," she stabbed the word's irony at him, "the Emperor insisted I speak not a word of our evening together. Otherwise, he would change his plans to restore our country's sovereignty. So forgive me for not ceding to your demand. I can only tell you that I faithfully carried out my pledge to *Pan* Potocki, and to Prince Poniatowski, and yourself. I do feel free to tell you that he demanded I return tomorrow evening."

It was all a lie. Napoleon had never made such a request to her. She had decided that the slight moments of intimacy the she had felt that evening for the first time in her life would linger all the longer if she employed it to drive her husband insane with jealousy. Not because she wished to stoke any ember of desire in him, but in revenge for his body being too old, his heart too cold to have enjoyed the full bloom of her youth. She wished to exasperate him by making him aware there were things in life even he could not control.

For no matter how noble a reason it might have been, he had given his own wife to another, more powerful man, and she wanted him to forever regret doing so. Even though, for the first time since it had been suggested to her, she did not regret, in any way, the evening she had spent with Napoleon Bonaparte.

The next evening she would honor her promise to return to him. It was that night that she reached the point where all she had to give was to be given to her new love. Marie would write:

"I could no longer shrink back. I had to move forward on the rocky road paved by my mad elation. The sacrifice was complete."

After *"reaping the fruit,"* Marie went back to the Royal Castle every night. One night, Napoleon said to her:
"Admit it, Marie, it is not me you love; it is the homeland that you love in me!"

To which she replied,

"Yes, Sire, it's true. I see the saviour in you, he who will regenerate the homeland that is so dear to us. You are the idol to which thousands of voices and hands are raised!

... All of the (country's) hearts are yours, can you doubt mine?" [79]

---

[79] *Diary of Marie Walewska",* Family Archives, 2006 by Alexandre Christian Walewski

Epilogue: Winter Quarters

January 1807

Snow and ice descended upon Warsaw in torrents as the *Grande Armée* went into Winter Quarters there. Its leaders were nestled in the warmth and shelter of the Royal Castle along the Vistula. The corps of the French army then radiated out like the ripples of a stone cast into the river: the cavalry closest to the castle's stables, the infantry bivouacked further out in the open. Each Marshal of France was responsible for sustaining the men of his own corps, resulted in their fighting amongst themselves for command of the best villages for foraging.

The oldest of the "Old Guards," *les Grognards, the Grumblers,* complained compulsively on behalf of their brothers of the conditions in Poland. The weather was too extreme, the roads too rough (nothing more than frozen serrations of mud), the food too scarce, and the girls far too chaste. Yet, here they would remain until the thaw of spring would bring about a recurrence of hostilities with the Russian and Prussian forces.

Yet, some were quite content with the lull in marching, of the scarcity of daylight, and thus of warfare. Night after night, Marie Walewska looked forward to the same darkness and the coach that would deliver her to the Royal Castle. There, she would share her nights with the man she found herself increasingly falling in love with - her Napoleon. Each morning, just before dawn, Roustam's knock would break her heart by announcing it was time to depart. She would then return to her home to torment her husband with no other detail than the obvious spring in her step.

Her child's governess, Magdalena, was most often there during the day. She watched over Marie's son while the Countess slept, restoring herself for the frivolity of that day's coming night.

Yet Magdalena had concerns of her own. Her daughter-in-law, Maya, had not spoken to her since Marek had revealed to his "wife" the truth that she herself for so long could not. Maya did not speak to anyone after that point, except her own children, as she was consumed by the overpowering shock of that stunning revelation from her now forbidden love, Marek.

And Marek Zaczek was no better. He survived each day by focusing his life only into his soldiering, ignoring his mother, his wife, and his children. He had rejected the happiness offered by any fictitious narrative. Not the one that Magda had created and Maya had given him a taste of in Paris. Not the one long ago when he was a peasant child, when he was so happy and full of life on the Duke's *folwark*. That, as it had turned out, was nothing more than an illusion. The father he so respected, Bronisław, was suddenly cleaved from him. The man he had for so long despised was now presented to him as his true kin; the thought made Marek question everything about his world. The only thing he knew to be real was soldiering, and so Marek continued to hone his skills for the battles yet to come.

It was those battles, and their after-effects that had created Magdalena's most pressing concern. Her sister-in-law Ewelina had lost two sons to warfare, and the life of her husband was claimed by the black spectre of Jacek's own hand. Ewelina had already been so bitter even before their deaths. She focused her hatred on Marek, blaming his defection to the French as the root of all of her suffering. Magdalena could not stand to witness the unraveling of Ewelina's sanity, just as one might wish to avoid the unwrapping of bandages from a grievous, gangrenous wound.

Magdalena worried each day just how the twisted, tortured mind of Ewelina might take revenge against Marek and herself.

The End

of

"The Life of Marek Zaczek

Volume 2:

Embers of Love and War"

Figure 27: Imperial Guard - Polish Light Horse Brigade 1807-1814 by Lucien Rousselot

Author's Notes

To the reader, I wish to sincerely say thank you very much for having finished the second volume in this serial historical saga that is **The Life of Marek Zaczek.** I hope you have enjoyed this amalgam of real historical drama and my fictional tale of Marek, Maya, Magdalena and the other characters. This novel required extensive research, and as a result it was three years in the writing. I hope to have the third volume out much more quickly, now that the bulk of that research is behind me. While I originally envisioned Marek's life story to be a trilogy, I realize now that the overall arc of that story is much more expansive than I had imagined initially, as it will span not only the Partitions of Poland, but also the period of the Napoleonic Wars which follow. I now foresee this series requiring seven full volumes to tell the complete tale of Marek Zaczek's life.

This novel was originally going to focus only on Marek's military contributions to Napoleon's armies. But as I began my research, I realized this volume would be foundational to those that will follow. It is as much about love as it is about war. In fact, I had an entirely different subtitle in mind when I began its writing, but settled on **"Embers of Love and War"** when I realized this second volume would include the love stories of not only Marek and Maya, but also of Nelson and Emma, and at least the beginning of Napoleon and the Countess Marie Walewska - perhaps the only woman who ever truly loved him. To me, it is interesting that both Nelson and Napoleon both fell in love with women trapped in affluent but loveless marriages to men far older than themselves. Did they see themselves as rescuers of trapped hearts?

If I have one question that I am asked more often than others in regard to my tales of historical fiction, it is, "How do you research the facts in your novels?" While I use many of today's modern internet sources, I always prefer to balance them against published historical references. I particularly love to read those accounts written and published either contemporaneously to the subject, or some thirty to fifty years later, those not necessarily colored with modern morals. I have included a listing of some of the reading material I consumed prior to and during the writing of this volume. I particularly enjoy including quotes from these sources, although sometimes, admittedly, they are intentionally not used in the original context, but in my own vernacular, to "thicken" the character's dialogue with their own historical words.

The expansive history presented was needed to understand not only this volume, but also the anticipated four additional volumes to come covering the rest of the era of the Napoleonic Wars. I find myself totally mesmerized by the often dizzying complexity of history, and challenge myself to weave an intriguing fictional tale within its bounds. I stay as true as I can to respecting the fullness of all historical accounts, but even in a subject as well documented and detailed as Napoleon's life, there are still gaps and disagreements among pre-eminent historians and military aficionados.

For instance, I suspect that no sooner is this book published that someone will argue that the Polish Lancers were not incorporated into the Emperor's Old Guard until April 1807. While this is accurate at the *regimental* level, I have awarded Marek Zaczek at the end of 1804 to become captain of a *battalion or company* of lancers within the Imperial Guard Cavalry. The lancers were an outgrowth of Dąbrowski's Polish Legions in the *Armée d'Italie*, and were highly regarded by Napoleon. It is only natural that there would have been a continuum of these loyal soldiers bridging between the legions of Italy and lancers of Poland.

Next, let us address two other gaps: first, the actual initial meeting place of Marie Walewska and Napoleon, and second, the nature of their first night together.

Despite all the historical sources I have researched, there is no concrete answer as to exactly when and where Marie Walewska first met Napoleon. It is clear that she sought him out and introduced herself as he was coming into Warsaw. She herself recounted in her memoirs that it was in the town of Blonie just to the west of Warsaw. This would have been on the route Napoleon took as he first approached the city in December of 1806. Other historians suggest it was actually at the town of Jablonie just north of Warsaw as Napoleon returned from the inconclusive Battle of Pułtusk in January of 1807. I have decided to base my story on the remembrances of the Countess as documented in her memoirs. In truth, either initial engagement does not materially change the story, but for the sake of disclosure, I document my decision here.

As for their first night spent together there is much speculation. Many believe the Emperor forced himself upon a resistant, most pious Marie. What all agree upon is the fact that Marie was requested by her countrymen to give herself to the Emperor in the hope of Napoleon reconstituting their nation. Marie, as both a married woman and mother at that point, certainly knew what she was being asked to sacrifice to his Imperial Highness. She certainly knew this was not to be the establishment of a platonic relationship.

Many historians account that Napoleon brutally forced himself upon Marie their first night alone with each other. Marie, in her memoirs detailed that there was no physical contact that evening. As I wrote this story, I envisioned the Emperor, during the course of his conquest of this beauty, recognizing the sadness within her. It was that perspective from which I imagined his own tenderness with her would stem. From that unexpected compassion, Marie rapidly grew in her intense affection for Napoleon. What nearly all historians do agree upon is the fact that Marie Walewska fell madly in love with Napoleon Bonaparte. I could not envision how a woman used so flagrantly used by others her whole life could fall in love with any other man who did so. So instead, I reasoned, Napoleon must have understood her needs, and was thus tender to her.

I have to admit here to having taken a few historical liberties with the Princess Czartoryska by placing her in a meeting with Napoleon and Talleyrand at Fontainebleau outside Paris just before the Emperor's coronation. That was purely fictionalized to advance the storyline, although it is true that Princess Izabela was known to have frequented Paris often for the joys of collecting art, among other pleasurable pursuits. The family palace at Puławy being sacked by the Russians in 1794, a fact central to the story of each of the first two volumes, is indeed true. The premise of her two sons being taken to Saint Petersburg as prisoners of Catherine the Great is also accurate. Her son, Adam Jerzy, becoming the Foreign Minister to Tsar Alexander I is, indeed, historically correct. Foreign Minister Adam Jerzy Czartoryski is mentioned by name throughout none other than Tolstoy's classic, *War and Peace*.

Another historically accurate precept was that General Tadeusz Kościuszko was living in the village of Berville, nearby to Fontainebleau at this time. In fact, the words of Kościuszko encouraging Marek to learn as much as he could from Napoleon is essentially a rephrasing of the words spoken by that general to the real life Polish Lancer Dzeydery Chłapowski as recorded in his *pamietniki* (memoirs).

Dzeydery Chłapowski was an officer of the Polish Lancers and was held in the highest regard by Bonaparte. He claimed to not only have met directly with the Emperor multiple times in the field, but also to have couriered some of his most sensitive correspondence. This lancer's memoirs give great insight into not only Napoleon's thoughts, but also to his movements throughout Poland and Prussia in the timeframe of this novel. For instance, it was from Chłapowski's accounts that we know Marshal Duroc, Napoleon's Grand Marshal of the Palace, broke his collarbone when his coach flipped over while negotiating the horridly unimproved winter roads of Poland.

Also, I have researched many of the historical facts contained in this novel by relying heavily on the published accounts of Napoleon's Campaigns as documented by historian David Chandler, as well as those of Horatio Nelson's life recorded by the American military biographer, Captain Alfred Thayer Mahan. I have the greatest respect for all historians, both professionals (like David Chandler and Captain Mahan) and amateurs (like Lancer Dzeydery Chłapowski and Countess Marie Walewska). I would never have the conceit to count myself among their ranks. I am, however, most grateful for their endeavors, and realize that my own meager efforts could never have been undertaken without the history they themselves have left behind.

I feel compelled to remark upon the joy I experienced during the research phase of this book. First, I was most grateful to come across the work of the artist Lucien Rousselot. His canvasses visually describe the military uniforms of all Napoleonic cavalry and his plates on the Polish Lancers of the Imperial Guard I found to be an astoundingly detailed resource. I wish also to thank the leadership at Greenhill Books of London for their allowing my usage of the print included by Mr. Rousselot in these pages as Figure 27 as well as prominently displayed on the back cover. I feel that this amazing print captures the pride, pageantry and patriotism of Napoleon's Polish Lancers.

I also came across the Diary of Marie Walewska, which I found to be an inspiring resource. My thanks to the Walewska family for translating and posting this incredible document. I varied from it only somewhat in describing the nature of her first night together with Napoleon, but I whole-heartedly recommend its complete and thorough reading.

Finally, I hope you have enjoyed my efforts, be they of Marek or any of my other characters in the various historical eras that I am so thoroughly excited to write about. If you do enjoy these works, please realize it is the timeless (and time-consuming) efforts of my wife Marie, who in editing and storyline consultation makes all of my works markedly better than they initially began. She is the love of my life, and her skills sharpen my tales with the deft agility not unlike that found in the blade of a surgeon's knife.

Appendices:

Appendix A: Source Materials/
Suggested Historical Reading

Appendix B: List of Image Attributions

Appendix C: Countries of the Coalitions
Within this Volume:

Appendix D: Countries of the Coalitions
Beyond this Volume:

Appendix E: Pronunciation Guide for Polish Terms:

Appendix F: Pronunciation Guides for
Polish Character Names:

Appendix A: Source Material & Suggested Historical Reading:

1) ***"The Campaigns of Napoleon,"*** David Chandler, Folio Society Edition (2002) in Three Volumes of the Orion Publishing/Scribner (1966) Original (One Volume).

2) ***"The Life of Napoleon,"*** William Milligan Sloane, The Century Company, New York, 1896, 4 Volumes.

3) ***"The Life of Napoleon Buonaparte,"*** J.G. Lockhart, Bickers and Son, Leicester Square, London 1889.

4) ***"The Life of Nelson,"*** Captain A. T. Mahan, Easton Press Edition (2014) of Little, Brown, and Company (1897) Original (Both Two Volumes).

5) ***"The French Revolution: A History,"*** by Thomas Carlyle, 1837, Easton Press 2008 Edition in 3 Volumes.

6) ***"The Czartoryski Family Residence in Puławy,"*** Idea Media Publishing, 1998.

7) ***"Napoleon's Polish Gamble",*** Christopher Summerville, Pen & Sword Military Publishing, 2005.

8) ***"Memoirs of a Polish Lancer: The Pamietniki of Dzeydery Chłapowski",*** Emperor's Press, 1992.

9) ***"Poles and Saxons of the Napoleonic Wars",*** George Nafzinger et al., Emperor's Press, 1991.

10) ***"Talleyrand",*** Duff Cooper, 1932, Folio Society Edition.

11) ***"The Diary of Marie Walewska,"*** Transcribed from Walewski Family Archives, March 2006 by Alexandre Christian Walewski.

12) ***"Marie Walewska (Les Maîtresses de Napoléon)"*** by Frédéric Masson, E. Guillium, 1897.

13) ***"Napoleon's Elite Cavalry, Cavalry of the Imperial Guard, 1804-1815, Paintings of Lucien Rousselot,"*** Text by Edward Ryan, Published by Greenhill Books (London) and Stackpole Books (Pennsylvania), 1999.

14) ***"Napoleon: PBS Four Part Documentary,"*** 2000, written, directed and produced by David Grubin, narrated by the historian David McCullough.

15) ***"The General Correspondence of Napoleon Bonaparte,"*** www.Napoleonica.org, Les Archives, Foundation Napoléon.

16) ***"Napoleon's Polish Lancers of the Imperial Guard"*** by Ronald Pawly, Illustrated by Patrice Courcelle, 2007, Osprey Publishing Ltd.

17) ***"Polish Soldiers During The Napoleonic Wars,"*** Soldiershop Publishing, May 2018, Edited by Luca Stefano Cristini.

Front Cover Layout:
Original Marek Zaczek Portrait by Madeline Trawinski
Age Progressed by David Trawinski
Composited Public Domain Images
Emperor Napoleon in his Study at the Tuileries by Jacques-Louis David, 1812.
Countess Marie Walewska Portrait by François Gérard, 1812.
Lord Nelson Portrait by Lemuel Francis Abbott, 1799.
Lady Emma Hamilton Portrait by George Romney, 1782.
The Explosion of the L'Orient by Thomas Luny, 1834.

Back Cover Image:
"*Garde Impériale - Cheveau-Légers Polonais, 1807 - 1814, Tenue de Parade après 1809*" by Lucien Rousselot, 1999,
Used under license from Greenhill Books, London.

Interior Images
Figure 1: *"Map of Europe 1804 - 1806,"* Created by David Trawinski, 2023
using licensed Adobe Stock Image #110535933 by Peter Hermes Furian
Figure 2: *"Map of Napoleon's Prussian Campaign of 1806-07,"*
Created by David Trawinski, Copyright 2023
Figure 3: *"Napoleon Crossing the Alps"* by Jacques-Louis David, 1801, Public Domain.
Figure 4: *"General Jan Henryk Dąbrowski in front of the Polish Legions in Italy"*
by Juliusz Kossak, 1882, Public Domain.
Figure 5: *"Captain Horatio Nelson, Age 22"* by John Francis Rigaud, 1781,
Public Domain.
Figure 6: *"Napoleon (unfinished)"* by Jacques-Louis David, c. 1797-98, Public Domain.
Figure 7: *"The Princess Izabela Czartoryska"* by Alexander Roslin, 1774,
Public Domain.
Figure 8: *"The Fight of the Ça Ira,"* Artist Unknown, 1795, Public Domain.
Figure 9: *"Battle off Cape St. Vincent, 1797"* by William Adolphus Knell, 1847,
Public Domain.
Figure 10: *"Nelson wounded during the Battle of Santa Cruz de Tenerife"*
by Richard Westall, 1806, Public Domain.
Figure 11: *"The Destruction of "L'Orient" at the Battle of the Nile, 1 August 1798"*
by George Arnald, 1825-1827, Public Domain.
Figure 12: *"Portrait of Tadeusz Kościuszko"* by Ramsay Richard Reinagle, 1817,
Public Domain
Figure 13: *Portraits of Lady Emma Hamilton,* George Romney, 1782-85, Public Domain
Figure 14: *Château de Fontainebleau, Seine-et-Marne,* Panoramic
Licensed Adobe Stock Image #113245733 by aterrom

Figure 15: *"A Polish Lancer,"* Wojciech Kossak, 1910, Public Domain,
as photographed by Kazimierz Olszański per Wikipedia.

Figure 16:: *"Illuminated Apse of Notre Dane de Paris at Night,"*
Licensed Adobe Stock Image #359598822 by SvetlanaSF

Figure 17: *"The Great Chase Between Nelson and Villeneuve (1805)"*
Created by David Trawinski using base map of the North Atlantic
from the Licensed Adobe Stock Image #271833867 by Tindo

Figure 18: *"Map of the Sea Battle of Trafalgar,"* Created by David Trawinski, 2023

Figure 19: *"The Battle of Trafalgar,"* William Clarkson Stanfield, 1836, Public Domain

Figure 20: *"The Death of Nelson, Daniel Maclise Nelson for the Houses of Parliament,"*
1859-64. Panoramic, Public Domain

Figure 21: *"The Death of Nelson, October 21, 1805,"* Arthur William Davis, 1809,
Public Domain

Figure 22: *"The Battle Map of Austerlitz,"* created by David Trawinski -
using Wikimedia Public Domain Image sourced as
The Department of History, United States Military Academy Archive

Figure 23: *"La bataille d'Austerlitz. 2 decembre 1805"* by François Gérard,
1810, Public Domain

Figure 24: *"Map of Napoleon's Prussian Campaign of 1806-07:"*
Created by David Trawinski, 2023.

Figure 25: "Letter with Seal on Table", Licensed Adobe Stock #384198481 by adam121

Figure 26: *"Napoleon i ks. Józef Poniatowski pod Lipskiem"* Janvier Suchodolski, 1837,
Public Domain

Figure 27: *"Garde Impériale - Cheveau-Légers Polonais, 1807 - 1814, Tenue de Parade
après 1809"* by Lucien Rousselot, 1999,
Used under license from Greenhill Books, London.

*** *** ***

Interior Chapter Heading Graphics and Dividers produced by David Trawinski
by modifying the following Licensed Adobe Stock Images:

Cannons/Fleur-de-Lis base made from Adobe Image # 52787187 by asmaker

with *HMS Victory* Rendering using Adobe Image # 86430238 by elenarts

with Napoleonic "N" image using AdobeImage # 392927897 by Alex Birch

Revolutionary War of the First Coalition (1793 –1797)
Coalition: Great Britain, Spain, Holland, Holy Roman Empire (led by Austria),
        Prussia, and Piedmont-Sardinia
Result: French Victory
        France annexes the Austrian Netherlands
        France annexes the Left Bank of the Rhine
        France establishes satellite republics in Northern Italy
        The Thousand-Year Ducal Empire of Venice is dissolved by Napoleon
Ended by: Several treaties including the Treaty of Paris (1797) with Piedmont-Sardinia

Revolutionary War of the Second Coalition (1798 -1802)
Coalition: Great Britain, Spain, Holland, Holy Roman Empire (led by Austria),
        Russia, Naples, Ottoman Empire and Portugal
Result: French Victory, Egypt occupied, French fleet destroyed
        at Battle of the Nile (1 October 1798), Italian territories regained by France
Ended by: Treaty of Amiens with British on March 25, 1802 and
        Treaties of Paris with Russia on 8 October 1801
        and Ottoman Empire on 25 June 1802

Napoleonic War of the Third Coalition (1805 - 1806)
Coalition: Great Britain, Holy Roman Empire (led by Austria),
        Russia, Naples, Sicily and Sweden
Result: French Empire Victory,
        The Thousand-Year Holy Roman Empire dissolved,
        Confederacy of the Rhine created,
        Combined Spanish/French fleet lost in Battle of Trafalgar
        Austrian and Russian armies defeated at Austerlitz
Ended by Treaty of Pressburg with Holy Roman Empire under Francis II
        Signed on 26 December 1805

Napoleonic War of the Fourth Coalition (1806 - 1807)
Coalition: Great Britain, Prussia, Russia, Saxony, Sweden and Sicily
Result: French Empire Victory
        Twin Battles of Jena and Auerstädt (14 October 1806)
            led to the fall of Berlin.
        Indecisive Battle of Pułtusk in January 1807.
        (Continued in next appendixIndecisive Battle of Pułtusk in January 1807.)

Appendix D: Countries of the Coalitions Beyond this Volume:

(Simplified)

Napoleonic War of the Fourth Coalition (1806 - 1807) (Continued in Marek Zaczek 3)
Coalition: Great Britain, Prussia, Russia, Saxony, Sweden and Sicily
Result: French Empire Victory
      Defeat of Russia and Prussian at Battle of Friedland
      Ended by Treaty of Tilsit (7 July 1807) with Russian Tsar Alexander I
         and Prussian King Frederick Wilhelm III
         Prussia lost half of its Territory with
            Napoleon's creation of The Duchy of Warsaw
      Creation of the Continental System of embargo against British trade.

The Peninsula Wars (1807 - 1814)
Coalition: United Kingdom, Portugal, Spain\
Result: War of Attrition which eventually gave the British army a foothold on the Continent and which brought them eventually into Southern France

Napoleonic War of the Fifth Coalition (1809)
Coalition: United Kingdom, Austria, Sardinia and Sicily
Result: French Empire Victory after Battle of Wagram
Ended by Treaty of Schönbrunn

The Russian Campaign (1812)
Combatant: Russia
Result: After Russia Lures Napoleon into a desolated Moscow, the French Empire Withdrawals, Resulting in the defeat and obliteration of the invading *Grande Armée*

Napoleonic War of the Six Coalition (1813 - 1814)
Coalition: United Kingdom, Russia, Prussia, Austria, Spain, Sweden and Portugal
Result: French Empire Defeated at Leipzig in the "Battle of the Nations"
Ended by Abdication of Napoleon, Exiled to Elba

Napoleonic War of the Seventh Coalition (1815)
Coalition: United Kingdom, Russia, Prussia, Austria, Sweden and German States
Result: French Empire Defeated at Waterloo
Ended by: Abdication of Napoleon, Final Exile to Saint Helena

Appendix E: Pronunciation Guide for Polish Terms:

Term	Meaning	Pronunciation
Pan	Sir	Pahn
Pani	Madame	PAHN nee
Proszę	Please	PRAH she(m)
Dziękuję	Thank you	Jeh(m) KOO ye(m)
Babcia	Grandmother	BAHPT tsha
Ciocia or Ciotka	Aunt	CHUTCHee/CHUTCHka
Do widzenia	Goodbye (informal)	Doh Vee ZEHN ya
Do zobaczenia	See you later	Doh Zoh ba CHEN ya
Dobronoc	Goodnight	Doh BRAHN oots
Dzien Dobry	Hello/Good day	Jane DOH bree
Dobrze	Good or Well	DUB zha
Dupa	Ass (Derriere)	DOO pah
Dupek!	You Ass (Insult)	DOO Pek
Dziękuję bardzo	Thank you very much	Jeh(m) KOO ye(m) BAHD zo
Nie ma za co	It is nothing! (Dismissive)	Nee ma zats so
Folwark	A Nobleman's Estate	FOL vark
Gówniarz	Sh**head, Punk	GOOV nash
Matka	Mother	MAHTka
Moja	My	MOI ya
Proszę bardzo	You are welcome	PRAH she(m) BAHD zo
Tata	Daddy	TA ta
Stare Miasto	Old Town	STAHRee Me AS to
Szlachta	Nobleman	Szlahta
Witamy	Welcome	VeeTAM mee
Zona	Wife	ZONE ah
Zupan	A noble's garment	ZUH pohn

Fictional Polish Character Names   Pronunciation

Fictional Polish Character Names	Pronunciation
Marek Zaczek	MAH rek ZAH check
Maya	MAI ya
Magdalena	Mahg da LEENE ya
Jacek	YAHT sek
Ewelina	Eva LEEN a
Rydek	RYE dek
Władek	VWA dek
Czesław	CHES wav
Bronisław	Brohn NIS wav
Bartek	BAHR tek
Andrzej	AHND jay
Duke Władysław	Vwa DIS wav

Historical Polish Character Names   Pronunciation

Izabela Czartoryska   **Izabela Char tor REE ska**

Princess, renown art collector, creator of first Polish Museum

Adam Jerzy Czartoryski   **Adam Yerzy Char tor REE skee**

Son of Princess Izabela, Patriot, Foreign Minister to Tsar Alexander I

General Jan Henryk Dąbrowski   **Yan HAHN reek Dom BRUV skee**

Patriot, Creator of Polish Legions under Napoleon in Italy

General Tadeusz Kościuszko   **TAH deush   Kohsh SHOOZ ko**

Patriot, American War of Independence Hero, Leader of 1794 Uprising

Lancer Dezydery Chłapowski   **Dez eye DER ee   Hwa PUV skee**

Patriot, Famous Polish Lancer in Service to Napoleon

Prince Jozef Poniatowski   **YO zef Pahn yee a TUV Skee**

Patriot, Nephew of last king of Poland, Ally to Napoleon

Stanisław Potocki   **Stan NIZ wav Po TOT Skee**

Magnate, Later Senator, Patriarch of the Polish State

Marie Walewska   **Marie Wa LEV ska**

Young Wife of Count Walewski forced by her countrymen to become mistress to Napoleon, with whom she fell madly in love

Novels by David Trawinski

***The Chopin Trilogy** (WWII/ Cold War Espionage)*
The Willow's Bend (2016)
Chasing the Winter's Wind (2017)
War of the Nocturne's Widow (2018)

The Deekie and Clay Series (Co-authored with Marie Trawinski)
Ever Blooms the Rose (2019)   US Civil War/Reconstruction
Guns of the Yellow Rose (2022)   Reconstruction/Western

***The Churchill Series** (World War I and II / Espionage)*
The Twins of Narvik Part I (2021)
The Twins of Narvik Part II (2021)

The Life of Marek Zaczek Series
(Partitions of Poland/Napoleonic Wars)
Volume I: Under the Wings of Eagles (2020)
Volume 2: Embers of Love and War   (2023)

All Proudly Published by